SERGEANT STONE,

SENTINEL

of the CRESCENT

CITY

Daniel Barker

 iUniverse®

SERGEANT STONE, SENTINEL OF THE CRESCENT CITY

iUniverse books may be ordered through booksellers or by contacting:

iUniverse
1663 Liberty Drive
Bloomington, IN 47403
www.iuniverse.com
1-800-Authors (1-800-288-4677)

ISBN: 978-1-4917-6677-4 (sc)
ISBN: 978-1-4917-6678-1 (e)

Library of Congress Control Number: 2015906517

Print information available on the last page.

iUniverse rev. date: 04/22/2015

CONTENTS

INTRODUCTION

This book is a sequel to *Sergeant Stone, NOPD,* the title character having been introduced in the short story collection *Tales From the Id* by James S. Prine. Familiarity with these volumes will enhance your reading pleasure but it is not a prerequisite for enjoying this book. This volume stands alone and, indeed, each story within it can stand apart as a separate reading experience. It is recommended that the stories be read in order, however, as certain characters and plot elements do weave progressively through them to the end.

It was a pleasure to return to the character of Sergeant Stone and write more of his adventures. I want to thank my uncle, author James S. Prine, for creating the character and letting me have some fun with him. It is like borrowing a Ferrari and taking it for a thrill ride. He also encouraged me to write the story of Stone's experience at Camerone, and I hope I did it justice in "Sergeant Stone in the Company of Demons." I want to thank my mother, Debra P. Mitchell, for her encouragement and proofreading help. She also suggested one of the story ideas, and "Crescent City Sentinel" would not have happened without her. Of course I must thank my wonderful wife, Danielle, for her encouragement in this non-lucrative hobby and for allowing me to spend valuable time on it. I wish to extend special thanks to Terri Schauf for editing the manuscript to make it fit for reading. Remaining mistakes are solely my fault.

Stone had to come back, you see. The last book reached a logical stopping point, but certain questions lingered. Whatever happened between Stone and Isis? Where was that relationship going? This book has the answers. What else did Stone do? Was he ever a Viking? Did he ever work in the Old West? Did he ever cross paths with biblical figures? Has he done anything meaningful in the future (from our vantage point)? Will Stone's enemies discover that he escaped retribution for detonating the Cosmic Eraser? Read on and find out. In the last book it seemed that only a few of Stone's adventures actually transpired in New Orleans. There are more "home games" this time out, as a bit more of the rich history of the Crescent City is explored and Stone lives up to the subtitle of the book. The rest of the wide world of history is not neglected, however, since our protagonist knows few boundaries. In the Afterword I will separate fact from fiction. Buckle up for a wild ride!

SERGEANT STONE AND THE TRIAL BY FIRE

A curious excerpt from "Frontier Lawyer: The Memoirs of Nathan Hodges, Esq."

1878--Okmulkee, Oklahoma

Thud!

I saw stars as some heavy, blunt object collided with the back of my skull. There was pain, but the shock of the blow was worse. My knees buckled and my vision narrowed, but I managed to throw my hands in front of my face to ward off the next blow. No matter. A hard fist slammed into my teeth anyway, knocking one of them free. So much for my winning smile, I thought ruefully. I tasted copper in my mouth as the blood flowed from the new vacancy. I crumpled to the hard, unyielding ground amidst a rain of blows from the mob. I was a fighter, but there was no fighting chance here.

So, this is how it would end. I'd been born a slave and had heard stories of lynch mobs my whole life, but I'd never actually seen one up close until today. When I was fifteen, freedom came with the end of the war. There wasn't much in the way of opportunity, of course. With mother having passed on and father long gone, I had to shift for myself through odd jobs and the occasional petty theft. My opportunities dwindled all the more once I had amassed an arrest record. I left Arkansas for the Indian Territory of Oklahoma where the laws of the white man had little sway. I settled with the Creeks near Okmulkee, a name which in English means "boiling water". The waters were sure boiling now.

I learned the Creek language and got on well with them, but white settlers followed. One of them was kind to me, however. Mr. Ackerman had lost his wife years ago and then lost his only son in the war. He welcomed my help with his dry goods business, even leaving it to me when he died a few years later. He had always stuck up for me. But, now there was no one, at least no one willing to challenge this mob on my behalf. When the popular widow Mrs. Gunther turned up violated and murdered in grisly fashion, suspicion fell on me in spite of the utter lack of evidence. Why? Had I been too familiar with a white lady? Had I crossed some line in returning her cordiality? Had the Creeks not been so powerful here, the whites might have blamed one of them. Probably because mine was the only black face around, it was far more convenient to settle on me since I was alone.

After what seemed like several minutes of kicking and beating, beating worse than I ever had as a plantation slave, they roughly forced the noose around my neck and began to drag me through the street. I was able to grasp the rope with my hands and force enough separation from my throat to avoid strangulation, but only just. They dragged me right past the Creek Council House, an impressive new two story brick building that was just being finished. The Creek authorities themselves were sitting this one out, not deeming it worth agitating the whites even more by intervening on my behalf. Through the legs of my tormentors I spotted our destination: the tree at which I was to be hanged. The beatings had slackened by now since I was quite helpless, but the threats and crude remarks about my race did not. A wave of panic swept over me, a foreboding of imminent death. My mouth went as dry as the dusty street and stinging ice flowed in my veins. So, this was it.

"String him up!" someone bellowed. The mob roared with approval. I was dragged into position and they made ready to throw the rope over a convenient tree limb. The line was tied to a horse.

"Release that man!" another voice rang out over the din.

It spoke with authority, as if actually expecting the deranged mob to comply. Everyone froze and turned to look for the origin of the voice. I turned also. My first reaction was disappointment: another white face. But this one was different. Half hidden by the shade of a wide-brimmed hat, the craggy features were unremarkable, except for the eyes that peered out of them. Those eyes bespoke irrevocable determination and not the merest hint of doubt. Then I took in the rest of him., He wore a long black duster coat and on his chest the badge of a Deputy US Marshal.

"He has to hang for murder!" shouted one of the ringleaders, a man who had once been a good customer of mine.

"If you are so certain of his guilt, then you should have no difficulty proving it in a court of law," the Marshal retorted.

"This is Indian Territory. There is no law here!"

"No Sunday west of St. Louis and no God west of Fort Smith," an angry townsman snickered.

"The eternal Law of right and wrong applies everywhere. You won't break it with impunity while I'm around," the Marshal sneered.

There was a motion in the crowd to the Marshal's right, and in a move too quick to follow, he whirled in that direction and fired his pistol once. A man screamed in agony and dropped his own pistol, clutching at his bleeding and shattered gun hand instead. The Marshal's move had been so terrifyingly swift and accurate that the mob stood dumbstruck as the wounded man wailed.

"I might have just shot the gun from your hand, but the gun did nothing wrong, you see," the Marshal explained icily. "You did." He continued, gesturing menacingly with the Colt Peacemaker, "I will say this only once more: release him."

The man doing most of the dragging grudgingly let go of the rope. I yanked the noose off of my own neck and gasped for breath. By then, a clear path had formed between me and my benefactor. I crawled toward him and he hauled me up to my feet with his free hand. I wobbled at first, but then steadied. He directed me to two horses tied up near the side of the Creek Council House. Its civilized grandeur seemed at odds with the scene in the street. The Marshal kept his Colt trained on the more truculent members of the mob who had been slow to drift away.

"You can present your evidence to Judge Parker in Fort Smith," he told them.

"If either of you makes it that far," someone in the crowd muttered in reply.

We rode out of town to the east without delay. I could feel angry eyes trying to stare holes into my back. I didn't dare speak to the Marshal until we were clear of town, our horses settling into a long distance stride on the dusty plain.

"Thank you," I said. "Never thought I'd have cause to say that to a white law man."

"Don't thank me; you are my prisoner. We are going to Fort Smith where Judge Parker can review your case," he explained.

"Judge Parker? 'The Hanging Judge'? No, I suppose you've done me no favor."

Judge Isaac Parker got his sobriquet three years earlier when he, almost immediately upon assuming office, hung several felons from the gallows at Fort Smith. It was a huge sensation in all the papers, and it was meant to be. He wanted to send the message that law and order had come to the territory. Not all took kindly to the message.

"Don't be fooled by the newsmen. You will get fair treatment. Or is that what you are afraid of?"

"I didn't do it! But that won't matter when the accused is a Negro, will it?"

"Considering how many marshals with your skin tone Judge Parker has appointed, you need not worry about that. One of them, Deputy Marshal Bass Reeves, is almost as good a shot as I am. Almost."

I was skeptical. I had heard of them but hadn't yet seen one.

"And what is your name?" I asked.

"Stone," he said simply.

"That's it?"

"That's all you need. You can preface it with 'Deputy US Marshal'."

"I'm Nate Hodges."

"So you are."

He wasn't the greatest conversationalist. Perhaps his mind was on the ride ahead, as was mine . It was a hundred miles to Fort Smith. Of course the rail ran through Muskogee to the northeast, but that track ran north-south and would take us far out of the way. It looked like we were headed due east through some of the most outlaw-ridden country anywhere. A lawman and a Negro, neither of whom could expect an eager welcome. We continued all that day, paralleling the Deep Fork of the Canadian River on our right, until stopping to make camp that night.

I noticed that Stone made no fire, and we ate only some jerky he pulled out of his saddlebag. This we washed down with nothing but water. He also kept noise to a minimum and bid me do the same. Consequently, we exchanged few words. Bandits roamed this area, so I guessed that Stone wished to avoid notice. He put my legs in irons, and he was standing watch when I dozed off, still aching from the beating I'd taken. He surely didn't wake me to take the watch since I was a prisoner, and he was already awake when I woke soon after sun up the next morning.

Stone had caught a couple of fish from the nearby river as I slept. He had me make coffee while he prepared the breakfast over a small fire. I noticed that he still took care to limit the smoke from it. After the coffee I was awake enough to attempt conversation.

"Do you have any idea who did that terrible thing to Mrs. Gunther?"

"Yes, I was about to pursue some suspects when that mob interrupted my investigation," he explained between sips of coffee. "There is a murderous gang of desperadoes raising hell in this part of Creek territory. They are suspects already in similar crimes. And then there is you. Apparently a bunch of folks have reason to think you did it."

"Me? But I'm innocent! If you didn't think so, why didn't you let them hang me?"

"See the badge?" he pointed to it. "You'll get a fair trial, assuming the prosecution makes a case."

After he unshackled me, we broke camp and mounted up, continuing east. We forded a couple of creeks, traversed the associated thickets of underbrush that grew beside them. Then, the trees thinned out, allowing us to ride side by side in the clear again. The ride grew dull and I struck up a conversation.

"So how many men have you killed?"

His expression grew grave, a contrast to the flippant tone with which I asked.

"I'm responsible for more deaths than you could possibly fathom," he said in a low tone I had to strain to hear.

"All in the line of duty, right?"

"You could say that. Most richly deserved it. Some didn't, but in every case it was necessary to save others, or so I was convinced at the time."

"Does it ever bother you?" I persisted.

"Not as much as those I failed to save. I'm only one man and I can do only so much."

"How about a woman? Is there a Mrs. Stone?"

"No."

"Some special lady?"

"Once."

"Only once?"

"If she could be so easily replaced, she would not be special."

Hard to argue with him. I thought fleetingly of Sarah, a girl I knew back in Arkansas before striking west. There had been no one like her since. I kept up with the questions and he kept giving short answers until he suggested that, as I liked to talk so much, maybe I could handle it for both of us. He said that if I told him my life story he would pretend to listen and even feign interest on occasion. I had to smirk at that, my first moment of mirth since the ordeal in Okmulkee. So I filled him in on what it was like to grow up as a slave with no father around, no one but my tired mother to look after me until she was also taken from me. I told Stone about my life of petty crime after the war and my decision to venture into Indian Territory. Then, how things turned up for me when I partnered with Mr. Ackerman, who improved my education and set me on a better path.

"Shh!" he cut me off with one wave of his hand and then withdrew his pistol.

We were approaching another creek crossing, the trees on the other side too thick to see through. A good ambush point, I thought. Crack went the first shot! It was quickly followed by others. Stone returned fire, but I could not tell at what. I got a glimpse of gun smoke in the trees, but that was it. Bullets smacked into the dirt and the tree stumps near us. Stone wheeled his horse about and yelled at me to follow. We galloped back the way we came, away from the ambush. More shots rang out behind us, bullets whizzed by our heads and impacted in front of us. I was as scared as at the lynching but rode as best I could alongside the Marshal. I could hear the splashing of horses in the creek behind us. We were being pursued! Stone pointed out a rock outcropping we'd passed earlier.

"Ride there!" he bellowed.

I didn't argue. It seemed to offer some cover, and we needed some quickly as they were gaining on us. Stone turned his horse and exchanged his pistol for the Winchester rifle tied to his mount. He worked the lever action quickly and sent a hail of bullets back at our pursuers, making them pause long enough for us to dismount and guide the horses up the rocky slope of the outcropping. Or so we'd hoped. My horse stumbled on a loose rock, fell backwards, and collided with Stone's horse, which got spooked and bolted. My own mount made a terrible, frightened whinny as it crashed to the earth, legs and gear flying in every direction. More shots from our attackers came, the bullets ricocheting off the rocks and sending fragments into the air. Horseless, we resumed our climb to cover. My horse finally found his feet again and bolted off in the direction of Stone's terrified mount. Our rides were gone.

We made it to the cover of the outcropping, though. At last we had some protection from the enemy rifles while lying behind the jagged rocks at the top. Stone continued to work his Winchester. That held them at bay and forced them to content themselves with ineffective potshots for the time being, but I could see them maneuvering for a better vantage point. We held the high ground, though, and I acted as spotter, careful not to present much of a target. Their bullets occasionally whizzed overhead or slammed into the rocks in front of us as an intimidating reminder that we were trapped. When I pointed out one of their attempts to flank us, Stone suppressed them with the rifle.

"How many did you count?" I asked.

"Seven. They're down to six now, though," he replied with a hint of satisfaction.

"Well, they still got more than we've got by a long shot."

"That isn't the half of it," he said, pulling back his coat to reveal the pool of deep red blood on his side.

"You're hit! You're hit bad!"

I felt a wave of panic. He was looking paler already from the blood loss. I had no chance against those bandits without him. Any medical supplies were lost with our mounts, mounts we could not search for without getting shot. He gave me instructions for fastening a makeshift bandage and applying direct pressure to the wound, but the dressing was soon soaked red.

"They know I'm hit, too. And low on ammo. It will be dark soon. Your best chance will be to make a break for it. Then, when you can, sneak away unobserved. I can't move," he said.

"Who are they?" I asked.

"They appear to be the gang I was telling you about before. Probably learned they were on my list and decided to strike first."

The sun went down quickly, it seemed. Stone was fading with it, but still gamely training the rifle on any movement below, occasionally firing to prevent a turning movement or to let them know that a frontal assault would still be costly. He sweated profusely. I did, too. We soon drained the only canteen we'd salvaged from the horse debacle.

"All right, it will soon be dark enough. Here," he handed me the Peacemaker. "Good luck."

"I can't just leave you like this. They'll come for you any minute, sneaking up in the dark."

He didn't reply. He just turned back to his task, watching in the failing light.

"Good luck to you," I said, and crawled to the opposite side of the outcropping.

The twilight was fading. I could just make out a pathway where I might crawl behind a row of rocks unobserved to the copse of trees below. I started down, low crawling as quietly as I could. I stopped when I heard a noise in the thicket beyond. My horse! What luck! If I exercised some care, I might reach it without incident and ride away while the bandits were busy finishing off the marshal.

That thought turned my blood cold. Those fiends would probably torture him for sport before they killed him; and, they would get away with it in this almost lawless land. They were the same bastards that did unspeakable things to Mrs. Gunther before they finally let her die. Who knew who else they'd murdered, or who else they would murder in the future. But, at least I'd be safe. For now. Maybe. They might track me down and shoot me in the back. I tasted bile in my mouth and felt sick all over. I'd been running my whole life long. Here I was again, leaving a man who'd rescued me. Another voice, that of self-preservation, tried to talk sense into me; but I couldn't press forward.

Staying put wasn't an option, and I couldn't bring myself to flee. There was only one thing left to do: I turned back, retracing my crawl back to where Stone still lay prone in his shooting position. He heard me approach and turned to me.

"Forget something?"

"Yeah, you could say that. I can't leave you like this, much as I might want to. I can shoot," I said, gesturing with the pistol. "Let me help."

He looked me straight in the eyes, straight into my soul, and said, "Greater love has no man than this, to lay down one's life, someone once said. So be it."

Then he astounded me by standing straight up in defiance of the enemy and his own condition. He deftly brought the Winchester up to his shoulder and fired five shots in rapid succession, working the lever action in a blur and changing his aim point slightly with each trigger pull. Each shot was rewarded by a grunt or yelp as the bullets found their marks, even in the darkness. He then turned around, took a few steps towards the back ledge of the outcropping where I had just climbed, and fired another single shot into the thicket below. This shot also found and felled a bandit who was apparently trying to take our position from the rear. I never saw him on my crawl down there. He would have almost certainly shot me down had I tried to mount my horse and ride away. Another Bible verse came to mind: "He who would save his life will lose it..."

My mouth was agape. How did he recover from such a wound? How did he shoot all those men? How...?

"Your trial is over, Nate Hodges. You are a free man."

"What are you?" I asked in astonishment. "One of the angels?"

"No, but they can count on me for an ally," he winked.

We climbed down from the rock, verified that the bandits were dead, and soon corralled both of our horses. As it was night, we made camp there, but I couldn't sleep. I interrogated Stone until the sun came up, and since I met with his approval, he permitted me some information. He allowed that he was not an ordinary Deputy Marshal, that he was from very far away, and that he had been serving in law enforcement for a very long time. He told me that he was not invincible and would die someday, but that it would take more than a bullet.

"So what can kill you?"

"Oh, I have faced mortal threats, but fear is not native to my nature. To understand mankind I have sampled it, and I now know it well. I greatly admire those who overcome this fear and lay their lives on the line for others. I often serve with them and help them in just causes when I can; it adds meaning to my existence, for I can never go home again."

It wasn't a statement of despair, but he seemed unutterably alone after saying that. I questioned him no more. We went our separate ways in the morning and I never saw him again. Since I clearly couldn't go back to Okmulkee, he left me the stolen money we found on the dead bandits so that I could make a fresh start. He said he would see to it that the rightful owners were repaid. I didn't try to argue with him. I pity anyone that does.

I never really figured out exactly who or what Stone was, nor did later inquiries about him shed any light. The events that day were so fantastic that perhaps I imagined them. Real or not, his example of justice and fairness inspired me to pursue a career in the law, but that is another chapter.

SERGEANT STONE VISITS ST. BERNARD

New Orleans, 1888

Isis climbed the staircase with all the elegance of a queen, which of course she was. Reaching the observation deck, she made her way toward Stone on the top deck of the steamboat. An exotic beauty, Isis attracted more than her share of curious onlookers, especially amongst admiring males. In its wake, the *Natchez VIII's* massive paddlewheel churned the Mississippi River's brown water into white froth as it pushed its way south out of New Orleans; ts two gigantic stacks brashly spewing forth white steam columns into the sky. Isis enjoyed the breeze on her face, the view of the river and shoreline, and the thrumming of the engines that reverberated throughout the ship. She strode serenely up to Stone's side as he conversed with an older gentleman. The older man wore long white whiskers and a uniform indicating that he was the master of the vessel.

"But Captain Leathers, I thought that the *Natchez VIII* had a reputation for speed. We seem to be plodding along so slowly," Stone needled him.

"I will show you speed, sir, if I have to dump ten gallons of bacon grease into those gears! By Jove, see if I don't!" the captain exclaimed loudly before stalking off in feigned anger, a tip of his cap to Isis as he passed her on his way to the engine room.

"What was that about?" Isis asked Stone, looping her arm through his.

"Captain Leathers, or 'Old Push' as he is called by some, is sensitive about speed since he lost the Great Steamboat Race to the *Robert E. Lee*. He is a proud man, and rightly so, but he knows he hasn't many cruises left. Business is drying up and he is getting on in years."

Isis stood beside Stone to look out over the railing. Her English had improved markedly in a short time. Transplanted here from ancient Egypt by Stone for her safety, she had made a difficult transition with grace. He hadn't explained the details to her, but she understood that Stone had powerful enemies who had threatened her in order to attack him. How it was that such a threat should be a problem for him, he hadn't explained, but he didn't need to. Isis knew in her heart that her passion for him was reciprocated. It was clear in how he looked at her and how he held her, if not in the things he said. His enemies knew he loved her, and that is why she had to leave home. It was the only thing that made sense.

When they had met, she was still married to Prince Osiris, the firstborn son and heir of King Sened. The night Sened died, Osiris' younger brother, Peribsen, had Osiris murdered so that he could claim the throne of Egypt. Stone, under the name Amun at the time, had been a friend of Osiris and conspired to hide Isis and their son, Khasekhemwy, from Peribsen. That wasn't the end of Isis' trials, however. An unusually passionate woman and a deeply pious priestess of Ra, she proved vulnerable to extra-dimensional predators who tried to lure her to her destruction by using the image of her late husband as bait. She was drawn into that other dimension and saw its fearsome inhabitants, but she was again rescued by Stone's timely intervention. Her recollections of the episode proved influential to later Egyptian mythological development, particularly in regard to its beliefs about the afterlife. Her tales of the alien architecture she saw led directly to pyramid construction in Egypt. Perhaps memories of that architecture were conjured when, from the deck of the steamboat she spotted inland a strange, half-completed stone tower surrounded by unkempt grounds overgrown with weeds.

"What is that?" she pointed inland.

"I thought you might notice that. It is an unfinished monument to a big, important battle that was fought here back in 1815. The Battle of New Orleans, it is called, and the most important engagement of that battle was right over there at a place called the plain of Chalmette. Almost fifty years ago it was decided to commemorate the saving of the city from foreign invaders by erecting an Egyptian-style obelisk. As you can see, the plans fell through and it was never completed," Stone explained regretfully.

"Were you at this battle?" Isis queried. She had had many history lessons from Stone in her effort to catch up on the last five thousand years, and she had come to understand that Stone was a participant in some of the events he described.

"Of course; I wouldn't have missed that one. I served in the Battalion d'Orleans under Major Jean Baptiste Plauche. Even before the battle this militia served as a night watch for the city since there was as yet no police department. When General Andrew Jackson--you've seen his statue in town--came with his federal troops, as well as volunteers from Tennessee and Kentucky, we joined them along with Jean Laffite's Baratarian pirates, Free Colored militias, even Choctaw Indians. A real polyglot coalition assembled to defend the city against the British invaders."

Stone pointed out the movements of the various units with the ease of an actual eyewitness, which of course he was. He seemed to take relish in describing the valor of both sides, especially the doomed march of the 93rd Highlanders and the fierce hand-to-hand fight waged by the American 7th Infantry to retake a redoubt captured by the British. He pointed to where the British commander, Sir Edward Pakenham, fell mortally wounded. Further down the river he pointed out the area of the 23 December night attack on the British camp, a bold move in an era when night attacks were rare. It was a confused melee that ended inconclusively, but it slowed the British advance and allowed for the bolstering of the defenses that led to victory in the main battle on January 8th.

"Old Hickory never lacked for aggressiveness. 'By the Eternal they shall not sleep on our soil' he'd said. He meant it, too," Stone smirked at the memory.

Isis enjoyed the history lesson and listened attentively as always. The lessons had begun upon her arrival in New Orleans, a place Stone described as a null region which made it much harder for extra-dimensional foes to locate them. Of course others knew this also, and so the area became a refuge for all kinds of interesting characters from throughout the multiverse seeking to lay low. This complicated life for Stone who played a two-level game: guarding the city from ordinary criminality as part of the NOPD, while also safeguarding it against alien threats from all over creation.

The first history lesson for Isis had been about her son who, from her current vantage point, had been dead for nearly five millennia. Khasekhemwy's eventual revolt against his uncle Peribsen was successful, Stone having prepared him well before they departed. Isis saw among their fellow passengers a happy couple with two cloying children. They made her miss her own child. She pined for another. Isis asked more questions to take her mind off of her heartache.

"So what is this place called?" she asked, referring to the mostly empty pasture lands spread out before them as the steamboat left the battlefield behind.

"This is the parish of St. Bernard. Down the river you'll see the homes of the Islenos, Spanish settlers from the Canary Islands, whom the Spanish government placed below the city to guard its approaches. They fought in the battle, also."

"How did it get the name of St. Bernard?" Isis, being of a religious frame of mind, had been investigating Catholicism as the predominant local religion, and was curious about saints.

"Well, it was called the Bayou Terre-aux-Boeufs before but was renamed in honor of St. Bernard of Clairvaux, the patron saint of the Spanish governor of Louisiana at the time, Bernardo de Galvez. You see, the famous Battle of New Orleans was not the first time that the city had been threatened by the British..."

Santa Rosa Island, Florida, 18 March 1781

Governor Galvez had been sympathetic to the cause of the American colonists from the beginning, and not only because Britain was a power hostile to Spain, but because he admired the principles of the American Revolution. Upon taking over the governorship of Louisiana he opened the port of New Orleans to American commerce. While Spain was still officially neutral, he communicated with Patrick Henry and other revolutionaries. He also schemed with an American agent, the New Orleans-based Irish trader Oliver Pollock, to supply the Continental Army with food and war materiel. In 1779, Spain declared war on Britain, and Galvez was able to take more energetic measures. The British controlled Florida at this time, and the border of the West Florida territory rested on the Mississippi River. To guard this territory and exert influence on the all-important river, the British maintained forts in the Mississippi River valley, from which their garrisons could potentially threaten the strategic port of New Orleans. If New Orleans fell, they could choke off supplies to the Continentals, threaten the rest of New Spain, and dominate the destiny of most of interior North America. Indeed, a captured letter for the British commander at Pensacola indicated that the British did plan an attack on New Orleans. Galvez sought to secure New Spain's control of the Mississippi and get payback for the loss of Florida by striking first.

Stone served in the New Orleans militia at the time, and his proficiency with languages made him valuable beyond his talents for training and drilling troops. The Spanish forces for the impending campaign included, besides soldiers from Spain, a variety of New Spain troops to include Creoles, Negroes, mulattoes, Acadians, Choctaws, Islenos, and assorted other inhabitants. Stone proved himself useful again by guiding the first of the big cattle drives from San Antonio, Texas to supply beef to the army in Louisiana. As a result, he became an informal enlisted representative on Galvez's war council. Galvez was a man of privilege from an important Spanish family who had attended prestigious military schools in Spain and France. He also had real combat experience, however, and had been badly wounded in fighting the Apaches on the frontiers of New Spain. He knew real soldiers when he saw them and he trusted Stone right away. That trust was rewarded when Stone's advice helped Galvez achieve lightning victories against the British garrisons in Manchac and Baton Rouge with few casualties. Galvez followed up by capturing the important gulf coast city of Mobile. New Orleans had breathing room, but the city was not safe with strong British forces still in West Florida, Creek and other British-friendly Indians in the hinterlands, British reinforcements in Jamaica, and a strong Royal Navy lurking in the surrounding seas. The British fortress at Pensacola, the capitol of West Florida, had to be taken.

Last year's expedition against Pensacola had been a disaster. A hurricane dispersed the fleet to safe harbors all over the Gulf of Mexico. Stone cursed hurricanes for what was not the first or last time. He had seen countless battles, but the vast majority were on land. There were some notable exceptions, of course. Actium, Dan-no-ura, and Lepanto come to mind, as well as several smaller engagements, but Stone usually fought with the grunts of the infantry. He'd been on the losing end of some fights at sea and disliked the extremely long swims afterwards since he did not use his ability to transit dimensions unless some extra-dimensional business called for it, or if it was time to move to a different epoch. Excessive travel of that sort tended to draw too much attention from the wrong entities anyway, and Stone would rather not be bothered unless the bother was his own idea.

Still, Stone's perfect memory and vast experience made him an excellent mariner. In his current guise he was but a militia member, however, so he did not flaunt his nautical knowledge and only assisted with sailing the ship when it was requested of him. Now he was back on terra firma on the barrier island at the entrance to Pensacola Bay, the Island of Santa Rosa. Overlooking it from the mainland side was the formidable Royal Navy Redoubt. Its guns probably had the range almost all the way to the mouth of the bay. Sailing straight into the bay would mean sailing right into a fierce cannonade from experienced artillerymen. The entire expedition could be sunk in minutes. The guns might be skirted by hugging the coast, but that risked running aground as attempts to get accurate soundings had failed.

There was some commotion behind Stone who turned to see the Commander himself, Field Marshal Bernardo Galvez, approaching. Stone saluted and Galvez returned it, joining Stone on the beach with his aides in trail.

"Sergeant Stone, I see you are pondering the same thing which is on my mind," he said, his eyes on the British fortress.

"A real Scylla versus Charybdis quandary. A miscalculation would be disastrous," Stone observed. The gravity of the decision was not to be minimized.

"Captain Calvo has made his decision. He intends to sail to Mobile to resupply the garrison. Only the Louisiana vessels that do not belong to him will remain."

Stone raised his eyebrows in surprise and then frowned in disgust. Then he softened and offered, "The *San Ramon* did touch bottom the last time he attempted to sail her in, and that was after lightening the ship. He is a highly experienced sailor and his opinion should not be discarded lightly."

"And yet we must gain entry. No roundabout landward assault will succeed. We'll never supply a large enough force through so much hostile territory. The longer we delay here, the greater the chance of another hurricane that could wreck the fleet."

"Are you asking my opinion, sir?"

"You know I have come to value it as much as those of the Council members."

Stone smirked. "I think you know which course I would urge, but the decision is yours alone. You alone will be pilloried if we fail. Without accurate soundings or a knowledgeable pilot, without a precise estimate of the enemy's gun range, any crossing will be daring. The British themselves have a saying, 'Who dares, wins'. I want you to go, to at least fail on a daring roll of the dice, but I will support you regardless," he finished with a slight bow.

The Field Marshal and Governor turned to Stone with a radiant smile. "Excellent! I was hoping you would say that. I'd already decided to commandeer the vessels not under Calvo and make a go of it. I did want to sound you out, though."

Galvez gestured down the beach to a waiting boat, "Join me on the *Galveztown*, my namesake vessel, and we shall make history one way or another." Stone was pleased to do so and even insisted on helping to row out to the brig.

The *Galveztown* was a two masted, 14 gun brigantine that had once had a different name, the *HMS West Florida*. She had patrolled Louisiana waters, wreaking havoc on vessels running supplies to the American colonists for their rebellion, until the fateful 1779 Battle of Lake Pontchartrain near New Orleans. In a bold ambush, American sailors using a Spanish-supplied vessel boarded and seized the *West Florida* from her British crew. The ship was renamed for the Spanish Governor of Louisiana who had already contributed so much to the American cause. Once Spain entered the war, he used it to even greater effect, particularly in the capture of Mobile. Pensacola would be a tougher nut to crack. Its garrison commander, General John Campbell, was a competent soldier who made careful preparations for defense.

The boat pulled up to the anchored ship where Field Marshal Galvez and his entourage climbed aboard. After greeting the officers, he directed that his personal ensign be raised atop the mast and announced that the attempt on Pensacola Bay was to be made immediately. This was greeted with a deafening cheer from the crew. A signal gun fired to cue the other ships to be prepared to follow. These were two armed launches and a single other sloop, all that remained from Louisiana, all that was under the personal command of Galvez. The rest of the fleet he'd had to beg for from royal authorities in Havana to wage this campaign. Those were under Calvo's command and would not take the risk.

"Our fellows will not be joining us. You, my loyal Louisiana brothers, are all that remains to force the entrance to the bay in the teeth of the enemy. The honor, the glory, of this day shall therefore be ours alone. For God, for the King, for Spain, for Louisiana, we shall sail at once!" Galvez bellowed loudly, but his last words were drowned out by the cheers of the crew.

Galveztown weighed anchor and set sail for the bay entrance, the green waters beyond beckoning them like a booby-trapped emerald. She rounded the spit of brilliant white sand that marked the extreme end of Santa Rosa Island, hugging as closely towards land as the helmsman dared to maximize the distance to the British guns. Running aground would be as disastrous for the campaign as getting blasted by the fort's guns. A ship was lost this way at the successful attack on Mobile, but a repetition in this unfamiliar bay would demoralize the reduced fleet beyond recovery.

Stone's sharp eyes saw the puffs of cannon smoke from the fort first. "Incoming," he warned. The blasts from the cannons were heard almost as soon as he spoke. Geysers erupted in the bay where the cannonballs fell.

"They are falling short!" one of the younger crewmen announced unnecessarily.

"They'll adjust fire," Stone reminded him.

Indeed they did, and the geysers grew closer with each following shot. A shot splashed close enough to spray the deck and the helmsman veered away from it.

"Steady on," Stone encouraged him. The danger of running aground was still great.

More ominous geysers followed the booms from the British guns, growing ever nearer. Finally a ball smashed into the rigging overhead. Some others passed over harmlessly. The ship began to veer again and briefly touched bottom before the helmsman corrected course. Even the experienced sailors grew nervous. More balls flew overhead, piercing the sails. Spirits were lifted, though, when a cheer went up from the army on Santa Rosa's shore. They were encouraging their fellows at sea in their perilous undertaking. Or could they tell that the ships were nearing safety?

The barrage from the fort was furious and the ships were taking hits. Galvez pressed on and the flotilla soon passed out of range of the guns and into deeper waters, safe from running aground. Success! No men lost and only minor damage to the ships. A passage was confirmed for follow-on vessels, too, for now Calvo would be shamed into bringing the rest of the fleet. Another cheer erupted from shore, which was answered by the sailors afloat. The British fire had slackened to nothing as they recognized their failure to stop the passage. They would need to save ammunition for the landward siege that could now begin.

Weeks later, that siege was still ongoing. The Spaniards had landed their troops and, after slowly slogging and fighting through the bayous and forests around Pensacola, constructed their siege works opposite the British fortifications which defended the city on the north and landward side. Trenches and redoubts were dug, bunkers and covered roads constructed, artillery positioned, and a mountain of supplies brought up to maintain the army. The main British fortress, Fort George, was further guarded by the outer redoubts called the Crescent and the Sombrero further to the north. As long as these stood, no assault on the main fortress could be made. Indian raids and sallies of the British garrison periodically interrupted the already glacial pace of the siege, but the Spanish force got a boost when reinforcements arrived from Mobile.

Galvez was wounded in the hand and abdomen on 12 April while trying to lead a force to cut off the retreat of a British harassing force, so

Colonel Ezpleta took command of the siege. Galvez continued to exchange polite letters with General Campbell, the British commander, in a futile effort to convince him to surrender. Campbell held out hope for a rescue force or perhaps a hurricane to turn the tide for him and declined.

Amongst the contingent of Islenos was a young man of about fifteen years of age named Joachim. A gregarious youth, he had many friends in his own unit. For some reason, however, he continually sought out Stone's company. Most of the older men recognized something about Stone which made them prefer to respect him from afar, but Joachim was oblivious to this and instead just found him interesting. Stone, for his part, was reserved but not unfriendly. The kid loved talking to him when the opportunity arose. It seemed to arise often since Joachim's duties consisted of moving supplies from the ships to the forward units, one of which was Stone's New Orleans militia.

A raid by British-allied Choctaws on the front lines took place while Joachim was there. Stone pushed the confused youth into the trench, telling him to stay there as he directed return fire. The boy had had a close call, but he showed no fear and kept on coming to the front to chat with Stone during slow periods, of which there were many. On 4 May the British troops from the Crescent executed a heavy raid on one of the forward redoubts held by the Hibernians, a unit composed of Irishmen serving Spain. The fighting was fierce, but after the redoubt was retaken, Joachim was discovered among the dead. The next day a storm flooded the trenches and drove the ships away for safety, stranding the army. To boost morale, Galvez authorized a ration of grog for the troops. Stone took none.

Stone saw to Joachim's burial in the saturated ground. He had the chaplain say some words and directed a salute with muskets. There would be no tears, for that was not Stone's way. He had buried numberless comrades on countless fields. There was no way he could protect them all. There never was. So it goes, Vonnegut would say. Joachim fell in the performance of his duty. Stone was doing his duty elsewhere, unable to help. The British, too, were doing their duty. There would be no regrets, but neither would there be regret for what Stone did next.

The weather cleared on 8 May. The shelling and counter-shelling at the Crescent continued ferociously all day. Around six o'clock in the evening, Stone advised his men to stand ready for an assault and stalked off to a nearby howitzer position. He approached the crew with a bag of Spanish reals and said, "I don't want to tell you how to do your job, so I am just going to bribe you to let me man the howitzer for a while."

After some hesitation, the crew accepted the offered coins, probably wondering why a sergeant carried such wealth in the field, and relinquished control of their howitzer to him. Stone studied the Crescent redoubt for several minutes. He seemed to take note of the winds. Finally he set up a shot, adjusting the aim point and doing all the loading work himself. When he was satisfied, he fired a round from the gun, not bothering to cover his ears in spite of the loud bang of the shot; he was intent on watching the result of his attack. The howitzer lobbed the shell over the redoubt wall and it crashed dead center atop the enemy powder magazine, resulting in a brilliant flash of orange flame followed by an earth-shattering roar from the exploding powder. Debris and soldiers flew dozens of feet into the air and a dense black cloud of smoke enveloped the wrecked redoubt. Pieces of what was once a fighting position continued to rain down around the area for several minutes as the smoke slowly cleared to reveal the devastation.

Officers readied their men for the assault and the infantry soon pressed forward with this opportunity. Stone likewise rejoined his militia and participated in the general attack which captured the destroyed redoubt and its shaken survivors. They had little fight left in them, so rattling was the apocalyptic explosion, so heavy the losses amongst their fellows.

The loss of the Crescent redoubt made the position of Fort George untenable once the Spanish artillery moved forward again. General Campbell surrendered the garrison to General Galvez two days later and Pensacola passed out of British control.

Back in 1888 Louisiana…

"With the surrender of Pensacola, all of West Florida fell back into Spanish hands. Washington defeated of Cornwallis at Yorktown later that same year and the two reverses convinced the British to end the war and recognize American independence. Galvez was later promoted to viceroy and moved to Mexico City where he was much loved for his efforts to improve conditions for the people, much as he had done for hurricane victims in Louisiana. The King bestowed on him the honor of placing the words 'Yo Solo' on his coat of arms since he alone risked all in the attack on Pensacola. Galvez Street in town is named for him, as is the town of Galveston, Texas, and St. Bernard Parish right here," Stone concluded.

"Sounds like quite a man. Did he ever marry?" Isis asked.

"He did. His married a New Orleans widow, Marie Felice de Saint-Maxent d'Estrehan. She was very beautiful, like you. The parish of Feliciana, later divided into two parishes, East and West, was named by Galvez in her honor."

"She must have been very special to win such devotion from him," she looked at him longingly. He didn't indicate whether he caught her hint.

"Galvez died young, though, in 1786. The British came back, of course, when New Orleans was part of the young United States. Over there on the West Bank is the spot where they were victorious, but the triumph was meaningless since Jackson's army had already defeated their main force in Chalmette." The *Natchez VIII* was now steaming north and back to New Orleans. Isis listened to Stone but strayed back over to starboard to look over the steamboat's rail at the main battlefield again. Stone joined her there.

"Something on your mind?" he asked.

"That monument. I want it to be completed," she said in a voice of queenly command.

"As you wish, my Queen," Stone smiled, addressing her as he did in Egypt.

"It will honor the people of my new home, and, in a way, those of my former home," she stated, referring to the Egyptian-style of the obelisk.

Then another thought struck her. "Will this city face another foreign invasion?" she asked, confident that Stone would know.

Stone's face grew impassive. "Yes," he replied simply, seemingly gazing at the event in real time through his mind's eye.

"Then there is another reason to complete the monument—to inspire the people of the future," Isis decided.

SERGEANT STONE AND THE
SECOND BATTLE OF NEW ORLEANS

New Orleans, 2067

Recollections of Officer Paul Saladino, New Orleans Police Department (NOPD)

The crisis had been building for some time and, in truth, Stone had helped build it. I had been on the force for about four years and looked up to him like he was a demi-god. I wasn't the only one in the NOPD that did so, and we were closer to the truth in our estimation of him than we could have dreamed at the time. But that would be revealed later. In the beginning he was simply the finest police officer anyone had ever met. He set a very high standard in police work for the rest of us and his influence grew well beyond his lowly sergeant rank. Stone hearkened back to the old ways, real detective work that was less dependent on biometrics and modern tracking technologies to find perps, and he was amazingly successful. Crime rates dropped, as did the number of unsolved cases. He consistently refused promotion and continued to work the beat as a sergeant and low-level supervisor, but no one made detective without his tacit approval. Soon the lieutenants, then the captains were his protégés as well. It basically became his department, especially the Sixth and Seventh Districts.

Soon, though, it became apparent that he was selective in the enforcement of certain laws. The anti-superstition statutes and firearm safety laws, for example. I never saw him arrest a Christian or seize a gun. After a few years it became apparent that there were even members of outlawed religious sects serving quietly amongst us in the NOPD. Persecution had caused them, the Christians especially, to grow like wildfire in New Orleans. Stone had predicted this, saying he'd seen it before. These laws were mandated by the United Earth Council. In fact, they made the return of tax revenue to the city dependent upon enforcement. Still, the NOPD focused less on UEC mandates and more on violent crimes. Oddly, violent crime dropped as the gun confiscations subsided.

Stone didn't do it all alone, of course. City leaders were growing more independent of the UEC and more skeptical of its promises. Soon it paid less attention to its threats, too. The economic collapse of the 2030s and the fall of the nation-states in the 2040s were ancient history. No one felt any loyalty to the faraway bureaucracy in Geneva, only some residual fear of retaliation. The UEC's military arm, called the Earth Security Force, better known as FiST (Force de Securite de la Terre in French, Fuerza de Seguridad de la Tierra in Spanish gave it the initials FST or FiST) had been busy suppressing Caliphate forces in Asia, but that war was winding down, freeing up strength to suppress dissent elsewhere. There were no rival militaries, nothing to protect the city if the FiST should show up to punish New Orleans for recalcitrance. Nothing but the NOPD, that is, and our weapons and numbers could not match theirs.

This was made all the more apparent when FiST showed up at Charleston on the east coast. That city had been even more vociferous in opposing UEC mandates, even allowing public Christian worship and other outlawed speech and demonstrations. The FiST restored order in ruthless fashion, first disabling any of the city's defenses with an EMP (Electromagnetic Pulse) detonation overhead, then moving the air and ground drones in to round up rebels, blasting with plasma bolts any who showed the least reluctance to obey. Thousands were slaughtered.

That taught the other North American cities a lesson. Many were cowed. Some cities, however, took the wrong lesson and stiffened their resistance. New Orleans was one of those. Mayor Fernandez declared New Orleans a "free city" with all ties to the United Earth Council permanently severed. In another show of defiance, the museum exhibits were cleared out of the old St. Louis Cathedral and the first public Mass in over twenty years was celebrated there. The Archbishop of New Orleans, technically a criminal, came out of hiding to officiate and Mayor Fernandez even attended. The gauntlet was thrown down. Most of us in the NOPD felt no loyalty to the UEC, but the law was the law, right?

"An unjust law is no law. A statute which does not square with the laws of nature and nature's God cannot command our obedience. It was once a self-evident truth that governments were instituted among men to safeguard the rights of all to life, liberty, and the pursuit of happiness. When governments do not do this, it is the right of the people to alter or abolish said government," Stone said, paraphrasing a document he called the Declaration of Independence.

"Sounds like treason," I said.

"It was to the tyrannical king at that time. The United States of America was founded by those words, by that sentiment."

"They taught us about the United States of America in school. It was one of the foremost nation-states up until a few decades ago when it all came crashing down. Isn't it discredited now?" I asked.

"It strayed from its founding principles and the people continued to choose leaders who bought votes with handouts from the public treasury. Civic virtue declined, civilizational confidence waned, and finally loyalty to the very concept of a free and sovereign nation-state evaporated, so much so that even something as basic as a definite border was no longer enforced. They no longer felt they had the moral authority to maintain a nation. Indeed, since they had squandered everything that made their country special when they abandoned those founding principles, what was left to fight for? So when the collapse came, no one did fight," he explained. These lessons weren't covered in our history books. UEC mandates were careful to oversee what went into the world's textbooks, he reminded me.

"How did they begin to stray, though, after such a promising start?"

"A complicated question. There were crossroads where they might have made better choices. Perhaps the decline and fall were inevitable once some idiot on the high court mangled the concept of liberty with his decree that,

'At the heart of liberty is the right to define one's own concept of existence, of meaning, of the universe, and of the mystery of human life.' As soon as that nonsensical assault on reality was enshrined in judicial precedent, the American experiment in *ordered* liberty was tottering. Once moral relativism became official state policy, the rational basis for all law and the constitutional order was undermined. Once the "self-evident" truths that could be arrived at by right reason were denied their force, the will to power had an open invitation."

"But a new spirit is rising," he continued. "People are fed up with unjust laws and overbearing, unrepresentative and unresponsive bureaucracy. The UEC demands obedience and revenue but gives nothing back but oppressive mandates. It was a matter of time before they would have to back up their rule by force of arms against people beginning to love liberty again."

"They can enforce their will through drones and mechanized troops. They don't have to risk their lives. We will, though," I protested.

"You think it is a strength for them to be able to fight without courage? Not if they meet determined opposition. Their technical advantage presents a tactical challenge, yes, but it is men who win wars, not weapons. War is fundamentally an exertion of the will. The UEC has for so long exerted its will on the cheap that it is no longer truly strong where it counts," he pointed to his chest. "Besides, you have me, and I'm not holding back this time. Their technology is so great that I have an excuse to cut loose with everything I've got."

"And what have you got?"

"You'll see. For one thing, I've got the brave men and women of the NOPD."

"But what will you have against the FiST troops? They can EMP all our plasma weapons and make them useless before we get off a shot!"

"Precision application of antiquated firepower will go a long way."

That was part of the conversation that was taking place in the break room at the precinct on November 12, 2067. I recall the exact date since that was the morning that Chief Wilson showed up at roll call. He strode to the front of the room and the normal chattering ceased. He was in full dress uniform, his star and crescent badge upside down to denote his position as Chief. Stone said that was a tradition that stretched back to the nineteenth century. How did that man know so much history that hadn't been taught in decades? All I had learned in school was that everything that came before the UEC was hopelessly corrupt and oppressive. Experience had taught me that the UEC was no better and possibly worse.

Chief Wilson stretched up to his full height, which was considerable at six foot five, and glared about the room sternly. "What I am about to say is deeply disturbing, but as you know the City leadership is doing great harm to our relations with the rest of the world. I have been contacted directly by the United Earth Council to take the mayor and city councilmembers into custody. There is also a list of rebel ringleaders that must be apprehended. I expect all of you to do your duty and secure this city from the insurrectionists infesting it before the FiST troops, already deployed, have to come in and do it their way."

The room exploded in noise from angry officers. The din continued for several seconds as the assemblage vented expressions of dissent. Some countered the dissenters with questions: "What choice do we have? You saw what happened to Charleston!" The murmurs died down as Sergeant Stone walked purposefully up the middle aisle to stand next to the Chief, his hands on his hips in defiance.

"Chief Wilson, you are hereby relieved of command and I place you under arrest for treason against the Free City of New Orleans. Take him away," Stone gestured to a couple of burly officers nearby who complied immediately. The stunned former Chief barely had time to register his complaint before he was ushered from the room.

"Now to the business of defending the city. As you heard our illustrious former Chief say, the FiST is coming down on us. Unlike Charleston, a town I liked, by the way, we know they are coming and have a couple of days to prepare. There is no time to waste."

"They're going to EMP us. All our stuff, weapons, vehicles, communications, even refrigerators for food will be rendered useless! What defense will we have?" an officer objected.

"Good point about the refrigeration and food storage. We will appoint a task force to work with the Fire Department to see to evacuations and to the feeding of those who remain. We'll stockpile non-perishable foods and pre-position replacement equipment outside the city to get the electrical infrastructure up and running again quickly once the enemy is defeated," Stone exuded strange confidence in the face of very long odds.

"Defeated? How are we supposed to defeat them, exactly?"

"Good question. I like good questions. We can't stop the EMP from happening; the bomb will detonate high over the city and we have nothing to intercept it. Almost all of their force is composed of drones which receive commands via encrypted satellite communication. That would be a weakness, but they are very adaptable and any cyber-attack of ours would only cause them a minor delay at best. We cannot match their technology; they've kept the best toys for themselves for years. We must counter them with older weaponry and other newer gadgets that are not vulnerable to the EMP. We can build a Faraday Cage to protect some of our plasma rifles, but they will still run low on power quickly since we must use high energy kill shots against their drone troops, not the stun shots that we use on humans. Our plasma generator can't be hardened and will be offline, so you get only so many shots until you capture enemy stuff. Now, we've got a lot to do and little time in which to do it, but this can be done. Here are some of the tactics I've developed for countering their hovering troop carriers and drones…"

A flurry of unusual preparations followed. Stone was full of unorthodox ideas that saved little time for inspirational speeches. The Mayor asked a large gathering of officers huddled in planning whom should be appointed the Acting Chief of Police (the City Council had evacuated with most of the citizens, so the appointment couldn't be confirmed). By universal acclamation, to include some high ranking officers that might have been in line for the job, we told her to appoint Sergeant Stone, and she agreed readily. Stone looked up in brief acknowledgement, muttered 'thanks', and got back to work. After some cajoling he consented to being sworn in with a very brief ceremony as Acting Chief of Police for the duration of the emergency. I guess the stakes were too high for him to refuse promotion this time, especially since it was offered in this way. He had mentored so many of us, and likely planted many seditious seeds along the way, that he was one of the principal fathers of this revolution anyway.

Chief Stone, now with his badge inverted with the star on top and the crescent on the bottom in keeping with tradition, sent out teams of officers around the city to gather unusual items. Somehow he seemed to know the locations of several caches of antique weapons and radios. A set of ancient vacuum tube-era radios was found which he said might work after the EMP. We trained on them and hoped to use them to coordinate defenses. The old gunpowder-based firearms would certainly still be usable, but only the higher caliber ones had any hope of damaging the mechanized drone troopers. Still, the word was put out to the citizenry that if they still had these firearms, we were no longer trying to seize them but to encourage their use or donation to our cause.

Stone led one scavenger hunt himself. Just outside the city was a place that had been called Jackson Barracks. Stone said it had been named for the last guy who'd successfully defended the city against foreign invaders. The place had been the headquarters of something called the Louisiana National Guard, long disbanded. States and their guard forces disappeared about the same time that nations and armies did when sovereignty was handed over to the world state. The barracks had been converted to storage of some kind and then forgotten. The buildings had been neglected for years. Sometimes we had to root gangs out of the dilapidated remains. Some were in better condition, though, and it was to one of these that Stone led me and three other officers (Sanchez, Johnson, and Lee –nicknamed the four musketeers), all of us carrying knapsacks he had given us. Inside, mine had a container holding liquid that sloshed around with my every step.

This sturdy brick building had once housed a museum, it seemed. Stone knew his way around and located an old vehicle that I'd only seen in pictures before—a jeep. He said its old engine would run just fine after the EMP as it was low on electronics. After inspecting it, he declared that it would be roadworthy after getting the proper fuel, lubricants, and a battery. Apparently I was carrying the fuel which he called gasoline. He said he had a source for the old gasoline, oil, and grease needed, and then produced those last two items out of Lee's knapsack. The battery he'd replace with a modern power source, but he said he could harden it against the EMP with enough insulation. The tires were in good condition and needed only air, which we provided via the air compressor he'd had us carry.

After an hour under the hood, the rest of us handing him tools or lubricants like we were assisting a surgeon, he declared it fit to fight. We cleared a space in the building's cargo loading area, which had a garage door suitable for exit. The ancient jeep's engine roared to life when Stone engaged the starter, and we all grinned at each other involuntarily. It had a charming sound of raw power, not like the electric wheeled and hovercars with which we had grown up. Stone drove the jeep outside the building and then switched the engine off after letting it warm up for a minute or so.

"We aren't done here," he announced, and he went back into the building. We followed him to a darker, windowless part of the building, using flashlights to avoid stumbling in the maze. Finally he stopped at an exhibit which showed scenes from some past war that wasn't covered in my history books. Yeah, my ignorance bothers me.

After we helped him move the exhibit, he ran his hands along the dust-free floor that was now uncovered. He found a seam in the floor and widened it with a chisel he took from his knapsack. Using it as a lever, he pried up a large section of floorboard to reveal a hidden basement. There was a ladder leading down into it which fortunately seemed sturdy. He climbed down and we followed. I was last down and found a space between my fellows so that I could see what they were looking at.

"Wow," Sanchez spoke my own thought, "what is it?"

Stone had opened a box in which lay a black metal contraption, an archaic firearm of some sort, but very large. It had a solid and sturdy barrel at least 40 inches long and grips on the back end for grasping with all fingers on each hand while depressing butterfly-shaped triggers with the thumbs. The blasted thing weighed 80 pounds if it was an ounce, and it took both me and Johnson to lift it out of the wooden crate. It was covered in some kind of grease to protect it from moisture and this gunk smeared all over my hands.

"That," Stone said with a smile, "is the Ma Deuce. The M2 Browning .50 caliber heavy machine gun. And over there," he gestured to some metal crates, "is the ammunition to feed this glorious beast."

I groaned. That small mountain of ammo crates, and a couple of spare barrels, would take some time to move out of here. Yet I smiled as I worked since Stone described the ballistic characteristics of this antique weapon, its range and the lethal impact of its heavy rounds. All the ammunition seemed to be in excellent condition, albeit very old. I remarked on this and Stone said simply,

"Let's just say that my grandfather knew how to take care of these things and left it here for a rainy day. The sky is clouding up."

We weren't done in that part of town. A little further down the road and we came to Chalmette. Stone said that the first battle of New Orleans had been fought here by that Jackson fellow. He led us to a large stone tower in a field which he said marked the site. The area was overgrown with weeds and there were no signs or plaques. Stone said that the new regime would have knocked over the monument as well, except they were lazy and saw no need—the people here had forgotten their heritage anyway.

We bypassed the neglected monolith as we marched to the river. In what used to be called the Chalmette Slip, we found an old tanker that was docked. Climbing aboard, we discovered that while it had sat unused for some time, it appeared to be in good working order. Stone managed to start the engine and declared that the ship was now part of the navy of the Free City of New Orleans and dubbed it the *Old Hickory*. He said he could harden its vulnerable components against the EMP as well and make good use of the old rust bucket. It was unarmed, so I didn't see how. Others were assigned to man the ship. I was to learn to drive the jeep.

We took the hovercar for the next scavenging mission since it was further away. We flew over Chalmette and some marshes, over Bayou Bienvenue and the Paris Road Bridge, which for some reason Stone referred to as the "Green Bridge, although it was clearly painted gray. He explained that it was painted green back in its heyday. He flew us over an abandoned industrial area he called Michoud (pronounced "me shoe") and set us down in what he said was once an assembly area for manned spacecraft, "back when humans still did that sort of thing," he said with more than a hint of reproach. What did humans need to go into outer space for when robots could do everything better out there? I made the mistake of baiting him,

"I learned in school that humans visited the Moon last century in one of the first great United Earth endeavors."

"Bullshit. You know that the world was still dominated by nation-states back then and the United Nations was powerless. No, a world united under one oppressive government would never have done such a thing then and probably still wouldn't have by now. It was achieved only because two of the world's great powers were locked in a struggle for dominance and each raced the other to get there first. Only one country's flag stands there today, the flag of an exceptional people, a free people that once dared do great things. Screw with your history books all you like, but no one will deny them that achievement while I still live to tell the tale," the Chief preached. It was my fault. I could have kept my trap shut.

We busted into the building, which seemed to have been abandoned at least as long as Jackson Barracks. The owners were not around for us to ask permission. If they objected, I suppose they could call the police. Stone didn't seem to know his way around here nearly as well, and there was much reading of wall and door signs by flashlight. Offices and cubicles dominated one area with only long outdated computers and dilapidated furniture. Papers were scattered all about, making the floor tricky to walk on in the dark. The air was stale and oppressive.

After some searching we found what appeared to be the assembly area, a large open building with massive, rusting machinery. Only Stone knew what we were looking for, and after rummaging in a storage area behind the main assembly building he called, "Eureka!"

We caught up to him and the sight of his find was far less impressive than the old machine gun. Stacks of beige plates. How boring.

"What the hell is this?"

"A special type of ceramic tile so durable that it was used to protect spacecraft from the heat of reentry into Earth's atmosphere from outer space. It could withstand temperatures similar to those dished out by modern plasma rifles," he explained.

The light bulb went on in my head, "Can we harness them to protect our officers?"

"That is my evil plan. It won't be perfect, but it will afford at least some protection and help our troops stay in the fight. There is enough here to give everyone front coverage, by my estimate. It is well; folks will be less likely to turn and run on the FiST mechs if their backs are unprotected, right? Anyway, fleeing will trigger an algorithm in the mechs' programming to begin an aggressive pursuit that will tear our people to pieces. Always do a fighting withdrawal with covering fire. They don't fear casualties as human enemies would, but they do try to preserve assets and will probe for your flanks as long as you keep them under enough suppressive fire. Let the fire slacken or retreat pell-mell and they will destroy you immediately." What the hell were we in for?

The next morning after a sleepless night full of battle preparations, we got word that the FiST troop ship had been spotted in the Gulf of Mexico, heading for the Mississippi River. No long distance hypersonic drones firing missiles like they do with the Caliphate forces. Then they hit with pinpricks, deliberately never fully defeating them since they served some political purpose. For a rebellious city under nominal UEC rule, though, they sent an occupation force. They were going to give us the Charleston treatment and wipe us out. The EMP would hit soon, followed by the sky filling with drones and unmanned hovering gunships. Then the troop carriers would drop in the mechanized infantry, fearsome drone soldiers. Lastly the automated troop ship would dock at the beachhead and unload the heavy vehicles and many more troops. Not a human in the entire operation except via SATCOM link to a headquarters in Europe, most likely, and that was only for the broad strategic direction. Everything else was automated. Life and death decisions made by programming and algorithmic responses to sensory data. Chief Stone gathered his top officers at Jackson Square for a last war conference. I was there too as the driver of his jeep, which had the Browning M2 .50 calibre heavy machine gun mounted on it for Stone's use. He said that he was the best shot with it in the NOPD, and no one doubted this or thought it bragging.

I parked the jeep in front of the Cathedral. It was flanked by the Cabildo and Presbytere museums. Across the street was Jackson Square itself, a courtyard surrounded by a wrought iron fence and dominated by the equestrian statue of General Jackson, one time savior of the city from an ancient crisis similar in many respects to our own. He hadn't been removed since the history had been forgotten. Stone had revived that history, however, and told us the tale. It was no coincidence that he chose this meeting place. I looked around to take it all in. The old French Quarter architecture of the Pontalba Apartments on two sides, Decatur Street on the side opposite the Cathedral and the Mississippi River beyond that. I could see a corner of the Café du Monde. The city was special to me, and now pitiless automatons dispatched by faraway bureaucrats were heading this way to take it all away. We'd just see about that. The other officers were thinking along similar lines as Stone climbed atop the jeep to address them.

"The cyber-attacks have already begun; communication with the outside world is virtually cut off except for some old style radios. The FiST troop ship is already sailing up the river and will soon be in range to launch its drones. This means the EMP will detonate overhead soon and you've all been briefed with what to expect. Nothing you were trained to rely on that is outside the Faraday cages will function. Those of you rich enough to spring for one of those cybernetic performance enhancers will thank me later for the old-fashioned conditioning program I insisted on since those will not work either. Enemy satellite imagery sees what we do, but we've been careful not to tip our hand so nothing they've seen should be helpful. The evacuation of the non-combatants is as complete as it will get. Those who remain are city militia that are helping us out."

"I am immensely proud of all of you. The risk is great and our victory will not come without cost. All of you know that, and yet here you stand. I will gladly fight beside you anytime, anywhere. And when we are victorious, other cities and provinces will see it. They will see that tyranny can be beaten and they will join us. Then we'll bring the whole corrupt system down! It starts here, today! The enemy shall not pass!"

We roared with assent and then the officers scrambled to their hover cars, taking off and flying low in case the EMP deactivated them without warning. Might as well expedite movement with them while you have them, of course. Ground cars were similarly vulnerable, but we expected the jeep to keep on running with its old engine. At least we'd have the streets to ourselves.

Sanchez was riding with us. She sat up front on the passenger side with that antiquated radio to operate our mobile command post. Johnson and Lee manned another radio at the static command post where they would receive messages from field units and relay the most urgent to us. Chief Stone manned the gun in the back and expected to be driven promptly to wherever he was needed most.

He confided that to us, me and Sanchez, that is, that he was not like other men. This we knew, but he elaborated. He told us that he was not as vulnerable to enemy fire as the rest of us, but that he wouldn't ask us to take any unjustified risks. He said that human technology was advancing to where even he, too, could be killed by it. To win the day he said that he would have to go into full "super-hero mode" instead of holding back like usual, so expect the unexpected. Of course I asked what the hell he meant by all that. He responded that since he helped instigate this particular fight instead of riding along, it was his responsibility to finish it. But did he just tacitly admit to being something other than human?

A distant boom thundered overhead. We looked up to see, in the middle of the bright morning sunshine, a strange splash of color akin to the aurora borealis, a phenomenon almost never seen this far south. The city went eerily quiet as motors everywhere stopped. Except ours. The jeep kept rolling as advertised. We passed several electric cars now motionless in the middle of the road as we drove to the Central Business District, or CBD. Arriving at Canal Street, all the lights were out and the cars stopped. The old streetcars weren't running anyway due to the evacuation. As far as I knew, no one was injured by flying their hovercars too high.

The main attack was expected to start at the CBD and then fan out if the FiST held to its normal model. Stone insisted that they were unimaginative and complacent and therefore unlikely to innovate. We made the CBD particularly risky for them by stringing high tensile wires between the tall buildings at the heights favored by the smaller drones and the troop hovercarriers. The wait for the arrival of the drones was short and they began buzzing all over the city, occasionally hovering like giant hummingbirds. Only these birds were not just dangerous in themselves; the enemy command net allowed all assets to access what every other asset was seeing through very robust datalinks. We would have loved to jam this net, but anything that might have done so just got fried by the EMP. The NOPD hadn't room in the Faraday cages to protect enough jammers to make this tactic work.

Speaking of the Faraday cages, they did manage to protect dozens of plasma rifles. Each would have four effective shots before exhausting their charge and no recharge would be available. With the EMP event now over, word went out on the old vacuum tube radio sets to start issuing them out. It was hoped that we would capture some enemy rifles. These could be detached from the mech troops' arms and used clumsily by humans, but once severed from their hosts' generators, these would also use up their charges quickly.

Overhead came the FiST gunship, an enormous flying saucer-type craft that parked itself over the city and hovered there. This was a weapon

Stone told us that we were bound to respect since its plasma cannons were very accurate and dealt out enormous damage. Moreover, we had nothing with which we could even try to shoot them down at their altitude. Fortunately, Stone had an idea on this as well.

"They are unmanned," he said. "An advantage when you want to send it someplace dangerous, but you don't want to waste them either, because they are expensive. So, they have defensive systems that must be automated. These process data from threat sensors and decide based on an internal algorithm whether or not to move the craft and evade the threat. Sadly, we have nothing that is a genuine threat at their altitude. Happily, I know the wavelengths of emissions that the defensive system will perceive as a threat anyway and move the craft out of danger. This will take them out of the fight since there is no human in the loop to realize there is no real threat and countermand the movement. In other words, we will tickle their threat receivers with arc welders modified to mimic surface-to-air missile launches and the automated system will not know the difference and honor the threat."

At the signal, militia volunteers all over the city began arc welding, emitting the faux threat signals. Seconds after the signal was sent we saw the gunship shoot off decoy flares and leave the area with a roar of its engines. Another part of the plan had succeeded! Chief Stone grinned and pulled back the charging handle on the Browning .50 caliber machine gun. Click-clack!

"Now we go to work."

Drones filled the city, their engine whines replacing that of the ordinary activity of the city cut short by the EMP. Their whine was high-pitched in level flight, somewhat less so when hovering. During hover was when they were dangerous. That meant they had either spotted something of interest to relay to the net for processing as a possible target, or the algorithm had already decided that a target had to be engaged and it was about to fire. They began to buzz through the CBD with impunity as if they owned the skies. The first indication that this was not entirely so was when some collided catastrophically with the high tensile wires we'd strung between the taller buildings. Flaming drone parts crashed on the street and I had to maneuver the jeep around the pieces of wreckage. It was about to get worse for them. We turned on to Canal Street where we had a long, unrestricted view to the north. Several drones could be seen approaching the heart of the city.

I thought they were still out of range, but Stone fired a shot at a drone far in the distance, the report of the M2 shockingly loud behind and above my head. One shot was all it took and the drone fell to pieces in front of us.

"Carlos Hathcock had nothing on that one," Stone said with a grin.

We went drone hunting, Stone swatting them like flies with deadly accurate single shots that conserved ammo. I grew accustomed to the noise, oh so much louder than the plasma weapons I was familiar with. But, I never got used to having the hot spent brass casings land on my neck, which happened all too often. Sanchez, to my right in the passenger side, relayed messages about where the drones were most active. I'd speed us in that direction and for very long range shots Stone had me stop the jeep as he sniped away at them unerringly. This happened several times, but on occasion we had closer engagements with several drones that returned fire. Sanchez was also helpful as a spotter while my head was down and focused on the road. I was beginning to like the old jeep and its strong engine; it made the electric cars seem wimpy.

"Keep moving unless I tell you to stop," Stone barked. "Stay unpredictable. Those fire control computers will not miss if you drive straight at a constant speed!"

This point was punctuated when a drone's blue plasma blast shot over the jeep close enough that the heat nearly singed my eyebrows. It spurred me to more evasive movement. Stone opened up with a burst from the .50 and dropped the cluster of menacing drones.

"Troop carriers on the move," Sanchez yelled. "Two approaching City Hall. One near Lee Circle, one near the Superdome, another hovering near Armstrong Park."

"City Hall is well defended. We have a team near the Dome and some in the 8th District. We're thin in the Warehouse District and it's the closest anyway. Take us to Lee Circle!" Stone ordered. Off we went. We were at Tchoupitoulas and Poydras, having just downed a pair of drones near the casino. I tore off north up Poydras.

"You missed the turn!" Sanchez scolded.

"What, you wanted Magazine? I was going to Camp Street."

"It's a one way on that side of Poydras!" she insisted, sounding just like my wife.

"No one else is driving!"

"Just take St. Charles; it's less likely to be obstructed," contributed Stone.

Fine. St. Charles, then. Stone had a point, though. St. Charles Avenue was nice and wide, accommodating as it did the streetcar line on the ample neutral ground between lanes. It also led straight into the wide open space of Lee Circle, which the FiST processor had apparently selected as a site to land mech troops. I revved the engine and we surged beyond Lafayette Square. A few blocks ahead we could see the troop carrier lower on approach and begin to hover, its jet engines in a higher whine now, much like the drones. It was similar in shape to the saucer-like gunship, only somewhat smaller. Hovering about fifty feet over the ground, it disgorged wires that fell to the pavement, down which the fearsome mechanical infantry drones rappelled. They looked like overgrown medieval knights from afar, but they were far less chivalrous. Stone opened up with the .50 on the troop carrier, the big lead slugs punching big holes in the aircraft's light armor. Seconds later it careened out of control and crashed spectacularly, destroying several deployed troops on the ground and, unfortunately, the statue of the uniformed, bearded man that stood atop a pedestal in the center of the circle. I presumed his name was Lee since that was the name of the place.

"The Old Man would have approved," Stone said of the fallen statue after finishing off the few surviving mech troops with another burst from the Browning.

"Getting low on ammo. To City Hall, and step on it!"

"Their gunship gets frightened away, they lose a startling number of drones, yet they proceed with the air assault. Unthinking, complacent, and foolish. Yet they still have deadly weapons," commented Stone as the jeep zoomed up Howard Avenue.

In our absence, a fierce battle was raging at City Hall. Two troop carriers flew up to the City Hall courtyard and began disgorging mechs. NOPD snipers were well concealed in surrounding buildings and opened fire once they stopped to hover. Each was instructed to take only one good shot before changing windows. The fire control for the carriers' plasma cannons could very quickly identify the origin of any shot and return fire in that direction. The volume of fire in this case was overwhelming, though, and the carriers' cannons could not keep up.

We had another ace up our sleeve since the Browning M2 was not the only ancient treasure Stone had dug up. He'd also found an M-79 40mm grenade launcher, but only a precious seven usable rounds. Sergeant De Noux proved handy with it, even taking down one of the carriers and accounting for several mechs before exhausting his ammo.

The charges on the plasma rifles ran out quickly as well. More NOPD officers poured out of the surrounding buildings to engage the mechanized infantry. Few shots were wasted and many mechs were destroyed, but it wasn't enough and more kept coming. The remaining troop carrier remained overhead to provide fire support to the mechs, inflicting heavy casualties with its cannon. The ceramic vests afforded some protection against the enemy infantry weapons, but could not protect against the more powerful weaponry of the hovering carriers, which rarely missed.

At this time, Corporal Cotton hit upon a brilliant tactic. She grabbed her net gun, which was a non-lethal weapon used to subdue rioters or nab fleeing suspects by shooting an ensnaring net around them. As it fired by using compressed air, it still worked post-EMP. Instructing nearby officers and militiamen to provide her with covering fire, she daringly charged out beneath the troop carrier and fired her net into the rear engine. The jet intake swallowed the net and the engine was ripped to shreds in an instant. The sudden power loss caused the carrier to lose control and crash into a squad of mechs on the ground, shattering them.

This was a blow to the enemy, but they still held the advantage with the NOPD plasma rifles running out of energy. The temporary chaos it caused in the enemy formation allowed our troops to fall back in good order to Duncan Plaza while snipers kept the mechs from a concerted advance. They could only delay the inevitable, though, and soon all the plasma was used up. Antique high-powered rifles were the only remaining weapons that could damage the mechs, anything smaller than a 30.06 being useless against their armor. But even these were in short supply after so many years of gun confiscations. Ammunition was more precious still. The NOPD and militiamen were gradually being overwhelmed, especially as drones showed up to provide the air support that was lost with the carrier.

Soon those drones started exploding in mid-air, struck by an unseen attacker. Then the source was clear as our jeep sped into view on Loyola Avenue and the battle was joined. The loud report of the .50 cal could be heard over the din of battle as short bursts from it mowed down the mechs' perimeter security, followed bylong bursts that tore into their main ranks from behind. Infantry drones burst asunder when hit by the big .50 caliber rounds, sparking mechanical limbs flying in every direction. The assault in their rear took them by surprise as they relied on aerial drone surveillance for early warning, and that was now lacking due to heavy losses. In short order, Chief Stone finished off that enemy force and the city defenders got a respite. Quickly the NOPD and militia harvested the fallen plasma weapons from the dead mechs to prepare for the next round while Stone replaced his barrel and replenished his ammo. More net guns were distributed with the idea of replicating Corporal Cotton's feat.

Sanchez and I drained our canteens of water and refilled them. War is thirsty work, and there was much more to do. I didn't need Sanchez's radio to tell me that there was a heavy firefight on North Rampart as I could hear the sounds of battle. Our roving fire teams were harassing the mechs marching this way from their assault zone in Armstrong Park. Chief Stone gathered some key officers around a map spread out on the hood of the jeep for a hasty conference. Sanchez fed him reports of enemy locations, which he marked. He then identified his desired ambush points and instructed the officers to deploy their troops accordingly.

"Don't shoot until you see the reds of their eyes," he told them. The mechs had glowing red eyes which made them quite intimidating. That and the fact that they were fearless, tough, and strong enough to break a man's back with the swipe of an arm.

A mixed unit of militia and cops armed with old gunpowder rifles was sent into the advanced position to meet the enemy first, up near Iberville. Hardy souls, they were. We hung back about one block behind them near the corner of North Rampart and Cana. Stone picked off aerial drones with single, well aimed shots from his sniper machine gun. A mass of enemy mechanized infantry marched down Rampart right at us. At the signal, the militia opened fire with everything they had. They managed to strike down some of the infantry drones, but nowhere near enough. The return fire was deadly, augmented by the fire support of the slow flying troop carriers that had brought in the mechs.

"Now!" Stone ordered. Sanchez transmitted the message, "Cowpens! Cowpens! Cowpens!"

On receiving this rehearsed signal, the forward unit ceased firing and turned tail to run back up the street as fast as they could. They'd been outfitted with vests that covered their backs as well, but several fell anyway to the searing plasma bolts of the enemy. We fell back and turned north up Canal Street before stopping next to the old Saenger Theater. This retreat triggered the pursuit algorithm in the mech infantry, much akin to the pursuit instinct of an animal predator, and they surged forward with double speed…

…right into the pre-planned kill zone. The troop carrier emerged into the open on Canal Street where Stone was waiting for it on the M2, which he promptly used to great effect, filling it with holes from devastatingly close range. When it crashed into the middle of Canal Street and erupted with a huge fireball, Stone exclaimed, "Audie Murphy has nothing on this!" Who are these people he talks about?

The FiST infantry found itself in a deadly cross fire from overlapping zones of NOPD plasma fire, also at relatively close range from vantage points atop and within adjacent buildings and from the street itself. Without their drones flying ahead to warn of danger, their pursuit algorithm led them directly into a withering ambush. Blue bolts crisscrossed the street and brought down scores of mechs. More NOPD and militia emerged behind them and cut off any escape. They also fired volleys of nets at the jet intakes of the remaining troop carrier and managed to bring it down. The carriers flew low to provide fire support but did not adapt to the new threat. They might have still provided adequate fire support from a higher altitude, but that was considered to be the role of the gunship, now absent, and they were not programmed to rethink their tactics. That enemy force was cut off and destroyed, but far more were about to pour into the city.

We got a report from our observation post atop the tall WTC building by the river that the massive FiST vessel which had launched all these robotic fiends had sailed up the Mississippi and was docking at the ferry landing at the foot of Canal Street. It immediately began to offload more infantry and also main battle tanks too heavy for the troop carriers to lift into the city. These mechanical monsters were too well armored for even Stone's mighty M2 to deal with. In spite of all their unusually heavy losses, the FiST would still win the day if it landed enough of those. We replenished our plasma rifle supply by taking many from the mechs we'd ambushed at the Saenger Theater fight, and Chief Stone led that ambushing force down Canal Street to attack the enemy beachhead. Another force gathered at City Hall under Captain Randazzo and marched down Poydras to join the attack. A third smaller force gathered near Jackson Square and moved west down Decatur and North Peters.

Over at the Chalmette Slip, the *Old Hickory* powered up and sailed down river on its mission. A team of volunteers from the New Orleans Fire Department was aboard with a skeleton crew to man the engine room and the bridge. Fire Captain Valdez sighted the enemy ship just as *Old Hickory* rounded the river bend at Algiers Point. It had just docked on the east bank of the river near the foot of Canal Street at Spanish Plaza. The broadside of the massive ship was presented to Valdez, a tempting target. There were no escort vessels protecting the troop ship in FiST's complacent deployment. *Old Hickory* had not slipped stealthily by the buzzing drones overhead, it was simply not deemed a threat since it was an unarmed cargo ship. The laws of physics, however, meant that 45,000 deadweight tons steaming at you at 13 knots was far from harmless. The FiST processors finally crunched the probability of collision and deemed the cargo ship a serious threat. All assets were ordered to open fire on *Old Hickory*. A dozen drones did so, the blue beams of their plasma guns sizzling desperately all over the ship, but they could not punch through the heavy metal hull to anything vital. The cannons on the troop ship then opened up. These had enough power to do far more damage, but the ancient cargo ship was closing fast now.

"I'm coming for you, you bastards," Valdez said under his breath. Then as the ship took more hits and his blood was up, he bellowed, "Valdez is coming!"

Valdez directed one last course correction to ensure the most catastrophic collision possible and then evacuated the bridge just in time. Moments after hustling his crew down the hatch and away from the bridge, a direct hit from the troop carrier's plasma cannon vaporized it and showered the deck with flames and molten metal. A crewman hit the alarm on the way down. Time to abandon ship.

The troop ship had already started to offload tanks and troops, so it could not maneuver. At this stage, that may not have worked anyhow. Even several direct hits at point blank range with the plasma cannon could not alter the course of the cargo ship, although the damage was impressive. The *Old Hickory* plowed ahead with its entire top deck ablaze like the fire ships of old that were used to disperse enemy fleets in the age of wooden ships and sail. The burning cargo vessel buried its bow into the FiST carrier amidships with a crash and scrape of metal on metal that could be heard for miles. The FiST ship nearly capsized with the impact but then righted itself after the initial shock. At least one heavy tank was lost in the river as it awaited transport ashore. The ship's troubles were only beginning, however. A severe hull breach made it take on water rapidly. Within minutes it had sunk into the muck of the river with only its top superstructure protruding from the water. *Old Hickory* sank next to it, mission accomplished.

A sizable force was landed before the fatal blow was struck on the ship, though. The force size would have been completely overwhelming had the ship not sunk, but the four tanks and two hundred mechs backed by aerial drones that were present still constituted a very potent enemy, particularly as we held no anti-tank weapons.

Our three-pronged assault met the invaders at the casino and a furious firefight erupted. Stone used the .50 as a sniper rifle to deadly effect again, swatting the remaining aerial drones quickly from the sky like a giant and inerrant fly swatter, thus denying the enemy the advantage of the air. Or so we thought. In the midst of this battle on Canal Street, above us a tremendous explosion engulfed the top of the WTC building where the most important observation post on the other end of Sanchez's radio had been, along with my friends, Officers Lee and Johnson. Fiery debris rained down all over the firefight on the street below. The blast had come from the gunship, now returned to the battle. Evidently there was a human in the loop somewhere who realized that we had fooled the craft's defensive system but had no actual surface-to-air weapons with sufficient range. They may have been slow to realize the error, but realize it they did since our modified arc welders no longer worked to frighten it away. The gunship and the cannons atop the tanks meant that the enemy held the advantage in firepower even with the loss of their ship and most of the aerial drones. That, and we were limited on functioning plasma weapons. They must have finally figured out our antiquated communications network too if they had zeroed in on our OP.

One of the tanks opened up with a cannon that emitted a great deal of light but no resulting blast. At the same time, almost all of the plasma weapons on the NOPD side fell silent. Only the old gunpowder weapons were still firing.

"Directional EMP!" Stone realized it first. "Have everyone fall back," he yelled at Sanchez, who got to work. He laid down covering fire and hit the tank with the .50 but the rounds had little effect. It was too late anyway as it had done its damage and cut our firepower by more than half. Another plasma blast from the gunship thundered into the casino, silencing the snipers we'd stationed there. After several improbable victories, the battle was nevertheless now going very badly for us. Stone laid down withering fire, each round claiming an infantry drone, but they had a surplus and surged forward. Finally one of the tanks scored a near miss on the jeep in spite of my crazy maneuvers, and we flipped over.

I was thrown clear, as was Stone. Sanchez was not as lucky, her leg pinned beneath the jeep and likely broken. Flames licked near her and drew closer, giving her another reason to scream. I was still clearing my head from my tumble when Stone slapped me hard on the shoulder and urged me to follow him. We crouched low and ran for the jeep as plasma bolts singed the air above our heads. The jeep was too hot to touch, part of it engulfed in flames already. There could be only seconds before the gasoline, the ammo, or both cooked off in our faces. Plus the enemy was closing fast. Stone grasped underneath the overturned jeep in spite of the blistering heat and heaved. As he stood he was exposed to enemy fire. I swear I saw him take several plasma shots as he incredibly lifted one end of the jeep off the pavement. He didn't even wear one of the ceramic heat shield vests, but he only grunted in pain when being struck by blasts that should have killed him instantly.

The jeep being lifted far enough to move Sanchez, I wasted no time in spite of my amazement and dragged her clear. Stone let the jeep down again where her leg had been and I picked her up to carry her to better cover since the mechs were drawing near. I couldn't imagine how we might make it, but Stone withdrew the .50 from its mount and hefted the 80lb machine gun bare-handed to shoot from the hip at the onrushing enemy. Of course he had just lifted a jeep, so this feat was small next to that, but I had no time to contemplate any of this as I made the best speed out of there I could while carrying the screaming Officer Sanchez. We found some temporary cover and I looked back at Stone. What I saw was completely unbelievable, and yet there it was…

End of Officer Saladino's recollection

Another failure, Stone thought grimly. Camelot, Atlantis, the Warsaw Ghetto, Constantinople, and how many others? Add this one to the list, his adopted hometown. But those failures were partly because he had held back. He didn't feel it his right to interfere with the unfolding of human history to that extent since he was an outsider. An overt intervention using his full otherworldly abilities was cheating, and so he had held back in spite of the cost. As he grew closer to Isis, however, that level of aloofness to the results of human affairs became ever harder to maintain. Failure in just causes became less and less acceptable. And now the humans possessed weapons that could hurt him, some that could even threaten his life. Surely the last reason for keeping the gloves on was now overcome by events.

He had helped instigate this fight. He had led it. These brave men and women took a stand because he said it could be done, because he promised to do everything in his power. Stone kept his promises.

The Browning made a glorious accounting of itself to the end, but finally the ammunition was gone. Stone laid it aside with respect and turned again to face the mechanized enemy. Their true enemies were many miles away, not risking their lives, not demonstrating even the courage tyrants once had in their quests to rule. Thereby fell away the last qualm Stone might have had about going full blown 'super-hero' mode. He charged them empty handed with a blood curdling roar that would make any berserker shiver. The mechs shot him with their plasma weapons, but these only stung his dense molecular structure, hurting without doing much serious damage. If he stood still and let them blast away at him with the tanks' heavy plasma cannons it would be different, but the smaller infantry weapons were not enough to stop him.

As he closed with the first infantry mech, he seized it in both hands and summoned the energy to execute an inter-dimensional transport of it, but he did so incompletely, thus for all practical purposes partially disintegrating the drone. He continued this process again and again, each drone he confronted hand-to-hand destroyed in like fashion. But there were dozens, and with the energy expense draining him, he couldn't take them all this way. He fought his way to the tank with the EMP cannon and climbed atop the turret, disintegrating at his Midas touch the mechs who 'manned' it, and took it over. He swung it around and with one well-placed pulse, disabled the other three tanks and a couple dozen infantry drones. The battle had seemed to take another turn until one of the remaining mechs tossed a silver grenade at Stone which burst into a cloud of countless fragments mere feet away from him, apparently harmlessly.

Picobots, Stone realized too slowly. A cloud of trillions of infinitesimally small killer robots. Too tiny to see with conventional microscopes, they attack at the molecular level. Durable as Stone was, the physics of his home universe was not so radically different that these were not a threat. He was still composed of matter, and these were a danger to anything so composed. Stone's tough exterior was of no avail to something so tiny which could slip through virtually any defense.

They worked quickly, devouring his cells at the molecular level where he was powerless to fight back. Almost powerless, that is. His immune response did counterattack, but it was overwhelmed by sheer numbers. A human would have succumbed already. He would lose his fight more slowly, more painfully.

Saladino looked on and saw Stone grimace, grasp his own head in his hands in torment, and then collapse to his knees with a scream of pain. Direct hits with plasma rifles had barely slowed him down, but the bastards found something which did. Saladino detached two plasma rifles from fallen mechs and charged the small remainder, including the one which threw the picobot cloud grenade. He aimed true and took out the three mechs nearest Stone. More NOPD officers came to back him up firing with old firearms or, like Saladino, recovering plasma weapons from the fallen mechs in Stone's wake. Soon, the remaining mechs were blasted into spare parts.

By now Stone was lying on the ground, unable to rise. He thought of transporting elsewhere, but the picobots would be along for the ride. Could he take them to an environment where he would survive and they would not? Perhaps, but it was too late now. Their attack was so intense that he didn't presently have the energy for inter-dimensional transport.

The overhead gunship, observing this reversal of fortune to its infantry, laid down devastating revenge fire. Several officers were killed in the initial blast while the rest fled for cover. Saladino managed to reach the EMP tank from which Stone had now fallen, seemingly unconscious. He crawled to Stone as the gunship blasted the area with another thunderous blow from its plasma cannon.

"Hit me with it. Point blank, full power," Stone managed to say, pointing to the EMP turret. Saladino understood. It wouldn't make sense to zap anyone else in the face with such a weapon, but in Stone's case and under these circumstances…

He climbed to the top, hoping he could complete his task before the gunship spotted him. A blast further up Canal Street indicated that it was pursuing fleeing city defenders. He reached the EMP turret and, fortunately, the controls were intuitively obvious: charge, aim, fire with safety off. Stone had been almost beside the tank, but he managed to crawl a few feet away while Saladino was figuring out the controls. This allowed Saladino to depress the turret enough to aim it right at him. Fire! A wave of blinding energy flooded over Stone, who lay still. Saladino hopped down to check on him.

"How do you feel? Did it work?" he asked.

"Yeah, it's over. Felt like being eaten by fire ants from the inside out," Stone replied weakly.

"What do we do about that? It could level the city," Saladino gestured to the gunship above. "Will that EMP thing reach it?"

"Doubtful. Too high, too well hardened against it. I'll have to take care of it myself," Stone said, rising slowly to his feet.

"How will you reach it?"

"Trade secret."

"You sure you're up to it? All those picobots gone?"

"No, I'm not sure, but yes, the EMP fried all the wee beasties, or enough that my body's own defense can eat the rest."

Stone steadied himself against the tank, looked up at the gunship, and took a deep breath. "Alright, here goes." Then, to Saladino's utter amazement, he instantly vanished.

Stone was weak, so he had to keep it simple. Not all avenues were open, anyway. It would be great to transport to a neighboring dimension, then pop back into Earth's dimension several minutes ago before the gunship started firing and save the officers it had killed. This would be akin to jumping out of the time stream as one would hop out of an actual stream of water, running upstream along the bank, and hopping back in at a different place for a do-over. Sometimes that could be done, and sometimes not. The non-rectilinear nature of space-time didn't always allow for it, and did not in this case. With his limited energy, Stone was only able to find a means of re-entering Earth's dimension in the same timeframe that he left, only moving about in space. In effect, he traveled instantly from beside Officer Saladino to the engine compartment of the gunship, which he quickly sabotaged.

From Saladino and Sanchez's vantage point, Stone had been gone for only a minute before reappearing suddenly beside them. They'd seen the gunship start to smoke as its engines failed before diving towards the ground. They could not see the crash site behind the nearby buildings, but they could see the column of smoke where it went down.

"We'll have to rebuild the Superdome again, I'm afraid," Chief Stone informed them. It had been the site of many gruesome public executions of Christians and other dissidents in recent decades, anyway. Bad memories. Stone slumped down next to the wounded Sanchez. He looked exhausted, his uniform destroyed, his skin burnt in places by plasma shots.

"So what happens now?" Saladino asked. Some other officers gathered around.

"The word will get out to the whole world what happened here. The UEC's ruthlessness was demonstrated at Charleston, but now its weakness has also been demonstrated. They are going to find it more and more difficult to keep their grip on the whole world," Stone predicted.

"And you? What exactly are you, anyway?"

"Just know that I'm on your side, Officer."

"Thank God for that," Saladino agreed.

Stone stood up again. "I am going to need a vacation, though. I must take my leave of you now. I am fiercely proud of all of you and would be happy to fight by your side anytime, anywhere."

The gathered officers all responded with variations on the same theme, namely, that they would be happy to fight by Stone's side at any time and place as well. Hands were shaken, backs slapped, hearty 'Well done' and 'Thanks' expressions were exchanged in what became Chief Stone's informal farewell. After a few minutes he bade them Godspeed, waved, and vanished from sight, leaving them to pick up the pieces in their shattered but free city.

SERGEANT STONE IN THE COMPANY OF DEMONS

New Orleans, 30 April 1993

NOPD Officer Ed Lewis interview excerpt:

There was another history lesson from Stone that I recall now. I met him once while I was off-duty and strolling through the Quarter. He was in uniform, as always, but outside the Sixth District on what was apparently a coffee break. He was sitting alone at a small table at the Café du Monde with a café au lait and a plate of three beignets covered with powdered sugar. Not his usual fare. I was going to keep going and pretend I didn't notice him. He was always intimidating but even more so at the moment since he had this thousand yard stare you see on veterans sometimes. It is like their mind's eye is seeing something that's not there, something awful. Best not to disturb them.

Too late. He spotted me and gave a slight wave and a big grin of recognition. Such a warm welcome was unexpected and I changed course to meet him, dodging a waitress on the way over to his table. It was morning and not too hot yet, the Quarter just beginning to fill with tourists. I really had nothing better to do than make fun of the mime at the corner anyway. My only plan was to grab a muffuletta at the Central Grocery a little further down Decatur, but it wasn't lunch time yet.

"Didn't expect to see you here, Stone. Don't you avoid doughnut shops to fight the stereotype about cops?" I ribbed him with a smile. Best to smile if you tease Stone.

"I make an exception for this place and this day," he answered. His smile had vanished, but he motioned me to the metal chair opposite him.

"So what's the occasion?"

"Don't you know any history?" he shook his head.

"Yeah, a little," I said, somewhat annoyed. Actually I had heard something on the radio that morning about the significance of the day. "Fall of Saigon. 1975, right?"

"Correct. Regrettable episode, but I can't be everywhere," he winked. "No, I commemorate a different incident that took place exactly 130 years ago today: Camerone Day."

"Not familiar," I had to admit. I took out my mild annoyance on a nearby pigeon, shooing it with my foot.

"I'm not surprised. It took place in Mexico in 1863, a year in which the United States was very distracted by internal issues. There was also a war waging in Mexico at the time between the French forces fighting to install their man, Maximillian, as Emperor of Mexico and the Mexicans who were fighting against foreign domination. You've heard of Cinco de Mayo, yes?"

"Mexican Independence Day?"

"No. May 5th, 1862 was the date in which a Mexican force defeated the French at the Battle of Puebla. That didn't settle things, though, and the French made another go at Puebla, the fall of which would open the way to Mexico City. The French sent in their Foreign Legion troops to bolster their force, but these troops, although they had served well in North Africa and Crimea, were looked down upon by the rest of the French Army and given all the dirty jobs. The Legionnaires had French officers but the men came from all over, many trying to *start* over. They were allowed to join under assumed names. Some were fleeing the law, or debt, or bad marriages and some just craved adventure. In any case, the Legion became home. It was to the Legion and each other that their first loyalty lay, not France. 'The Legion is our country' was their refrain. In any case, the French commander had long supply lines to protect for his siege of Puebla. He assigned the Legion to convoy protection in the fetid plains on the road to Vera Cruz where the main enemy was yellow fever and malaria. That is, until Camerone."

"But why do you commemorate this with coffee and beignets?" I interrupted.

"Ah. Therein lies the tale."

Chiquihuite, Mexico, 30 April 1863

The 3rd Company, 1st Battalion Legionnaires stepped out smartly from their regimental headquarters shortly after midnight, packs on their backs, muskets in hand, and accompanied by several pack mules loaded with supplies. Each wore the distinctive Legion uniform with white kepi cap, blue tunic with red epaulettes, and red zouave-style pants. The uniforms were impeccable upon leaving garrison, but would show the dust of the march when the sun came up. They marched in silence, the tromping of their feet the only sound. The company drummer, Legionnaire Casimir Lai, did not touch his drumsticks during this night recon march in hostile territory. They maintained light discipline as well and no man lit up a smoke in spite of tobacco cravings. The stars above were the only light.

3rd Company had 120 men assigned, but only 62 ready to fight due to the toll of various tropical diseases. Its regular officers, too, were out of the fight. Captain Jean Danjou, the battalion adjutant, was placed in command by Colonel Jeanningros for this mission. Danjou was a proven veteran who had lost his hand to action in the Crimea and wore a wooden prosthetic replacement. Joining him were 2nd Lieutenant Vilain, the paymaster, and 2nd Lieutenant Maudet of the headquarters company. Both were decorated veterans who'd risen through the ranks, but some of the enlisted men resented the low pay issued by Vilain.

The assignment was to safeguard a 64-wagon convoy hauling ammunition, supplies, and, most notably, chests filled with gold for paying the regular army troops besieging Puebla. The Mexicans had learned about this convoy and the French had learned what they had learned thanks to an Indian informant. The Mexicans would certainly attack the convoy; where was not known. Colonel Jeanningros ordered Danjou to take 3rd Company back down the road to Vera Cruz as far as Palo Verde to link up with the convoy. Failing that, it was to return to Chiquihuite.

There was a brief rest at Paso del Marcho where a company of grenadiers was stationed. Danjou politely declined the offer of a platoon of reinforcements from the grenadier captain since he was anxious to get going to effect the link up. A few gulps of coffee and a few bites of black bread and then it was time to pick up the packs and get moving again. As much ground had to be covered as possible before daybreak.

Stone was in the rearguard, keeping the march orderly as one of the high-time NCOs. Like many in the Legion, he had an assumed name, but in his case it was an entire assumed identity. Here he was Sergeant Louis Morzycki, a Polish national who had already seen Legion service in Italy. He was also in his vulnerable mode, susceptible to injury, exhaustion, fear, etc. every bit as much as his comrades in arms. He was not likely to actually perish by the force of human arms, but for an authentic experience of human life under extreme circumstances, he was temporarily suspending his knowledge of his superhuman sturdiness. It was a sort of self-inflicted and selective amnesia that he could cure himself of at the conclusion of the experiment. It was not a thorough amnesia, either, since he retained knowledge of his true identity, if not the full truth of his nature. He respected human courage but could not share in it while knowing that the bullets would not kill him.

The other men in the unit, while not from as far away as Stone, nevertheless had remarkably varied and interesting backgrounds. Some were nearly kids, two of them being only seventeen years old. Several were grizzled veterans in their forties. Corporal Berg had been an officer in the regular French army but was broken for misconduct, so enlisting in the Legion gave him a fresh start. Some missed sweethearts back home, some had fled woman trouble there. They hailed from all over Europe and, in some cases, beyond. For all of them, the Legion was now home, fellow Legionnaires their family.

As the sun came up the marchers could now see ramshackle buildings and abandoned hamlets on either side of the road. One of these, the map indicated, was a place called Camerone. The countryside before them consisted of scrub brush and it rolled gently down towards the Jamapa River. Another collection of abandoned farmhouses, the hamlet of Palo

Verde, lay two miles ahead and was the extent of their planned march. A small lake was adjacent to the Palo Verde ruins and adjacent to that a small hill which Danjou chose as a campsite. Eerie silence prevailed near the ghost town. Nothing stirred besides the Legionnaires and, ominously, some vultures.

Danjou posted sentries and set a perimeter. Other men gathered some wood and set a campfire. The men let down their packs and sat on or beside them, wiping their sweaty brows. Soon, ribald jokes and teasing were the order of the day as they rested their weary bodies after the long march. With the fire started and water boiling to brew coffee, the men's spirits lifted. With no enemy in sight, this could turn out to be an easy mission.

Just as that pleasant thought was starting to take hold, a sentry called out. Dust rising in the west. Wrong direction for the convoy. Perhaps the main force at Puebla had sent back a security detail for it? Distant shapes came into view, a large cavalry formation. Sun glinted off their rifles and lances. Danjou raised his field glasses for a better look.

"To arms! It is the enemy!" he announced.

The just boiling water was tossed into the campfire, extinguishing it. No coffee for now. The men hustled to their weapons and packs from whatever they were doing, being it sitting down or relieving themselves in the bushes. Mules were rounded up to resume the burdens they'd so recently set down. Stone, aka Morzycki, and the other NCOs, Sergeant Major Tonel and Sergeants Germeys, Palmaert, and Schaffner, wasted no time getting the men back into order.

The company was exposed here, a dreadful place for infantry to meet cavalry. Danjou determined to make for the cover afforded by the Camerone hacienda. Scouts were sent in that direction and the company was formed into two parallel columns marching away from the road and into the thistles and scrub bushes of the plain, the only cover immediately available. The two column formation would be able to quickly form a last ditch defensive square, the only hope infantry had against the far more mobile cavalry. If caught in the open while in columns they would be quickly overwhelmed by the onrushing horsemen.

They neared the abandoned hacienda. Its buildings and courtyard surrounded by a ten foot adobe wall promised some protection. They had still not been sighted by the Mexican cavalry. Then a shot rang out.

Legionnaire Pierre Conrad, Danjou's batman, dropped his musket and clasped his hip before collapsing to the earth. Danjou knelt to help him and dispatched a four man team to trap the sniper. The hacienda was not as abandoned as hoped.

Danjou quickly consulted with Vilain and Maudet over a map. There was an Indian village nearby, further to the west. He decided to make for it instead. The march resumed and the columns moved west and bypassed the hacienda. The four counter-snipers returned from it and reported that the shooter had vanished. Unfortunately, the shot had alerted the cavalry, which was now unmistakably headed towards the Legionnaires.

"Form square!" Danjou commanded. The NCOs repeated the order and got the men formed up. The Mexican cavalrymen rode ever closer, their long lances gleaming in the sunlight. In short order the square was formed and no flank was left unprotected. The Mexicans split into two groups, but either way they attacked from would face heavy musket fire from the disciplined Legionnaires. All was made readiness within the square, officers and NCOs barking orders, bellowing that the men were moving too slowly, although they weren't. Sixty-two muskets were ready to pour fire on the enemy. The smoothbore muskets were already antiquated by the newer Minie rifles, with less accuracy and range, but the .70 calibre balls would destroy what they hit and the Legionnaires were proficient marksmen.

"Do not open fire until my command!" Danjou ordered. With the limited range of the muskets, the tactics would have to match. This would be an old Napoleonic-era engagement wherein the infantry square would hold fire until the cavalry got close enough that their volley's effects would be maximized.

The two Mexican columns slowed and regrouped, the horses moving at a fast walking pace. Then, at about seventy-five yards, the cry went up from them, "Viva Mexico! Viva Juarez!" and the charge came. The horsemen leveled their sharp lances at the Legionnaires and spurred their mounts to a thunderous gallop, covering ground at a startling pace. The high bushes of the plain helped disorganize their formation somewhat, but on they came with ever greater speed.

The Legionnaires coolly held their fire, waiting for their captain's order. Finally, at about fifty yards, he yelled, "Fire!" and the first volley of musketry erupted from half the men in the square. Gaps were torn into the cavalry columns, men and horses spilling chaotically all over the hard-packed earth. The remaining cavalrymen charged on with even more determination to wipe out the Legionnaires and aiming their lances with murderous intent. The infantrymen quickly reloaded while the second volley aimed. "Fire!" Danjou ordered again. Another thirty rounds tore into the onrushing cavalry with similarly catastrophic results, but on they came.

"Fire at will!"

Go to half-cock on the hammer, grab a new charge from your pouch, tear it with your teeth, pour the pre-measured powder down the muzzle, follow with the ball and wadding from the packaged charge, withdraw ramrod, tamp it all down the muzzle, replace ramrod, replace percussion cap on the nipple near the hammer, go to full cock, take aim, fire. Feel the recoil in your shoulder, see the flash and smoke of the powder and assess your shot to correct the next. Repeat. More Mexicans spilled from their horses in front of the infantry square. No weak points could be found in the formation; ready muskets and bayonets faced the cavalry at every point. The surviving cavalrymen withdrew and began circling the square outside of musket range.

They'd never make the Indian village and they couldn't stay in the open against cavalry. Danjou decided to move back to the hacienda. The square was an awkward formation to maintain on the move and even more so on uneven ground with tall shrubs everywhere. Stone kept his men in line, but inevitably the formation lost its former cohesion. The Mexicans formed for a second attack. Quickly the Legionnaires firmed up their square to meet it.

On they came with another fearsome charge, their bravery evident after that first sharp repulse. As before, Danjou directed two organized volleys before clearing individual fires. The first result was repeated, the Mexicans driven off with heavy loss, but not driven far. This time the noise of the musketry was too much for the pack mules which broke and scattered in several directions. Some of the men tried to corral them, but to no avail. This chaos disrupted the all-important cohesion of the square, leaving some Legionnaire stragglers vulnerable to enemy lances. The Mexicans rode them down with glee, getting revenge at last for many dead comrades. The cries of the stragglers pierced by lances was dreadful, but Stone and the other sergeants forbade the men from breaking up the formation even more in running to their aid. They were beyond help, run over by enemy horses in the open field. Gone too were the pack mules, and with them all the reserve ammunition and most of the company's water supply.

The formation loosening, Danjou sensed that they might not repel another charge. So, he decided on making one of his own and ordered an assault on the hacienda. After a volley at the cavalry between the wavering square and Camerone, Danjou gave the signal and the Legionnaires executed a ferocious bayonet charge on the enemy horsemen. Stone was in the thick of it, smothering his own fear with the anger he felt over the men they'd lost.

"Give them the bayonet! Vive le Legion!" he cried and surged forth with the others. Some cavalry were taken by surprise by this and failed to get away from the angry, charging Legionnaires. Some payback was issued for the Legionnaires run down by the lancers. Bayonets were jabbed in horse bellies and in cavalrymen's legs, spurting blood and knocking over mounts into the dust and confusion of the melee. The cavalry broke and fled the onslaught initially, giving the Legionnaires free run to the hacienda. Soon they reformed, however, and pursued the running infantry which could not outpace them. More stragglers were cut down, but forty-six Legionnaires somehow reached the relative safety of the hacienda walls, drenched with blood and panting from the sprint as they reloaded. Some of the blood was their own, but not all.

Danjou took stock of the courtyard, assigning men to various entrances and outbuildings to form a perimeter defense once the wooden gate was shut. Almost immediately the men took fire from a second story window in the main farmhouse on the north side of the courtyard. Infuriatingly, there was no entrance to the second story from the courtyard itself, nor from the first floor which the Legionnaires quickly occupied, but only from the outside which was already raked with fire from the surrounding dismounted cavalry of the enemy. The courtyard walls afforded some protection from the enemy rifles outside, but that protection was reduced by the presence of enemy snipers in the farmhouse, snipers they apparently could not reach. Precious rounds had to be expended on suppressing them and vigilant sentries had to be detailed for this, thus reducing the hands available to defend the perimeter.

Initial defense preparations set, Danjou now found that he was blind inside the courtyard walls. The outbuilding and farmhouse windows were poor vantage points for observing the enemy, especially as they were frequent targets of enemy fire. Stone, with his exceptional eyesight, volunteered to be hoisted atop the highest point of the stable on the south side to reconnoiter the enemy. He studied the enemy dispositions for a few moments but had no good news.

"Hundreds of them. We're encircled. Some are trying to sneak up to closer firing positions, so have everyone keep a sharp eye out." Stone proceeded to do this himself, taking a shot at any Mexican who strayed within range of his musket. He wasted no bullets and the Mexicans soon learned to avoid the sector under his watch. His reloading was dizzyingly fast even in his awkward prone position atop the stable's roof.

The other Legionnaires followed suit and directed well-aimed fire at any attackers that got too close. More firing positions were created by punching holes in the courtyard walls. This made forays against the gates even more problematic for the Mexican troops, as they could take fire from multiple directions. At that range, even the old muskets were deadly in Legionnaire hands. Soon Mexican casualties began to pile up, but the Legionnaires lost some men too, and they had far fewer to spare.

The fight had started around 0800. At around 0930 the Mexicans ceased fire. Stone sighted a horseman approaching under a white flag of truce. The Legionnaires also ceased fire as the lone Mexican rider, a lieutenant, rode to the gate and shouted over the wall in excellent French.

"You have earned our admiration. I guarantee you and your men safety and the best we can offer you as prisoners."

"Non!" Danjou replied with anger.

"But there is only a handful of you, and you haven't a chance. My army is 2,000 and we have more men on their way here. As a fellow soldier, not as an enemy, I ask you to surrender."

"Merde! We have plenty of ammunition. No surrender!"

The Mexican officer rode back in exasperated silence. Danjou called to a Legionnaire nearby to bring him the bottle of wine he had brought on the march and somehow kept through the chaotic fight to the hacienda.

The men were thirsty, the water scarce, and the hot sun still rising in the sky. Captain Danjou crawled to each man on the perimeter to offer a sip of wine. It was only enough to moisten the tongue for a moment, perhaps only enough to aggravate the thirst of the men, but they appreciated the gesture. Danjou did not give the drink for free, however. From each he extracted the same oath.

"You promise me to die rather than surrender?" He stared each man down with ominous eyes glaring out over his impressive handlebar moustache.

"Oui, mon capitaine!" each man swore in turn before taking a small swig of the wine.

The Mexican bullets started to fly again, smacking fiercely into exterior and interior walls, splintering wooden beams, throwing dust in the air with impacts into the adobe bricks.

"Here they come!" Stone warned from above as he fired, dropping a charging enemy soldier and immediately reloading.

The Mexicans came on in earnest, sending waves of men at every possible entryway into the hacienda. The Legionnaires poured withering fire into their ranks, killing scores of them, but on they came, closing to point blank range. Fire was exchanged by men separated by mere feet, powder flashes burning the faces of the enemy, screams from men on both sides punctuated by yet more musket fire. Some Mexicans closed to hand-to-hand range with the Legionnaires and got the bayonet in the belly or butt of a musket to the face for their audacity. Legionnaires and Mexicans traded fire at each other from both sides of windows or wall openings. A Legionnaire would poke his musket out, fire, invariably hitting a Mexican soldier, and withdraw to reload. An angry Mexican would retaliate, sticking his rifle into the opening and firing quickly but blindly at the unseen enemy, usually missing but not always. The defenders had the better kill ratio, but the attackers had overwhelming numbers. The fight raged on. The sun rose higher, lessening the available shade and broiling the courtyard defenders, already weak from thirst.

Concerned about the flagging defenses on the east wall, Danjou dashed across the courtyard to bolster them. Crack! A shot from the upper story of the farmhouse felled him. Fire was returned on the enemy sniper, but he had retreated from his window after taking his shot. Lt. Vilain ran to his captain's side and dragged him out of the line of fire against the farmhouse wall. Danjou looked him sternly in the eye as he struggled against the pain of his wound.

"Never…" and he breathed his last. Vilain sadly closed his sightless eyes and set him neatly on the ground. Then he took the captain's sword and bellowed for all to hear,

"Mes enfants! I command you now. We may die, but will never surrender."

If the Legionnaires had formerly disdained the paymaster, that was now forgotten in this shared crucible. They fought on. They fought on even as their tongues dried to the roofs of their mouths and their muskets became too hot to touch. This wasn't for nothing. Vilain realized, as had Danjou, that the Mexican force facing them was absurdly large. It could only have been meant to intercept the convoy, but instead it was tied down by this much smaller force. The longer the Legionnaires held out, the better the convoy's chances. The success of the siege, and therefore the war, rested on that convoy reaching Puebla. Around noon the men heard the drums and bugles of approaching troops.

"The relief column! We are saved!" someone said excitedly.

"No! Mexican infantry. About a thousand of them," Stone corrected from his vantage point.

Shortly after the Mexican lieutenant returned under the truce flag.

"I renew my offer to accept your surrender and guarantee your safety. Your bravery is wonderful, but fruitless."

"Merde!" Vilain eloquently retorted.

"Then prepare to die!" the officer rode away in disgust.

The Legionnaires were down to thirty-four men effective and the Mexicans came at the barricades again. Again they met devastating fire that reduced their ranks. The Legionnaires, who should have been mad with thirst, maintained excellent firing discipline. Their ranks, too, thinned with every assault. A well in the courtyard was probably dry, but it could not even be approached to be sure due to the sniper fire from the second story. It served only to mock the men, but none lost composure and rushed it lest they be cut down. The men resorted to drinking their own urine and even the blood from their own wounds. And the merciless Mexican sun kept baking them. Barely any shade could be had in the courtyard.

Another assault came, the Mexicans more determined than ever. They brought pickaxes to tear away at the courtyard wall. The infantry reinforcements poured continuous fire on the hacienda from every point on the compass. The Legionnaires, their ammunition replenished by taking it from fallen comrades, grimly fought on. The Mexican onslaught was repelled again, but this time they left burning bushels of grass by every opening, the heat increasing the misery within the hacienda and the smoke obscuring the vision of the marksmen.

During yet another assault around 1400, Lt. Vilain was dashing to inspect the defenses at a certain point and, like his captain, was cut down by a sniper's bullet. Command fell to Lt. Maudet, who also urged the men to fight on. They did so and repelled this assault as well, albeit at cost. The water was completely gone now and neither did the urine and blood suffice. The courtyard was littered within and surrounded without by the dead and dying from both sides. The wounded groaned in misery, many begging for water. The flames and smoke rising from the entire perimeter turned the scene into one straight from Hell.

Stone had climbed down from his perch since the smoke now made it useless. Next to him inside the stable stood a young man named Grant, who asked if he had any water. Stone did have a tiny amount in his canteen, which he handed over. During a brief lull in the action, Legionnaire Grant could no longer restrain himself. Taking the canteen and braving the sniper fire within the courtyard, he crawled over to a wounded man begging for water and let it dribble into his mouth. The man's miserable groans ceased, but he expired soon after. His suffering had been eased by the tiny amount of water and Grant's reassuring words in his ear, the last things he heard. Stone took note of this.

"What's your name, son?" Stone asked him.

"Grant," he said with a Belgian accent.

"Your real name. My real name isn't Morzycki; it's Stone."

"Catteau. Victor Catteau."

The assaults continued. Peering through the smoke with burning eyes, the Legionnaires fired at any movement, exacting a heavy toll on the attackers. Lt. Maudet got his chance to refuse a surrender offer, too, and did so with a gusto equal to that of his predecessors. By 1700 only a dozen remained still able to fight. The battle had raged for nine hours. Outside the Mexican commander could be heard haranguing his men. Another full scale attack came. The Mexicans, now further bolstered by the arrival of guerilla fighters marching to the sound of the guns, did not need to hold any of their force in reserve and committed everything to the attack. An irresistible human wave charged the hacienda, every man contributing to its roar with loud battle cries. The best sharpshooting could not stop that many men from reaching the main gate, which finally burst under the weight of the angry mob of troops. They poured through with bayonets fixed and looking for targets. The dozen Legionnaires countered with a volley that felled the first rank of the enemy, then met the second with their own bayonet charge.

Musket butts bashed skulls and ribs, bayonets pierced chests, abdomens, legs. Cries of anger, cries of pain, furious curses and some prayers too. Both sides confronted not just the enemy, but their own inner fears and howled at the frightening exultation of the confrontation. Stone took a heavy toll with his bayonet skills. Thrust, parry, advance, lunge, retreat, advance again and repeat the cycle. A dozen men and more fell to his bloody bayonet or to a smashing blow from the butt of his musket. Finally a bullet to the face dazed him and the mob rushed over him, clubbing him and stabbing him. Sergeant Morzycki was dead as Stone fell to the overwhelming force along with five other Legionnaires. Stone himself was not dead, of course, but he was out of this fight. He would resuscitate only later.

The last six Legionnaires fell back to the stable and barricaded themselves within. Lt. Maudet, Legionnaires Wenzel, Catteau, Constantin, Leonhart, and Corporal Maine each had a single shot remaining. One final offer of surrender terms. One final, "Non!" in refusal. The men looked at each other in silence. All knew what was to follow.

"Load," Maudet ordered. "At my command, fire. Then follow me through the breach. We'll end this with our bayonets."

They stripped away the barricade and fired their last volley into the army waiting for them, then formed a wedge and charged with bayonets. The Mexicans prepared to reply with their own volley. As they did so, Catteau threw himself in front of Lt. Maudet in an effort to save him. Catteau went down with nineteen bullets in him, but did not save Maudet, who was also mortally wounded. Leonhart was killed also and Wenzel was wounded in the shoulder, but he stood again with Constantin and Maine to renew the battle. They stood back to back and ready to face all challengers.

The Mexican soldiers stood in awe for a moment, but then encircled them with a ring of bayonets. The end was upon them, but then a Mexican colonel barged into the circle, slapping men aside with the flat of his sword.

"Do you now surrender?" he asked quietly in French.

"On the condition that you allow us to keep our weapons and equipment and treat our wounded lieutenant here?" Corporal Maine offered.

"One refuses nothing to such men as you," the colonel replied.

And with that, the battle was finally over. The wounded received treatment, such as it was, and the survivors were taken prisoner. Upon seeing them the Mexican commander, a more senior colonel, asked,

"Is this all that is left?"

The officer who brought them in replied, "Yes, Colonel."

"Truly, these aren't men—they're demons!"

The body of Stone, aka Sergeant Morzycki, vanished before being collected for burial, of course. Stone had relocated at the conclusion of this interlude to parts unknown. Years later from his perspective, but mere moments later on April 30, 1863, he returned dressed in a Mexican uniform to avoid attracting attention. He was recruiting help for a very important assignment, the seizure of the most dangerous weapon of mass destruction this universe had ever seen. He needed the best and all of the demons of Camerone fit that description. One young man stood out even in that elite group, however. He found the bullet-riddled body of Victor Catteau, aka Grant. The young Belgian was on the verge of death, but Stone placed him in a stasis that halted his demise for trans-dimensional travel. Away from curious human eyes, he could perform a minor medical miracle using the techniques of his advanced home world, a world long since destroyed by a weapon like the one he was seeking. A team of all stars selected from the many brave souls he'd served beside would help him in his quest to stop such destruction from happening again. Grant had surely earned a spot on that roster.

New Orleans, 30 April 1993

"Wow, those guys must have clanked when they walked. What a bunch of bad asses. I feel inadequate now. Thanks," I said sheepishly.

"Not only brass balls but iron wills. Life left them but courage never did," Stone got that faraway look again.

"But I don't see the connection with coffee and beignets."

"The Legionnaires were boiling water for coffee that morning but never got to drink it, so here I drink it for them in memorial. They didn't get a real breakfast that morning, nor did they eat later, so French doughnuts are as appropriate as anything else. Besides, I rather like them. Café du Monde always serves a glass of water with the coffee and beignets, too, as you can see. The water commemorates the grueling thirst they endured that day. I drink that in their memory, too," Stone explained.

"Strangely personal and intimate memorial that would make more sense if you'd actually been there," I observed. "Which of course you weren't."

He smirked. Before he could reply, if he intended to, his radio crackled. A Code Three somewhere in the Sixth District. No time to waste and he stood to leave.

"You finish those beignets for me, please. I hate waste. I got to drink the coffee this time, at least." And off he went.

But what did he mean, 'this time'?

SERGEANT STONE UNDONE

[Note: this story takes place before the events of the first volume's "Sergeant Stone Unbound" which brought the inter-dimensional war to a conclusion.]

In a reality outside human-perceived space-time...

Supervisor 17 had a name, of course, but it remained secret for operational security. It helped in dealing with free agents like Stone who may or may not accept an assignment or might even defect and bring their knowledge to the other side. Of all of these, Stone was the most nettlesome. While the universe he watched over was a backwater this was no problem, but enemy activity had heated up there recently and it even focused on the very planet in that universe which had most of Stone's attention: Earth. Unremarkable at first glance, closer inspection revealed a substantial fault line of space-time ran through it, and its populace could eventually have outsized impact once it figured out the larger game. This meant that Stone's beat, and consequently Stone himself, had grown in importance to the Commonwealth in its efforts to frustrate the Syndicate's expansionist aims.

Stone entered the office and sat down without a word. The Supervisor spoke, "Glad you could make it so promptly."

"I wasn't on anything urgent. Just watching the first performance of Hamlet at London's Globe Theater."

Supervisor 17 could not imagine enjoying that, but he let it pass without comment. "Well I have something rather urgent for you. We have intelligence that the Syndicate has placed an agent in newly reborn Poland in 1920 to bring about an outcome to the Russo-Polish War favorable to the Russians. War weary Europe and America have disarmed after the Great War and the Soviet Union will be able to spread communism over the whole continent if they can steamroll Poland. This is to the Syndicate's advantage but bad for us, as we think you will agree. We want you to look into it."

Stone nodded, "I do agree that it must be prevented. I will see to it at once, but I could use more details to go on."

"Yes. Drusus down the hall will brief you on everything we have. Good luck."

That was that and Stone departed for his brief. Drusus, the intelligence officer, was thorough in his brief. Unfortunately there was still much that was not known. It was believed that a single Syndicate operative was posing as a Soviet officer, possibly a political officer, and was directly aiding that side in the campaign. The unit was not known but he could be expected to turn up at the decisive point in the battlefield in order to guarantee a Soviet victory. Stone opted to join a Polish unit that would likewise show up at the decisive point in order to neutralize this enemy agent and allow history to proceed as it should. Drusus agreed to facilitate this plan. After Stone left, he also thoroughly briefed his Syndicate handler about Stone's plan since he was a double agent.

16 August 1920

The Red Army was on the march and appeared unstoppable. Marshal Tukhachevsky's victorious legions had ejected Polish forces from Ukraine and now threatened Warsaw itself. Outnumbered, outgunnedand dispirited, Polish troops hastily formed defensive lines before their capital and the industrial center of Lvov. Marshal Pilsudski, the Polish commander, was preparing an unorthodox counterstroke. He had disengaged large forces from the Bolshevik onslaught and moved them to the south where the enemy had lost track of them. This he knew since brilliant Polish cryptographers had broken the Reds' codes. Polish intelligence could intercept and decode Bolshevik transmissions and now had a far clearer picture of their troop dispositions than the Reds had of theirs.

As the Red tide broke into two large forces around the unpassable Pripet Marshes, they would lose cohesion and leave a gap that Pilsudski could exploit with his counterattack. French and British advisors called his plan amateurish and doomed to failure. Indeed it was a huge gamble that required precise timing and luck since his assembly areas were dangerously close to the enemy. If the Reds should accelerate their timetable they could be caught unprepared and the thin forces left guarding the roads to Warsaw would be overrun as the counteroffensive was blunted. It was paramount that the Polish right hook not be discovered too soon or all would be lost. Warsaw would fall and with it Poland. Lenin would then have a clear path to spread the Communist Revolution to vulnerable post-war Germany and beyond.

Stone had a huge battlefield to search for his opposite number. Normally he marched with the infantry since that was where the most pain was usually found. This time he might have opted for the mobility of the cavalry, but he had a better idea. The aircraft was a new weapon but it had proven itself in the recent Great War. With it he could survey vast reaches of the enormous campaign area and be ready to strike far afield. Left with an infantry or even cavalry unit, he could become stranded far from the decisive action and miss the intervention of his adversary. It was a pity about the cavalry. This war would feature not only the biggest cavalry clashes since the Napoleonic Wars, but also the last such battles by modern forces. This was a transitional period for human warfare. Cavalrymen wielding sabers would charge machine gun positions alongside tanks and armored cars with airplanes zooming overhead.

At Lewandowka, Stone found the Polish 7th Escadrille, which was composed mostly of American volunteer pilots. He joined them under an assumed name and quickly demonstrated his flying skill to their satisfaction. Later he would make sure the records were lost and that there would be little evidence that he had ever served with them; this was a standard procedure. The 7th Escadrille had recently changed its name to the Kosciuszko Squadron in honor of Tadeusz Kosciuszko, the Polish military architect who volunteered and ably served the American Revolution's cause, even designing the fortifications at West Point. He maintained a friendship with Thomas Jefferson afterwards and in his will left some of his wealth for the cause of slave education and liberation in the United States.

The Kosciuszko Squadron was led by Major Fauntleroy and Captain Cooper who, like most of the men they commanded, were American veterans of the air war on the Western Front. Ground support and maintenance personnel were native Poles and the squadron was equipped with a mobile headquarters that moved by rail. The same train carried aircraft and supporting equipment from one operating location to the next. In this case, the aircraft consisted of a mix of German Fokker DVIIs, Albatross fighters, and the Italian-designed Ansaldo A1 Balilla (Hunter) fighter. The latter had missed action in the Great War. It was popular with air racers for its speed, and it carried fuel for longer missions than most of its peers. Many pilots complained of its poor handling, but its inherent instability was a necessary tradeoff for greater maneuverability. Unforgiving and treacherous for a rookie pilot, it was a potent machine in skilled hands. Stone was highly skilled, naturally, and proved himself quickly by checking out in all three aircraft right away. The Fokker DVII was a dream to fly and his favorite. It was so feared by the Allies at the end of the war that the Treaty of Versailles, along with bringing Poland back to life and imposing heavy indemnities on defeated Germany, also stipulated that Germany surrender all of them. To Stone's advanced species these 1920 state of the art aircraft were so antiquated and simple as to be charming and quaint. It was as simple to him as riding a bicycle was to an ordinary earthling. The trick was to keep in mind the limitations of these craft and not demand too much of them.

In August Tukhachevsky was making his big push on Warsaw. Although he might have used the 1st Cavalry Army under Budyonny to guard his flank, he did not do so. If he had, Pilsudski's plan would have been derailed and Warsaw would have fallen. Instead Budyonny laid siege to the city Lvov, partly because of the influence of one glory seeking political commissar named Josef Stalin. If he could take it quickly enough, he could join the general battle and seal Warsaw's doom. As it happened, the Poles would put up stiff resistance there, most famously at the train station at Zadworze which was defended by old men and boys not of military age using cast off rifles. They were wiped out almost to the last man, over three hundred of them, but their sacrifice delayed the Bolshevik advance for a full day and earned comparisons with Thermopylae.

Overhead, the Kosciuszko Squadron was aiding them and other Lvov defenders with relentless bombing and strafing. The Americans flew tirelessly, each pilot flying five sorties a day as the maintainers struggled to keep the aircraft airworthy. They adopted tactics of very low strafing of cavalry columns which served to frighten and scatter the horses. This was very daring flying and the aircraft came back with many bullet holes. When they came back, that is. Stone was not to be outdone in this, of course, and did his part in attacking the Red columns, while also flying reconnaissance and hoping to sense the presence of the Syndicate operative. As this was not a null region, he should know if the enemy agent was within several miles. In the meantime he enjoyed flying and making life hard for the communist hordes.

Pilsudski's counterstroke was to start within 24 hours. It was imperative that the Reds not detect the troops massing at the jumping off point lest they close the gap they had left in their advancing armies. Bolshevik recon flights had been few and far between, none of their pilots willing to challenge the Kosciuszko Squadron. Stone gulped some coffee and hopped in his Balilla fighter for the day's second sortie. The first sortie had been satisfactory. His bomb had scored a hit which flipped a Russian armored car on its side and disabled it. His strafing run had decimated the accompanying infantry. He had gotten very low to achieve this result, but the ground support crew did not complain when they had to unwind small tree branches from around the wing spars. They knew he and the others were doing good work.

The ground crew pulled the chocks and cleared the area except for the engine troop. He placed a canvas sock over the topmost propeller blade and stood to the side. In his hand he held a rope connected to the canvas sock. With a signal from Stone he yanked hard on the rope and turned the prop, whereupon the sock flew off the blade. The engine coughed to life and the prop spun faster until it was invisible and the engine roar drowned out every other sound. The plane surged forward and bounded over the uneven ground of the taxiway. An aircraft was taking the runway ahead of him in a prearranged flight order. The times were carefully regimented by squadron leadership and only aircraft problems forced changes. The other aircraft took off and Stone took the now vacant runway.

Lining up the aircraft on the runway, he did a last minute flight control check. His walk-around inspection of the aircraft had been done before engine start. The control surfaces all moved where they should in response to his stick and rudder inputs. Satisfied, he placed his goggles over his eyes and his scarf around his neck. Not only did it get chilly in the slipstream at ten thousand feet, but the engine might spew oil all over your goggles and then a pilot wants his scarf handy.

Stone checked his watch. It was time. He pushed his throttle up until the 220 horsepower engine's roar more than doubled and released the brake. The Balilla surged forward like a racing thoroughbred out of the starting gate. The plane rolled quickly down the runway and Stone felt it lighten on its wheels, seemingly wanting to go airborne. Not just yet, give me a little more speed, he thought. Just a little rudder to counteract the P-factor. It wasn't rational to expect the aircraft to hear and understand his thoughts, but Stone indulged the human tendency to anthropomorphize the aircraft and establish a close working relationship with it the way he would a horse in the cavalry. Then it was time. He eased back on the stick and adjusted the trim; the aircraft leapt away from the ground eagerly, as if it had no further use for terra firma and never would again. Or at least not while the fuel lasted.

The plane continued to soar up and away, leaving the summer heat of the surface for the wild blue yonder. I must do this more often, Stone thought. He was thankful this mission profile allowed him the indulgence of flight since so often he slogged through the mud with the infantry. Everything was more beautiful from five thousand feet. He banked to the east and pointed towards Lvov and the heavy fighting there. Once at altitude he trimmed out the plane for straight and level flight and just enjoyed the time in transit; work would be at hand soon enough. Since this was the second sortie of the day and they'd worked admirably that morning, there was no need to test fire the twin .303 Vickers machine guns.

Stone sighted another plane at his altitude, which was heading in the opposite direction and coming from the Lvov area. Probably a friendly, Stone thought, though the markings were too far to see. He was ready on the trigger just in case. After a minute he could identify it as a Fokker

DVII with the red and white checkered markings of the Polish Air Force on the tail. As the two planes passed each other, the pilot heading back to base flashed Stone a grin and gave a thumbs-up. Stone waved in acknowledgement. It looked like Captain Corsi, but he was not certain. In any case, the greeting meant a successful sortie. Business was good and a target rich environment lay ahead.

He began his descent and changed his course to approach the east side of the city, where the armies were slugging it out from a south to north heading. Ahead of him and spread out below he could make out the two armies, the Russians on his right and the Poles on his left. He smiled when his battlefield survey revealed that he was arriving in time to unleash hell on a Red cavalry charge that was about to begin. Normally he looked for a lucrative target for his two-hundred fifty pound bomb, first to lighten the aircraft for the follow-up strafing attacks, but this would have to wait. The Poles needed strafing on the line of attacking horsemen now. The bomb could still be employed afterwards. Stone set up for his strafing run, lining up his sights on the far left flank of the cavalry. On this heading he was perpendicular to the whole lot of them and could saturate the entire line with machine gun fire.

Stone poured on the speed and dove on them. The Reds noticed him and some anti-aircraft guns opened up on him; he ignored them and pressed home his attack. He smiled at the timing since the charge was just beginning and he could inflict maximum chaos from his position. The cavalry had their sabers drawn and were focused on the Polish line ahead of them, more concerned about the machine gun nests ahead. Too late they heard the roar of Stone's engine off to their left. Stone came in at fifty feet and 140 miles per hour. The low altitude would not only startle the horses but increase the accuracy of his guns. The speed would make him harder to hit.

The first enemy horsemen neared Stone's sights and he laid on the trigger. The twin Vickers guns hammered away and Stone dragged the tracers over the line of cavalry, mowing down many and scattering the rest. He felt some enemy rounds hit the plane, but nothing disrupted the plane's controllability and he ignored them. Flying past the last of them, he released the trigger and pulled up out of the strafing run to survey the damage. The cavalry charge had been completely disrupted and the survivors fell back in disorder. Riderless horses scattered about the chaotic battlefield. Stone scanned behind the Bolshevik lines and noticed a likely command post. He pointed the Balilla towards it and throttled up again, leveling out at 200 feet. More tracers arced up to meet him. Most missed, but some rounds punched through the fabric of the fuselage or wings. Nothing vital was hit and Stone readied the bomb. Just one chance to get it right. The target disappeared beneath the engine cowling and he counted another beat before pulling the bomb release. The plane bobbled upwards with the sudden weight loss and he quickly corrected. Banking away, he looked back in time to see the explosion very near his target and grinned as the thunder of the detonation caught up to his ears.

It had been a good morning's work, but the bomb was gone and the ammo was low. There was still a bit more fuel than was needed to get home, though, so he could do some reconnaissance before returning to base. On the way back to the airfield, he sighted another aircraft flying north away from Pilsudski's assembly area and toward Tukhachevsky's lines. On a hunch he took an intercept course on a northwest heading. Bolshevik planes had been rare, but if this was one then the pilot had just seen what he needed to see in order to alert Tukhachevsky to the threat to his left flank. As the range closed Stone identified it as another Balilla fighter. Even before he made out the communist Red star on the tail he knew he had found his opposite number from the Syndicate.

The enemy agent must have sensed him as well and turned his fighter to face Stone's. The planes charged at each other like jousting knights of old. Muzzle flashes appeared from the other aircraft. Stone answered the incoming fire with some of his own. Both planes took hits but suffered only light damage. The fighters roared by each other close enough for Stone to distinguish the other pilot's whiskers. Stone didn't recognize the other agent, but he may have altered his appearance. There was no question he was Syndicate, however.

As soon as the other plane roared by, Stone banked hard into it to try and line up his sights on him. It wouldn't be that easy, though, since the other pilot had performed the same maneuver. The planes twisted back on each other like the heads of two coiled vipers and spit their venom as before, only this time the window for the engagement was brief as the duelers zoomed by each other again. They became locked in what fighter jocks call the 'scissors': two fighters each kept trying to turn into the other to get a tail shot but would end up going nose to nose for quick shots at each other, then flying by and repeating the attempt. The twisting maneuver formed a double helix path in the sky with each pilot hoping for the other to make the first mistake.

The extra-terrestrial pilots could withstand far more g-forces than could the wood and fabric planes they drove. The bullets would not prove fatal to either aviator, either, but destruction of their machines would mean mission failure. If Stone could shoot down the other plane, its pilot could not warn the Bolshevik leadership to close the dangerous gap in their forces that the Poles were now positioned to exploit. If Stone were shot down, he would survive but fail to stop that vital military secret from being learned by the Reds and they could march over most of Europe.

Stone's guns went silent as his ammo ran out. He had to bring the other plane down by colliding with it, but the 'scissors' he was locked in wasn't helpful for that since the window of opportunity for ramming was so small. If the other pilot figured out that he was out of ammunition, he might disengage from the fight and just fly home with his information. Stone decided to lure him into a trap and after the next pass extended into straight flight instead of turning into his foe. The other plane did turn and closed on his six o' clock to make the kill, but Stone went vertical and the tracers shot harmlessly below him. The other plane climbed to follow and when it got behind him again for another shot, Stone cut his engine power to idle and kicked his rudder for a hammerhead stall that quickly snapped his nose back around to face the still climbing enemy fighter. Stone applied power again and aimed directly at the other aircraft. The distance was too small and the closing speed too great to avoid the collision. The enemy pilot tried to break left in a last ditch maneuver, but Stone broke right and into him, smashing his right wings hard into those of the other biplane.

The wood of the wing spars snapped and Stone ducked as support cables, now released from their anchors, slapped back at the cockpit. The plane tumbled and Stone's view shifted rapidly back and forth between earth and sky. He spotted the other aircraft tumbling in similar fashion, the wings on its right side also missing. Gravity tugged at him against his shoulder straps, then slammed him into his seat again. This process continued several times until Stone hit the release and fell out of the cockpit the next time the aircraft inverted. He tumbled through the air until assuming proper skydiving body positioning, stabilizing him as he fell. Now he could see the other aircraft and the other pilot bailing out as he had. Stone brought his arms down to his sides, pointed his head towards his falling foe, and moved towards him through the air. Impact on the ground was seconds away. They would both survive, but the experience was unpleasant enough to avoid. Stone anticipated that his foe would transport away and enter the interphasing spheroids of space-time to find another location. If he could get close enough before he did so, he might follow.

The other pilot righted himself and fell in skydiving fashion. Then he noticed Stone's approach and vanished as Stone guessed he might. Fortunately, Stone had closed the gap enough for trans-dimensional pursuit and likewise vanished, leaving Poland and 1920 behind.

The two combatants exchanged the sensation of falling to the earth for the even more disorienting experience of careening between dimensions in the matrix of interphasing space-time spheroids, a complex web of crisscrossing universes. Navigating it was always a challenge and pursuing someone through it even harder, but Stone was a practiced hand at this and managed to keep his quarry in sight. Finally the Syndicate agent picked an aperture into a particular universe and entered it, Stone hot on his tail. Stone dropped into the portal a second after his opponent and emerged right into a stasis net. Its paralyzing energy coiled around him and painfully immobilized him. He crashed onto the hard, dusty surface of a planet he had never seen before, the net preventing him from rising. He could barely move his head for that matter, but he glimpsed a purple sky with three moons over a distant mountain range.

Given a few moments, he could break out of the stasis net, but he would not get that chance. The agent he pursued was now accompanied by three others. He recognized three of them from the Commonwealth briefs he had received on enemy operatives that had been seen in his area of responsibility. The one he had the dogfight with over Poland and followed into this trap was Severus, a cunning enemy tactician, Stone was now learning to his dismay. Another was Nimrod, who had a bloodthirsty reputation. The team leader was Ahriman. He was the task lead for Syndicate operations in this sector of the multiverse which included Earth. Stone had frustrated his plans before but never confronted the man himself.

Unlike the other three, the fourth of these was not in humanoid form. A black gelatinous blob about the size of a small automobile, it could morph its shape and extend tendrils from its amoeba-like body. Some of those tendrils wrapped around Stone's leg and dragged him across the dirt towards itself. A large gaping maw opened as he was drawn near.

"Not yet, Grendel. The time for that will come, but we must converse with our guest before dinner," Ahriman told him. The other two snickered.

Ahriman addressed Stone. "So, you foiled our little gambit in Poland on your precious little Earth. No matter; we will achieve that objective another way. Our main objective today was you. We knew the Commonwealth would move to block our communist project and we knew they'd send you. That is why we let them know what we were up to," he grinned.

That did not quite explain it, Stone thought. They were too well prepared. They must have a mole within the Commonwealth's Inter-dimensional Service.

"So now that we have you in our clutches, what we will now do is also predictable," he continued. "We will torture you for information on Commonwealth strategy and operational plans and then kill you," the grin vanished.

"Nothing to say? That is fine. We don't need you to say anything. Grendel here can extract the information from your mind without coercing verbalizations." The open 'mouth' on Grendel began to salivate, a sticky gray substance oozing out and dripping down to the ground.

Well, this was bad, Stone thought. Even if he could free himself from the stasis net, there were four of them and each was, if not quite a match for him, very close to it. Four of them together would be insurmountable. He did not have thorough knowledge of Commonwealth operations since it was compartmentalized and he never had a need, or even a desire, to know the higher secrets. What he did know could still be very helpful to the Syndicate, however, and this information he must not allow them to have under any circumstances. He would fight to keep them from getting that information at the cost of his life, an outcome that appeared highly likely at the moment.

Grendel's cold, gelatinous form crept over the immobilized Stone, sending a shiver through him. It covered his lower half up to his waist in two seconds and kept flowing over him.

"Any last words?" Severus asked with a sneer. Stone said nothing. Turning to the others, "I really thought he would have something witty for us."

"Disappointing," Nimrod agreed.

The black gelatin rose up to Stone's neck, then over his face and enveloped him completely. If he had been subject to fear, he would have felt it then, Stone reflected. He plunged into a sensory deprivation chamber upon being completely covered by Grendel's disgusting body, alone with his thoughts and unable to breathe. He could go without oxygen for extended periods, but he was now completely trapped with no idea when, or if, he would breathe again.

Soon he was no longer alone with his thoughts. Grendel was not only a shape-shifter but a tactile telepath, able to forcibly enter the mind of a being with which he was in physical contact. He was telepathically invading Stone's mind, looking to wrench free the valuable information Ahriman sought. He was not being discriminatory in it, though. This was no pinpoint strike but rather an onrushing horde seeking to loot everything in Stone's psyche. Grendel was possessed of very powerful mental energy and steamrolled Stone's outer mental defenses. He began to sift through Stone's memories and toss aside those that didn't interest him as if he was ransacking a house for valuables.

Stone was not without some resources, however. With all the strength he could summon, he withdrew his memories into an interior mental fortress and locked it up so securely that even he could not enter. If he survived, hopefully he would recover them eventually, but survival did not seem likely just now. Securing the information was the uppermost concern. Grendel would have to kill him to break into that fortress, but once he did so the information would be irretrievably lost. Grendel strained against Stone's interior mind castle with all his might but failed to breach it. He lost his temper and his focus as he made another attempt. Once he did so, Stone, or what remained of him mentally, saw an opportunity to counterattack. Not unlike Tukhachevsky's assault on Warsaw, a flank was left open for exploitation and Stone rushed into it to repel his enemy with all the mental strength he could muster.

Outside, the interrogation seemed to drag on and so Ahriman had dismissed Nimrod and Severus to other duties while he kept watch to see Stone's demise. It grew boring as he could see nothing of what he assumed to be a one-sided mental struggle. It seemed to be going well, judging by how eagerly Grendel was going about his work. With Stone out of the way, Ahriman's primary obstacle in this sector would finally be removed. In certain projected futures, the so-called western civilization of Earth would eventually become a major problem for the Syndicate's ambitions. Now Ahriman could complete its destruction and move on to more interesting worlds. If he played his cards right, he could be viceroy for this entire sector. That would give him absolute power within his little fiefdom and he would be answerable only to Syndicate High Command. Yes, the future looked much brighter now. Hopefully Grendel's devouring of Stone's mind would yield enough intel to accelerate this grand future.

Grendel quivered a bit and Ahriman walked closer in curiosity. He must be nearing completion, he thought, since this surely has dragged on. Grendel suddenly erupted in a geyser of black gelatin spraying everywhere and causing Ahriman to instinctively cover his face. Stone jumped to his feet, his whole body smeared in black goo but free of the stasis net which ripped off him when Grendel exploded. Ahriman was stunned. For an instant his gaze locked with that of Stone who just glared back in unspeakable wrath. Suddenly Stone grabbed his throat with both hands in a superhuman vise that Ahriman struggled vainly against. Ordinarily his strength was in Stone's league, but he was helpless against Stone's mindless rage. He fell backwards, Stone on top of him. Stone bellowed in anger and wrenched Ahriman's head sideways, breaking his neck with a crunch.

In his last death throes, Ahriman had attempted to transport away. He opened a portal but was dead before he could use it. Stone passed through it instead, accidentally. He had no memory of who he was, where he was, or what was going on. He certainly had no knowledge of how to transit the interphasing spheroids of space-time, but he willed himself through it; he knew not where. Instinctively he made his way to Earth's universe and then Earth itself because somehow the route was familiar, though not in a conscious way. Finally he emerged back into ordinary space-time with a splash into a cold ocean, but with no idea where or when…

SERGEANT STONE AND
THE VIKINGS

9 August 1062

Stone bobbed up and down, treading water in the freezing sea with the black night sky above, the many stars his only companions. He had no idea how he had gotten there. Worse, he could not even recall his own name. He struggled to remember anything at all, and his efforts yielded only a series of images that he did not recognize. What's more, they seemed to bear no relation to each other. He saw places and people all stridently different from one another. He conjectured that his full brain contained a rich panoply of memories, but somehow he had lost access to most of them and, crucially, the narrative string which tied them together. There was just enough to let him know that a great deal was missing, and this was vexing. Most vexing of all: who the hell was he?

He was still smeared with some unrecognizable black slime that was gradually washing off in the seawater. He did not recognize the garb he wore, but he quickly figured out that it did nothing to protect him from the water's bitter cold. A normal human would succumb to hypothermia after this many hours, but Stone did not realize that he was made of sturdier stuff. All he knew was that he was cold, wet, and miserable and wished to be no longer.

No land was visible in any direction. After lengthy scans of the horizon, some lights appeared in the distance. They were headed Stone's way, multiplying as more came into view. Torches. Many of them. He could tell as the distance closed that they were affixed to dozens and dozens of large boats. An entire fleet was headed this way. The boats each had a single large square sail. As they inexorably drew nearer, more details became evident. Stone could spot circular shields, the type men would carry into battle, arrayed on the sides of the boats which also sported long wooden oars. These oars were being rowed in unison by the crews to the beat of a drum and propelling the boats forward. They modified this rhythm on occasion to avoid collisions with other torch-lit boats in the otherwise impenetrable darkness. The prow of each of the long wooden boats curled upward and terminated in a stylized carving of a dragon's head. Stone felt a hint of recognition at the sight that gave him hope, but it quickly subsided and left him as before.

Soon the boats drew close enough to spot him in the torchlight. Stone waved his hands and called to them, "Ahoy!"

One of the crewmen of the nearest boat saw him right away and alerted his fellows. They responded to his hail and somehow Stone understood the words perfectly. He had no personal memories but somehow the language center of his brain was untouched. He did not know the name of the language, but he knew it. Odd.

"Greetings stranger. Friend or foe?" one of them asked.

Stone almost laughed. Who would respond with anything but 'friend' in this circumstance? "Oh, friend. Absolutely friend."

"Are you with King Harald or King Svein?" the voice rejoined.

Stone had no idea how to respond. "Whichever one pulls me out of the sea first." It was honest, at least. Hopefully it would be enough.

The boat whose lookout had conversed with him altered course and someone threw him a rope, which he grasped. They pulled him aboard and regarded him for a moment as he dripped on the oak planks of the longship's deck. He was strangely attired and beardless. One of the crew threw a cloak over him while others stood by with hands on sword hilts.

"What is your name? From whence do you hail?" the boat's commander asked as he stepped forward.

"I wish I knew. I have no meaningful memory prior to a few hours ago when I found myself adrift at sea," Stone answered. "Perhaps I hit my head and fell overboard."

"He could be lost from the Danish fleet," one of the others suggested.

"Not likely," the commander doubted this theory. "His appearance is strange, but it isn't Danish. Maybe Saxon or…I don't know," he rubbed his red bearded chin.

"Anyway," he addressed Stone, "welcome to the fleet of King Harald of Norway. I am Earl Hakon Ivarson. You owe your life to me and to this ship. Serve it and you will live. Betray it and we will cut your throat and put you back where we found you."

Stone was allowed to dry off and rest from treading water, but once they deemed him fit for service they put him at an oar. He did not mind this; it gave him time to think. In spite of his adventure in the sea, he did not seem to tire easily from the rowing.

Soon the lookout on this and other ships threw up a cry and all eyes strained forward. A line of torches appeared on the horizon signifying another fleet approaching. Judging by the length of the line, it was a much larger fleet than that of the Norwegians. This caused some consternation and murmuring among the crew.

"A signal! My lord, the King signals for a war conference," the lookout reported.

"Very well. Bring us alongside the King's ship."

Hakon and other earls gathered on the King's ship for the conference, but the meeting was short. The decision had to be made quickly whether to flee the superior enemy force or engage. Minutes later, Hakon returned to his own ship to announce the verdict.

"The King says, 'We'll win or fall heaped on each other sooner than flee! Each man shall fall across his brother!'"

The roughly ninety hearty Viking warriors on the longship roared with approval, and similar reactions from the other ships echoed over the open sea. The ships maneuvered into a line formation. Oars were stowed, sails were trimmed and the ships were lashed together for mutual support. Earl Hakon's ships anchored the right side. Weapons were made ready and the men awaited the enemy. An extra sword was found for Stone and placed in his hand where it felt oddly comfortable and familiar. It was a standard Viking sword, single handed, double edged, well balanced and sturdy. Stone was placed in the front line near the bow with some spears at his back should he prove less than reliable. He was a stranger, after all. He was grateful that he had been given a weapon in the first place.

The approaching torch lights grew larger and their light threw long dragon shadows on the sea in front of them. The Danes lashed their ships together as well to form a long chain of floating wooden fortresses. The two lines of ships drew closer. The men tensed as the thrill of impending action struck them. Stone felt the energy of it, too. It felt oddly familiar. Even though he had no memory of any others, he knew somehow that this fight would not be his first..

The lines of ships continued to close, propelled only by inertia and the oars of the ships at the extreme ends of the lines. Orders were given and archers made ready. When the signal was given, volleys of arrows were exchanged. Some of them were lit with flame to act as a guide for the archers to adjust their aim via the pre-modern tracers.

"Shields!" screamed Hakon to his crew. The men with shields raised them in response. Arrows embedded in them or bounced off with the fury of a hail storm. Screams erupted from wounded men as some of the arrows inevitably found a target. More volleys were exchanged across the open water between the closing ships. Finally they drew within range of grappling hooks, and these were used to close the last bit of the gap allowing the close combat to finally commence. Soon a mass of ships connected by the grappling lines formed a wooden island in the sea that was crawling with men determined to kill each other. Land war was brought to the sea. Battle cries of rage interspersed with the cries of the stabbed and slashed wounded and the splashing sounds where men fell or were pushed into the sea.

Hakon's ship anchored the extreme right flank of the Norwegian line. A Danish ship closed with it and the two adversaries grappled with each other. The two crews glared at each other over their shields as the ships were pulled together. At last they crashed against each other and the fight was on. Stone had no shield and was in the front facing the spears of the enemy. A strange calm came over him right before the clash. And then it was all a blur of activity as the opposing warriors exploded on each other.

A Dane launched a spear at Stone, but he batted it away with his sword and delivered a blow to the offending spear-wielder that split his helmet and felled him. No, this was certainly not Stone's first time at this kind of thing. The fall of the man he had fought left a gap on the enemy ship which Stone quickly filled by leaping aboard and continuing the fight. He slashed at enemy shields and parried their counters as the Norwegians joined him in the attack. The fight quickly devolved into a confusing melee of slashing, screaming, and bleeding Vikings. Several men, including Stone, slipped on the blood which soon covered the oaken deck. After several minutes of brutal fighting the Norwegians took the Danish ship, the last Dane falling overboard after a spear thrust in his gut.

The neighboring Danish ship, which was lashed to the one Stone helped take, had several hearty fighters who were still resisting Earl Hakon's men from the neighboring Norwegian ship. But the men on the captured ship now had a vantage point from which to attack them. Two volleys of arrows into their unshielded backs finished the fight on that ship.

The fight was going well for the Norwegians on this side of the battle, but that was not true everywhere. Then the lookout announced that the King appeared to be hard pressed by several Danish ships converging on his position in the center of the line. Earl Hakon broke six of his nearest ships out of the line formation, resuming use of the oars to make the best possible speed to the place of the King's difficulty. Announcing their arrival with volleys of arrows that thinned the ranks of the warriors facing the front of the battle, the Earl's task force swung around behind the Danish ships pressing the center of the line.. Return fire was paltry since those Danes were now suddenly engaged on two fronts. Earl Hakon's ships each deployed their grappling hooks and snared a Danish ship for close combat.

Blood was already up by now and the Norwegian Vikings surged over the sides of the enemy ships with loud yells. The Danes had by now recovered from the shock of envelopment and resisted stoutly. Stone was in the thick of it and would have felt out of place had it been otherwise. Why was such a brutal scene so terrifying and yet oddly comfortable at the same time? Yet he was far from alone in feeling the thrill of battle. He was surrounded by Viking warriors on both sides who evidently also took some pleasure in this gruesome work.

He took a couple of sword slashes on his arm and shoulders but the blades did not bite even though he wore no armor. They stung but did no apparent damage. That was also odd. He repaid the warriors who hit him with interest and they were not as unscathed. Stone turned around in the middle of the melee at the sound of a Dane going the berserker way and charging at Earl Hakon. The berserker, already wounded, raised a battle-axe over his head and came at Hakon who raised his shield in response. The battle-axe came down and shattered the shield, knocking Hakon's arm aside. With his other arm he plunged his sword into the man's abdomen, but the berserker did not even slow down. He embraced Hakon in a fierce bear hug while the sword protruded from his gut and he bled out on the deck. Hakon struggled to free himself, biting the man's ear, but he failed to get loose and they both fell overboard with a splash.

Stone cast his sword aside and dove after them. They were sinking fast in their armor and the torchlight on the surface barely penetrated the murky deep. Stone dove down farther, straining to reach them before he lost sight of them altogether. He found that he did not weary of the effort and did not require another breath. With another lunge he snagged Hakon by the back of his cloak and arrested his fall. The other man was almost dead by now and Stone was able to kick him away at last while dragging Hakon upward. They broke the surface after what seemed a long time and Hakon gasped for the air he had sorely missed. Stone took only a normal breath.

"I give you thanks, stranger. I will reward you, too, assuming we live," Hakon told him after catching his breath.

"You plucked me from the sea; it seemed sensible to return the favor," replied Stone.

The ship they had been fighting for was now firmly in Norwegian hands and they boarded it with no difficulty. Fighting continued but now the tide seemed to turn in favor of King Harald's forces, and the Danes began to retreat at daybreak. Harald wanted to pursue in hopes of capturing King Svein, but in the confusion this was not possible. The Norwegians had won the day, but the Danes lived to fight again as most of their ships withdrew safely.

Later Stone learned that King Svein was a wily opponent, so there was disappointment but not surprise in his escape. The two kings had agreed to a meeting time and place for their fleets to battle it out, but Svein's ships did not show. Harald then dismissed the half of his fleet manned by paid bondsmen since they were expensive to maintain in the field. The noble half he kept for raiding the Danish coast to convince the populace that Svein could not protect them. This was part of his long term strategy to assert his kingship over Denmark, but so far he had failed to do so. The clever Svein brought out his fleet when he learned that Harald had dismissed half of his and intercepted him near the mouth of the Nisa River.

King Harald triumphed anyway, partly thanks to the maneuver of Earl Hakon but also because he was inarguably one of the greatest soldiers of the age. Harald 'Hardrada' (the Ruthless) Sigurdson had been a soldier since fighting the Battle of Stiklestad at the age of fifteen when his half-brother, the saintly King Olaf, fell at his side. He escaped into exile where he served the Russian ruler Yaroslav the Wise against the Pechenegs and later led the elite and feared Varangian Guard for the Byzantine Emperors. After many successful battles against the Arabs and the Bulgarians, he returned to Norway when he learned that his nephew, King Magnus, had ascended the throne. Arriving home he contested with Magnus for the throne but an agreement was reached that gave him half of Norway. He gained the other half when Magnus died. He had spent much of the time since trying to gain the Kingdom of Denmark as well, but King Svein had managed to frustrate this.

So Harald Hardrada sailed back to Norway with a resounding tactical victory against the odds but was no closer to the throne of Denmark since Svein had escaped. Earl Hakon was highly regarded for his role in the victory and he in turn now held Stone in high favor for saving his life. Upon return to his dominions in the Uplands of northern Norway, he sponsored Stone and made him a permanent retainer. Stone took the name Bjorn Hakonson since he knew no family. The Earl had commercial interests in Iceland and Greenland, so Bjorn got into the business of sailing longships and trading for walrus tusks, rope, and the occasional polar bear. He earned the Earl's trust so thoroughly that he was put in charge of his own ship by the time he grew a full beard.

During a visit to Greenland, Bjorn's first mate Thorvald spoke up during a drinking session when the subject of Bjorn's amnesia came up.

"I might have an answer to your problem. Since the recovery of your memory is long delayed, it may be that you are bewitched somehow."

"That has been suggested before," Bjorn replied, unimpressed.

"But I know where you might find someone to break the spell. Back in Norway, and even in Iceland, the Church makes volvas who practice the old seior magic hard to find. Here in Greenland, though, I happen to know where one lives," Thorvald grinned at his secret knowledge.

"Nothing I've tried on my own has worked. Lead the way. After our drink, of course," Bjorn said before he downed another horn of mead.

After three more rounds of mead, the two men left their fellows to continue drinking and walked out into the frigid night. Thorvald led Bjorn out of the small fishing village and then beyond several more secluded huts. Trudging further, they passed the last of the huts and the sounds of carousing behind them faded until only the crunching of the light snow under their feet could be heard. Finally the trail ended, but Thorvald led the way beyond it and into somewhat deeper snow. At last they spied the dim light of a lone hut's fireplace.

"You go on. I want nothing to do with that old witch," Thorvald told him. "They say she has the power to cause men to forget things, so perhaps she can help you to remember them."

Bjorn was bemused at this stalwart warrior who would singlehandedly face a whole ship of Danes and sail resolutely on seas he believed held monsters of incredible size, yet seemingly preferred the cold to the warm hut of an old woman. Bjorn made his way alone to the humble hut and knocked on the door.

A woman did answer, but she was not as old as he anticipated. Her fair hair was turning white, but it was hard to see which color predominated in the dim firelight.

"Yes?" she asked suspiciously.

"I am told you can help those that are bewitched."

"What kind of bewitching?"

"I have no memory of my life before one year ago, only senseless dreams."

"What kind of dreams?"

"Dreams of battle, mostly, but in settings I can scarcely describe. In some of them I am seemingly killed."

"Did you bring any silver?"

"Very little, I'm afraid."

She grunted and looked him up and down before deciding to let him inside her plain, one room abode. There were few furnishings other than her bed. A bear skin blanket on the floor was the only extravagant adornment. It was there that she bade him sit and collected from him the few pieces of silver he had. She did not seem satisfied with the amount, but she did not turn him away, either.

Retreating to a corner of the hovel, she returned in ceremonial dress. Her cloak was a deep blue and bedecked with gems. She also held a wand that was likewise bejeweled. This she waved over him as she chanted. She invoked various gods and goddesses, Freyja in particular. She concluded by touching the wand to his cheek three times while saying some magic word.

That part of the ceremony over, she laid down the wand and disrobed without a word. When the cloak fell, she stood there before him naked. She was remarkably attractive for her age, but then she was apparently only in her fifties and not the decrepit crone he had been led to expect. Her skin was still taut and her runic tattoos did not sag. She wordlessly helped him to remove his clothing also. When she embraced him, he found that he was quickly aroused. When she lay back on the bear skin rug, he joined her there. Somehow he was aware that this was not his first time at this kind of thing, but no distinctive memory surfaced. Was this part of the ritual itself or part of the transaction since the few silver pieces were inadequate? In any case, he continued until she was clearly satisfied this time.

When they were finished and put their clothes back on, she sat and faced him gravely for a moment, dabbing sweat from her brow with a cloth before speaking.

"I cannot see your past. It is shrouded as if in a deep fog, a fog that may one day lift. All I can say is that you are from very far away."

"Of course. I sailed here from Norway."

"No, much farther away than that. Farther than I can see. What I did see was your future. Your dreams of death—they are omens. You are destined to fall in battle."

"Then a good death awaits me and I welcome it. I only want to remember who I am before that day comes. Will I?"

She shook her head, "I cannot see. I am sorry. The gods did not see fit to reveal that to me. Perhaps if you sail back to the distant land you came from you might recover your memories."

That was that, and Bjorn left the hut to rejoin Thorvald who was still star gazing in the cold.

"Well? That took longer than I expected," he said at Bjorn's approach. "I was afraid she had eaten you."

"No. I didn't suddenly remember everything, either."

"Perhaps it takes time. Was she as old and ugly as they say?"

"Hideous."

That night Bjorn was troubled by warlike dreams again. He was in a strange battle and surrounded by fellow warriors all dressed alike with sky blue helmets and tunics. They faced an unseen enemy that could launch devastating blows from afar that crashed with a roar rivalling anything Thor could wield. To shield themselves from these deadly attacks, they had dug crevasses into the ground deep enough to stand in without being seen. To emerge above ground from these mud pits was to court death. The enemy could also sling deadly projectiles from smaller weapons to take down a single man from great distances. These slings were no mystery to Bjorn, somehow. Within the dream he seemed familiar with these weapons and he and his fellows each carried one on their persons. These contraptions were not like any bow or sling but appeared to be wooden staffs mated to metal rods that one aimed from the shoulder. The projectiles were made of metal and uniform in appearance with each having a pointed tip like an arrow head. These metal arrows were propelled with a loud thunderclap from within the staffs, though not as loud as the enemy's bolts that threw enormous geysers of dirt into the air, sometimes with blood and body parts as well.

"Incoming!" someone yelled. All in the pit ducked their heads and waited for the impact of the enemy strike. No thunderous crash came, no pelting with dirt clods. There was a faint whizzing sound instead. Even in the dream, the blood in Bjorn's veins froze as he realized what it was.

"Gas! Gas! Gas!" he bellowed. All scrambled for their masks, but it was too late. The air had been poisoned. Bjorn fumbled with his mask and donned it, but he could no longer see. His eyes burned and so did his lungs. He couldn't breathe…

Finally he awoke, puzzling over the dream. He was sweating even though the hovel he stayed in was cold. Another strange death in another battle with weapons he could scarcely understand. Did he once die from the poison breath of a dragon? Somehow he knew that was not the case, but he could come up with no satisfactory explanation. Gradually, he drifted back to sleep while thinking idly of the volva, hoping that the pleasant memory of her would ward off another nightmare.

It did, but soon the witch was replaced in his dream by another woman. She was younger and dazzlingly beautiful. She had darker skin, long jet black hair, and a statuesque figure. It seemed that he knew her in far warmer climes. Visions of her were accompanied by radiant sunlight and hot sands underfoot. His feelings about her were warm as well. Not mere lust as with the witch, although that was certainly in the mix. No, he felt a deep and meaningful bond with this woman that he ached to reestablish. This time he awoke wishing to experience more.

The next day Bjorn instructed Thorvald to have the crew gather provisions and make ready to launch.

"On to Vinland again, then?" the first mate asked.

"No. We go back east and then south. We'll go south until the sun's heat is unbearable," Bjorn smiled.

"I could do with some of that," Thorvald replied with a grin of his own.

Months later that grin was replaced by a grimace. Thorvald had kept smiling during a recent fight with the Saracens, but the current storm was enough to steal the mirth from any man. The ship was tossed to and fro fiercely by the merciless waves. Each man clung for dear life to whatever part of the ship he could grab. Thorvald's brother Thorkel cried out to Odin for deliverance. Some others called out to one or more of the other gods, some called out to the God of the Christians, and some simply cried out. Bjorn had not begun the habit of prayer but was starting to consider it in the heart of this maelstrom. He wished fervently to move the ship out of danger or to anywhere but where it was.

Quite suddenly his wish came true. The storm was gone in the blink of an eye, replaced by calm seas and sunshine. Prayers of thanksgiving to the various gods replaced the cries of anguish. The sail was unfurled again and the men rowed on happily for a time. Then they heard an ominous noise in the sky. All eyes searched the heavens for what it was that could make the horrible, rapid thumping noise.

"There! A dragon!" cried Ulf in the prow.

All eyes followed to where he pointed. A dark shape could be spied against the white of a cloud. It approached and they could see more detail. The dragon's wings beat so rapidly over its head that they could scarcely be seen, but their noise was monstrous. The dragon paused and hovered over the ship, its horrendous breath pushing down on the crew from high above. In the fearsome maw of the dragon, two terrified men could be seen. They pointed at the ship and looked at each other, perhaps hoping that the ship's warriors could deliver them from their plight.

Or so it seemed to the crew, but Bjorn disagreed. This, he knew, was no dragon. He had seen it's like in one of his dreams. It was a flying machine of some kind and controlled by mortal men. In his dream he and others had been aboard one. He and his group were wearing matching tunics and helmets, green in color this time, and they carried a version of the thunder staff arrow-slingers that had no wooden component. What was the flying machine called? A chopper! The chopper in the dream had let him and his group down in a clearing and they had run into a dense forest filled with green vegetation. Their green tunics helped them blend in to their surroundings as they went hunting for some enemy hidden within. Then the chopper had taken off again under the control of men. This thing was one of those, only it was white while the one in the dream had been, like so much else, green.

Thorvald took aim at the dragon with his bow and let an arrow loose. Odin must have smiled on the shot since it defied the dragon's downward breath and hit the dragon in the belly where it bounced off its scales. The dragon flew off and the crew cheered Thorvald for his great skill. The crew continued sailing on its previous course. Presently Ulf sighted land and the men rowed for all they were worth.

On reaching the beach, the men hopped from the ship with their weapons ready, excited from the fight with the dragon. Nearly naked slaves, most with tattoos marking them to signify their owners, lay strewn lazily about the sandy shore. Although clearly slaves since they were unarmed and marked, they were doing no work. The Vikings slapped them aside with the flat of the sword and proceeded inland where they raided a mysterious land full of strange wonders. Bjorn remained near the ship trying to assimilate the 'dragon' of their encounter and the chopper of his dream. What did it mean to finally encounter in the real world something which had previously only been in his dreams? It could mean that the dreams were more accurate as memories than he had believed.

The crew did not raid long and came back with only a few captives. They told tall tales of dragon-fry darting along the ground with helpless human captives in their mouths. Other humans here seemed nonplussed by these fearsome creatures, however. The Vikings fought with the dragon-fry, but their armored skin proved impervious to harm. Bjorn got a glimpse of some of these 'dragon-fry' and saw that they matched the man-driven ground conveyances which he had seen in a dream. With no animal pulling them, these carts rolled along the ground at great speed. Bjorn knew he had previous experience with these carts but, exasperatingly, he could force no clear memory to the surface of his mind while awake. Only in dreams did it all seem so clear. In the dreams he seemed to know not only how to operate the carts, but also details about their peculiar method of propulsion.

Just as Bjorn felt the urge for more exploration in hopes of jarring more memories loose, the crew was earnestly desirous for a prompt departure. They did not wish to anger by too long a stay the god of this strange land, nor did they wish to chance another duel with the dragon. Bjorn assented and the crew shoved off, rowing out to sea with all available speed.

One of the male captives spoke up, "What the %$&* is going on, man? You can't do this! I have rights! This is the twentieth century, man, not the tenth! Is this some kind of…ughkk?"

The pommel of Sigurd's sword knocked his front teeth in and he stopped speaking. Only Bjorn understood his words, and that was a mystery in itself. Twentieth century? That might explain the fantastic machines. But what magic brought them here? And why was Bjorn already familiar with things from the distant future, even if only via dreams? The startling possibility confronted him that they were now in the far future and, what's more, that this was not his maiden voyage.

Bjorn desperately wished to return his crew to their homes, but had no idea how. At that moment the ship pitched violently as if tossed by a rogue wave from out of nowhere. When it passed, the ship was now in a roiling sea under a storm-darkened sky. Gone was the sunshine of the land of the dragon and dragon-fry. It now seemed that the ship was near to the storm it had encountered earlier that day, though conditions were not nearly so bad. They sailed on and the next day raided a Saracen coast in Iberia. All seemed to be normal with no more incredible monsters or machines. They had made their way back to their own time and place, if indeed they had ever actually left it. The ship and crew finished an uneventful return voyage to Norway after that, but the men were still frightened. They dubbed Bjorn 'the far-traveled' and boasted of their 'adventure in the unknown land' but none volunteered to sail with him again. Almost none, that is.

"I would sail with you anywhere, Bjorn, even though it terrifies me," Thorvald told him with a slap to his back. Thorkel, Sigurd, and Ulf spoke likewise.

Bjorn smiled. "Let's drink to that. I'll buy." This elicited a hearty cheer so loud that the rest of the crew was hardly missed.

Things had changed in Norway while Bjorn and his crew were away. Unable to subdue Denmark, King Harald Hardrada had turned inward to solidify his control over the kingdom at the expense of the earls. Tax resisters and recalcitrant earls found themselves roughly treated by the royal army. Earl Hakon resisted mightily in the north but was overcome and driven into exile in Sweden. It was there that Bjorn and his men finally rejoined him.

Earl Hakon, for his part, grew restless in exile and sought means of reconciliation with Hardrada. Informants told him that Earl Tostig, another exile, had convinced King Harald to assert his claim to the throne of England. Tostig was the former Earl of Northumberland who had been overthrown by the late King Edward the Confessor. When King Edward died with no heir, Tostig's brother, Harald Godwinson, assumed the throne but did not restore Tostig to his earldom. Tostig accordingly sought revenge and urged Harald Hardrada to invade based on his line's old claim via relation to a previous king of England, Harthacanute. Hardrada took up the challenge and issued a call to arms throughout Norway. Hakon reasoned that if he sent a few ships of his men bearing his standard to assist, then he might eventually be restored to the King's good graces. Stone, aka Bjorn, took on the assignment and equipped three vessels to carry seventy men each on campaign and set sail in September of 1066, joining the rest of the invasion fleet at its assembly point at Solunds. Hardrada was not inclined to reject any help on an enterprise of this scale, and Bjorn's Vikings were permitted to join the fleet.

When the winds were favorable, King Harald sailed across the North Sea, gathering more friendly forces from earls in Orkney and the Shetlands. Gaining small victories and reducing small fortresses along the coast, the fleet then sailed up the River Humber and offloaded the bulk of the army below York. Local English earls responded with alacrity and assembled a large force to repulse the Vikings. This force met Harald in battle between the river and a large ditch. Beyond the ditch was an impassable marsh which would prevent either army from outflanking the other. Harald bore his 'Land-Ravager' standard before him and led his troops directly at the English line. These local militia were no match for hardened Viking warriors and were put to flight with great loss. Such was won the last great Viking victory on English soil. The important town of York submitted to Harald Hardrada shortly thereafter, but the English King, Harold Godwinson, had quickly amassed a more professional force to the south where he had been waiting for the landing of William of Normandy, another claimant for the throne. He marched his army north with startling speed to confront Hardrada's troops. Meanwhile Tostig arrived with reinforcements for Hardrada.

Bjorn and his men had been in the forefront, of course, eager to represent their earl well. These men included some who had been with Bjorn since the Battle of the Nisa River where Earl Hakon had plucked him from the sea, like Ulf and Sigurd. They, along with brothers Thorvald and Thorkel, had voyaged with him to the unknown land. Still others had sisters who had slept with him. All in all, they were a hearty bunch and close knit after so many adventures together. They enjoyed each other's company while camped near Stamford Bridge where Hardrada had just accepted the surrender of Stamford Castle. The army was not disposed for battle with the bulk of the men encamped on the south side of the bridge, a smaller portion on the north side, and a third component guarding the ships. Most had discarded their armor due to the heat of the day. Bjorn forbade his men to do this, however, and they grumbled but obeyed.

Not a half hour passed before dust on the horizon signified the approach of a large party. The English cavalry appeared first, the sun glinting off their armor and spears as they formed up in battle array. The infantry followed soon after and lined up behind the horsemen. It was an enormous force and Hardrada was caught with his army divided. A quick war council decided on making the best stand possible while sending word to the rest of the army to march quickly to their king's aid. Hardrada tried to buy even more time with a parlay. He and Tostig rode out to meet King Harold Godwinson's messengers under a flag of truce.

One of the English horsemen said, "Is Earl Tostig with this army?"

"We won't deny that he might be found here," Tostig replied.

"Tell him that his brother the King will restore him as Earl of Northumberland, and moreover make him master of a third of the kingdom to rule alongside himself."

"This is a welcome change of heart," Tostig replied. "But if I accept this offer," he dropped the pretense, "what shall be offered to King Harald Sigurdson, my ally?"

"We shall give him six feet of good English earth. Nay, perhaps more since he is taller than most men."

"Never will the Northmen say with truth that Earl Tostig betrayed their king. We shall fight, then, and either die with honor or gain England by victory." And the parlay was concluded with each party riding back to their lines.

"Who was that who spoke so well?" Hardrada asked.

"That was my brother, King Harold Godwinson," Tostig answered.

"It is a pity you did not say so; I'd have slain him right there."

"I will not betray him, either, in such a manner. We must beat him in battle."

"So be it."

The Vikings made a wall of shields and spears and made ready to receive the English cavalry. At first the English rode around them, probing for weakness. Their assaults were light in the beginning, testing the defenses. Succeeding assaults increased in severity, but the Vikings held firm. If they could hold out long enough for reinforcements to arrive either over the bridge or by ship on the river, the day might yet be won.

At the center point in the line however, discipline broke down and some of the men broke formation to pursue the English horsemen and launch their spears at them. This created a gap that the cavalrymen were quick to exploit and a fierce close-quarters battle erupted in that part of the line. Hardrada himself led his reserve force into the gap. He was strong and skilled with the sword and hewed a path through the English. None seemed able to stop his onslaught at first, but then came wave after wave of English arrows. Their impact was especially telling now that the shield wall had collapsed. Some of the arrows hit stray Englishmen, but one of them struck Hardrada himself in the windpipe. He collapsed and died instantly. Tostig tried to rally the men, but the cohesion was now broken and the cavalry rode men down. English infantry now closed in for the kill.

Bjorn had his men fall back to the bridge. Most of his men had remained with the ships. Some that he had with him were already lost to arrows. Thorkel was run down by cavalry. Forming a circle of shields, the remainder of about eight men fought their way backwards towards the bridge. They made a much harder target to challenge than the random individuals that could be run down in the open field and, with fierce fighting, they managed to reach the bridge. From there they witnessed the carnage of the field where most of their fellows lay and saw the rest fleeing the victorious English. Tostig had also fallen by now. The rest of the army behind them on the other side of the bridge and the Derwent River was still not ready to meet an assault. More time had to be bought or they, too, would be run down by this English army that had seemingly appeared from nowhere.

Bjorn spoke to his men, "I must bid you all farewell. You must go and I must stay so that you can get away. Please do not disobey me in this. Nothing will be served by your staying. Hardrada and Tostig are dead and you've done your duty for the Earl. Please send him my regards."

"What are you going to do?" Thorvald asked, itching to stay.

"I am going to remain and ensure that you can get home and live a long life in the fields and fjords of home. You have already lost a brother, Thorvald. Don't make me lose mine. Go. Take to the ships and make for

Norway; this battle is lost. I must leave you as I came to you. Valhalla awaits," he pleaded.

"We would have stayed with you," Ulf said.

"I know it. You sailed with me over the whole ocean to help me find myself, and find myself I did. I found my home with you as part of this band of brothers. Accept this last gift from me. For my part, I could never hope for a better death," Bjorn answered.

They bowed, not without silent tears, and left him alone on the narrow wooden footbridge before running across it to the other river bank. The English had mopped up on the north bank and now turned their attention to the bridge. A single Viking stood there in the middle of the bridge with full armor and helm, a long black beard, and his hands resting atop the hilt of a fearsome battle-axe. They approached incredulously. One man against an army? The launched a salvo of arrows. These bounced off his chain mail and helm to no effect. The infantry moved forward slowly.

Four men abreast were all that could march down the bridge. The first of the infantry stopped just outside of striking range. Bjorn raised the axe to the ready and waited. He was not the one in the hurry. Let the English tarry all they like. Finally the first group raised their swords and shields and came on to commence battle. Bjorn swung the axe and it whistled through the air before crashing through a man's shield as if it were made of foil. The swing continued through the ruined shield and buried itself through the man's chain mail and deep into his chest. He fell into the man next to him and Bjorn quickly dislodged the axe for another mighty swing to his left and down, beneath another man's shield and severing his leg. The man screamed and fell, the blood from his stump squirting all over the wooden bridge planks. A swing back to the right hit another man in the chest with the flat of the axe, the blunt trauma knocking the wind out of his lungs and the man himself completely off the bridge and into the water with a splash. Another mighty swing back to the left sailed over the man's shield and decapitated him, his head bounding back down the bridge in front of his startled fellows.

Follow-on assaults were met with similar ferocity and Bjorn did not tire. He was fueled by berserker rage, by frustration at his fractured memory, and the desperate need to save his companions. Also, the next attackers had to negotiate the slippery blood pool and work around the bodies or body parts of fallen comrades. Distance attacks with javelins, spears and bows produced no results, so the infantry continued to feed men into this death machine. With the death of Harald Hardrada, the Viking Age had essentially come to a close. One Viking stood on Stamford Bridge to make sure that the last page of that saga was covered in blood and glory.

The foot soldiers continued to come on at the urgings of their officers who could not believe that one man was stopping an entire royal army. The men did so in spite of the treatment they saw meted out to their predecessors. With every swing of that dread axe, another man or two men were sent to the next life. This went on for nearly an hour, giving the remnant of the Viking army on the other side of the bridge time to rally. One enterprising Englishmen found a barrel in the river and floated unseen beneath the bridge. He steadied himself and took careful aim with his javelin at the unarmored groin of this invincible warrior. He launched his weapon straight and true through the slats in the bridge and into Bjorn's unprotected underside.

Bjorn, that is, Stone, was caught by surprise. His recent very lucid dreams had shown him scenes of battles and in some of these he had been gravely injured. These recollections and the prediction of the witch that he was destined to fall in battle had unconsciously triggered his vulnerable mode. The prophecy of his fall became self-fulfilling. The unconscious notion of vulnerability was actualized and since Stone did not recall his true nature, he could not restore his innate invulnerability to weapons such as the English javelin. It struck home and inflicted great pain. He sunk to his knees and the infantrymen facing him moved in quickly to finish him. They tried to cut off his head, but the blades only bit so far. Finally he fell off the bridge and was lost in the river.

The English flowed over the bridge at last, minus forty men they lost fighting Stone, and continued the battle with the remaining Vikings. The Norwegians had lost their top leaders and were beaten back to their ships in this battle. They never again troubled England which remained in English hands for a whole two weeks until William of Normandy landed in the south. Harold Godwinson rushed his men down to meet him and repeat his performance of Stamford Bridge, but his exhausted men were not up to the task and the Normans vanquished them at the Battle of Hastings. Godwinson took an arrow in the eye and was given his own six feet of good English earth while William earned the sobriquet, 'the Conqueror'. Thorvald, Ulf, Sigurd, and the other companions of Bjorn made it back to their ships and home.

Bjorn's name was lost to history, but his stand on Stamford Bridge went down in legend. Stone recovered after floating down river for several miles. The javelin could not kill him even in his vulnerable mode and he healed rapidly. Still, the grievous injury and the fall into the water combined to open a closed channel in his mind that freed his suppressed memories. He climbed up on the river bank and lay there assimilating his newly released memories and sorting out his last few years as a Viking in relation to the rest of his long life. He had succeeded so well in locking up his own memories away from the Syndicate interrogators that he had blocked them from himself for four years as well. Only then did he realize that he had inadvertently transported his ship and crew to the twentieth century and back during the foray in the 'unknown land'. At last the long amnesia odyssey was over. Onward to new adventures…

THE WEDDING OF
SERGEANT STONE

New Orleans, September 1890

Isis had assimilated well into New Orleans, but then the place was such a heterogeneous mixture of cultures that her exotic origin was not a huge obstacle. She hailed from ancient Egypt, but with her dark complexion she passed easily for a Creole woman in 19th century Louisiana. She mixed well with the Creole women and learned their cuisine if not their language by many visits to Congo Square and Treme' Market. Stone had tutored her in English and she had mastered the language so well that she was now exploring other languages of the city such as French and Italian, but those were a work in progress. Those languages she practiced in shopping at the French Market for the produce unloaded from the nearby wharf on the Mississippi River. With Stone's help she was also picking up Latin, a language she took interest in so that she could better understand the Masses she attended daily at St. Louis Cathedral.

She and Stone lived in one of the Pontalba Apartments whose distinctive balconies with wrought iron railings overlook Jackson Square in the heart of the city's French Quarter. The rent was high for a New Orleans police sergeant, but Isis did not know that. Stone had no money worries for some reason in spite of his meager pay, but they lived simply except for the somewhat glamorous location of their apartment. Isis had been raised a princess and was accustomed to the finer things, but she was content in her exile and largely let go her royal pretensions if not her dignified reserve. Of course even a modest lifestyle in the nineteenth century surpassed high living in the Bronze Age. She did relish the pomp of the Mardi Gras parades with their elaborate costumes and faux royalty. Stone did not tell her that peasants like them were not invited to the krewes' royal balls.

With the vantage point from her apartment veranda, Isis could not ignore the impressive cathedral and naturally became curious about the ceremonies within. She had much time to herself while Stone was at work to visit the Poydras Market, the shops on Royal Street, and the food vendors on Decatur. While fascinating, these did not hold her interest all day. Inevitably she began to attend Mass and this inexorably led to curiosity about the religion itself. Isis had heard of Christ because of history lessons from Stone, but here in this place Christ was believed to be physically present in the sacrament at Mass. This notion was irresistibly fascinating for her.

Isis had been a priestess of Ra in her former life. She had seen her husband Osiris apparently return from the dead. She had a very religious frame of mind and was captivated by the Christian belief in the Resurrection of Christ and eternal life for believers. She asked questions of the believers at the cathedral and was directed to Father Manoritta of the nearby St. Anthony of Padua Church, a parish devoted to serving the onrushing waves of Sicilian immigrants entering the city. He and Father Gambera, a colleague of Mother Frances Cabrini (later Saint Frances Cabrini) gave her thorough instruction in the faith and she was an eager student.

As she learned more and the date of her baptism approached, Isis realized that she was living in sin with Stone per the belief system she was entering upon. An unusually passionate woman, she struggled with herself but through an exertion of the will, began to abstain from relations with Stone, something she had pursued avidly before. Stone seemed nonplussed by this and went about his business, something which irked Isis. Actually it made her want him even more, made her wish to make him want her, but she resisted this urge. Finally Isis was baptized into the Catholic faith. Stone was in attendance and he suspected what would follow.

On their short walk home from the cathedral, Isis' normally regal self-confidence gave way to uncharacteristic nervousness. She was downright fidgety. Clearly, something was on her mind but she wasn't sure how to express what she wanted to say, and it wasn't due to any residual difficulty with English. When she wanted a private conversation with Stone she often reverted to ancient Egyptian anyway, and she did so now.

"There is something important I would like to ask you," she began. "We have been together…as man and woman…for some time now."

"Stop right there. If we are going to do this thing, we are going to do it right," Stone cut her off. "It is not your place to ask me. I must ask you. That is how it goes."

They had reached the center of Jackson Square, the former Place d'Armes. Stone and Isis had the center spot to themselves for the moment, even free of pigeons, and Stone took her by the hand. He went down on one knee and presented her a sparkling diamond ring. Isis was familiar with this ritual, too, but was taken by surprise. Stone had observed her reactions as she'd beheld other couples do this. She caught her breath and looked down at him lovingly as he asked, "Will you be my wife?"

He barely finished before she said yes and they embraced. The ice queen's green eyes shed a tear each, which Stone wiped from her cheeks. After a beignet and coffee breakfast at Café Du Monde, at which both could hardly stop smiling, they wandered back to the cathedral to start the process for holy matrimony.

Stone had been married before, of course. Guinvyr, the beautiful Celtic princess with the flaming red hair had been his wife in 6th century Britain. Stone's search for the Cosmic Eraser, a device similar to that which had destroyed his home universe, was misremembered as the quest for the Holy Grail. He went down in history as the legendary Arthur and Guinvyr as Guinivere. Like Isis she was a queen and, also like Isis, lived on in legend. Stone reflected wryly that he sure knew how to pick them. Guinvyr was long dead in the 19th century, so Stone was free to marry. To dodge any bigamy, he would consciously avoid any return visits to her era.

The clerk at the Presbytere adjacent to the cathedral naturally requested baptismal certificates from the happy new couple. This was a simple matter for Isis since the ink on hers was barely dry. Stone had one, too, albeit a forgery as part of his self-created identity as a New Orleans native. He had been baptized, just not on the date specified on the paper. It specified his first and middle names as well. Stone always went by Stone as his last name for it contained a link to his past, to his long lost home. The other names fluctuated as needed to blend into human society in different eras. John was a frequent choice and was what he was using in 1890 New Orleans. It was simple, strong, and he had actually encountered John the Evangelist once. The middle initial was M, which stood for the more exotic name of Melchizedek. Therein lies a tale.

Stone was a keen observer of humanity to include its many religions, but it was his friendship with Pope Julius II which made him pay attention to the details of Christianity. That worldly warrior-pope might have been the only one that could have done so. Stone assisted Julius in his many wars and intrigues to reestablish the authority of the Papal States in Italy and became his most trusted advisor, a fact neatly hidden from history. As they became closer, Stone revealed to Julius in the seal of the Confessional his true nature and origin. The intrigued Julius instructed, baptized and ordained Stone, even offering him a cardinalate, but this Stone refused.

The question arose whether the sin of Adam's fall stained Stone's species, whether it was redeemed by the Christ. Julius decided that any rational being was made in God's image and that since Stone's species had destroyed itself, it must be considered fallen even independent of Adam's fall. As such it was also redeemed by Christ who, though human, was God incarnate as a creature and therefore representative of all God's rational creatures who needed redemption. Other questions remained, such as how the rest of Stone's species might ever hear the gospel and be saved since their entire universe had been wiped out and none were left. Julius seemed assured that nothing could finally snatch souls from the hand of God, not even the obliteration of a universe. This wasn't a full answer, but then what answer could there be? Stone didn't argue.

Of more immediate concern to Julius with his new knowledge was that there existed, in addition to Stone himself, otherworldly creatures that were able to shift back and forth through time, for whom the events of the past were not necessarily beyond their ability to influence. Julius feared for the stability of sacred history, particularly events recorded in the Bible. At Julius' behest, Stone went back to work security for various sacred events which the shape of the time stream laid bare to possible outside intervention. He marched with the armies of Israel under David and Jonathan. He was there part of the time when Moses led Israel in the desert for forty years, even helping fight the Amalekites. He returned to see the fall of Jericho. The truculent Samson challenged him to a wrestling match and Stone could not refuse, only stipulating that it take place in private to avoid it being recorded in Sacred Scripture. The duel was worthy of any legend and lasted an entire day until the pair agreed that it was pointless to continue and that they should declare it a draw.

Stone was less than completely successful in avoiding biblical attention, however. He was very careful, but everyone makes mistakes. While observing the patriarch Abram he got too close. Abram spotted him and came up to start a conversation. Of course Stone had been involved in blown stakeouts before during his years of police work, so he played it cool. Vanishing from the time stream while under eye might lead to his inclusion in Scripture as an angel or something.

"Greetings! My name is Abram. By what name are you called?"

Crap, he saw me, Stone thought. Stone had picked a deliberately mysterious name for his cover that wouldn't be connected to any of the neighboring peoples. "Melchizedek. I give you a blessing from the Most High." Stone gave him a real blessing, complete with the Sign of the Cross. Abram couldn't recognize it, but Stone hoped it would seem awe-inspiring and mysterious enough for him to back off. No luck.

"Where have you come from?"

"I come in the name of the King," Stone, aka Melchizedek answered. Lots of kings around here. He can take his pick and assume what he wants.

"Which king?"

Damn. Inquisitive fellow. "The King of Peace, of course." Not a lie, at least.

Abram bowed low in homage. Oh crap. Stone quickly raised him to his feet. This was getting out of hand. There would be no quick way to brush this guy off, so Stone, as Melchizedek, involved Abram in a complex religious ritual in an effort to satisfy him and so make good his escape. Falling back on his ordination training, Stone gathered wine and bread and celebrated Mass, chronologically the first in history. It was elaborate and reverent and all in Latin to add to the majesty and mystery, which impressed Abram, so much so that he insisted that Stone take a tenth of his goods. Great, I overshot, Stone thought. He would find a charitable outlet for his new wealth in goats at the first opportunity.

"May the Most High God bless and keep you, Abraham, er, Abram. I must depart," the mysterious Melchizedek intoned solemnly.

Abram bowed low again and pronounced an even more elaborate blessing, to Stone's discomfort.

"Yeah. Thanks, man. You too," he responded with a departing wave. Now if only Abram will forget that this very minor incident ever happened, all will be well. Or hopefully no one will know any different, Stone hoped.

A quick review of Genesis upon Stone's return to the sixteenth century revealed, to his horror, that he was now a featured character! A preliterate society, one insignificant chance meeting, and it was recorded for all time! Failure.

Then there was the most important assignment, the one covering the central event of Christianity, indeed of human history: the Crucifixion. Stone was there as part of the execution detail, but his angle was crowd control. No outside interference occurred here, either. Stone's mere presence might have deterred any other extra-dimensional interlopers. That, or another Power, was at work. In any case, Stone was able to witness up close the carrying of the Cross through Jerusalem to Calvary.

Stone was very familiar with human pain and suffering. This man, Yeshua of Nazareth, suffered as much or more than anything he had seen. Even before being scourged, he had been beaten mercilessly. The scourging itself left barely any undamaged skin on his rack of bones. The crown of thorns added yet another cruel torment. Then it was time for him to carry the patibulum out to the site of crucifixion, suffering more indignities and assaults along the way.

But he had the power to stop this at any time, yes? He didn't. Most condemned men spat at their tormentors. What had they to lose now? They cursed at the jeering crowd with impressive obscenities. This one said nothing, did not defend himself in any way. The most powerful being in or out of creation was apparently set on a different display of power.

Stone had witnessed other crucifixions. When the condemned were raised upon the cross, the vilest words could be expected to spew forth from them, calling down curses and wishing the cruelest fates on their enemies. In spite of the pattern being set here, Stone half-expected something similar. Probably nothing obscene, but perhaps a prophetic warning of divine retribution.

"Father forgive them; they know not what they do."

What was this? And it was no act. He was in great pain, but in his eyes burned a compassion even greater. He prayed for his enemies. Forgave them. Stone respected strength. That was what one normally expected from gods; thunderbolts from Zeus or Thor and the like. But this was strength like he'd never seen. He truly was suffering this in order to save. Couldn't there have been an easier way? No. He was determined to show his love by giving absolutely everything he had.

And it got worse as the afternoon dragged on. Yeshua, his wrists and ankles nailed to the cross, had to heave himself upward to catch every breath but was gradually asphyxiating anyway. The pain grew exponentially. Finally, he screamed in agony, "My God, my God, why have you abandoned me?"

In that moment of supreme torment, of absolute weakness and seemingly on the verge of despair, Yeshua had won a convert in Stone. Yes, for Stone, who so admired strength, this was the moment he realized he had found a God he could follow. Not another powerful god of wrath who commanded mindless obedience. Not another guru who promised deliverance from suffering through self-denial. No, this God did not remain aloof from the suffering and degradation in the human condition. He embraced it as fully as possible by sharing in it to the hilt. Accusations against the Deity about how he could allow so much evil and suffering in the world fall mute here before the cross of Christ. He didn't make it all go away. Instead he drank it to the bitter dregs himself and promised to his followers, if they were willing to do the same, that they could be saved. The destruction of Stone's home universe, seemingly an insurmountable disaster, still loomed small next to the Creator of all universes being nailed to a tree to suffer and die. Surely nothing was beyond His care or ability to save, then.

When it was over, Stone momentarily lost situational awareness and spoke his mind aloud where nearby witnesses could hear.

"Truly this man was the Son of God."

It was after this that Stone was inspired to make the habit of subjecting himself to human weakness. He could suffer pain and fear as humans do, even suspend his own knowledge of his invulnerability in order to experience authentic fear of death. He had 'died' by falling in battle several times. At Camerone, Teutoburg Wald, Troy, Warsaw Ghetto, Verdun, and so many other horrific events, he had faced down death. These experiences magnified his respect for the fighting men and women who laid down their lives throughout human history for worthy causes.

Pope Julius gave him a dispensation, freeing him from his vows. He was no longer a priest and was free to marry. Again, that is. Stone thought of Guinvyr. He could not make her happy as his wife since his heart already belonged to Isis. He could not blame her for running off with Lance Corporal Lott (who also was misremembered in legend as Sir Lancelot). Hopefully the two of them had lived happily ever after. Marrying Guinvyr had been politically necessary to solidify bonds between Stone's band of searchers for the Cosmic Eraser and the local Britons, whose support was essential. Lance Corporal Lott had been one of that band of searchers recruited from history, in his case Chosin Reservoir, North Korea, in 1950. He had helped Stone stand against the ChiCom army as rearguard so their fellow Marines could withdraw to avoid encirclement by the vastly larger communist force. His steadfastness under fire impressed Gunnery Sergeant Stone, who recruited him for the mission in 6th century Britain where he proved invaluable again.

But why had Stone's heart belonged to Isis? Why did it still? By nature Stone was not subject to such emotions. Similarly to how he could make himself subject to the human condition in other ways, though, he had decided to make himself vulnerable in this way as well. His new feelings settled on the strikingly beautiful and remarkably passionate Isis, whom he met while observing pre-pyramid Egypt. She was married to Prince Osiris, of course, so nothing could come of it. That is until Osiris was cruelly slain by his brother and rival for the throne, Peribsen, who later took the name of Seth. Stone could have switched off his romantic interest in Isis as he could his other experiments in human feelings, but he chose not to do so. He told himself that it was because it would make for a false experiment since humans could not so easily switch off their feelings. In truth, it was probably because he simply did not wish to do so. Stone could no longer be certain, but neither did the uncertainty bother him. As a result of all this, he loved Isis and denied her nothing. She wished to marry him. So be it.

Saturday, 14 September 1890

A bright sunny morning and, in New Orleans, still quite warm in mid-September. Isis was thankful that she lived near the cathedral and that every step to it was cobblestone; so much of the rest of the city had muddy streets due to a recent rain. That would have been an unwelcome problem for her wedding dress. Stone had been living in a separate apartment to avoid the sin of cohabitation but had spent the previous night at the house of Police Sergeant Richard Walsh, the best man.

Isis had but few friends, it being in her nature to make a small number of close friends rather than a large number of acquaintances. These were composed of a handful of ladies she met through the church. Isis had to maintain some distance because she had to keep her true origins a secret. There was simply no way that she could avoid striking someone as odd after a few in-depth conversations. She was a quick study, but there were still many common frames of reference she did not share with the nineteenth century ladies. Still, she grew close enough to one of them, an Isabella LaRosa, to ask her to be the maid of honor, to which she agreed. Isabella was a relatively new immigrant and also trying to fit in with New Orleans, so there was some commonality.

Attendance was good for the wedding of a police sergeant and his rather mysterious bride. The New Orleans Chief of Police, David Hennessy, gave away the bride himself. He needed little persuading since he respected Stone and was intrigued by the lovely Isis. A bachelor himself, he lived with his mother and focused on fighting city crime, a task lately made more difficult by an increasingly violent feud between rival factions of Italian immigrants to the city. Still, he couldn't help but notice the loveliness of the bride and must have reconsidered his bachelorhood.

The attendees assumed their places. That of the bride and groom, she in her white wedding dress and he in his police dress uniform, was in front of the altar where they would kneel for most of the lengthy ceremony. Fortunately, some cushions were provided for the purpose. Father Gambera spoke the opening words in a strongly Italian-accented speech:

"Dear friends in Christ: As you know, you are about to enter into a union which is most sacred and most serious, a union which was established by God Himself. By it, He gave to man a share in the greatest work of creation, the work of the continuation of the human race. And in this way He sanctified human love and enabled man and woman to help each other live as children of God, by sharing a common life under His fatherly care. Because God Himself is thus its author, marriage is of its very nature a holy institution, requiring of those who enter into it a complete and unreserved giving of self."

The formulaic words struck Stone. If he hadn't taken the proceedings seriously enough up until now, this opening bid him do so. Hitherto he had focused on doing something pleasing for Isis, but this commitment was a grave one and lasting. If he respected her, and he did, he would have to commit himself to her with every fiber of his considerable will. Perhaps he had come to view the human race as a race of children with their brief and fragile lives. He had not set out to adopt a patronizing attitude; indeed he held them accountable for misdeeds and dealt with them as the rational, responsible, and free moral agents they undoubtedly were. Still, he could be forgiven perhaps for holding aloof from certain of their rituals and taking them lightly. He could no longer do so. In effect, he was joining the human race today. All previous excursions into their shared experience paled before this. Also, for the marriage to be valid, he could no longer avoid the "work of the continuation of the human race" the priest mentioned. Isis wanted children and he would not refuse her. Fatherhood, Stone thought, would be, in the words of Peter Pan, an 'awfully great adventure.' Of course Peter had been contemplating the adventure of death. Stone was acquainted with death. This adventure, more than any he had undertaken before, would be about life.

Father Gambera continued, "This union then is most serious, because it will bind you together for life in a relationship so close and so intimate that it will profoundly influence your whole future. That future, with its hopes and disappointments, its successes and its failures, its pleasures and its pains, its joys and its sorrows, is hidden from your eyes. You know that these elements are mingled in every life and are to be expected in your own. And so, not knowing what is before you, you take each other for better or for worse, for richer or for poorer, in sickness and in health, until death.

"Truly, then, these words are most serious. It is a beautiful tribute to your undoubted faith in each other, that, recognizing their full import, you are nevertheless so willing and ready to pronounce them. And because these words involve such solemn obligations, it is most fitting that you rest the security of your wedded life upon the great principle of self-sacrifice. And so you begin your married life by the voluntary and complete surrender of your individual lives in the interest of that deeper and wider life which you are to have in common. Henceforth you belong entirely to each other; you will be one in mind, one in heart, and one in affections. And whatever sacrifices you may hereafter be required to make to preserve the common life, always make them generously. Sacrifice is usually difficult and irksome. Only love can make it easy; and perfect love can make it a joy. We are willing to give in proportion as we love. And when love is perfect, the sacrifice is complete. God so loved the world that He gave His only-begotten Son, and the Son so loved us that He gave Himself for our salvation. 'Greater love than this no one has, that one lay down his life for his friends.' "No greater blessing can come to your married life than pure conjugal love, loyal and true to the end. May, then, this love with which you join your hands and hearts today never fail, but grow deeper and stronger as the years go on. And if true love and the unselfish spirit of perfect sacrifice guide your every action, you can expect the greatest measure of earthly happiness that may be allotted to man in this vale of tears. The rest is in the hands of God," he concluded and began the nuptial Mass.

After obtaining the consent of both parties to be married according to the rite of holy mother Church, the priest bid them join their right hands. The moment of truth. Stone and Isis turned to each other.

"I, John Stone, take thee, Isis Panthea, for my lawful wife, to have and to hold, from this day forward, for better, for worse, for richer, for poorer, in sickness and in health, until death do us part."

"I, Isis Panthea, take thee, John Stone, for my lawful husband, to have and to hold, from this day forward, for better, for worse, for richer, for poorer, in sickness and in health, until death do us part."

Father Gambera did the Sign of the Cross over them and intoned, "Ego conjugo vos in matrimonium, in nomine Patris, et Filii, et Spiritus Sancti." Both replied, "Amen."

The rings were blessed and exchanged, after which the Mass continued with the normal liturgy, but it was mostly a blur to the bride and groom. Stone had allowed himself to be subject to the human emotions of the event and found it was as turbulent as any combat. Finally it was over, and they were proceeding down the aisle together; saints on the high cathedral ceiling looking down, friends and neighbors smiling from the pews, sunlight streaming with the full spectrum of colors through the stained glass, and the organ music in their ears. Then they went through the large wooden doors into the full sunshine, down the few steps and underneath the raised ceremonial sabers of the NOPD coterie that Sergeant Walsh, the best man, had assembled for the occasion. Finally they boarded the coach and it sped away to the cheers of those gathered and the clopping of the horse's hooves on the cobblestones of the square.

Tomorrow they would board a ship for Rome as part of their honeymoon. Isis was also keen to see Egypt. Stone obviously had sources of finance well beyond his police salary, but this would be one of the few times they would flaunt it. They would spend their first night as husband and wife in their own apartment, however. There the business of consummation took place which, in the interest of modesty, shall not be detailed here. Suffice to say that both were very pleased at the result and when Isis expressed her approval Stone replied,

"Not to boast, but I was a consultant for the authors of the Kama Sutra."

"What is that?"

"I just showed you," he winked.

Subsequent events would demonstrate that Stone chose bad timing for a lengthy honeymoon. He could not see the future at all while he stood still in time. While jumping dimensions he got a limited view, a glance really, of the broad strokes of history, but very little detail. He could find the big pivot points of history, often the vulnerable ones most subject to hostile intervention, but disasters like that which shook New Orleans in his vacation absence could not be easily seen. He did not use his powers of mobility to instantly go back and forth from his vacation destinations since it might expose him, and more importantly Isis, to the observation of hostile forces. If he had, he might have seen what was coming, but there is no guarantee. As it was, he set sail with his bride just before the real troubles began in the Crescent City, unaware of the crisis that came mere weeks later.

There was always trouble when new waves of immigrants arrived at a place. In the 1890s, it was the turn of the Sicilians just as it had been for the Irish a generation before. Sicilian immigrants dominated the all-important stevedore business, unloading the near constant flow of cargo, mostly produce, arriving from ships at the city's river docks. The Provenzano family had once dominated this business but recently lost out on important contracts to the Matranga family. Back in May, a group of Matranga employees were driving a carriage loaded with fruit from the docks to the waiting shops for morning delivery. It was still night when they turned onto Esplanade Avenue, one of the streets that had received new electric lamps to replace the old gas lamps. The new lights, while the wave of the future, were still unreliable at this stage of their development. The street at certain corners remained dark under the trees. Such was the case at the Claiborne intersection where the stevedores were ambushed by shotgun-wielding assailants shouting in Italian. Several were wounded; Tony Matranga himself losing his right leg below the knee, but the victims could not recognize their attackers in the weak light, or so they said initially. Later during the investigation they implicated members of the rival Provenzano family and associates.

Chief Hennessy investigated, but the evidence was scanty. He was an experienced detective and had greatly improved the NOPD with his reforms, reforms which Stone heartily supported and personally enforced. The New Orleans police were becoming a more professional force, but the project was a long term one and much had yet to be done. Hennessy was a good candidate to begin the process, having been a lawman for most of his life, beginning as an errand boy for the Reconstruction-era Metropolitan Police. His dad had been a cop and was shot and killed in an off duty quarrel. David Hennessy was less quarrelsome than his father, but had also seen his share of scrapes, even killing a man in a gunfight. He had a good record of tracking down fugitives and, while working for the Boylan Detective Agency, had successfully provided security for the 1884 World's Fair at a time when the NOPD was unreliable. Now he was in charge of the force and changing it for the better. He was also making efforts to keep up good relations with both the local Italian community and the black community. He had even been on friendly terms with both the Provenzanos and the Matrangas, but that line was getting ever harder to walk.

The investigation into the shooting on Esplanade revealed little, but the Provenzanos clearly had motive. Some members of that family and their stevedore associates were arrested for the crime on circumstantial evidence. The prosecution's case was weak and the trial had many irregularities, but the jury convicted the accused anyway. Another judge, after touring the crime scene and seeing the improbability of recognizing the assailants at the dark intersection, set aside the verdict and scheduled a new trial. Hennessy was scheduled to testify at the retrial himself. It was speculated that his testimony would be helpful to the accused.

Hennessy attended a police board meeting along with Mayor Shakespeare (?) the night of October 15, 1890. The meeting addressed, among other things, disciplinary actions for some cases of police corruption that had come to light. Afterwards, Hennessy dodged the rain to take a late night snack of oysters and milk at the Virget Saloon with a Boylan friend named Billy O'Connor. Bidding his friend goodnight, he then made his way down muddy Girod Street to the home he shared with his mother. Near the corner of Basin Street, not far from his home, he was met with a hail of bullets and gravely wounded. He withdrew his Colt and returned fire at running figures in the dark, but the damage was done. O'Connor, hearing the sound of gunfire, rushed to the scene. He was joined by another Boylan man and some cops who were also responding to the noise.

Hennessy sat on a doorstep, clutching his bloody side. He recognized O'Connor and said, "Oh, Billy. They gave it to me, but I gave 'em back the best I could."

"Who gave it to you, Dave?"

"It was the dagoes."

Nothing more specific was forthcoming. Further questioning by Sergeant Walsh revealed no more information about the culprits. The Chief lingered painfully well into the next morning, but his wounds were irrecoverable. By nine the next morning, the Chief of New Orleans Police was dead and the bells tolled around the city. Their tolling signified more woe to come to the city. The unhelpful identification, "dagoes", led to the rounding up of dozens of innocent Italian citizens and immigrants for questioning. Fear of the Mafia gripped the city, a fear that would turn vengeful. More deaths would follow; law and order would also be casualties before all was over.

THE HONEYMOON OF
SERGEANT STONE

Rome, Italy, 19 October 1890

There was no better tour guide for Rome than Stone since he had known it in many eras. Outside of New Orleans, it was the city in which he had spent the most time. He had known it under the Etruscans, the Republic, the Empire, the barbarian kings, the Byzantine reconquest, the so-called 'dark ages', the Middle Ages, the Renaissance, and more recent times. Today he had shown Isis the Vatican and St. Peter's Basilica, a destination of particular interest to her as a recent convert. He was quite familiar with the Vatican as well, having spent much time there with Pope Julius II, a pope who was not on the fast track to canonization but was certainly a formidable personality.

Their trip had been a very pleasant one. The wonders of Egypt's pyramids and other monuments captivated Isis and she was gratified that history had not forgotten her, although the cult of worship was somewhat embarrassing. The mighty pyramids had been inspired by the architectural marvels she witnessed when kidnapped by malevolent aliens from another dimension, a terrifying adventure from which Stone had rescued her. She described the pyramid-like structures she'd seen and early Egyptian builders took up the task. For her to see them in person and know that they had stood so long a test of time was very meaningful to her.

A telegram awaited Stone at the hotel lobby. It was from New Orleans, sent by Sergeant Walsh. "Chief shot dead STOP Killers unknown STOP Investigation struggling." The news was horrible, but Stone exhibited no reaction other than to fold the message and tuck it away. He turned to Isis.

"Duty calls. I may have to leave you here for a few days. There are worse places to be left, and I'll be back shortly."

Back in the room, Stone simultaneously packed for his trip within a trip, explained to Isis the events they'd missed in New Orleans, and started his own mental investigation from afar. Hennessy had made his share of enemies, but which one might take the bold step to assassinate the police chief of a major city? The Mafia had a history of such bold strokes at the heart of civil authority, but which organization? Matranga, Provenzano, or other? The Provenzanos would seem unlikely as it was expected that Hennessy's upcoming testimony would help them in their retrial. The Matrangas seemed too obvious for the same reason since suspicion would immediately fall on them. Hennessy had other enemies, too. Back in 1881, he had shot and killed a man named Deveraux who had wounded his cousin Mike Hennessy and was about to finish the job. Hennessy was not charged with murder, but hard feelings clearly lingered in the Deveraux family and with those sympathetic to them. Dave's cousin Mike was gunned down again, fatally this time, by an unknown assailant in Houston in 1886.

None of these leads could Stone explore in timely fashion from Rome. The original crime scene in New Orleans would be long since desecrated by now and utterly useless by the time he returned. There was one thread he could pull on from this side of the Atlantic, however. Also in 1881, Hennessy, while working for the Boland Detective Agency, had captured the notorious Mafia bandit Giuseppe Esposito who was then extradited to Italy. Esposito, who had changed his name to Vincenzo Rebello and married a New Orleans woman in spite of having a wife already in Sicily, had already escaped from Palermo authorities once. He was the lieutenant of the vicious Antonino Leone, the notorious Sicilian brigand. His band was most well-known for kidnapping an Englishman and mailing back first one ear and then another along with ransom notes. Hennessy, tipped off by an unknown informant, used good detective work and managed to track him down in New Orleans. Several in the local Sicilian community, including Charles Matranga, his close associate Joseph Macheca, and some of the Provenzanos, vouched for 'Rebello'. However, he was recognized by the carabineri sent to bring him back to Italy where he was sentenced to life in prison in Palermo. That city was but a short boat ride from where Stone now stood. Perhaps it would pay to visit Esposito, since he was already in the neighborhood.

The Ucciardone Prison's walls were forbidding. Built in 1807 during the troubled Napoleonic years, they protected several stone buildings that splayed like spokes from a center complex to make a star-shaped fortress overlooking the port of Palermo. As a professional courtesy, Stone had stopped at the carabineri headquarters in Rome to visit his contact there, an Officer Cardona. Cardona had answered information requests from the NOPD about certain immigrants that were suspected of Mafia ties, and Stone in turn had answered Cardona's requests. All of this had taken place by telegraph and the mail, so it was gratifying to meet in person. . Cardona was eager to help when he learned that Chief Hennessy had been assassinated. He had lost too many of his own colleagues to Mafia killers.

The Ucciardone Prison administrators were suspicious at first, but Stone's fluency in Italian and natural charm put them at ease while a letter from Cardona sealed the deal. He was soon led to the waiting area for his interview with Esposito. After several minutes, the guards escorted in a forlorn looking man in prison garb and shackles, chained him to the wall, and left the room. He was short and muscular but with defeat in his eyes.

Stone spoke, "Vincenzo Rebello?"

The man looked at him without a hint of recognition of the name he had assumed in New Orleans. After a moment he answered quietly,

"I am Giuseppe Esposito."

"Sarah sends her love," Stone told him. This was the name of his New Orleans wife, but again, this name did not register with the man and he stood in silence. Stone examined him more closely. Right age, build, and similar facial features. A good likeness, really, but the wrong man. This was not Esposito. The tell-tale scar between the eyebrows was missing. None of the defiance and rebel spirit could be seen in this dejected man. He did not recognize names that were important to Esposito. The real Esposito should have enthusiastically accepted being called Vincenzo Rebello, the identity he wished all to accept as part of his alibi.

"You are not Esposito. What is your real name?"

The man's eyes widened in shock and met Stone's gaze for the first time. "How did you know?"

"They threatened your family unless you played the part, didn't they?"

The man nodded and spoke softly so the guards outside would not hear, "Please don't tell anyone. My momma and sisters, they will kill them."

"I can only help you, and them, if you tell me everything."

The bewildered man did so, explaining how bandits had threatened his family unless he agreed to serve their chief's sentence. Unfortunately he had been singled out because of his resemblance to Esposito and secretly substituted for him upon the latter's escape. This was done by Mafia infiltrators within the guard cadre at Ucciardone, and those agents kept him under watch to make sure he played his role or else. Stone got all the details from the hapless man that he could and promised not to betray his secret. He also promised to help him and his family when able. For now, though, Giuseppe Esposito was at large again and Stone's prime suspect in the murder of the New Orleans Chief of Police.

Stone could alter his appearance and did so now. In his disguise as an elderly street sweeper, he could spend all day outside the main entrance to the prison and observe. After a stakeout of only four hours it was time for shift change and a new group of guards showed for work. About fifteen minutes later, the guards they relieved came off duty and began to emerge. Stone recognized one of them as one of the two which had brought the Esposito impersonator to him. The man had shown an obvious and unhealthy interest in the proceedings while the other had merely gone about his business. Stone didn't need to be a brilliant detective to guess that the interested guard was a Mafia informant paid by them to keep an eye on their actor in order to make sure he did his job and did not spill the beans. If Stone's next guess was right, the informant would make haste to tell his paymasters that the fake Esposito had a nosy police guest today. No doubt that word had spread through the prison grapevine that the visiting guest worked for the New Orleans Police Department. If Esposito's gang had anything to do with the murder of Hennessy, that bit of information would be of keen interest to them, although they would likely wonder how Stone could have arrived so quickly over the ocean if he was investigating that crime.

The man had changed out of uniform and hailed a taxi. Stone had paid one to standby about thirty minutes prior, suspecting that shift change was imminent. He instructed his driver to follow the carriage the guard had boarded. The driver did so, heedless to the traffic already moving on the street and nearly colliding with an overtaking wagon, but he pulled back on the reins just in time. In spite of the many careless Palermo drivers, horsemen, and pedestrians, they proceeded down the avenue uneventfully after that..

The guard's carriage rolled quickly eastbound down the Via Roma with Stone's carriage trailing behind. It seemed to be laundry day as most of the many balconies on either side of the avenue were covered with clothing left out to dry, streaming in the breeze off the Mediterranean like colored flags. The guard's carriage finally stopped and let him out at a busy piazza in front of St. Dominick's Church. It was late afternoon and an outdoor market was still doing a fairly brisk business selling produce and seafood. Not unlike the French Market back in New Orleans, Stone thought as he paid his driver and disembarked to follow the man.

The guard walked quickly, forcing Stone to do likewise even in his old man guise. Finally the off duty guard stopped at a booth near the church entrance to get the attention of a fish vendor with a wave. The man looked up and nodded, washed his hands and moved out from behind his table, joining him for a brief conversation. Then they both left and entered the church. Stone waited a moment and followed them inside. The church was Romanesque in style but still well-lit by ample windows. The smell of candles with a whiff of incense was a welcome change from that of the fish market outside. The guard had yet to notice his tail, so Stone kept him in sight. Only a few other people were there praying or lighting candles. The fish vendor left the guard alone at a pew and left. For several minutes it appeared that the guard was now there only to pray, but finally another man, very well dressed, entered the church with the fish seller. This well dressed fellow entered the confessional booth in the center box reserved for the priest, and the fish man motioned the guard to one of the adjoining penitent boxes. No one besides Stone, regarding the activity from the corner of his eye, seemed to notice. The fish vendor stood outside, his arms folded, apparently on guard to prevent eavesdroppers and shuffle away any penitents who thought to go to Confession. Stone moved to a pew nearer the box to listen, but did not arouse suspicion since he was well outside human audible range. With concentration, and pretending to pray as his perfect cover, he could hear everything said in the confessional box. The fish vendor could never have guessed that was the case from such a distance.

The well-dressed man spoke first, "You have something for me?"

The guard replied, "A visitor came to see Ragusa today." This was the name of the fake Esposito.

"And who was this?"

"An American policeman. I didn't catch his name, but he came with a letter of introduction from Rome which I was not shown. My superiors saw it. I can find out tomorrow," he said, hoping for approval.

"What was said?"

"I could not hear through the door. Their interview was very short."

"What reason did the American give for wanting to see him?"

"I-I don't know. I do know he was from New Orleans," the guard said, trying to be helpful.

"New Orleans?" now the well-dressed questioner showed genuine interest. "Are you certain?"

"Yes. I know I heard that. A New Orleans policeman."

"There is no way they could have sent an investigator here so quickly. Unless they already had a man over here and sent a telegram. Hmm. I wonder…still, the Americans would not send a city cop for such a thing. Odd. Did you have anything else?" he asked.

"That is all I know. Shall I find out his name?"

"No, I can use other sources for that. It wouldn't do for you to be so curious about it now. Thank you for the information, as always. You will be rewarded, of course."

"Grazie. If there is anything else I can do…"

"You may go now."

The man left immediately, and Stone let him go since he had a new surveillance target now. The passing thought occurred that the Mafia lieutenant would indeed learn his name from his sources in the prison staff. Normally this wouldn't be a huge problem since there was little the Mafia could do to him, but he was a newlywed with a bride to protect now. Even he couldn't be at her side all the time and could not protect her while away. Indeed she was currently back in Rome alone, a city rife with Mafia agents. Stone was now neck deep in a confrontation with the Sicilian Mafia since they would undoubtedly conclude that he had learned the Esposito secret. Moreover, the Mafia lieutenant was very interested in the fact that Stone was from New Orleans. None of this would hold up in court, but Stone had enough to confirm his hunch that the Black Hand (a name for the Sicilian Mafia) played a role in the Hennessy murder. In light of Isis' vulnerability, Stone decided to act fast by going on the offensive.

The Mafia lieutenant and the fish vendor soon departed as well by taking separate exits. Stone waited a few counts before leaving also, changing his appearance as he did so since he was seen in the church. He now appeared young again, but not his normal self since he had appeared that way at the prison. He was the same height and build since he could not alter his body mass by much and his clothes he could only change by turning his coat inside out. A sharp eye would have seen that he had the same pants, shoes, and undershirt as the old man who had entered the church, but no one was observing him that closely. Outside the Mafia lieutenant was easy to reacquire due to his hat and because the crowd automatically parted before him.

The Mafioso strode wordlessly up to a personal coach and boarded, the driver speeding off immediately. Stone had to quickly hire another cab to follow. The Mafia coach made haste with all possible speed out of Palermo towards the hill country to the southwest. Stone's driver had to exert himself to keep up and Stone had to assure him of extra payment. The drive lasted a couple hours into the late afternoon. Finally the mafia coach stopped for a rest in the town of Altofonte. There, Stone's driver refused to go any farther and demanded payment, which Stone gave him. He quickly turned around and drove back to Palermo, wanting no more to do with this chase. Stone had to find new transportation while the Mafia man and his driver rested at a pub. There were no horses available for purchase on such short notice, forcing Stone to borrow one without permission for his hot pursuit. He was way out of his official jurisdiction, but now was not the time to quibble over such legalities. He did not take the time to borrow a saddle as well, but fortunately the horse was cooperative with bareback riding. Stone mounted him not a moment too soon for the coach was off again, tearing up the road to climb the ridge to the south of town. Stone and his new friend rode after, careful not to follow too closely.

It would have been a pleasant and picturesque ride had the circumstances been different. Occasionally the road would twist and the trees would part to provide a great view of Palermo, stretched out below and the blue of the Mediterranean beyond. As they climbed higher along the ridge the road became more desolate until finally there were no more houses to be seen. The coach disappeared around a bend in the road. After Stone rounded the bend, he was confronted by two men armed with double-barreled shotguns, their faces covered with tied handkerchiefs and the wide-brimmed hats they wore.

"Ciao!" one of them offered. A third armed man stepped from out of the woods into the road behind Stone as he slowed and then stopped his horse shy of the two in his path. Highwaymen, but not only that since they let the expensive coach through unmolested. They were guarding the road for someone. The three of them converged on Stone, one on either side of his horse and one behind. The leader who had spoken drew nearer and spoke again.

"Please dismount and empty your pockets, Signor."

"I have no money for you, but what I do have I freely give," Stone replied to him, his hands up but staring him in the eye.

The man grinned beneath his mask and asked jovially, taking one hand off his shotgun to reach for the reins, "And what might that be?"

"Justice."

As he said this, he spun his horse to the right using only his legs, bringing the reins out of the armed robber's reach. Being within reach of the shotgun barrel, Stone quickly seized it. As soon as he had grasped the shotgun, Stone flipped backwards off of the horse in a rodeo-worthy move that left him in possession of the shotgun and threw off the aim of the other two men. One of them fired anyway, hitting nothing but spooking the horse into spinning and kicking wildly. The man Stone had disarmed was trying to rise and draw a sidearm out of his coat, but Stone interrupted this with a savage blow from the butt of the shotgun to his throat. The man's neck collapsed under the impact with a squishing noise and his head lolled back awkwardly before he crumpled in a heap and lay still. The other two robbers were trying to dodge the bucking horse and get a clear line of fire, but Stone beat them to it, rolling to his right and coming up firing both barrels, dropping both men.

The horse had had enough and it bolted back down the road the way it came. With any luck it would find its way back to its owner in Altofonte. Stone disarmed the highwaymen and dragged their bodies off the road to conceal them in the woods. There was still enough light, and it was a simple matter for Stone to track the recently passed coach. The complication now was that shots had been fired which were doubtless heard for miles. Accordingly he marched by the edge of the road, ready to dart into the woods at a moment's notice. The coach turned off the main road onto a driveway leading to a large villa surrounded by a stone wall. Stone approached through the woods and was able to observe the courtyard without being seen. The coach he had followed all the way from Palermo was there, its two horses being led away to the stable to be brushed down. A half dozen men with shotguns and rifles roamed the grounds and seemed to be on alert, perhaps due to the shots from the direction of their road guards.

Stone observed them for some time. The guards were thorough and backed up by trained Rottweilers. Sneaking in would be next to impossible unless he 'cheated' by teleporting in. Even that wasn't always possible to do at the exact time he wanted. No, for these hardheaded and wicked men a direct approach was called for. He could not talk them into letting him search the place for Esposito and he was way out of his jurisdiction to invoke the law. Since he was far from New Orleans and unknown here, a superhuman display would not have to be explained away to maintain his low profile. Also, he intended to leave the stable hands as survivors to tell the tale and spread terror amongst the Mafiosi. A lengthy stakeout would give them a chance to learn his identity and therefore that of Isis as well. It was time for a little of the old ultra-violence, Stone decided, borrowing the term from a terrible movie he once saw almost a century from now.

He readied two of the shotguns and stuffed more shells in his pockets. He also recovered a six shooter from the ringleader of the highwaymen and readied it. The third shotgun he abandoned as too cumbersome. He expected to acquire new weapons as he went anyhow. The sun was setting and the light was getting dim. He crept up slowly through the woods so as not to make a sound and approached near to one of the eight foot stone walls. From here he lost the vantage point he had on the small hill in the woods and could no longer see activity inside the courtyard. He climbed a tree for one last reconnoiter and got an idea as he did so. Noting the positions of all the men inside, he climbed back down. The tree was young enough to be springy and flexible but sturdy enough to support his weight. He clasped it and, exerting his great strength, began to bend it back to the ground and away from the wall, slowly so as not to attract attention.

Even an unusually strong human could not have bent such a sturdy tree this way, but it was also flexible enough not to snap. He threw his leg over it, clasped a shotgun in each hand, and then hopped up to release all the pressure on the bent tree. It immediately shot upward to right itself, flinging Stone thirty feet in the air to sail well over the wall and deep into the courtyard. His well-aimed slingshot launched him right at two of the guards who were standing near the center of the courtyard, smoking and chatting. They looked up at the noise of the springing tree and saw a man fly over the wall directly at them, a shotgun in each hand. They could not react before Stone brought a shotgun barrel down on each of their heads with enough force to crack their skulls and send their lifeless bodies flying into the dirt.

Stone landed on his feet and took aim at two more guards at different points along the outer wall, one with each shotgun, and fired, dropping them. He repeated this process again as the remaining two guards tried to take aim. They were too slow and Stone's salvo from the second barrel of each weapon felled them just like their comrades. Barely four seconds into the attack six Mafia men were already down. The courtyard was not yet secured, however. The two Rottweilers rushed at Stone at full speed. He let the lead one clamp down his jaws on the empty shotgun in his left hand. The one in his right he brought down on the snarling beast's head with a crunch and it fell limp. The second fell to a swipe to the side of its skull from one of the steel barrels.

Instead of reloading, Stone dropped his empty weapons and took up a shotgun from one of the first men he had killed before running full speed towards the main villa's front door. It was of solid oak construction but exploded into splinters from his savage front kick. The guard inside was surprised by the door's larger pieces flying towards him, but he was recovering to aim his shotgun at Stone. Too late. Stone got his shot off first and blasted the man into the wall behind him. The interior of the villa was unexpectedly ornate given the more humble exterior. Fine art hung on the walls and expensive chandeliers from the carved wood ceilings. The tour would have to wait, however. The well-dressed Mafia lieutenant he had followed from Palermo fired a couple of pistol shots from the upstairs balcony. The shots went too high but the man didn't wait around for Stone to return fire, instead running down the hallway to the right. So that is where Stone ran at considerable speed.

He got up the stairs quickly and peered around the corner from a low firing position, exposing little of himself and only for an instant. He was able to see which room the man ran into before the door slammed. Stone followed quickly to maintain the initiative, ramming his shoulder through the closed door and barging into a large, well-decorated office. The lieutenant raised his pistol to fire, but Stone gave him a blast from the shotgun's second barrel that sent him careening into the far corner where he lay still.

There was another man in the room behind an ornate wooden desk. From this desk he drew a revolver and fired at Stone. Four shots reverberated loudly in the room. No effect. The man took more careful aim and fired two more. Stone, unharmed, flung the empty shotgun at his assailant, striking him in the hand and causing him to drop the empty six shooter. Stone drew his.

"That stings. Now sit down and keep your hands where I can see them. If you do not answer my questions I'll let you experience that stinging sensation."

"I couldn't have missed. I know I hit you," the man said in wonderment and fear as he slowly sat down and placed his hands on top of the cluttered desk.

"Actually you did miss with one of them in your panic. The other five stung pretty badly," Stone explained, kicking a flattened bullet across the floor, "Mr. Esposito." The man matched the description right down to the scar between the eyes. Stone had let him futilely empty the pistol at him to elicit terror and cooperation. It seemed to be working.

"So you recognize me. No point in denying it now. You found me. Now what?"

"The Italian authorities believe you to be in Ucciardone Prison."

"Some do, yes. Not as many as you suppose, though; we bought off many of them. The Black Hand has enough money to corrupt anyone. What is your price? You've got my attention now. What can we do for you? I can offer you almost anything," Esposito recovered some of his confidence as he spoke.

"Can you restore the life of the New Orleans Chief of Police, David Hennessy?"

Esposito's eyes went wide at this, then narrowed again. "What are you talking about?"

"Hennessy arrested you years ago, ending your bid to dominate organized crime in New Orleans. Once you got free again you plotted revenge, didn't you? Who did it for you? The Matrangas?"

Esposito spat. His eyes had gone black with hatred. "A curse on them! They betrayed me to the lawmen and then pretended to support me!"

"The Provenzanos, then?"

He spat again. "A curse on them as well; they were no help to me, only got in my way."

"So you sent agents from here, then, and made it look like local Italian Mafiosi."

Esposito turned smug. "A triple vendetta and I executed it flawlessly. I wanted revenge on both families. What better way than to pit them against each other?"

"The Esplanade Avenue shooting. Your men?"

Esposito nodded with a grim smile. "And how elegant that in the bargain I get revenge on that stupid cop who did their dirty work? Kill him and make it appear they did it. If the two families don't kill each other, enraged Americans will crush both of them."

"The truth is going to come out when I haul you in to testify," Stone asserted. That would be problematic. The Italians wouldn't extradite but couldn't seem to hold him, either. The confession he had wouldn't stand up in court under the circumstances.

"You are a remarkable man, whoever you are. If anyone could make me talk, it is you. But you don't know the Black Hand. Even I am but a small player. If I betrayed them, no place on earth would be safe for me. Or you," he hinted darkly.

He put his hand up to his face nonchalantly as if to scratch his nose and a shot rang out. He keeled over out of his chair and crumpled onto the wooden floor. Stone rushed to him, but it was too late. Blood gushed from a small entry wound under his chin where he had evidently shot himself with a derringer hidden in his shirt sleeve.

"Damn," Stone muttered in frustration.

A day later and Stone was back in Rome, thankful to be with Isis again to spend the last few days of their honeymoon together before catching the ship back to the States. He informed Officer Cardona, his trusted counterpart in Rome, that they had the wrong man locked up in the Ucciardone Prison under the name of Giuseppe Esposito. Furthermore they needed to protect the man and his family upon his release.

His side trip to Sicily had been illuminating but ultimately unsuccessful. Revenge was exacted for the murder of Hennessy, perhaps, but Stone could never prove the truth of it, at least not to anyone that mattered in the affairs of the city. Terror was struck into the heart of the Sicilian Mafia for a time, especially because the surviving stable boys insisted that a single attacker who flew through the air was responsible for the entire bloodbath. Nevertheless, the deceased Esposito would get what he wanted with a Mafia war in New Orleans and the inevitable backlash that would fall on the innocent Italian immigrants in the city. The trip home would be a long one and Stone dreaded what he would find upon return to New Orleans.

THE TEMPTATION OF
SERGEANT STONE

New Orleans, 13 March 1891

"Get out!" Isis screamed at Stone. "Just go to your precious work! You don't understand me and you never will! You are not even of this Earth!"

"Good idea. Talk to you later," he said as he finished getting his uniform on and ducked out the door of the apartment. He could hear her sobbing after he closed the door. Sigh. What had he said, anyway? Stone felt that he had joined mankind in another meaningful way: the inability to comprehend the enduring mystery that was the human female. If native males had never surmounted this challenge, what hope had he? Best to go to work and hope for the storm to blow over. Usually so self-possessed, Isis had become a bundle of sensitive emotions lately. The marriage had started very well, the honeymoon had been an incredible tour of Egypt and Italy, far more than most police wives could expect. This a result of Stone's wise investments informed by his time travels. They lived well. He treated her well, yet somehow she had become difficult to please in recent weeks. The honeymoon phase was already over.

Perhaps he had allowed frustration at work to slip into the happy home? It was not easy to frustrate Stone, but New Orleans had gone mad during his lengthy vacation. Perhaps that was why he had never taken one before, he thought ruefully. None of the triggermen were apprehended the night of the Hennessy shooting. Even Stone could not interrogate Esposito in Sicily before he killed himself, so that promising lead was lost. The physical evidence amounted to some bullet holes and some modified shotguns found in gutters in the neighborhood. There was little to go on besides Hennessy's statement that it was "the dagoes."

Of course it was, Stone thought. They were Black Hand assassins from Sicily, but he would never know whom, nor had he any evidence. Justice had been served to the man who had sent them, but the shooters themselves would likely remain mysterious. Predictably and tragically, the NOPD began rounding up scores of Italian immigrants in mass arrests and holding them until they had reason to clear them. This took place in Stone's absence or he would have opposed it. Finally suspicion fell, as Esposito would have hoped, on the family that had obstructed his rise in New Orleans organized crime by betraying him years ago, or so he thought: the Matrangas. They had the most to gain by seeing to it that Hennessy did not testify at the Provenzano retrial over the Esplanade ambush, a retrial which resulted in acquittal for the Provenzanos anyway. They had publicly sparred with the Chief in their anger. Witnesses claimed that they threatened his life. So with little evidence the grand jury indicted nineteen men associated with the Matrangas, including Joseph Macheca, suspected of being the ringleader.

The trial for the first nine of the nineteen accused began on February 16, 1891 at St. Patrick's Hall, a dilapidated and stuffy court building on Camp Street. The lighting and the acoustics were poor, but this was the venue for the New Orleans trial of the century. Police Sergeant Stone had access to the proceedings and soon concluded that the prosecution's case was appallingly bad. Witness testimony was contradictory. Prosecution witnesses who claimed to identify the defendants as the shooters at the scene were not credible. As at the Esplanade shooting, the electric lighting at Girod Street was very poor, electric lighting being still a new feature in New Orleans, making identification of the running shooters next to impossible from the vantage points claimed.

Still, the city newspapers, while giving lip service to due process and the sanctity of the law, contributed to the anti-Italian animus building in the city. Much was made of an alleged confession by one of the defendants, but it was no confession at all, merely the rambling statement of an unbalanced man. To those so eager to see justice done it was an open and shut case, however, and facts be damned. Mayor Shakspeare appointed an extralegal Committee of Fifty to investigate ways to curb the violence brought by Sicilian mobsters. Italians, immigrants and citizens alike, were constantly taunted by street punks yelling, 'Who killa da Chief?' Stone introduced some of these to the business end of his nightstick, but he wasn't omnipresent.

Italian flags were all over the French Quarter to honor the upcoming birthday of King Umberto and St. Joseph's Day. Bad timing, Stone thought. It would enflame things. He headed over to the trial location at St. Patrick's Hall to help provide security in case things got rough. Today was verdict day. The *Daily States* and *Daily City Item* predicted a quick return of a guilty verdict. Other newspapers made similar predictions. Stone wondered just what trial they had been covering since he would certainly vote not guilty based on the evidence presented. The case surely did not meet the 'beyond reasonable doubt' standard, but then Stone knew about the Esposito angle to frame the Matrangas, an angle for which he unfortunately had no evidence.

Shortly after Stone arrived, the trial's presider, Judge Baker, ejected everyone from the building besides members of the bar and the press. A crowd of curious citizens spilled outside to join the rest of the gathered onlookers on Camp Street. The cigar smoke was as heavy as the air of anticipation. The morning dragged on with no verdict. Spittoons filled and tempers grew short in the heat. Angry jeers flared up when the paddy wagon from the Parish Prison arrived with the accused only to be turned back to the prison by Sheriff Villere for lack of a verdict. Stone was on watch lest a riot erupt in Lafayette Square, but it did not. Not yet. The crowd was disappointed that the verdict was delayed, but it still expected justice to be served on the accused since their guilt was a foregone conclusion.

Around one thirty in the afternoon the paddy wagon showed up again, this time to disgorge the defendants. The police were ready with extra manpower on hand, Stone helping direct crowd control. He scanned faces, looking for murderous intent. While doing so he found one face looking directly at him and not at the proceedings involving the prisoners. The face belonged to a beautiful woman with flawless cheekbones, blue eyes, blonde hair, and a made-to-order figure clad in the latest fashion. Normally such a bright and shiny object would not have phased Stone, but this woman was more than a pretty face. He felt immediately drawn to her and not simply because of her beauty, although that didn't hurt. Stone worked his way through the crowd and over to her. It seemed imperative somehow that he do so. She watched him approach and waited for him to arrive.

"Madam," he tipped his hat. Looking into her eyes at close range he discovered the reason for the connection. The realization was exhilarating, but he maintained outward control. This woman was of his own kind, a survivor from his home universe, long since destroyed! For eons he thought he had been the only one left, but here was another standing before him.

"Greetings, good sir," she realized it, too. "I think we have much to discuss."

They remained long enough to learn the verdict: most of the defendants were found not guilty and a few got mistrials. No convictions. Hardly a surprise to Stone, but most of the crowd was taken aback apart from some Italian folks in the crowd who smiled but mostly kept quiet. The defendants were elated as they were paraded back to the paddy wagon for the trip back to prison. They were being kept there for the night because, technically, they had yet to receive their verdict on some lesser charges that hinged upon the murder and conspiracy charges. Now that those were decided, the lesser ones would be dismissed in what was a mere formality. The crowd was surly but dispersed without incident. Stone got relief from his supervisor and strolled away from the scene with his new acquaintance down Camp Street back towards the Quarter. It had rained again and Stone, playing the gentleman, helped her dodge the worst of the puddles in the now muddy streets.

"I am Stone," he said by way of introduction. "For a very long time I thought I was the last of us."

"I go by the name Lilith," she said. "For just as long I have believed the same. How have you come to be here?"

"I was transiting dimensions in pursuit of a deranged nihilist armed with a Cosmic Eraser. I found him, too, but not before he had hidden the device. I did not find that Eraser until later. It didn't matter since it was another Eraser used by another group which eradicated our home universe while I was away. I had been led to believe that I was the only one besides the lunatic I pursued that was outside our home dimension when it was annihilated. Apparently that was not so," he smiled.

"I was also working law enforcement and on a similar task. I was aware of your mission but thought you had failed and perished with everyone else when our home was wiped out. I searched for a time anyway but eventually gave up all hope. Now, to discover you in this backwater after so long. Amazing," she smiled also.

"I kept looking for the missing Eraser in this universe, before finally happening on a planet I liked and staying. When war erupted over control of the interphasing spheroids of space-time between the Syndicate and the Commonwealth, I naturally joined up to assist the Commonwealth as by far the lesser of two evils. The null area here makes it difficult to find me when I'd rather not be found, too," he admitted.

"That was what drew me at last. I have been pursued by malevolent trans-dimensional travelers as well and sought a refuge. The Syndicate has been destroyed as a trans-dimensional power, by the way, and that war is over. Someone destroyed all links between their home universe and the rest of the multiverse, isolating them forever," she reported.

Stone grinned broadly, "Heh. Yeah, I'd heard that."

"Something else to tell me?"

"Did I mention that I later found that missing Eraser?"

"That was you?!"

"Yeah."

"I'm impressed. Gutsy move. You have made powerful enemies. No wonder you stay here."

"That, and I like it."

They had walked several blocks in what seemed no time at all and were back in the French Quarter. Stone guided Lilith to a place where they could continue the conversation over drinks, The Absinthe Room at the corner of Bourbon and Bienville Streets. The light was low to begin with in the old building which dated to early that century and they found an even darker corner for some privacy. Over absinthe frappes, a specialty of the house made from a hallucinogenic fermented wormwood, they traded war stories about life after the destruction of their common home. They watched the barkeep make the unusual drinks by dripping cool water from a distinctive marble fountain over sugar cubes that were then added to the glasses of absinthe. The sweetener was necessary since the absinthe by itself had a very bitter licorice flavor. The effects of this powerful potion were telling on the humans in the bar rather promptly, but for the two aliens in the corner it took more time and greater consumption. The storytelling took hours and absinthe does not help anyone to keep track of time.

In human terms, both were many centuries old and had no one for most of that time with whom to share so much. There had been no one since the loss of home to reminisce with about what was lost, how glorious it was and how awful its destruction. They had expected to live centuries more until entropy overtook them in such utter loneliness, such isolation from the rest of creation. But here now they had found in each other "bone of my bone and flesh of my flesh." It was also of enormous consequence that one was male and the other female. Lilith broached that subject first.

"Perhaps we have the chance now to begin again. You are here and so am I. We might rebuild the glory of what was. Our race has not died out after all," she pointed out.

Stone could not deny that this was a hope he had once cherished but finally gave up on. Now here it was sitting across from him in a New Orleans bar. How long had he carried the burden of being the last, the burden of survivor's guilt? Now there was a chance to recover from the ultimate calamity that had befallen the ancient and noble race that had spawned him. It sweetened the deal that she was very lovely as well. There was one problem: he was now a married man. What of Isis?

All these thoughts occurred rapidly to Stone and his hesitation in responding was brief but still too long for Lilith. She leaned over and planted a passionate kiss on his lips. The smell and feel of her was more intoxicating than the absinthe. A woman of his own kind. She could please him in ways no human female could hope to do. She could live as long as he and truly understand him as a true helpmate. She could provide children whereas Isis might or might not due to their physiological differences and children by Lilith could rebuild their species and their once glorious civilization. He allowed himself to respond to the kiss, but then felt a pang of conscience.

"I'm married," he told her.

"What?" she sounded incredulous. "To one of them?" She nodded towards some of the fellow bar customers. Humans.

"Yes," he asserted in all seriousness.

"Well, so what? What is that to us? These little people and their little ceremonies. We have a chance to rebuild everything together!" her eyes shined with excitement.

"I gave my word to be faithful."

"A word given to a human is of no consequence. Use them as playthings, sure, I've done the same, but to actually commit like this to one of them…" she shook her head.

"A given word is never without consequence. My word is my bond. I always keep my promises," Stone said in deadly earnestness. The former Gunnery Sergeant had in mind the Marine Corps motto, Semper Fidelis, Always Faithful, at this moment. This was something Stone was determined to never compromise. Moreover, he refused to hurt Isis.

"I can't believe you take one of their primitive rituals so seriously," she said with rising anger.

"The ritual was solemn before God."

"You believe in God? Even after everything?"

"I suppose you created yourself?"

"Of course not. But…"

"Then how can you behave as if you are responsible only to yourself?"

"I stopped believing in a Benevolent Creator when our home was destroyed. What did God do about that?" she asked, her voice rising a little.

"God didn't make that happen. We did. Our choices brought that about."

"But now we have the opportunity to undo that catastrophe. To recover what was lost. To save our species! How can you refuse me? How can you dare? Am I so repellent??"

Stone shook his head in the negative, "No, you are very beautiful, but that changes nothing. I am bonded to another."

"Not to another equal. To one of them," she gestured with a sneer. "They and their pathetically short lives stuck in linear time are of no meaning to such as us. They are inferior, to be crushed underfoot if they become inconvenient!"

"So that is how you would raise our offspring? A lordly master race born to crush lesser beings under heel? Perhaps that is why our kind was permitted to perish. You have already lost your soul; I will not compromise mine. I am sorry to discover that the many ages you have lived alone have made you grow cold and harsh. If I had not reached out to care for these 'inferior' beings, started to care for someone besides myself, no doubt the same thing would have befallen me. They have been my salvation, for I nearly became like you," he said with dismissal.

Lilith did not receive this well. She let out a screech which shattered some of the glass in the bar as she stood and delivered a smashing front kick to Stone which propelled him through the wall behind him and out into the muddy street. She followed through the newly created opening to continue the confrontation. Stone stood in the middle of Bourbon Street, his uniform no longer its pristine blue but now covered in mud and horse dung.

"Alright, the absinthe is getting to us. Let's both try to calm down," Stone proposed.

She heard none of it and charged him, ramming him through a wooden fence and into an alley. At least they were now away from gawkers, Stone thought, but the problem of two superhumans having it out on Bourbon Street was still a problem for the police sergeant, and calling for back up would not help. He needed to move the venue of the battle to someplace safer for people and property. Stone also wished to maintain his human identity in this time and place, so he did the unexpected and pulled his revolver. The bullets would not kill her, of course, but she would be unaccustomed to their sting and distracted for his next move. She came on in a rage and Stone unloaded all six shots quickly into her face. She instinctively covered her face with her hands to deflect them and Stone used the chance to seize her in his grip. Once he did so, he opened a portal into the nexus of interphasing spheroids of space-time to find another battle site. They vanished from the Bourbon Street alley and any onlookers who heard the shots and came to investigate would find empty space. Most of the onlookers at that early morning hour were likely drunk already and would blame intoxication for their odd recollection of events.

Now away from 1891 New Orleans, Stone had to quickly find a landing zone in some different time lest Lilith recover and try to pick it for them. Staying on the same point on the Earth would be simpler and staying within the New Orleans null zone would help avoid the attention of other trans-dimensional travelers who would complicate things. It would be great to land in New Orleans prior to the city's 1718 founding when there would be nothing but woods and Indian trails, but that would take more than one connecting flight from Stone's current location and he had to make this quick. Another option emerged and he quickly chose it before Lilith freed herself from his grip.

22 March 1788

The previous night, Good Friday, saw eighty percent of New Orleans destroyed by fire. Only one person perished in the conflagration, but 856 of 1100 buildings in the city were utterly destroyed . The French Quarter, to include the Cabildo and Cathedral, was effectively wiped out. Reconstruction would be in the Spanish style since Louisiana was now a colony of that nation, but the name "French Quarter" would nevertheless endure; its charming architecture would be associated with the French. That reconstruction under Governor Esteban Miro with plans drawn up by Madame Gravier and funds from Don Andres Almonester y Roxas would be rapid and effective, one of the few bright spots in the history of the city's governance.

Stone and Lilith crashed into a burnt out wooden building near the corner of Bourbon and Bienville not far from where they'd stood a few seconds before and over a century later. Ash and soot exploded from their landing and sent a cloud in the air, but this was hardly visible in the dark of night. This part of the city was empty since few sought to rummage for valuables at night besides looters and Stone didn't care for their safety. Any destruction they wreaked here could only aid the reconstruction effort since the burnt buildings for blocks around would have to be razed anyhow to make room for new construction.

"That's better," Stone said to no one in particular. Then to Lilith, "Now, you were saying?"

14 March 1891

The trial verdict was not the final word in New Orleans on the Hennessy case. The newspapers reacted with indignant rage and proclaimed that the jury had been bribed. "Rise People of New Orleans!" urged the *Daily States*. A meeting was called for concerned citizens to gather at ten in the morning at the feet of the statue of Henry Clay on Canal Street to consider how to respond to the unjust verdict. Eight thousand angry people crowded around the statue and listened to the meeting's organizers and their haranguing speeches.

William Parkerson, John Wickliffe, and Walter Denegre were the foremost of these, opportunistic men seizing upon the public anger. Parkerson warmed up the crowd and offered himself for leadership in an as yet unnamed 'action.'

Denegre addressed the mob next, "The law has proven a farce and a mockery. It now reverts to us to take upon ourselves the right to protect ourselves. Are we to tolerate organized assassination? Not one of those jurors told the truth! They were bribed…I am not after the Sicilians or Italians as a race, but I want every man who murdered David Hennessy punished! Are you with me?"

The crowd roared, "Yes!"

He continued, "As a member of the Committee of Fifty, I have come back to tell the people that the power they delegated to us to employ has failed, and that the committee is powerless. The courts are powerless! Citizens of New Orleans, protect yourselves!"

Wickliffe helped build the rising tide to a climax, "Within the walls of the parish prison are confined a number of men declared innocent by a jury of the murder of Chief Hennessy. Are those men to go free? Is execrable Mafia to be allowed to flourish in this city?"

"No!" the crowd exploded.

"Fall in under the leadership of W. S. Parkerson!"

"Yes! Hang the dago murderers!" yelled the mob.

"Get your guns and meet us at Congo Square!" Parkerson ordered.

The human wave pushed through the streets towards the prison, overwhelming everything in its way. A few policeman tried to disperse the rabble but were dissuaded from further efforts when guns were pointed at their heads. Women and children were shoved aside if they didn't clear a path. At the prison, Warden Davis was warned by telephone that a mob was headed his way. He instructed the guards to open the cells. The desperate prisoners who were the mob's targets tried to hide themselves, but hiding places were wanting. Joe Macheca managed to squeeze himself into a doghouse.

The mob found the main entrance to be a formidable obstacle, swarmed around the prison and discovered a small door on the Treme Street side which soon burst asunder after their repeated assaults. The guards offered no resistance after the door was smashed. Dozens of armed men poured into the prison searching for vengeance. The outside door had been a private entrance to the apartment of Captain Davis. An iron door on the inside barred further access to the prison and the captured prison staff were not helpful in producing the keys. After several minutes of battering, this door too succumbed to the weight of the mob which now had access to the prison yard. Wickliffe announced the intention to kill only those acquitted, not those given mistrials or yet to undergo trials.

A vigilante thought he spotted one of the targeted men and a barrage of fire was poured into one of the upstairs cells from the ground floor of the prison yard. Warden Davis emerged and begged the crowd not to shoot indiscriminately. And so the search was on. Outside the crowd heard the gunfire and cheers went up, "Give it to them! Death to the dagoes!"

The vigilantes combed the prison and shot down the 'dagoes' as they found them, the defenseless and petrified men trying to hide and in some cases pleading for their lives. Shotgun and rifle blasts decorated the prison walls in gruesome sprays of blood and brain matter as the men were hunted down in turn. Trapped in their cells, knowing what was coming and utterly helpless, they could do nothing but listen as their fellows were shot to pieces and await their turns. Two of the men were roughly captured and dragged outside to be hung for the mob. One of them, a man named Polizzi, was hung on a streetlamp by a clothesline which broke, then hung again by a rope but with his hands unbound, allowing him to grasp the rope and haul himself up. A boy perched on the streetlamp punched Polizzi in the face until he loosened his grip, but the desperate man kept clawing at the rope again to save himself. Finally he was lowered so his hands could be bound and hung again. To be sure of the job, armed men in the crowd riddled him with bullets. The other fellow, Bagnetto, was hung in a tree. After the first branch broke he was hung again. He was less entertaining since he had already been beaten into a bloody pulp by the mob. Joe Macheca survived the ordeal by staying in that doghouse until it was all over. Ironically, he would later be the reputed Mafia kingpin of New Orleans while eleven others, likely innocent, were massacred.

Their bloodlust sated, the armed vigilantes dispersed. Curious members of the mob toured through the prison for hours afterwards, some collecting souvenirs of the citizenry's great victory over lawlessness. Slowly the police wagons arrived to clear the streets. The two hung bodies were cut down. One of the victims in the prison, Antonio Marchesi, survived the shooting but was gravely wounded. Still, he received no medical attention and was allowed to linger until he finally succumbed nine hours afterwards. That evening the ringleaders reconvened and proudly announced that a stain had been wiped from the city. The citizens had risen up and fulfilled their righteous duty, but now the brave men must disperse lest mob rule replace rule of law.

The ringleaders would never be tried for the massacre of eleven men whom the law had not found guilty of anything. The public officials made excuses for failing to protect the prison or to later charge those responsible. Public opinion was divided in the country about whether justice had been well served or not. Diplomatic relations with Italy collapsed and war looked likely. Italy's fleet was not inconsiderable at the time, either. Eventually reparations were paid by the US government to family members of those murdered. For many years afterwards the words, 'Who killa da Chief?' would be chanted whenever citizens or immigrants of Italian descent needed to be cowed.

Sergeant Stone would not have permitted this grave injustice on his watch. The mob would have stormed the parish prison only over his dead body. Of course in practice this would have meant that many of the mob would have died in a failed attempt, and the survivors would have learned to be more content with the verdict of due process. But when law and order in the city needed him most, Stone was very distracted by urgent matters of a personal nature, such as preventing an enraged woman of unusual strength from scratching his eyes out…

22 March 1788

Lilith came at him for the umpteenth time. The woman was relentless and the fight had dragged on, greatly aiding the work of demolishing the burned out buildings of the city as the two combatants punched or slammed each other through walls and smashed large chunks of charred debris on each other. She had started well in the fight as she was fueled by a rage that augmented her strength and Stone had held back in hopes of de-escalating the confrontation. He quickly disabused himself of that notion as her attacks became truly dangerous and he had to use his full strength. Fortunately his full strength exceeded hers even in her rage, but she was not without skill as a fighter. Here, too, though, Stone's well ran deeper and he had more combat experience to call upon. She started to recognize that she was overmatched and redoubled her efforts in desperation.

Stone deflected Lilith's kick and when she attempted to follow up with a spin kick, he was waiting for it and caught her leg. He then swept her other leg, dumping her head first into the ground with a thud. The time for chivalry gone, he pressed his advantage and pinned her arm, threatening to break it.

"Okay, we've both gotten some good exercise. Now how about we just go our separate ways and forget this ever happened?" Stone offered.

"Oh, I'll never forget this insult. Or forgive it. I will make sure you never forget it, either," she spat back at him.

Lilith began to try to open a doorway and slip to another dimension. Stone was able to block this since he was in close contact with her, so Lilith redirected her energies towards trying to transport him instead, though in a disruptive manner that would fatally transport only part of him. This he was able to block as well, but as he did so she switched tactics and moved to completely transport them both. Before Stone could stop this, they were both careening through the interphasing spheroids of space-time and Stone lost his grip on her. He was about to disengage and return home when she seized hold of him. Lilith, in suicidal desperation, aimed towards a point in space-time that would have them emerge in the center of a black hole and kill them both. Stone strained to break free but her grip was ferocious. With time running out, Stone hit her as hard as he could with a bone jarring blow to the face. As with the bullets to the face before, it was just enough of a distraction and he twisted free at the last instant. She apparently plummeted into the singularity and oblivion, but

Stone didn't wait around to verify, jumping for the nearest exit to avoid that calamity himself.

14 March 1891

Stone made his way back to New Orleans, reappearing late in the same day that he had left. He discovered later to his chagrin how eventful the city had been in his absence. It was an unfortunate consequence of his perambulations that he had clearer views of the past and future than of any present he might choose to stay in. In spite of many visits to the future beyond 1891, once here he could not tell with certainty what would transpire in the near term. He did know with certainty that he had had his last absinthe, but he did not know what to expect when he finally darkened the door to his own apartment. He last saw Isis yesterday morning in what now seemed a lifetime ago and it had not been on the best terms.

She opened the door at his knock. He looked awful, his uniform tattered, muddy, and stained with soot from the 1788 fire. She had a look of concern and let him in, closing the door behind him. A whiff of gumbo hit his nose and made him feel at ease. The place was tidier than usual, as if Isis had busied herself with even more cleaning than was ordinarily the case. The neatness of the room clashed with the chaos of his ruined uniform. Before he could speak, she embraced him warmly in spite of the mud on his torn clothing.

"Forgive me for the harsh words at our last parting," she breathed. He felt relief but decided not to tell her that he had spent the night with another woman; she would misunderstand the joke.

"I am sorry also," he told her. He wasn't actually conscious of wrongdoing and never apologized to anyone else, but those others were not wives.

"I have news of great import," she leaned back and looked him in the eyes. She had maintained the custom of formal speech from her days as royalty.

"Oh?"

She nodded. "I am with child."

"Ah," he smiled. "The next big adventure begins."

SERGEANT STONE VERSUS THE BELOVED OF THE GODS

18 May 1756, Vaishali, India

Leftenant Edward Percy of His Majesty's Army, now in service to the East India Company, was pleased that his long range patrol had, thus far, been a success. He had shown the flag, reconnoitered a vast area, and established contacts with numerous local leaders. Now the time had come to begin the long march back to Fort William in Calcutta. That fortress was being steadily improved and the Company's grip on the city growing ever stronger, but the Nawab, Siraj ud Daulah, was growing ever more truculent about that.

Percy returned to his platoon. Sergeant Stone had secured provisions and already had the men ready to march. Percy had come to rely on Stone, and thanks to him never had to worry that his orders were not carried out or that the men were not ready to move. This time the platoon had stopped near a stupa, or stone mound. Near it was a stone pillar roughly fifty feet high. On top of it was carved a fierce looking stone lion. Percy was pondering its origin when Sergeant Stone came over to report the men's readiness.

"I wonder what this is," Percy wondered aloud. He didn't expect an answer.

"Oh, that's one of Ashoka the Great's old edict pillars," Stone replied in heavy Cockney accent.

"Never heard of him," Percy stated dubiously. How did the comparatively uneducated sergeant know about this when he did not?

"He ruled these parts over two hundred years before Christ. Huge, powerful empire he had."

"So this is yet another arrogant eastern potentate's monument to his own power," Percy concluded.

"Not exactly," Stone replied.

265 BC, near the Daya River, India

Stone stood in the front lines, as usual, and observed the approaching enemy force. He was a veteran of many such battles and stood with the outnumbered side in most of them, but this opposing force was truly vast. The entire army of the Mauryan Empire stood in battle array before them, determined to completely conquer the budding Republic of Kalinga and make it yet another imperial province. Hundreds of thousands of infantry and archers accompanied by thousands of horse cavalry and war elephants slowly made their way to the battlefield. The logistical organization for fielding such a force was itself a marvel. It was a colorful assemblage from all over the vast empire ruled by the merciless Ashoka, the so-called 'Beloved of the Gods' and the grandson of Chandragupta Maurya, the founder of the dynasty who learned from the example of Alexander the Great himself.

The Mauryan Army was a well-organized combined arms force based on the tactical unit of the patti, a mixed platoon containing one elephant-borne mini-fortress with three archers and a driver, three horse cavalrymen armed with round bucklers, javelins, and a long spear, and five heavy infantry armed with a large shield and a khanda broadsword. Three pattis formed a senamukha, or company, three senamukhas formed a gulma, or battalion, and so on. The Kalinga Army, to which Stone had attached himself as a volunteer, was similarly organized but far smaller.

Kalinga was a feudal republic and fiercely independent. Councils elected by the upper castes made all the important decisions. There was a raja, but his power was limited and could be overridden. His power was at its zenith when acting as a war leader, as Raja Anantha Padmanabhan was forced to do on this occasion. The people of Kalinga enjoyed a far greater degree of freedom than their counterparts in the Mauryan Empire that dominated the subcontinent. They practiced the teachings of Jainism and did not aggress other nations. Healthy maritime trade enriched the province, as did its fertile soil, making it a tempting target for Ashoka. The fact that Kalinga was the only part of India not under his direct rule, or at least paying tribute, rankled him. Kalinga's people were proud, stiff-necked, and determined to preserve their freedom. That was why Stone stood with them and why Ashoka the tyrant massed his forces against them for cruel conquest.

As Stone beheld the massive horde before him, comprising conquered peoples from Afghanistan to the Himalayas and down to Ceylon, he doubted that he could save hopelessly outnumbered Kalinga. He had killed at prodigious rates at Teutoburg Wald, Troy, Camelot, and others, but could not stop the overwhelming attackers even at his full strength. At the least he would ensure that the Mauryans paid a heavy price for their unjust conquest. He unsheathed his dual katar daggers which he preferred over the khana swords and shields his Kalingan allies offered. He had forged these Indian-style blades himself. They were push daggers with 'H' shaped grips between two parallel braces that allowed the user to jab the sturdy triangular blade forward in a mighty punching motion. In the hands of a wielder of Stone's strength, no armor or shield on this battlefield could withstand it. They were also sharp enough to slash and could parry, but Stone was offensively focused and therefore wielded one with each hand, eschewing any shield. The especially long daggers he'd forged, once he donned them, made each of his upper limbs appear to have grown huge steel talons out of the forearms. He was not in his vulnerable mode today anyhow, and none of the Mauryan weapons could stop him, but they had such a huge army assembled that he likely could not stop them all before they overran Kalinga anyway. His conscience demanded that he try, nevertheless, to assist the young republic against the tyranny of its stronger neighbor.

The Mauryan army paused its march to leave a no-man's land between it and the opposing Kalingan force. Soldiers from all over India had gathered to take part in Ashoka's conquest, the different colored turbans and other head dresses distinguished the many different tribes and regions from around the empire. One group, the Nagas, a tribe of mystical cobra worshippers, wore serpent-head helmets to intimidate their foes. The Mauryan line stretched far longer in both directions, leaving encirclement a likely outcome. The Kalingans knew the odds and stood manfully against them anyway, their courage earning both Stone's admiration and his assistance. Elephants on both sides of the line roared impressively, nervous with anticipation of the impending carnage. Horses, too, neighed and some bucked. The men were as nervous as the animals but all maintained military discipline. For a time the two armies regarded each other from opposite ends of the plain. Behind the Kalingan army was the Daya River. The raja had deliberately chosen a battle site that made retreat for his men impossible. No later stands could be made anyway. Today they must conquer or die.

Horns sounded on the Mauryan side and their army advanced slowly in keeping with the elephants' walking pace. The Kalingan horns responded in kind and the two armies began to converge in the center of the plain. As the range closed, orders were issued and waves of steel-tipped bamboo arrows were launched by the archers on both sides, their powerful bamboo longbows delivering effective volleys from considerable distance. Men on both sides screamed in pain and fell as some of the arrows found soft, fleshy targets. Most stabbed into the ground or glanced off armor. Stone had no armor but raised his katars in an 'X' block over his head. The arrows could not injure him, but he didn't wish to distract his superstitious comrades in arms who might react in unexpected ways to witnessing arrows bouncing off him.

More signals were given and the chariots and cavalry were unleashed. Thundering hooves and spinning wheels kicked up so much dust that the armies were obscured from full view of each other. Mauryan and Kalingan chariots clashed in the center of the battlefield. Frequently they crashed into each other, flinging occupants onto the ground where they were trampled by the cavalry or other chariots. Javelins flew and the injured cried out, the tumult punctuated by the roar of elephants waiting to join the fray. Soon they were given the order they anticipated and joined the general advance of the infantry.

Stone urged the infantry of his patti ahead and ran at full speed to engage the enemy. Into the swirling maelstrom of dust, blood, screaming, and cruelty he waded, quickly dispatching any Mauryan combatants that came near and then rushing towards the next group of them he could find. With fierce punches he impaled one Mauryan soldier on a katar, kicked him off and then pierced another. He deflected javelins thrown at him or spears jabbed toward him with deft parries using his twin katars and then closed the gap with the attacker to stab them as well. Bodies clashed around him in a chaotic melee, but this was home to Stone. He threw horsemen off their mounts and mercilessly slashed or pierced them, then moved on quickly to kill another. With his twin blades he was a veritable dervish of death, spinning through the sea of combatants and chopping down those in the wrong uniform. Frequently he would deflect a spear or sword stroke with one katar and then punch the other forward to kill his opponent. No armor on this field withstood the force of his dagger punches.

Quite unexpectedly, a counterpart in the Mauryan army was cutting down Kalinga warriors as rapidly as Stone was dispatching his opponents. At first Stone suspected a trans-dimensional interloper like himself, perhaps an enemy agent. That had happened before. A second glance revealed that this enemy fighter was thoroughly human but very highly skilled in an unusual martial art. He wielded in each hand an even more unusual weapon called the urumi, a sword with several long, flexible steel blades that behaved like the tendrils of a whip but were razor sharp. He spun them around himself very rapidly but not chaotically. With his high degree of skill he maintained control of each of the flying, bending blades with unerring precision that he used to cut down several men at a swipe. Shields, if not severed by the flying steel, were able to parry one blow at best. This did nothing for the rapidly succeeding blows that followed. Swordsmen would likewise raise their khanas in defense but were not quick enough to block all the blades or the follow-up strikes that were too fast for them. The skilled dual urumi-wielder effortlessly blocked javelins launched his way, the bamboo shafts falling to pieces at his feet, and no one seemed able to charge through the whipping blades without getting sawed nearly in half.

A worthy adversary, Stone decided. He could simply survive the brunt of the urumi blades and close in to kill the guy; surely he had killed many in such artless fashion today since this was war, not a friendly sparring session. Still, this man was very highly skilled and deserved respect. Stone decided that he would beat the man on fair terms, not allowing the multiple blades to touch him. It was not often that Stone found such a worthy foe among the humans without rendering himself vulnerable.

Stone dashed in, blocking the flying blades with quick slashes of his katar, and tried to close the gap. The man danced away with impressive spin moves, hopping in the air and landing further away while keeping the heat on Stone with continuous attacks. Stone had to keep up a dizzying pace, exerting considerable mental energy to track each of the flying blades to time his jumps, parries, and dodges to evade them all. Whenever he gained some ground, the martial artist extended the gap again with another spin or flip and closed off pursuit with another deft urumi swipe. The man was good and quickly recognized that he had a worthy adversary in Stone. He changed up the order of his attacks, showing more creativity with each new swing. The steel blades slashed rapidly through the air, whistling menacingly, some impacting the ground and kicking up dirt, some clanging off Stone's parrying daggers, others sailing overhead and swinging around for another strike. Stone was at a serious range disadvantage. He could not step out of the strike zone nor could he close the distance enough to use the katars offensively, as they were designed. He had to continuously dodge, weave, jump, and parry with his blades.

Stone caught a couple of the urumi blades with another 'X' block of his katars and trapped them underfoot. The snagging of his bendable sword blades under Stone's weight momentarily threw off the graceful timing of the warrior's dance of death, and he nearly stumbled. Catching himself, he swiped desperately at Stone with his other urumi sword, preventing him from closing the gap more than he had. Freeing his trapped urumi blades, he spun away again to extend the gap. Stone was waiting as he did so. A katar dagger is not designed as a throwing knife and would not fly far, but for Stone's purpose it would not need to. Having read the pattern in his adversary's movement, Stone waited for that precise moment when the man's back was turned to him in mid-spin where he could not see Stone prepare to throw his knife. He let it fly straight and true to where he knew the man would land and hit the jackpot, the blade burying deep into the urumi fighter's side before he could block it. He gaped in surprise at the hilt now sprouting from his torso, the blood already streaming out in a great rush. Stone wasted no time in closing in to finish him with the other katar and withdrawing the thrown one from his foe's ribs.

The killing continued unabated; the din of clashing arms and yelling combatants reaching a crescendo. Stone easily navigated this chaos and he went on dispatching the invaders without mercy, without letting up. Though overmatched numerically, the Kalingans did not want for courage and continued to fight and die against the hopeless odds. Even Stone's high killing rate could apparently not stop the inevitable. An angry enemy elephant roared and lumbered towards him. The archers atop its back bounced an arrow off him. He charged the elephant and ducked beneath its swinging tusks before stabbing at the belly. It howled in pain and reared up, colliding with another elephant nearby. The crash of the two behemoths was disastrous, one being impaled by the tusks of the other and both howling in deafening roars, drowning out the screams of the men astride them and the infantry near them who were crushed.

More elephants rushed into this nightmare, sending men and horses scurrying in terror. Stone stood his ground and stabbed at the rampaging monsters, but not doing enough damage. One of them managed to grab him about the waist with its trunk while he was engaging an infantryman. It hoisted him high in the air with the intent to smash him into the ground but roared in pain and dropped him when he stabbed its trunk with a katar. It reared up and tried to plant its foot on Stone to crush him, but he was already back on his feet and caught the huge foot on his daggers. The force wrenched them from his grip but also wounded the mammoth creature which then angrily tried to mash him under its massive foot. For anyone else that would have worked, but Stone was strong enough to stand up under the animal's weight. Or he could until a second wounded and crazed elephant barged into the proceedings, knocking Stone over and collapsing atop him. The beast died a moment later but Stone was crushed into the dirt beneath its weight and immobilized while the battle was finally coming to its conclusion.

By the time he emerged some time later after finally working himself free of the enormous carcass, the entire world had changed.

The smell was overpowering. Flies buzzed by the thousands. Several dead elephants were strewn about, all of whom apparently emptied their bowels in their death throes. The dead horses added their own aroma to the mix, but dead human soldiers lay so thick over the ground that scarcely any patch of grass could still be seen. Mauryan and Kalingan soldiers lay where they fell, some seemingly still grappling with each other although they were now bereft of life. Spears protruded from torsos, severed limbs and even heads were scattered about. In places the ground was saturated with blood. It rivaled anything Stone had seen in his long experience of war and bloodshed, but the worst was yet to come. Stone saw a thick column of black smoke rising from the other side of the Daya River in the direction of the Kalinga settlements. The Mauryan army had finished off the Kalingan fighters and moved off to attack a softer target. Stone trudged towards the smoke, his tunic destroyed and his torso smeared with dirt and blood. Perhaps he could wash in the river.

It was impossible to avoid stepping on bodies during his trek, so he no longer tried. Occasionally he came across wounded, and these he did avoid, but they were all beyond help. Not stepping on them was the best he could do for them. At last he reached the river. All thought of washing in it vanished when he beheld the carnage there. Not only was it choked with the bodies of dead warriors but it literally ran red with the blood of the slain. Not a metaphor, not a figure of speech. The river was red with human blood.

Stone waded in to cross. The red river water rose to the middle of his chest. He kept going. It rose to his chin. He stumbled in the muck and was completely immersed. How symbolic he thought. He was now covered in blood. He had killed so many, contributed mightily to this epic bloodletting, and for what? The disaster he'd wished to avert had still happened. Kalinga had fallen anyway. What a damned waste.

He emerged from the river now completely bathed in blood. He looked like some kind of war god from mythology, unsated and wandering the earth in search of more victims. But Stone was sated. The last thing he wanted was more blood. So many lives had been extinguished today. What had his intervention achieved? He had made the Mauryan victory more costly, perhaps. That was cold comfort now. He was covered in flies but ignored them as he tromped along.

He marched on towards the column of smoke. He could hear wails of terror and torment from women and children even from miles away. By the time he reached the outskirts of town, which by now had almost finished burning, the wailing had subsided; so few of the victims remained. The Mauryans had moved on, so there was no one for him to exact revenge upon. There were survivors, mostly women and small children and a few old men, but all too few. Most were wailing over the bodies of dead relatives lying in the street or because someone they loved had been seized and taken away by the invaders. Some cried quietly, watching their homes burn and their neighbors and relatives mourn inconsolably. This experience, too, was not brand new for Stone, but that fact did not dull the effect. These people had lost…everything.

The imperial invaders swept on like a wave of locusts, devouring all in their path. Stone could offer nothing to the victims left in their wake. He could not restore their loved ones, their homes, their way of life now gone forever. Some had finished crying and stared at him blankly, numb to the pain. It was no surprise to see the old men that way, but the thousand yard stare from children was a different level of disturbing. Some had seen their mothers raped and killed, their fathers and older brothers tortured and killed, their older sisters taken as slaves. So it goes.

Stone could not undo this. He was not even susceptible to the chemical reactions which, in human bodies, caused physiological rage or sorrow responses. What he did do was recognize intellectually that a grave injustice had taken place. This determination he made with an unswerving and irrevocable finality that would not ebb and flow along with transient and fickle human emotion. He could not make all of this better. He could, however, see to it that Ashoka, the Beloved of the Gods, did not celebrate his conquest for long…

The following day, Stone finally found an unsullied water source and washed himself. His peerless tracking skills were not needed to find the Mauryan army camp; they had left a broad swathe of destruction through Kalinga. Still, it took him most of the day to catch them on foot because of their head start. They were encamped in a grassy plain, the sprawling camp for the huge force nearly filling it from one end to the other. Stone observed it from a rise at the edge of the plain as the sun began to set. There was no stockade, only some sentries. Security was lax now that the

Kalingan army had been completely destroyed; it had died where it stood. Stone watched them until nightfall, careful to avoid being observed by their scouts. He didn't want any trouble. Not yet.

The night brought the noise of revelry in part of the camp. The victors were enjoying their spoils and dividing the booty they had seized. Stone had located the royal tent that doubtless held Ashoka, the author of the savagery he had passed on his march here. He could teleport himself there, but that would be cheating. It was the same reason that he did not teleport out from beneath the dead elephant and would have conceded defeat to his urumi-wielding opponent if he had struck him a blow sufficient to kill a human combatant. Stone's code of fair play demanded that he sneak into the camp as a human attacker would. Human means for human ends.

Of course he was up to the task having honed many human skills. He did not lazily rest on the superhuman abilities natural to his species. Earth was his adopted home, so he unleashed the full powers of his nature only when the situation called for it. He slipped into the Mauryan camp using stealth, having carefully observed the sentries and timing his breach of their screen just right. Once inside the camp it took him little time to find a soldier unwisely drinking alone. Sneaking up behind him and choking him into unconsciousness was accomplished with no one the wiser since the noise of celebration easily drowned the sound. Stone took his clothes but not his life. The time for killing the soldiers had gone; that was for the war which was now over. There was only one life left to take now. Anyone coming across the soldier would assume that he had stripped off his own clothes and passed out in a drunken stupor. Stone strategically placed the soldier's gourd of rice-based liquor where it would reinforce this assumption.

Now dressed as a Mauryan soldier, Stone made his way to the imperial tent. The sounds of celebration receded as the party was kept away from this area. Finally he located the tent he was looking for. It stood out for its many vibrant colors evident in the light of the torches lit at its four corners, the half dozen sentries who guarded the entrance, and because the sheer size of it dwarfed most of the other tents. As Stone wished to avoid a ruckus, he ruled out engaging the front entrance guards and sought another way in.

There were no guards posted on the other side of the tent. He extinguished the torches at the opposite corners, thus casting that side of the tent's exterior in darkness. Withdrawing the dagger he had borrowed from the soldier he had relieved of his clothes, he cut a small entrance into the tent's exterior fabric almost noiselessly. He then bent low and slipped into the dark room inside. Dagger at the ready, he stood and glanced around. An empty bed chamber, fine pillows and Chinese silk sheets scattered about. There was a light in the tent's main chamber that he could dimly see through the tent's interior curtain 'walls'. He exited the bedroom and made for the main chamber, a receiving room for the Emperor. A single lamp suspended from the center high point of the tent cast a weak light about the large room to reveal large sitting pillows, a field table with maps, some idols of Hindu gods on an altar in one corner. A lavishly dressed male figure with uncovered black hair lay prone before the altar, his face buried in one of the pillows.

The head raised a bit and said in an annoyed voice, "I gave strict instructions that I was not to be disturbed!"

"I do not obey instructions from you," Stone said evenly.

"Who dares?" the young man spun to face him, his face streaming with tears. "You dare enter the imperial presence unbidden?"

"I do. I have come to exact justice for Kalinga."

At those words Ashoka, for he could be no other, deflated, his royal arrogance gone in a flash. He saw the dagger in Stone's hand and assumed a kneeling position in front of him. Then he ripped the bejeweled, saffron colored garment he wore, exposing his breast.

"I did not expect to receive justice so promptly; my prayers must have been heard. Strike!"

This was not expected. Arrogant condemnation, pathetic begging, crying out for the guards, maybe even a fight, but certainly not this. Ashoka closed his eyes to await the blow. It didn't come. Stone sat down in front of him. Ashoka opened his eyes and then assumed a similar posture opposite him.

"What stays your hand? When I held Kalinga in my power, I did not stay my hand. Now the land trembles at my name," he said this as if he was aghast rather than boastful.

"I am curious about why you seem to want me to take your life."

"I do not want it," Ashoka said tiredly. "I do not want any more deaths, not even my own, although I may deserve it. I am sick of death. Death to my enemies. Death to my own soldiers. Death to women and children who were not even on the battlefield. Death, death, and more death, all to extend my empire."

"Yes, your empire is triumphant. Conquest complete. Was it worth it?" asked Stone.

"After the battle I rode through the battlefield and was shocked by how many soldiers on both sides perished in the fighting. But it was in riding through the destroyed city of Rajapura that I saw how the entire populace suffered. A woman ran up to me, not caring that my guards were ready to kill her, and she rebuked me saying, 'Your actions have taken from me my father, husband, and son. Now what will I have left to live for?' I saw the devastation in her eyes which surpassed any of the material destruction of the city. I had no answer for her," he locked eyes on Stone searchingly, hoping his intended assassin might have the answer he sought. "Nothing is worth causing that."

"Was this not the result you wanted? Did you not set out to conquer Kalinga? Did you not know that conquest means death? Indeed you are a great conqueror. Countless dead bodies testify to that. Too many to bury, too many for the vultures and dogs to eat," Stone coldly replied.

"Yes, I am Ashoka the Great Conqueror. Yet I am the one diminished. I am the one conquered."

"The Buddha said, 'Though one man conquers a thousand men, a thousand times in battle, he who conquers himself is the greatest warrior'," Stone reminded him.

Ashoka brightened somewhat at this. "And also, 'It is better to conquer yourself than to win a thousand battles. Then the victory is yours. It cannot be taken from you, not by angels or by demons, heaven or hell.' That is the victory I want, the conquest I must make. As for bloodshed, I will have no more of it, not of man or beast. If my empire endures, it will be because it governs justly, not because it spreads terror. I will embrace ahimsa for the rest of my days, for truly, to injure another is to injure oneself. I am more convinced of that than ever, for I deeply feel the injury I have inflicted."

Stone regarded him in silence for what seemed a long moment. He could not read minds, but a long career in law enforcement enabled him to almost invariably detect deceit. He could detect none in the young emperor. "What makes you think that your reign will continue beyond tonight?" he asked, showing the dagger.

"Nothing. I do not deserve such a reign and will still accept your verdict. I have learned too late that I must rule with gentleness and improve the lives of my people. Never again will I seek to expand my rule through brutal conquest. Whether you kill me or not, I have fought my last battle. I so swear," he said with apparent conviction.

"If you do this, you will become the Buddha's greatest legacy. If you break your word, you will see me again," Stone said gravely. Ashoka bowed and Stone left the way he came in.

18 May 1756, Vaishali, India

"So this Ashoka renounced violence but continued to rule a vast empire? How did that work out?" Percy asked incredulously.

"Very well during his time, actually; the empire only fell well after his death. He was a man of his word and strove ever after to improve living conditions for his subjects. He fought no more wars, never resorted to the death penalty, got rid of torture, and even tried to suppress cruelty to animals. He spent considerable energy spreading, but not imposing, his Buddhist beliefs. He truly earned his sobriquet of 'The Great' more than Alexander or Peter ever did," Stone's accent had slipped during this pedantic interlude, but it was time to go and he stepped back into character.

"Get up, you maggots! The Company doesn't pay you to sit on your arses!" he bellowed at the men who hurriedly complied. Percy tipped his hat to Ashoka's stone lion and joined his men.

Sergeant Stone, Warrior Monk

12 March 1894, New Orleans

Isis thrust the crying two year old at Stone and yelled so as to be heard over the child's cries, "Take your daughter! I can't fight her and fix your dinner."

Stone, who wanted dinner, grudgingly took the angry toddler into his arms. The kid was a lot of fun when she was in a good mood. She was not currently in a good mood.

"Easy, Cassandra," he cooed to her reassuringly, "it isn't so bad."

For all his many years, he was still inexperienced in handling children. Isis, who had had one child by her first husband, the late Osiris, was much better at this sort of thing. Unfortunately, she was also better at making dinner, or at least the jambalaya that Stone was hoping for. To complicate things, Isis was pregnant with their second child and had to negotiate her kitchen tasks around a bulging belly. Still, Stone was a quick study and soon the little pig-tailed girl was napping on his shoulder. He laid her down gently on the bed in her room and came back to the kitchen to assist his wife.

"We will have to get a bigger place soon with the family getting bigger," he said.

"I've been telling you that."

"Yes, but it had to be my idea before I did anything. We have to start looking for an actual house."

Indeed the Pontalba apartment overlooking Jackson Square was getting cramped with all the baby stuff and another child was on the way. Isis would miss the view and the proximity to the cathedral and the French Quarter environs, but it was a needful sacrifice.

"This is the first family of your own, isn't it? In spite of your great age," she teased.

"My great age?" Stone repeated. Isis was getting quite the sarcastic sense of humor. Where on earth had she learned it? "Need I remind you that you were born nearly five thousand years ago? I don't have you beat by as much as you think," he rejoined.

Isis smiled. "Still, I can tell that this is your first time with fatherhood."

"It is," he admitted. He had no family of his own back in his home universe and had started no other until now. With her. It made her feel quite special to know that.

"What were you like when you were young?" she asked. "If you can remember back that far?"

"The same, only more so," he smirked. Then turning somewhat more serious, "I was less wise."

"Hard to imagine you that way," she said. It was a compliment.

"We all have to start somewhere."

10 April 1553, Shaolin Monastery, Henan Province, China

The Cosmic Eraser was certainly in this universe and most likely on this planet, but where and when? Stone had given up his active search until some helpful clue turned up. In the meantime he would make the best of his new life on this planet while he waited for that to happen. If it did. He had cornered the last of the fugitive nihilists on this planet but he had already ditched the Eraser. Before Stone could interrogate him, he had destroyed himself with a lesser weapon. Lesser only in that it was less powerful than the Eraser which could destroy an entire universe for all time. The explosion destroyed an entire island and with it a promising civilization called Atlantis.

Upon leaving that disaster behind, Stone tried to go home only to find one far, far worse. The nihilists had developed another Eraser and used it to completely destroy Stone's home universe in every timeframe. He could never go home. Such a magnificent civilization, trillions of souls, all lost as if they had never been. Except Stone because he had been outside. Of course the magnificent civilization was a victim of its own success. Only a staggeringly advanced society could even develop the Cosmic Eraser in the first place. It could not then uninvent it or, ultimately, prevent its use.

It would be a long time before Stone discovered that he was not the only survivor and for now it seemed that he was the loneliest being in creation. Having lost everything he held dear helped make him completely ruthless as well. What value had life, after all? He returned to Earth in hope of finding the remaining Eraser. In spite of his callous view of life, he would do his remaining duty and try to avert another such catastrophe. At least it gave him some purpose.

The utter loss of his home and all whom he had cared about filled Stone with rage he could not resolve. Those responsible had already perished and he could not get revenge. Landing in China upon his return to Earth, he soon heard about monks at the Shaolin Monastery at the base of Mount Song. They granted him permission to stay with them. He did not become a Buddhist, but the teachings about renunciation of desire to avoid pain still resonated. Perhaps someday he would travel back in time to speak to Buddha himself.

Another attraction of the monastery was the intense martial arts training. While Stone's species was far more powerful, his physical body was still a close enough match (and some minor shape-shifting made him indistinguishable) that human movements were relevant for him. Stone was already a skilled warrior, but he did not complacently assume that he had nothing to learn from humans. He found that he learned a great deal from them, as they did from him, and all benefited from the constant training. Stone also benefited from the calming meditative practices he learned there.

Stone had been living with the monks for five years under the name of Tianyuan. He bore the same shaved head and wore the same orange robe as the ordained monks. It was just after dawn and before morning exercise that Stone rose and wandered the Pagoda Forest outside the monastery.

The slender, many-tiered towers and the trees amidst them made for a picturesque meditating location, especially at this hour with the sun rising and the towers casting long shadows and the early morning mists wafting gently upward.

Stone was lost in thought as he wandered amidst the many towers when a flash of orange caught his eye. At the last possible moment, Stone dodged the flying kick and his assailant landed hard on his feet nearby, following up with another kick which Stone blocked. More blows followed, the man quickly raining fists upon Stone who deftly parried each one before responding with a palm strike to the solar plexus. The man grunted, doubled over, and sunk to his knees.

"Good one, Lu Cheng. I wasn't paying enough attention. How long were you waiting atop that tower?" he helped the man up.

"Almost an hour. I knew you'd come this way. One of these times I'll get you," the monk said in between breaths.

"Come. We will have the morning meal together. If you're still hungry, that is."

"Of course. It takes more than that for me to lose my appetite," he smiled.

Returning to the monastery, Lu Cheng rushed in to join his fellow monks in the morning chant. Tianyuan seldom joined these sessions and when he did substituted his own meditations for the chanting. The chanting complete, the monks assembled for their morning meal of bean soup. That was generally followed by some more chanting and then the kung fu training commenced. Today was different, though. At the conclusion of the meal, Chou Zheng, the aged lead monk, stepped to the center of the chow hall to address the assembly.

"We have a visitor this morning who brings an urgent message. He has traveled far and I ask all of you to give him your attention," he said as he relinquished the floor to a man dressed as a magistrate who appeared about fifty years of age but with the weight of the world upon his shoulders.

"My name is Wan Biao. I am the Vice Commissioner-in-Chief of the Nanjing Chief Military Commission. As you may or may not be aware, trouble with the wokou has increased dramatically in recent months. Due to harsh economic conditions, the Emperor's government is low on funds and on trained troops. The wokou pirates raid up and down the coast with impunity, raping and pillaging at will. Now they are so bold as to capture and hold towns since they do not think that we can dislodge them. Even now they control both Hangzhou City and the entire Huangpu delta region. I ask you, in the name of the Emperor, to lend us your renowned martial prowess to beat back this menace," he bowed as he concluded.

Stone had heard something of these pirates but had paid them little mind. They were far away and did not seem special. Called wokou, they were bands of mostly Japanese bandits but also included many Chinese, some Koreans, and some desperadoes from as far away as Portugal. Ruthless and bloodthirsty, only now did they seem to be a genuine threat to the Ming Dynasty's grip on China.

Debate began at once. Some monks protested that taking action would violate their pacific Buddhist beliefs. Others pointed out that they trained heavily in martial skills to include not only open hand techniques but all manner of military weapons—why should these skills be wasted? Spearmen, archers, swordsmen, and especially experts in the staff were to be found here. They had even trained the Emperor's troops before. Training was one thing while active participation was something else entirely, it was countered. These skills were honed to defend the monastery from attack, not for waging war. More than once, outsiders had plundered the monastery's riches, killed its monks, and destroyed everything. The devastation of the 14th century Red Turban Rebellion was well remembered. Others countered with more history in pointing out that the monks, way back in the 7th century, had actively fought on the side of Tang Dynasty to solidify its rule over China. The Tang Dynasty emperors richly rewarded the monastery for its service. This precedent seemed to carry the argument. Everyone acknowledged that the danger from the pirates was dire. It was decided that the monks would aid the Emperor.

By universal acclamation, Tianyuan (aka Stone) was chosen to lead the monks of fighting age into battle. The great masters were too far in years for active campaigning and Tianyuan was the top student. Most master one or two styles, but Tianyuan was deadly with all of them after only five years at the monastery. Truth be told, he had taught as much as he had learned, sharing some techniques from his home. He was also uncommonly deadly with the staff.

Stone accepted this charge. The pirates reminded him of the lawless nihilists that wiped out his home. They left nothing but destruction in their wake. Stone was a law and order type no matter where he was and so he was more than willing to take on this mission. These pirates would be sorry.

After seeing to provisions for the trip, Tianyuan led fifty monks out of the monastery on foot. They traveled with light packs, accustomed as they were to doing without comforts. The regular practice of self-denial would benefit them greatly on the march. Tianyuan kept the monks at a hard pace with little sleep. This would further harden them for the trials ahead. They did not stay dependent on roads but cut directly across rugged terrain. Carrying little, they lived mostly off the land. When they did set up camp, half slept while the other half stood guard and they switched halfway during the already brief sleep period. The men arrived at Nanjing a full day ahead of Wan Biao who had traveled by donkey along the roads.

Two other contingents of fighting monks had been summoned by Wan Biao for the campaign. Thirty came from the Wutaishan temple in Shanxi province and another thirty from the Funiu temple which was also in Henan. The Shaolin monks suggested that the leader of the largest contingent, theirs, should be the overall commander. The Wutaishan monks did not object, but the leader of the Funiu contingent, one Yuekong, hotly rejected this course.

"Shaolin kung fu is weak compared to Funiu. We have the strongest skills in war, therefore, we should lead. I have the most experience in strategy of anyone here. Besides, Tianyuan is not even an ordained monk. The gods will not support him," Yuekong insisted to general murmurs of agreement from his men.

Stone was not subject to emotions in quite the same way that humans are. He did not see red, exactly. There was no physiological response. However, his pride was affronted by the insult. Who were these weakling humans to challenge him? How dare they? Who did they think they were dealing with?

Tianyuan climbed the staircase leading to the front of the town hall and stood atop them before the large wooden gate. From there he towered over the courtyard and his booming voice reverberated off the walls as he yelled, "I am real Shaolin. Is there any martial art in which you are good enough to justify your claim to superiority over me?"

Challenge made and challenge accepted. Yuekong did not even consider going after Tianyuan alone. He chose his seven best men and led them in a charge up the staircase. Once Tianyuan was brutally beaten, fair contest or not, his pathway to leadership would be clear.

Tianyuan did not wait for his opponents to reach him but instead attacked the fastest man, knocking him backwards with a hard straight punch to the face. The hapless monk rolled down the stairs like a barrel, the man immediately behind him gamely jumping over him but the succeeding one was not as quick and the resulting collision left them both sprawled on the ground at the foot of the stairs.

A rapid kick from Tianyuan ejected another man over the railing of the stairs and into the dirt. Two more monks reached the top of the stairs and attacked. Tianyuan ducked one kick and caught the leg of another, throwing the man into his fellow attacker and sending both down the stairs. Another attacker reached the top, and Tianyuan caught that man's arm as he punched and launched him with a hip throw into the path of another monk charging up the stairs. Yuekong reached him next, sending a string of skillful blows at Tianyuan who blocked each in turn before nailing him in the chest with a hard kick that sent him down the stairs as well. The last man attacked with a punch that Tianyuan blocked. In the blink of an eye, Tianyuan swept his leg and sent him crashing to the bottom of the stairs to join his fellows.

The eight vanquished monks recovered themselves and stared up at him in disbelief. Murmurs spread through the crowd. They heard some comments that were less than complimentary about Funiu kung fu. Their anger rose to new heights in their injured pride. Yuekong ordered his men to grab swords. Now armed, the eight men split into two groups with half proceeding to the back entrance of the town hall while Yuekong led the remaining three up the stairs again. Shortly the large wooden door of the hall behind Tianyuan opened and the other four emerged, swords at the ready.

Before they could commence their attack, Tianyuan grabbed the iron bar which was used to bolt the door shut. Wielding it as a staff, he attacked the four who had emerged from the hall to encircle him on the terrace. Moving with blinding speed, he deflected their sword strokes with clanging force, forcing one attacker into the path of another to break up the cohesion of their assault. He parried, dodged, and then swung or jabbed the iron bar with a vengeance, breaking blades and eliciting grunts and howls from the men who fell under the fierce blows. Those four down, he turned to face the four who had climbed the stairs.

He hit them like a whirlwind, each swing of the staff knocking a blade aside or sweeping a leg, each thrust doubling a man over in pain or knocking him senseless. His speed was too great for his opponents and in seconds it was all over. Eight men lay groaning in pain on the ground or the stairs. Tianyuan came to the wounded Yuekong who was cradling his ribs.

Yuekong bowed low, "Forgive me. I submit. You are more than worthy to be our commander." He bade his followers do likewise and they quickly complied.

That's better, Stone thought. Now to plan for the pirates and the business at hand.

Tianyuan examined a map with Wan Biao to select a target small enough for the one hundred twenty monks to tackle and yet important enough to damage the position of the pirates. All eyes soon fell on the temple they occupied atop Mount Zhe from where their modest occupying force controlled the Qiantang River's outlet to the Hangzhou Gulf. Tianyuan agreed that a small 'special ops' force of well-trained monks might have strategic impact there well out of proportion to their small size. Biao organized the transportation to move the force to within striking distance while Tianyuan planned the assault on the complex.

It would be a night attack, something difficult to coordinate in modern times, but Tianyuan had his troops rehearse the assault on a similar compound while en route to Mount Zhe. The first practice run went badly, but the next two went much better and Tianyuan decided that they were ready. On the night of 27 May, he assembled his force at the base of the mountain. Tianyuan personally led a small force up the slope to deal with sentries, but they encountered none until reaching the wall of the compound. A pair of monks were sent back to quietly lead the rest of the force back up the mountain while Tianyuan and the remainder surveyed the target. Another pair of monks reconnoitered around the circumference of the wall and reported back. The distinctive tower of a Taoist temple could be seen in the center of the compound, surrounded by humbler out-buildings that served as a barracks. The guards were few and the moonlight was dim. The entire force crept up close to the main gate without being spotted.

The Shaolin monks specialized in the staff. These staffs were of iron and eight feet long. The compound wall was ten feet high, but Tianyuan had trained an elite few in the art of pole vaulting. At his signal, archers took out the two guards strolling lazily atop the main gate. Tianyuan and six other monks charged the wall and stabbed their staffs into the ground just shy of it, vaulting themselves over the wall and landing in the courtyard with their staffs in hand. At least one of the iron staffs made a clanging noise as its wielder flew over the wall. The guards were now alerted and a tocsin was sounded, but the monks were still on schedule.

Two of the monks made it to the main gate and opened it from the inside while Tianyuan and the others dispatched the first three guards who ran into the courtyard to challenge them. With the gate open, the other one hundred-plus monks charged into the compound with yells, swinging their swords and staffs with ferocity. Most of the pirates had been asleep but they rapidly grabbed their weapons and joined the fray. The monks held the advantage, however. They were ready and held the initiative. Swords and staffs swung and clanged with frenetic energy throughout the compound, the orange robes of the monks distinguishable even in the gloom of the night. The pirates fought gamely but could not prevail; the attack had been too well planned.

In minutes it was over. Forty pirates lay dead and the compound was back in imperial hands. The government could begin to reassert control on the river and the gulf. Tianyuan began planning the next battle.

That next challenge involved wresting the Huangpu River delta from the pirates. This delta lay south of Nansi (modern Shanghai) and provided many small inlets and hiding places for the wokou. Their predations were so severe that the cash-strapped Ming government was building a defensive wall around Nansi. Wan Biao again provided transportation and provisions to the monastic force and also gave intelligence on a likely wokou base. Intelligence reports also estimated enemy numbers at the base as approximately equal to that of the monks at one hundred twenty. Tianyuan planned an assault using several small and fast canoes that would sneak up to the enemy base with little warning, hopefully too little warning for them to man their junk and its cannons.

It was the morning of 21 July 1553 and Tianyuan's riverine force launched before dawn, led down river from Nansi by a local boat pilot. As the sun rose, the enemy junk and river dock came into view, the monks rowing swiftly but quietly towards it. Beyond it on land lay the enemy base, a compound similar to that on Mount Zhe.

The canoes reached the dock free of incident until a watchman aboard the junk called out an alarm. An arrow silenced him, but the surprise was over. No matter; the monks went smartly to their assigned duties. A team of them boarded the junk and killed the skeleton crew in a short but sharp fight. Other teams set up ambushes for any pirates who emerged from the compound. The team aboard the junk set it on fire and tocsin bells soon sounded in the enemy compound and the nearby hamlet to warn of the blaze. Pirates opened their main gate and streamed out to fight the fire only to be cut down by the arrows or spears of the monks. The pirates learned quickly and forgot about the fire, streaming out with weapons to fight the monks instead.

These pirates were overwhelmed in numerous small engagements where the monks' superior training gave them the upper hand. Monks seized the main gate and the entire compound lay open to them. The pirates were given no chance to surrender and death came quickly to most of them by way of sword stroke or a vicious blow from an iron staff. Four monks were killed and several others wounded, but the wokou dead numbered at least sixty. The remainder fled the compound in various directions. Tianyuan quickly organized his troops for pursuit. Even this early in his earthly career, Stone was already a superior tracker. He employed those skills now to hunt down the fleeing pirates.

The years of renunciation of self, the recent hard marches, the iron discipline of the monastery, all these now paid off during the pursuit. The pirates were systematically hunted down over several days and for nearly twenty miles. When one group was hunted down, the monks had the stamina to backtrack and then pursue a different group that had splintered off. In this way they ensured that few escaped. Even in fear for their lives, the pirates had to rest. The monks needed little and quickly made up ground on them.

Finally, after ten days of heavy pursuit, the last group was tracked down to a bamboo forest by the river. Stone was remorseless and relentless in his pursuit. These lawless bandits would pay for their many crimes. He could not make those pay who had destroyed his home, but he could punish dangerous outlaws in his new one.

Early morning mist seeped between the immensely tall, green bamboo stalks that were so dense in some places that the rising sun could scarcely be distinguished between them. The morning reminded Stone of that last peaceful morning in the Pagoda forest at the monastery before this quest started. Perhaps today some resolution would come. His monks were spread out in a long skirmish line and marched as quietly as they could through the dense bamboo. Unfortunately, any movement against the bottom of a bamboo stalk could be seen very far off thanks to the corresponding shaking of the top of the same stalk.

"Aieeee!" The sound came from above in the tops of the bamboo, but soon enough the ambushing pirates jumped down to ground level and took the advancing monks by surprise. A chaotic battle in the forest ensued, every combatant finding difficulty in landing any sweeping slashes because the bamboo stalks blocked them. Tianyuan commanded a change in fighting styles to emphasize jabbing and stabbing attacks or overhead strikes while demonstrating on the pirate fighter in front of him. The monks understood and adjusted their fighting techniques, turning the tide against the ambushers.

After another brisk struggle, the outnumbered and overmatched pirates fled as their casualties mounted. A chase to the river followed, individual pirates being cut down by groups of monks who showed no mercy. Stone joined in the chase and in the slaughter, sending several pirates to the next life with his iron staff.

The last group of pirates was trapped against the river up ahead. Stone dashed quickly through the bamboo to be present at the end of the fight. By the time he got there, only one armed pirate remained. His face was terrified as he confronted hopeless odds. Before him he held his sword and behind him he was shielding an equally terrified woman, likely his wife, who clung to him desperately. He slashed at the approaching monks but could not hold so many at bay from so many directions. Finally a spear head caught him in the leg and he went down under a flurry of spears, swords and staffs.

The woman shrieked, "No! Please!" She had no weapon, but one of the monks quickly stepped forward and struck her on the head with his iron staff, silencing her screams forever.

Stone walked over to where she lay. She was no pirate. She had held no weapon. Her only crime was her choice of husband. Perhaps he had lived badly, but he had died defending her. Stone thought of the desperate look of terror that had been on the man's face and thought how he might have felt had he been in his place, if he had a wife shrieking in terror behind him and begging for their lives. He looked up at his fellow monks. And what of them? How had it come to this? They had begun as near pacifists and now were killing unarmed women begging to be spared. The one who had struck the fatal blow was none other than his friend, Lu Cheng, the gentle young monk with the quick smile. Were they hypocrites? Perhaps, but how much of this was Stone's fault? How much had his thirst for justice been translated into bloodlust as it rubbed off on them?

"We're done here," he said aloud, but he was speaking to himself. He snapped the iron staff over his knee as an exclamation point to the surprise of the onlookers. 'Tianyuan' departed alone into the thicket of bamboo until he was out of their sight. They never saw him again.

4 September 114, Petra

The Romans were in charge in Petra now, but life there had not changed much. It was still a crossroads, a key trade intersection for the region. It also contained interesting architectural features carved out of the sandstone and approachable only via narrow winding passages through the rock. Stone made a habit of visiting since it attracted people and news from all over. Sometimes this included people and news from off-world.

The experience in China had chastened Stone somewhat. He decided that while his experience more than qualified him for leadership roles among the humans, it was not proper for him to assume them except in extremis. They had to follow their own path and all he could do was gently encourage them to choose the right one, not choose it for them. If they chose to fight evil, they would have in him a staunch ally. Where they faced threats from beyond their world which they could not cope with, they could certainly count on his help. Day to day, however, he would be content with a lowly role, influencing at the micro level. He would be a non-commissioned officer in their ranks. A sergeant.

One of those off-world threats was on his mind now. Stone's species had been far from the only one capable of inter-dimensional universe hopping and time travel. Other beings were soaring through the inter-phasing spheroids of space-time, many of them intent on using their newfound abilities to subjugate others. Such was the way of things, but Stone was committed to opposing them, especially if they made trouble for his adopted home. Such was his way. A coalition of these beings called the Syndicate was forming to seek domination over the whole multiverse. Stone's people would have stopped such an effort when they were still around, but with them out of the way, the Syndicate could move forward. Fortunately, a rival coalition called the Commonwealth was forming to oppose them. Stone had spotted an agent of that coalition here in Petra and approached him now.

Stone dismounted the camel and strode over to the temple façade with its statues of Castor and Pollux flanking the doorway. In that doorway stood the man he came to see, a fellow traveller from elsewhere. The man watched him warily, no doubt sensing the extra-dimensional energy buzz that emanated from Stone like an aura. Beings such as they could usually detect one another by such means. Was he friend, foe, or neither? No doubt he would shortly learn.

"Good evening," Stone said in Greek, a lingua franca for the area.

"Good evening," the man replied. "Is there something I can do for you?"

"There is something we can do for each other since we have a common cause. Demetrius, is it?"

The man nodded in the affirmative. "And you are?"

"Your best chance for stopping the Syndicate. Call me Stone."

12 March 1894, New Orleans

"It is hard to picture you as a monk. Or Chinese. Or bald," Isis mused.

"I have become all things to all men so that I might by all means save some, to quote Saint Paul," Stone answered.

"But what happened to the monks?"

"I left but later learned that they kept fighting the pirates until suffering defeat under a less competent commander. C'est la guerre; I had other causes to fight. I've never run out of causes and suspect I never will."

"I am glad you were there to fight for me," she told him.

"I will do so as long as I am able," he kissed her hand gallantly.

CRESCENT CITY SENTINEL

Der Fuehrer had declared war on the United States and he tasked the Abwehr to strike at the mongrel enemy on his home turf. Lieutenant Walter Kappe recruited me and eleven other loyal party members fluent in English for Operation Pastorius, the mission to infiltrate the United States and sabotage war production sites. After initial screening, four were eliminated, but this was a partial ruse. Two were eliminated, or so I was told, but two others, myself included, were kept on in secret, compartmentalized from the rest. The other eight were divided into two teams to be brought near the east coast of the USA by U-Boat. They would then embark on small boats to land on the beach with their explosives, bury them, and proceed inland disguised as American civilians. Loaded with cash and handkerchiefs with invisible ink that revealed safe house locations, they were to contact friendly agents, recover their explosives, and begin striking at the enemy's war industries with the side benefit of spreading panic in the American home front.

Klaus (I never learned his real name; I was going under the false name of Dietrich) and I were trained for a different approach. The other teams were striking at targets along the USA's eastern seaboard, but we were to operate along the southern coast in the Gulf of Mexico. Lieutenant Kappe, while verifying my racial purity and my absolute loyalty to National

Socialism and Der Fuehrer, discovered that my family had lived in New Orleans for four years when my father held a job there. I knew the city well and could find my way with ease. Klaus had lived in the western United States, but his English was excellent. Still, I was to be team leader for the New Orleans operation.

Kappe feared that the other teams might be compromised during too long a stay behind enemy lines. He was determined to achieve at least one success, so he hedged his bets by training our team for a more conventional commando raid. The means we would need to reach the target and extract ourselves were not quite conventional, however. It was early May of 1942 when Kappe summoned me to his office. He bid me sit down and handed me an American newspaper, *The Miami News*.

"Read this one," he pointed to the article he wanted me to look at with his chubby finger.

The article was entitled, 'Boat Builder Makes Big Business Out of Small-Craft Construction'. A photograph of a torpedo boat had a caption boasting how it was, "giving the Axis plenty of trouble." Below that was another photo of what appeared to be a shallow draft landing boat disgorging armed sailors onto a beach. Another offloaded a truck so far into the shore that it did not get bogged down as it disembarked. The caption described the practice maneuvers as taking place at a Louisiana lake. I knew where that was and Kappe knew that I knew; it was why he called me. I scanned the article with interest.

Andrew Jackson Higgins specialized in constructing small boats before the war, mostly pleasure craft and shallow draft boats that could negotiate the swamps and marshes of Louisiana. A Nebraska native, he found his niche in timber and then wooden boat construction. It seemed many of his customers had been smugglers who favored his craft for their ability to reach out of the way places. Now the US government was paying him to mass produce not only fast torpedo boats but thousands of these landing craft, which could one day threaten the Reich with their ability to land huge forces at an almost unlimited variety of landing sites in Europe. The Wehrmacht could not possibly defend every inch of coastline these boats could reach.

"They are building several plants around the New Orleans area, but the biggest one so far seems to be," he paused as he laid a large, detailed map of lower Louisiana on the desk, "here." He was pointing near the center of the city near the City Park. My father had taken us to that park when I was a teenager.

"Let me quote the article, sir: 'The city stands 120 miles from the open gulf and is reached only by a winding channel flanked on either side by the wide and well-nigh impassable swamps. And the gulf itself, and the Caribbean, too, have been converted into inland lakes by a great chain of offshore air and naval bases'."

He waved dismissively at that last sentence, "Our U-Boats have already operated with impunity there, sinking many of their vessels. That other part, about the city being 120 miles from the gulf, therein lies the difficulty. I dare not ask even my brave secret Kriegsmarine unit to take a U-Boat so far up the Mississippi River."

"No," I nodded. "Suicide mission. The river is treacherous, heavily trafficked, and way too long to stay unobserved. A miniature submarine might land commandos and might stay unobserved, but they haven't the range."

Kappe smiled. He didn't do it often and it was not pretty, but what he said made me smile with him, "Don't be too certain. The Reich's mini-subs are not yet ready, still on the drawing board, but our Japanese allies have devoted attention to this area for years and they have suitable craft. They've already used them with success in their Pearl Harbor attack."

"Great, but how do we get one from them?"

"Leave that part of the operation to me; I will tell you when you need to know. For now, suffice to say that we can employ a two man submarine with a range of one hundred miles."

I stopped smiling. "Remember the article? New Orleans is well over that on a one way trip. Plus, I assume that such extreme range can only be achieved by keeping the speed very slow. That will extend the trip well into daylight and increase the danger of detection."

Kappe and I frowned together. I glanced down at the map.

"Wait a moment," I said, suddenly inspired. "Forget the river. Look here," I pointed east of the city on the map.

"The mother ship U-Boat sails here," I said, indicating Lake Borgne, a small body of water surrounded by land on three sides but opening to the gulf on its east side, "and releases the mini-sub. The big boat won't want to stick around in that small lake, either, lest she be found, so she sails back out again and returns the next day for the rendezvous and pick up. The mini-sub proceeds here," I pointed to a narrow pass labeled 'The Rigolets'.

"The Rig-o-lets?"

"They pronounce it 'rig-o-lees'. The mini-sub can get through there, into Lake Pontchartrain, and sail west." I moved my finger along the south shore of the lake. New Orleans lay between this large inland lake on its north side and the winding Mississippi River to its south. Instead of attacking from the river and the south, a treacherous, lengthy, and winding passage, we could plunge the dagger through a chink in the eastern armor and then down from the north into the heart. My finger stopped at a point on the lake shore almost due north of the target factory.

"And then what?" Kappe asked, the suspense making him impatient.

"Well, it doesn't get any less interesting from there. The good news is that the City Park is huge and we could conceivably stay within its confines almost all the way from here to the target." I gestured from the sub's stopping point on the lake shore and through the large, north-south running park to the Higgins Factory target. "Approaching on foot during the night, there is a very good likelihood that, having gone unnoticed thus far, we could continue to do so right up to the factory gate."

"What is the bad news?"

"The tyranny of distance, of course, as our brothers are discovering on the Eastern Front. On foot it will take too long to trudge with the explosives through the entire park, in the dark, set the explosives, march all the way back to the submarine and launch again in the same period of darkness. Not during summer. The sub can be submerged while underway in daylight, but we dare not leave it exposed in the sun. The entire commando raid must be executed at night, from anchoring the sub to launching again."

"So...what if..." he trailed off, out of ideas.

"Hang on. The mini-sub can haul a small motorized boat like the ones the other teams are using. Much faster than walking and it can haul those heavy explosives most of the way."

"Through the park? How?"

"Not through it. Beside it, parallel to it. Here," I pointed, "is Bayou St. John. We'd have to drag the boat around a seawall or two, but it is still vastly preferable to doing the whole trip on foot. We disembark around here," I pointed near the southeast park entrance by the museum, "wherever there is the best concealment, and then cross the park on foot heading west to the target. We set the explosives and then retrace our steps through the park back to the boat. At a sufficiently late hour there will be few if any in the park to even see us. Regaining the boat we go back north through the bayou, dragging the much lighter boat now around the obstacles, and then return to the mini-sub before sun up. We launch and submerge and navigate back through the Rigolets and the rendezvous with the U-Boat. Simple. Not easy, but simple."

"Finalize your plans. We have U-885 at our service. It is not officially commissioned, completely secret, and outside of the Kriegsmarine chain of command. It leaves Brest in two weeks for operations in North America. You and Klaus will be on it."

We left in the U-Boat as scheduled. Its crew had been recruited by the Abwehr from the Kriegsmarine for special operations and they were sworn to secrecy. U-885 was a Type IXD2 with double the range of most other U-Boats in service. We sailed first for Argentina, however, not for the United States as expected. Arriving at General Lavalle, Abwehr agents introduced us to a new passenger, a member of the Japanese Imperial Navy who specialized in mini-subs. He then introduced us to the Type A Ko-hyoteki two man submarine itself. He knew no German but did know English, so he was able to instruct me and Klaus in the operation of the sub. The irony of using the enemy language to learn to attack the enemy was not lost on any of us. The brush up on thinking and speaking English was also helpful. We did not plan to speak to any Americans on our short visit, but it would surely pay to be able to if plans met with the unexpected, as they tend to do. Klaus and I soloed after a week of lessons and successfully negotiated the inland channels around General Lavalle, Argentina, which was good practice for navigating the Rigolets. For our graduation exercise we launched from the U-885 and then navigated to a rendezvous and recovery.

The Japanese navy man joined the crew for the duration. After departing Argentina for the Gulf of Mexico, Hideki (the only name I was given for him) continued to drill us on mini-sub operations and emergency procedures. He would also assist with the launch and recovery of the mini-sub just as he had with the first mating of it to the U-885. He would have been valuable to take with us if a Japanese man would not have been so obvious in New Orleans. He could also have been useful in staying with the mini-sub during the raid, but alas there was only room for two, and two men would be needed to haul the explosives to the factory and set them.

28 June 1942

D-Day had arrived. This very first phase was one of the most dangerous. U-885 arrived on station in Lake Borgne and observed the sea and sky for an hour before stirring so as to guard against surprise by enemy patrols. Surfacing in daylight in this inland lake was extremely risky, but the launch would be expedited to limit exposure as much as possible. It was deemed crucial to use some daylight for the tricky navigational feat of finding the mouth of the Rigolets in the mini-sub and also to preserve as much of the period of darkness as possible for the ingress, the factory raid, and the egress.

Finally, when the captain deemed it safe, the U-Boat surfaced and Klaus and I quickly exited onto the deck and climbed into the mini-sub. Other crewmen manned the deck gun but it was for self-defense only. If we came under attack now, the mission would be scrubbed and the U-Boat would proceed with ordinary torpedo attacks on shipping, something it intended to do after the raid anyhow.

Our mini-sub was already loaded with all of our gear so we buttoned up and performed pre-launch checklists. The mother ship did the same. After comm checks verified that both vessels were ready, we submerged together. On command, we detached from the mother ship and maintained neutral buoyancy at periscope depth while U-885 continued its descent and then proceeded out of Lake Borgne and back to the relative safety of the open gulf. We engaged our motor and proceeded northwest, Klaus steering by my commands as I peered through the periscope.

We found the mouth of The Rigolets with no difficulty and proceeded through. Though submerged, it was still daylight and our periscope was still visible. In fact it cast a shadow on the water in the setting sun. Still, the waning daylight made the tricky navigation far simpler. The area was sparsely populated and we saw only a couple of fishing boats in the distance. If any had come near we would have withdrawn the periscope and tried to wait them out. Fortunately, as we had but little flexibility with our timetable, this did not prove necessary. In the twilight we navigated around the first bend of The Rigolets and the passage widened a bit. We proceeded west, clunking along at the snail's pace of six knots and hopefully leaving no wake with the periscope. Off to port I could see what remained of an abandoned nineteenth century fortification called Fort Pike. It was no longer manned since it was obsolete. How ironic that if it had been we may have been spotted. Instead I observed no one on shore and only two small fishing boats too far away to see us.

Rounding the bend around the fort, the waters opened up as we entered Lake Pontchartrain itself. We turned the mini-submarine due west into the sunset. No longer in the tight confines of The Rigolets, I was comfortable withdrawing the periscope for minutes at a time and navigating by dead reckoning. This kept us safer from observation since leaving the periscope silhouetted against the setting sun was risky.

We chugged along under the murky Pontchartrain waters. With the sun now set and darkness covering us, I felt my confidence soar. Even submerged, the passage through The Rigolets was a phase I feared almost as much as the actual commando raid on the factory. The lights of the city now appeared on our port side and through the periscope I could identify points of interest. New Orleans apparently feared no air raids; light discipline here was no help to ships running the gauntlet of our wolf packs at sea. I still kept a fairly wide berth from the shore to limit the odds of detection, but not so far that I could not navigate well with my sightings.

My biggest concern in this phase was the new airfield constructed on reclaimed land that now jutted into the lake. Built by Louisiana's Bolshevik governor, Huey Long, the airfield now hosted Army Air Corps units. It was exhilarating to pass under their noses. Once west of that airfield I had Klaus steer us to 210 degrees, my estimated heading to the mouth of Bayou St. John. In the periscope I could see a gap in the lighting where the scarcity of homes on the lakeshore north of City Park could help point us in the right direction. By this point I longed for a breath of fresh air. The dank, diesel-soaked air of the tiny sub was getting oppressive. The Japanese sailors who performed much longer missions in these cans have my respect.

At long last we neared shore at an oblique angle and I sighted the mouth of Bayou St. John. I had visited the lakeshore a couple of times as a kid, but those memories were of little use and from the wrong vantage point, but a thorough map study paid off here. We slowed in the dark shallows. I observed the beach very carefully for what seemed like long minutes. No night fishermen. No passers-by. Our luck was holding; we would proceed.

Klaus opened the hatch as quietly as possible and set an anchor which we hoped would keep the submarine from floating away during our visit. It was very dark here, but car headlights could be seen in the distance. Discovery of the submarine was a very real risk and would seal off our escape. We wore ordinary civilian clothes and large amounts of cash. Plan B for escape would involve a bus to Texas and trying to cross into Mexico. The one upside to the discovery of the mini-submarine was the panic it might spread through the American homeland, particularly a Japanese one in the gulf coast. With luck, the Americans might overreact and intern every Japanese person in America.

We closed the hatch and made ready our two man rubber-hulled motorboat. We knew the engine had been fully serviced so we set it in the water and loaded the explosives aboard. Once ready, we boarded with Klaus as lookout and myself in the back at the motor. I pulled the cord to start it. Nothing. My heart jumped into my throat. I pulled again and the little motor roared to life; we were on our way.

But not for long. Soon we were confronted by the seawall, which was part of the flood protection system. This was the part I dreaded, but we had thought ahead. We beached the boat and killed the engine. Climbing out, we fastened small wheels to axles we had mounted on the underside of the rubber hull. We screwed them on quickly with wing nuts and had the motion down so well that we did not need to employ flashlights. We had quickly transformed the boat into a wagon. With Klaus tugging on the pull rope in the front and me pushing, we maneuvered the boat on land around the seawall and over the levee and, in a matter of minutes, had regained the waters of the bayou on the other side, huffing and puffing from our exertion.

I started us up again and now we were really on our way. Few residents witnessed us motor down the bayou, and if they did they could see nothing nefarious anyhow. Our boat was also loaded with a couple of fishing poles on the off chance we got stopped on the water and questioned. I recognized some points of interest from my youth, although, once again, my vantage point was different now as I had never been boating in this bayou before. I allowed myself to enjoy it. I like boating. The wind hit my face and washed away the stale stench of the submarine in my nostrils. I was on a glorious mission for my Fuehrer, about to strike a deadly blow at enemies of the Reich!

On the left I could see the top of the Orthodox Cathedral and, remembering its position relative to the park, I knew just where we were. The bayou widened and I pushed the motor to top speed, enjoying myself immensely. Klaus was getting wet from the water kicked into his face by the bow at my unnecessarily high speed. He turned and gave me a dirty look, but I smiled back at him and he softened. I backed down the speed a little.

We passed under a bridge. On our left, the east side, we could see the lights from many residences, but there were none on the west, our right side. We were already passing alongside the rather large 1300 acre City Park. A whites only park, I recalled from my youth. That was as it should be, of course. Yet this was still a nation of mongrels and it was about to be taught a lesson by its proper masters. Another reason to target the Higgins factory was that it hired Negroes to work right beside whites and even paid them the same wages! Surely the Fuehrer would appreciate our extra attention to detail in target selection.

We motored by Demourelles Island, a small island in the bayou which contained several homes of wealthy people. No other boats were out this night and we saw only a few kids fishing from land. A couple of them even waved. How ironic. I waved back. We proceeded under some more bridges, both car and rail. Traffic was light at this hour. It was a Sunday night and most everyone was resting for work tomorrow. We had chosen the right day and time, I thought, since activity at the target should be minimal.

Passing under a major bridge, we beached the boat on the west side just prior to a major bend in the bayou. The bridge we had just passed beneath led to the main automobile entrance to the park adjacent to the

Isaac Delgado Museum of Art. I had been there once, but the memory was vague. I recalled more about chasing ducks in the lagoons outside than any of the art within, but such are the priorities of children. Here the traffic was somewhat heavier and we were certain to be seen. The key here was to act as if we were up to absolutely nothing unusual. The large sacks on our backs, which contained explosives, would have to be carried openly across the intersection of Esplanade Avenue and Wisner Boulevard in full view of the equestrian statue of Confederate General P.G.T. Beauregard, a native of the area. He doubtless would not approve of our raid but was helpless to stop us.

We waited for a quiet moment when no passersby and few cars could be seen and marched casually across the avenue with our heavy sacks. Here Klaus proved very helpful. His size was not convenient for submarine duty but his strength was invaluable for carrying many pounds of explosives, not to mention in moving the boat over land.

Reaching the other side of the street without incident, we entered the park, avoiding the road and sidewalks. We picked a route that would take us west across the park and which paralleled City Park Avenue to our south. Beyond our route were the lights of the city as well as a lagoon to the north which we kept on our right side. It extended almost the entire east-west length of the park. Walking between these two in the dark and steering clear of well-worn paths, we avoided attention from pedestrians and cars on the street. Marching quietly through the ancient oak trees and open spaces of the park, we remained unnoticed by late fishermen on the lagoon.. We had to watch our step to avoid the tree limbs that dipped down to the ground, so old were these trees. While we watched our feet, the Spanish moss hanging from higher limbs would brush our faces and startle us sometimes. The crunching of twigs and acorns was louder than we might have wished, but there was no one to hear; we had the park to ourselves at this dark hour. One odd sight: across the lagoon on the north side and in the middle of nowhere was a large peristyle with numerous Greek style columns.

Marching on through the dark and working up a sweat, we finally emerged out of the darkness of the park on its west side and saw the Delgado Trades School before us. Many of the workers at the target factory were also students at this school. Our target lay just beyond, on the other side of the campus. Careful to time our emergence from the park onto the sidewalk so that no one saw since that would look suspicious, we crossed the street nonchalantly, ignoring fellow pedestrians, of which there were few. No one seemed to notice us. Crossing the Delgado campus, we avoided well lit areas, but not so scrupulously as to appear strange. Or so we hoped. If questioned here we would pretend to be students and claim that our sacks held books. Failing that we would have to resort to our knives.

We crossed the campus without incident, our careful map study paying off again, and there it was: the Higgins boat factory. It was quiet at this time, about 2330 hrs. The factory was surrounded by a fence and well lit but with only a single watchman at the gate, so luck was still with us. We found a patch of fence that was not so well lit and quickly cut through it. Klaus and I did not have to speak since the rest was well rehearsed. He knew which structures to target and so did I. We went about our work quickly. There was no way to hide from all the street lamps so we did not try. Speed rather than stealth was our ally here.

Not explosive experts ourselves, we had been well briefed by those who were about how to place the bombs to do maximum damage and how to set the timers. I kept my knife handy in case a roaming guard got too close, but apparently the man at the gate was alone. And why not? What were the odds that Nazi commandos would attack this facility?

I did steal a look in one of the windows. Several Higgins boats were there in various phases of construction. A large banner was hung over the workroom which stated, 'The Guy Who Relaxes is Helping the Axis'. I smirked. Well, soon enough that banner and all the work within the factory would be consumed. America would know its vulnerability.

After about ten minutes of work we met again at the hole we'd cut in the fence and proceeded out. We retraced our path through the campus and crossed into the park, barely containing our glee. We had succeeded in setting the charges! The target would be destroyed! Now for the drama of our escape. We made our way through the park much faster and easier than the way in, no longer burdened by the weight of the explosives. We still considered it best to limit exposure to the local residents and used the same route through the quiet and dark middle of the park until reaching Wisner Boulevard again. There we crossed nonchalantly again and I nodded smugly at General Beauregard, confident in winning a victory over his home town.

Recovering our boat, I started the engine and we launched into the bayou again heading north. The boat moved much faster now with the reduced weight. In what seemed like mere minutes, we reached the seawall again. Though tired, this time the act of portaging the boat was far easier without the explosives. Now the question: would we find our mini-sub where we had left it?

Motoring up to the anchored location, for a moment I felt a tinge of panic. Where was it? Never mind, it was there, bobbing up and down. The black hull was just so hard to see in the night and we dared not use flashlights. But there it was. We dragged the boat back on board and secured it. Opening the hatch, we took one last look around and took a last breath of fresh air, or as fresh as the lake air can be, and plunged back into the tiny sub to begin pre-launch checks. It was almost 0100, the time our bombs were set to go off. Pity we could not wait for the early Fourth of July fireworks, but we needed to make haste to achieve our rendezvous. U-885 would not wait in Lake Borgne for long.

The rest of the trip was, thankfully, uneventful. We cruised serenely through Lake Pontchartrain heading east. For several miles we did not even submerge in order to make better speed. In the dark, the danger seemed minimal. Before passing the Army airfield we did submerge again and stayed that way through The Rigolets since a slower speed was preferable to navigate the narrow passage. By 0330 we reached the pickup point in Lake Borgne and U-885 was waiting, flashing a directional light in response to my own periscope's flash. We executed the well-rehearsed recovery procedures flawlessly and mated the Japanese mini-sub again to its German mother ship. Re-boarding U-885, Klaus and I were all smiles. The crew cheered us heartily. Success!

Sergeant Peter Stone of the NOPD had been on the force for seven years. In this identity and in this era, anyway. The total time he had given to law enforcement in the Crescent City spanned substantially longer. It so happened that at this stage of this tour he worked in the mounted police. It also happened that during this time the NOPD maintained its horse stables on the grounds of City Park. It further happened that Stone was on duty the night of 28 June 1942.

Stone sometimes stopped at the famous Dueling Oaks during his mounted patrol. These ancient oak trees had trunks as wide as most people's bathrooms and limbs that arced to the sky and back down to the ground again, giving much pleasure to the children of the city who found them irresistible for climbing adventures. They were quite picturesque, especially in the evenings with the setting sun's pink light splashing on the Spanish moss which hung languidly from almost every limb. The Dueling Oaks have their name for a reason, of course. When dueling was legal, and even for a good while after, duels did indeed take place here with either sword or pistol. The causes of the duels were often over trivial slights, but the ceremony and procedure surrounding them was elaborate and rigidly governed by a code of honor. Stone had himself been challenged to several duels which he fought here in the 1830s. He would carefully avoid killing any of his opponents since none of them could hope to kill him, but victory could be had by only drawing first blood. As the challenged party, Stone would always choose the sword since he enjoyed the fencing practice and honor could be satisfied by a scratch. He always won, but his opponent always walked away. Most often they walked together for drinks once the wound was attended. A couple of lasting friendships were even forged, Stone recalled with a smile.

This night Stone happened to reach the Oaks late. He had to break up a drunken altercation which delayed his usual rounds. He missed the sunset, but no matter. With his flawless night vision he could still enjoy the scene almost as well. This night his vision spotted two figures trudging quietly through the dark on the south side of the lagoon and not using the more convenient sidewalk. They apparently did not wish to be seen. This made Stone wish to see them all the more. He urged his mount forward silently and rode parallel to their line of march, staying on the north side of the lagoon. One of them nearly spotted him when he turned his head north to look at the peristyle and its Greek columns.

Stone observed them as they carefully timed their departure from the park to avoid traffic. They crossed over the street and entered the campus of the Trades School, still carrying their heavy sacks and not wishing to be seen. Stone crossed as well after waiting an interval to make sure they did not see him. The horse seemed to know this was a surveillance mission and accordingly kept his steps light and quiet.

Through binoculars he observed them as they cut their way through the outer fence of the Higgins Boat Factory, thus erasing any notion that they may have been trying to deliver Santa's gifts early. Watching them place what gifts they did bring at points along the outside of the building, it was not hard for even a less practiced eye than Stone's to guess that they were planting bombs. He could stop them now, but he wanted more. They were probably part of a larger cell of saboteurs and he wanted to catch them all. Still, he would have to act quickly to save the plant and still follow the two saboteurs to their friends.

He watched as the two figures completed their task and reunited at the hole in the fence before walking quickly back to the campus the way they had come. Stone guessed they would follow the same route back, but with their incriminating bundles now offloaded they might opt to walk back as ordinary pedestrians on the sidewalks. Either way, Stone gambled that he could track them down. For now, he had to take his eye off of them. If he called for backup they would get spooked and he would never catch the whole ring. Department procedure would have to wait on this one.

Trotting over to the hole in the fence, Stone dismounted and ran through it to the factory buildings. He found the first bundle and, sure enough, it was a potent bomb set by a timer to explode in one hour. So at least he would have time to find them all. He disabled it and hunted for the others. He found the ones on the near side of the building immediately since he had observed their placement. Those on the far side he did not see directly, but he found these quickly as well since he knew their pattern and knew where he would have placed them himself. With his sharp vision he was sure that he had missed none of them. He even found the sacks discarded by the saboteurs and employed them to once again hold the now deactivated bombs. The factory was safe. Now to quickly return to his horse and continue the surveillance.

Stone rode to the sidewalk on City Park Avenue, the street which formed the southern boundary of the park. No pedestrians could be seen all the way to Esplanade. He rode in that direction. If they had been picked up by friends in a car, they would have gotten away. Stone had a hunch, though, that not only were they still on foot but that they probably went back through the park again. He rode to the corner of Wisner and City Park Avenue and looked north. A couple of people on the sidewalks, but none were his quarry. He might have screwed up. He calculated how long it would take them on foot to traverse the park again, now relieved of their cargo. On horseback he should have beaten them, but not by this much. He waited.

There they were, emerging from the shadows during a pause in the car traffic. They crossed Wisner going eastbound. One of them gave a slight bow to the statue of General Beauregard. Smug bastard, Stone thought. He kept them in sight as they crossed the sidewalk on the opposite side and kept walking down to the bayou. This brought them to lower ground and out of Stone's sight. He crossed the street as well. Before he quite finished he heard a boat motor fire up. He spotted them motoring north up Bayou St. John at a high rate of speed. The chase was on and he urged the horse forward at a gallop. Stone's trusty steed charged forward with alacrity up the grassy ground that separated Wisner Boulevard from the bayou but began to tire as the chase wore on. The noise of the engine drowned out the sound of galloping hooves, but this was less of a concern as Stone lost ground before the speeding boat. It pulled away and the horse slowed even more in his exhaustion.

Stone caught a break when the two saboteurs had to drag their boat around the seawall. They were still unaware of the pursuit and took their time attaching wheels to the boat. Stone slowed his approach so as to not be heard and to give the horse a chance to catch his breath. Before long they were back in the water and heading to Lake Pontchartrain. But why?

Stone now had to hazard a guess as to which side of the bayou he should be on. If they were heading straight into the lake it would not matter and he would call the Coast Guard and end this, but he had a hunch that he might yet be able to follow them to an important rendezvous. He played another hunch and decided to cross over to the east side of the bayou by riding over the seawall levee. That side had less lighting and activity; it was the more likely site for secrecy .

With his superior night vision, Stone was able to observe the two men from far enough away to not alert them. He watched as they found their miniature submarine and placed their boat upon it. Even he had to suppress a tinge of respect for the audacity and inventiveness of their raid.

They took a mini-sub into Lake Pontchartrain and a boat down Bayou St. John before trudging on foot through the park and setting explosives at the Higgins plant. Amazing. And now it seemed that they might actually get away with it. Unfortunately for them, they tried it on Stone's watch.

After sealing themselves back into their submarine, Stone galloped to them with all possible speed to reach the sub before it cast off. He dismissed his mount to some needed rest and stepped down the seawall steps with the sacks of bombs on his shoulder. He needed superhuman effort to wade out to the sub under this weight, but the distance was short and he reached it in time to climb aboard. He clung to the conning tower as the sub made its way east and out of the lake. Stone knew these subs had limited range and reasoned that it would sail to rejoin a larger submarine which acted as a mother ship. That was his target.

Things grew less comfortable when the submarine submerged. The water was cold and dark and while Stone could go hours without oxygen if he needed to, it was not an experience he relished. Hopefully this would be worth it. The small sub chugged along at a maddeningly slow rate. Even Stone's endurance and patience were tested. This was unpleasant in the extreme, but he had been through worse. He let himself feel righteous anger to fuel his determination to see this through.

Finally, hours later, the mini-sub surfaced in Lake Borgne. He watched as it exchanged brief light flashes with directional beacons with what had to be its mother ship. He slipped off the sub's hull and into the water and watched the impressive recovery operation. He heard German voices congratulating the two saboteurs he followed all the way from City Park. He started swimming stealthily over to the U-Boat as the crew climbed down the hatch. They closed it just as he splashed aboard the deck. He dragged the sacks of bombs behind himself and knocked three times on the hatch.

Klaus and I climbed down into our mother ship. The crew slapped our backs and gave us every congratulation for a job well done. Der Fuehrer would be most pleased. Now U-885 could wreak havoc on American vessels with her torpedoes. We joyfully saluted Der Fuehrer and the Fatherland when the captain called for the crew to prepare to dive. Debrief and a fuller celebration would have to wait a bit longer. There was a knock on the top hatch. Had we left someone topside in the excitement of the moment?

A sailor opened the hatch to recover his forgotten ship mate. Something knocked the sailor down and he fell to the bottom of the ladder with a thud. Then two recognizable sacks fell on top of him and spilled our explosives all over the deck floor. The timers were set and ticking down. A voice called in perfect German from the top of the ladder,

"The City of New Orleans returns your gift with kind regards." And the hatch closed. We frantically dove for the explosives to disable them. The captain glared at me in accusation and started to speak. I never heard him...

Wump!

Stone opened the hatch and black smoke billowed out. In he went for the gruesome work of killing the rest of the crew since the explosives could not have reached sailors in the far reaches of the submarine. That done, he detonated a torpedo to scuttle the ship, blasting it into so many pieces that he doubted it would ever be found at the bottom of Lake Borgne. A mystery of the war that would never be solved. As for that war, Stone decided that this tour with the NOPD had come to an end. There was work in Warsaw where he would smuggle Jewish children out of the Ghetto and then kill some Nazis when the time came for the Jews to make their stand. After that, Peter (the name means 'Rock') would join the United States Marine Corps in time to serve at Peleliu and Okinawa. Higgins boats brought him to both locations. Staying in after the war, Gunnery Sergeant Stone would join the 1st Marines at Inchon and then go MIA in the Chosin Reservoir in North Korea when the time came to move on again. But that is another tale...

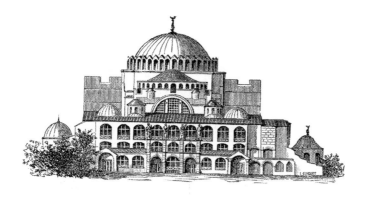

SERGEANT STONE AT THE
FALL OF THE EMPIRE

5 February 1900, New Orleans

"Tell us a story, Dad."

It was Cassandra, the oldest, asking Stone for a bedtime story. She was eight years old but still relished her father's tales. Her younger brother Gideon, who was six, readily seconded her motion.

"So few stories that I know are fit for children."

It was sad but true; most of his interesting recollections were not suitable for young and impressionable minds. He usually had to rely on fiction for bedtime storytelling or strictly edit his own experiences. Still, the kids loved even the edited versions of his own adventures.

"Tell us one about a war," Gideon urged. "A great big battle."

"No, how about one with you rescuing a fair maiden, a damsel in distress," Cassandra pleaded.

"There weren't so many of those," Stone told her.

"What about Mom?" Gideon asked.

"Well, yes, I suppose she qualifies," he allowed.

"Mom has told us that story a bunch of times. There must have been some other ladies you met in your travels," suggested Cassandra, hopping on the bed and causing her long black hair to spill over her face.

"All too few. I usually hung out with stinky guys in muddy trenches or sweltering jungles or blistering deserts or…you get the picture."

"How about the Battle of Troy? Tell us about Cassandra of Troy," Cassandra asked, bouncing again.

"Never actually met her; she stayed locked up and I was busy with the fighting. Had to make sure Aeneas survived so that there would be a Rome. Also I wound up resuscitating Hector so he could help me on a special mission. He did, too, and wound up dying a second heroic death," Stone trailed off thoughtfully.

"Were you always on the losing side?" Gideon queried as he, too, bounced on the bed.

"No, smartass. But often," Stone admitted.

"So you were there when Rome started?" Cassandra again.

"Yes, I was. And many visits after that. In fact Rome is probably the only city I served longer than New Orleans."

"What about the end? Were you there, too?" she persisted.

"That gets complicated. The fall in the West was a slow, agonizing process. The fall in the East came much later, but it did have a more definite end when the Turks took Constantinople."

"And you were there?" Gideon this time.

"Yes. I would not have missed that. When your friend is on her death bed, you go and see her."

"There must have been a girl there," Cassandra interjected.

"Yes there was, now that you mention it."

"Tell us that story, then. The fall of Constantinople. A battle for me and girl stuff for Cassandra," Gideon was proud of what seemed to him to be a diplomatic breakthrough.

"Not a story for the timid. Are you sure you are up for it?" Stone asked seriously.

"We won't tell Mom if we get scared," Cassandra promised and Gideon nodded assent.

"Very well, then. It was in April of 1453 that the last siege began…"

6 April 1453

Alethea Christopoulos was fourteen years old when the Turkish army of Mehmet II pitched its tents outside the walls of Constantinople. Her father Gregos was one of the minor barons serving Emperor Constantine XI, so she was privy to political developments. She paid them more attention than her pious mother Alexandra did. That poor soul determinedly avoided all discussion of politics and frequently retreated to prayer. She was more often found at the Hagia Sophia basilica than at her own home. She knew things were not going well and took refuge in contemplating the holy icons.

Perhaps prayer would save them again. Constantinople had, after all, withstood centuries of sieges. Only once had she fallen to the Crusaders in 1204 who were supposedly allies against the heathen. By 1261 the Latins had been kicked out and Constantinople was once again under Greek rule, but the empire never regained her glory days. The Turks had whittled away at Byzantine territory until now the Emperor ruled Trebizond, the Peloponnese, and the city itself. All the rest had been swallowed into the Ottoman Empire. Last year the new Sultan constructed an imposing new fortress across the Bosporus from the city which dominated all sea traffic in and out. Constantinople would have great difficulty receiving reinforcements and supplies from the outside now. One Venetian vessel ignored the Sultan's demand to stop for inspection and the crew paid with their lives, the captain's impaled corpse left on display as a warning to other vessels.

The ship had been sunk by a single shot from an enormous cannon, the brainchild of one Urban of Germany. This cannon could propel a stone shot of twelve hundred pounds over two miles. Not only did it threaten any sea traffic, such a monster spelled ultimate doom for the ancient walls of Constantinople itself. Diplomatic efforts proved fruitless until finally Mehmet II slaughtered the last ambassadors sent to him. There could be no doubting what would come. In desperation the Emperor had consented to ending the schism with Rome and reuniting with the Roman Catholic Church. This was not greeted with enthusiasm in the city which still remembered the cruel sacking it had suffered from the Fourth Crusade. Some even announced that they preferred to be dominated by the Turkish turban over the Latin tiara.

Alethea's family was not in that number, but neither was the reunion a cause for joy. They treasured the old liturgy and knew the Emperor had only agreed so that the Pope would appeal to the western leaders to come to the aid of the Byzantines. This he did in addition to outfitting galleys at his own expense, but reinforcements were slow to come. It was all too little and too late. Seven hundred Genoans under Giovanni Giustiniani Longo, an expert in siege warfare, had come to join the defense. Other foreigners had come also, especially Venetians, but even with all the Greeks, monks included, the city could muster only seven thousand to defend fourteen miles of walls. The Sultan had over one hundred thousand camped outside and a fleet which dwarfed that of the Byzantines.

Gregos did not try to give his family any false confidence. The situation was grim and deep down everyone knew it. One person made Alethea feel better whenever he showed up, a man called Stone. He was a foreigner who had come to aid in the defense of the city. He worked closely with her father Gregos since the latter had been tasked by the Emperor with strengthening the wall near the San Romano gate, a weak point in the ancient bulwark that was likely to face attack. Stone exuded cheerful confidence that helped build morale and spur the workers to greater efforts in bolstering the ancient walls.

Stone was neither Greek nor Italian, and yet he spoke both languages flawlessly. He was allegedly from England, but that was so far away to Alethea that it might as well have been the Moon. He did seem otherworldly, like a man out of place. Perhaps that was why she felt better around him, because he reminded her that the world was more than Constantinople and all was not lost. The Emperor was entitled the 'Most Serene Emperor' but the label of serene even better fit this man. Though she thought of him as otherworldly, almost angelic in his calm demeanor, in fact he could mix with any company. She heard him cajole lazy stone masons working on the wall with frightful profanities to motivate them when he did not know she was within earshot, but she also heard him eloquently defend the positions of Aristotle and Aquinas against the Greeks who mostly favored Plato and Augustine.

The Byzantines stretched a great chain across the harbor and defended it with galleys. Any seaborne assault on the walls would have to first breach that obstacle. With the seaside walls relatively secure, but still watched over by a ready reserve force, the bulk of the defenders were attached to the landward wall facing Mehmet's enormous force. That force was now bolstered by the enormous new German-designed cannons which were slow to load but so devastating in their effect. On the twelfth of April the bulk of the Ottoman fleet arrived, roughly one hundred and twenty warships versus the Byzantine and allied force of less than twenty.

Daily bombardment began and almost never ceased until the final day of the siege. The noise from the huge guns was staggering and like nothing anyone had ever heard. They shook the ancient stone battlements to their foundations, the crash of the huge cannonballs reverberating menacingly through every quarter of the city. Initial assaults on the walls were thrown back with heavy loss. Crossbowmen, arquebusiers, and stone throwing men drove back the Turks, but there was no rest for the defenders. As soon as the attack was over they had to busy themselves with rebuilding the damaged parts of the wall.

It was here that Alethea played a role as part of the corps of women bringing stones to those rebuilding the defenses. Her mother remained in prayer, but Alethea took these opportunities to check in on her father. She had to admit that she also wanted to see Stone. She stayed busy, doing her part for the city by bringing water or ammunition to the defenders as well. She prayed also, albeit silently and not before a tabernacle as her mother did. There were frequent processions of icons through the city appealing to the Blessed Virgin to save it from the unbelievers, and for these she would stop respectfully to pray. After a particularly heavy Turkish assault on the wall was repulsed on the eighteenth of April, her father sent her back for more crossbow bolts.

"Bring more, Alethea. I promise not to waste them," Stone winked at her and Alethea thought her heart skipped a beat as she smiled back at him. Then she was off like a shot to get the needed ammunition.

Her budding crush was one of the few things that made Alethea smile in those days. She was in constant fear for her father's life at the wall. She feared for the city itself, for everyone in it, her mother and herself included. She did not know what she would do if the walls were breached and she should fall into the clutches of vengeful heathen soldiers. In the meantime there was the privation of the siege itself since food had to be rationed. Water was still plentiful from the many cisterns and wells, but the city could not feed itself forever. Then there was the noise of the constant bombardment. Every boom of the giant cannons was terrifying, like an eruption from Hell itself. She saw with her own eyes the terrible damage they inflicted on the once mighty stone walls that for so long had defended the city. The defenders labored endlessly to repair this damage, but they were showing signs of weariness. It was a pace they could not maintain indefinitely.

Morale was lifted briefly on the twentieth when four Genoan galleys somehow managed to fight their way through the Turkish blockade and into the harbor. This was a boon to the Byzantines and an embarrassment to the Turks, but it changed little. The bombardments and the assaults continued while conditions in the city gradually worsened. On the twenty-second matters took another turn for the worse. On the Asian side of the Bosporus, the Turks had labored to build a road over the hill near Galata and, with teams of oxen and greased rollers, managed to transport seventy-two medium-sized warships overland around the harbor defenses. The relative safety of the seaward wall was now gone; the Byzantines had to fully man the defenses that had once fallen to the Crusaders. An attempt to destroy this fleet with fire ships met with costly failure when the lead galley was quickly sunk by a Turkish cannon shot. The noose tightening, Emperor Constantine sent out a ship to search the seas for any signs of the promised reinforcements.

By mid-May the situation in the city was becoming desperate. During one of her visits to the San Romano gate on the sixteenth, Alethea happened upon some excitement. The Megaduke Loukas Notaras was on hand and there was furious digging. Stone's otherworldly hearing had picked up the sound of some digging beneath the wall. Mining was suspected and those with digging experience had been sent for. Digging at the spot which Stone directed, the workers did indeed stumble upon the tunnel which the Turks were digging under the wall. From there they could have set explosives that would have collapsed a large section of the wall.

Stone volunteered before any volunteers were called for; someone had to go deep into the dark enemy mine and set fire to the supports for the tunnel to collapse it. Dangerous duty, but Stone insisted on going alone. His confidence won over the Megaduke and this was allowed. Alethea was frightened for him and clutched her father's hand during her fearful vigil.

Nothing was heard for long minutes except the castanets, drums, and tambourines of the enemy camp and the occasional shelling. The music from their camp was thought to have the objective of frightening the city's populace since it was intimidating indeed. They may also have had the objective of covering the noise of their digging. In this, at least, they had failed.

Finally, smoke billowed from the dark cavity leading to the enemy tunnel. Moments later Stone emerged from the smoke, his clothing disheveled, dirty, and splattered with fresh blood. Alethea gasped but it was soon apparent that the blood was not his but rather that of some unlucky Turk who had opposed the raid. Stone reported success and soon a rumbling deep in the earth confirmed the tunnel's collapse. With but little delay, Stone rounded up a team of workers to go back to fill in and seal off the remnant of the Turkish tunnel so that they could not try again.

Any boost to morale by this reverse to the Turks was short-lived. On the morning of the eighteenth there appeared in the Turkish camp an immense tower, apparently constructed overnight, that was taller than the Byzantine battlements. This impressive structure was made of strong wooden beams covered with camel skins and filled with earth. It was impervious to the crossbows and small cannons on the wall and provided cover for the Turks to approach the wall closely without fear. It also gave them a vantage point from which to shoot at the wall's defenders, demoralizing them further.

The weary defenders still manned their posts and remained vigilant. Inside the walls priests and women were organized into work gangs that kept hauling barrels of earth to bolster the battered walls. Alethea was one of these and she worked ceaselessly. All knew that the day and hour were soon approaching when they would meet their ultimate test. Some held out hope that a friendly army would come and lift the siege, but others knew better and continued to do their grim duty if only because submission was hateful. Despite her youth, Alethea was in the latter camp.

In the coming days the Turkish fleet tested the harbor defenses and rowed towards the chain in hopes of severing it, but the allied fleet sallied forth quickly and deterred the attempt. More Turkish mines were discovered and successfully countered, but the battering of the walls continued as well. Ill omens appeared in the sky that disheartened the Byzantines. There was a lunar eclipse, a strange fog, and St. Elmo's fire appeared on the dome of the Hagia Sophia. Many took these as signs that God was abandoning the city to the heathen. When a holy icon slipped and fell during a procession, the ill omens seemed to be confirmed. The Venetian ship that had been dispatched to search for the promised reinforcements managed to sneak back into the harbor and report that no such reinforcements were coming. Emperor Constantine briefly fainted at the news but recovered himself. His advisors counseled him to flee while he could and to set up a government in exile, but he steadfastly refused to abandon his people.

The Turks showed their growing confidence by keeping fires lit in their camp and playing loud music constantly. They could be heard boasting about how many Christian slaves they would soon have. Said Christians within the city increased their prayers and petitions to Heaven, Catholic and Orthodox forgetting their differences and worshipping together. A pall of doom seemed to encompass the city as it waited for the inevitable attack which could not be long delayed. In spite of herculean efforts, the workers could no longer keep up with the damage done to the walls by the Turks' enormous cannons. San Romano gate was in particularly sad shape. No one doubted that the main attack would take place at that chink in the armor, and yet the threat was sufficient at other points that the city's defenders could not wholly concentrate there.

On Monday, the twenty-eighth of May, a spontaneous procession of the icons took place and was joined by all who were able, including the Emperor. It paused for additional prayers at points by the wall that were under particular threat. At the conclusion of the procession, the Emperor addressed the throng. He encouraged stout resistance by calling to mind the great heritage of the Empire and the perfidy of the enemy as well as the fate of the city's inhabitants should it fall. After having played diplomat, having to settle quarrels between the city's Greek defenders and foreign allies, he called for unity and told the foreign defenders that he loved and trusted them as his own subjects since, apart from all of the rest of Christendom, they had come and stayed through this dark hour. Finally, he appealed to all gathered to think of the four great causes for which one must fight: faith, family, country, and sovereign. All four were now threatened. He, for his part, would fight to the last for his faith, his country, and his people. He then went about thanking all gathered and asking pardon from each for any wrongs done them, thus making ready to receive the sacraments for what was likely the last time.

Alethea, who had held back tears for so many grueling weeks, finally broke down and sobbed quietly, clutching her father's arm for strength. He embraced her warmly, his own eyes welling with tears, his normal fatherly reserve now gone.

"If we win, we save our city. If we lose, we go to a better city, the Heavenly Jerusalem, where the Lord will wipe the tears from every eye," he assured her. She nodded.

Stone took all of this in. He was not in any great danger of death from Turkish weapons, yet he felt the impending loss of this city keenly. He had served the Empire, both East and West, for countless years. Now the end had come. He would make sure that a toll was exacted for that end, but there was no way to stop it this time. He was here as he would be to aid a good friend in his passage to the next life. The fall of this city, the end of this civilization, reminded him all too well of the loss of his own home. It, too, had reached great heights of achievement and glory, suffered declines and recoveries, periods of decadence and renewal, only to finally be done in by a group of barbarians. This final result Stone hated to see, but entropy made it inevitable. Entropy would finally even claim his own life one day if nothing else cut it short. Like Gregos, he had hope for a better City. In the meantime the Turks would have to tear this one from his determined grasp. This was not his first 'last stand' since he made a habit of them. They showed him humans at their best and worst. They provided the acid test. Do you really believe what you claim about causes greater than yourself or life after death, or will you give in to the instinct for self-preservation? Stone experienced some of these crucibles himself as a mortal. He had faced the fear and passed the test, but it was not easy. Others who passed this test had his everlasting admiration.

Three hours before dawn the Ottoman artillery batteries opened up in earnest to prepare the way for the general assault. The tocsin bells sounded throughout the city to summon all available defenders to their posts. Alethea awoke from her bed with a start. Today would not be like other days. Her mother woke, too, and they embraced for a tearful farewell. They feared it would be their last and they were right to fear. Alexandra made her way to the Hagia Sophia to begin more fervent prayers. Alethea headed for the San Romano gate to assist the defenders at the most critical point, the point her father guarded along with Stone.

The Turks lined up their poorest troops first to soften up and weary the defenders. Behind them stood the regular infantry and behind them the elite Janissaries in their distinctive white turbans and flowing robes. With loud cries of determination the first wave came on. The defenders responded energetically with arrows, crossbow bolts, arquebus bullets, and stones. The stones hurled from the top of the high wall were as gruesome in their impact as the bullets, dashing brains from unfortunate skulls when they found their mark. The Turks were so tightly packed that few of the stones were cast in vain. For his part, Stone stayed good to his word to not waste a single crossbow bolt. He directed others to throw off the scaling ladders that reached the wall. He gave profitable advice on aiming bows, crossbows or arquebuses to those within earshot.

The first wave of poor quality troops suffered grievous casualties but most pressed on. Some that did not were sliced by the scimitars of the troops behind them to encourage them to return to the fray. Nevertheless, the first wave was soon exhausted. They had had their intended effect and the defenders were beginning to tire. Ammunition was still plentiful, however, and they knew they had the rest of their lives to use it.

The second wave of Anatolian regulars, a more professional force, now pressed their attack against the weakening defenses. The San Romano gate was a particular target since it had suffered much from the preparatory bombardment. Mehmet II intended to give the defenders no rest for he knew that only such a relentless attack would succeed even now. The defenders still had plenty of fight in them at this point, though, and they inflicted frightful losses on this second wave.

The huge German cannon opened fire and hurled a twelve hundred pound stone ball against the wall near San Romano gate, collapsing a section of it. The smoke from the tumbled wall obscured the approach of the third wave. Day was dawning, and with it came the fresh, elite troops of the Sultan. The crisis point had now come with the walls in near ruin and the defenders near physical and moral exhaustion. The fierce Janissaries came on with loud cries accompanied by castanets and tambourines. The defenders unleashed a devastating volley of arrows, bolts, bullets, and stones, felling many of them, but still more came and breached the outer wall. The hand-to-hand fighting began with unspeakable ferocity, sword and scimitar clashing savagely. Alethea, hauling stones to the front, watched her father leap into the fray and she called out to him. He could not hear her in the tumult. Stone laid his crossbow aside, drew his sword, and followed close behind him.

She approached as close as she dared, but the noise and smoke were disorienting. She could distinguish the tall white turbans of the Janissaries and it seemed that the tide of them receded. The defenders climbed back up to the inner bulwark. Stone was covered in blood again and carried a body over his shoulder. She recognized the cloak of her father and ran to meet them. Stone laid Gregos down as she arrived. He was still alive, barely.

"My child," he recognized her, tried to reach for her but had not the strength. She hugged him gently so as not to cause him more pain. The wound was a serious one, a sword stroke through the abdomen. She looked at Stone. He nodded grimly in the negative. Nothing would save him and his time was running out.

Gregos turned to Stone as well and said, "The city will not be saved, nor the Emperor. God has willed it so. But you, Stone, I ask of you, please save my child. Can you do that for me?"

Stone nodded in the affirmative. "I will see her through this."

Gregos looked on his daughter again and smiled. He said a prayer over her and then expired. She buried her head in his chest and wept bitterly. Stone stood and sheathed his bloody sword, giving her some privacy.

Another huge cannonball collapsed a section of the wall, widening the breach and sending smoke and debris high into the air. Stone covered Alethea as it rained down on them. When the smoke cleared somewhat, a cry of dismay went up from the defenders. A nearby tower showed the Ottoman banner, signifying that they had entered the city. Actually it was only a small band that slipped into an unsecure door in that tower. They were trapped and close to annihilation, but their banner disheartened all the Byzantines and their allies. The wounding of the Genoan leader Longo had a similar effect. Word spread that the city was lost. It need not have been so yet, but once that word spread it was inevitable.

Nearby, Constantine XI, the last Eastern Roman Emperor, was good to his word. He threw off his imperial finery and charged into the breach with sword raised as another wave of Janissaries came on. He was never seen again.

Stone grabbed a torch and lit several wooden hoops aflame that he had stored nearby.

Alethea asked, "What are you doing?"

"Just a little trick I picked up from the Knights of Malta for this particular enemy," he told her.

With unerring precision, Stone tossed several of these burning rings of fire into the ranks of the onrushing Janissaries. Their tall turbans and flowing robes ignited right away and the fire spread freely amongst their tight ranks. Cries of bloodlust were quickly replaced by cries of torment. The afflicted men could not free themselves fast enough from their robes. In terror, these human infernos darted around madly and spread the flames to their fellows. Chaos caused the charge to lose its impetus for a few precious moments. A handful of others dodged the spreading flames unscathed and continued forward. These men were felled in quick succession by rocks smacking into their skulls, Stone's aim again proving flawless.

"They don't call me 'Stone' for nothing," he said under his breath.

But suitable stones were soon wanting, crossbow bolts were exhausted, and the flaming hoops were spent. Now the Janissaries were re-forming their ranks to press the charge forward again. This next wave he would have to meet with the sword. Such a close range engagement would be dangerous for Alethea. The city was now lost anyhow and Stone judged that it was time to leave. He took Alethea's hand and pulled her from the scene. She took one last look at her father and they fled the approaching horde.

"Don't worry for him," Stone said to her, referring to Gregos. "'The souls of the just are in the hand of God and no torment will touch them,'" he quoted.

They fled east down the avenue leading into the old city. Other defenders from the walls, realizing that the fight was lost, choked the road in their panicked flight. Stone dodged and weaved through them, dragging behind him the frightened Alethea who struggled to keep up. They were too far from the harbor and the roads in that direction too crushed with people to make a friendly galley in time. Some of these would escape since many Turkish sailors had abandoned their ships in favor of joining the rape and pillage in the city. They ran instead towards the old city where the buildings were more numerous and a hiding place might be found.

They ran for a couple of miles, past the old Constantinian wall, past the Forum of Arcadius and St. Athanasius Monastery. At the Forum of the Ox, Alethea stumbled and hit her knee hard on the stone road. She was too tired to maintain the frantic pace. Stone hefted her over his shoulder and was able to make even better time through the fearful crowds. The bells continued to peal, warning the populace and urging more prayer, but the minutes left for Constantinople as a Christian city were dwindling fast. The sun was fully up now and casting long morning shadows on this final morning of Byzantine rule.

The rest of the trip was a blur to Alethea and she mostly saw cobblestones from her vantage point atop Stone's shoulder. She recalled some of the churches they passed, the Forum of Tauri, a glimpse of the Great Nymphaeum on the city's Third Hill, the Forum of Constantine, and the old Hippodrome. At long last they reached piazza before the Hagia Sophia.

"Mother will be in there," Alethea said.

"Worst place to be; big fat target," Stone told her.

"There is a prophecy that the heathens will be turned back and not enter the basilica."

"Trust me, that prophecy is wrong. They have barred the doors and there is no time to search for your mother. We have to hide."

She wanted to argue but did not. Instead she asked, "Is this the end of the world?"

"No, not even close. But a page of history is certainly turning."

Stone found the humblest house he could find, an old one in disrepair in the shadow of the ruined Great Palace. The ancient home of the Byzantine Emperors was now empty except for the beautiful wall and floor mosaics. It had never been refurbished after the Latin conquest. Indeed the city's heyday was long behind it and the empire never had recovered from the Fourth Crusade.

The house was inhabited by a frightened family of four, an old couple and their two overweight sons. They were evidently a noble family but no longer prosperous. The two sons looked well fed enough but did not appear to have labored for the city's defense in any meaningful way. Stone disliked them immediately, and when one objected to his entry into the house his hand went to his sword. That ended the argument.

Stone reassembled the wooden door he had busted, but it would no longer serve as much of a barrier. The moans of despair outside grew and soon enough the sounds of the looting could be heard with the approach of the Turks. Women in particular could be heard screaming as they were brutally violated. Those who would fetch nothing at the slave markets were slain without mercy. Special attention was paid to the churches and monasteries for they held most of the riches the city still had. Of course many Turks had women and girls as their targets. Others went after boys.

Alethea found a corner and tried to shut out the din by pressing her hands against her ears, but it was no use. The others in the house looked stricken and terrified but said nothing. Soon their worst fears came true and Turkish soldiers reached the house. The ruined door proved no obstacle and a scimitar pointed through the doorway followed by an Anatolian infantryman. In a flash, Stone's blade had knocked his aside and found his throat which promptly spurted blood all over the entrance as the hapless man fell backwards.

Stone charged into the daylight in the street to confront the man's companions. He smiled at them, grateful for the opportunity. One of the keys to prevailing in these kinds of fights, he had found, was deep down someplace to actually enjoy it. Killing soldiers doing their duty was one thing, but he had a special dark place in his heart for rapists. Even during his career as an amnesiac Viking leader he had never permitted this.

There were only six of them but they all rushed him at once. No matter. He side-stepped the first to reach him, deflected the blade of the second into the third which forced him to parry the blow. He slashed at the back of his first attacker, the one who passed him as he dodged, and that man went down with a scream.

Stone wielded a hand-and-a-half sword, commonly called a 'bastard' sword. As the name implies, it could be used single handed or with both hands for extra power. Stone moved back and forth gracefully between styles as the situation warranted. Facing multiple opponents from multiple axis at first called for deft one handed fencing, but he would use both hands for a killing blow or to throw off an enemy's balance with a fierce parry.

Stone's steel flashed with a speed his adversaries could not match. In seconds one man lost his sword hand, another his head, another clutched his bleeding stump of a leg, and the last man was impaled through the chest and died instantly. The man who lost his hand ran away cradling his truncated arm and crying in agony.

Stone called after him, "Send all your friends! I can do this all day!"

For the sake of his charge, Stone would actually prefer to avoid attention. One of the fallen Turks had dropped a flag. The Turks were in the practice of hoisting their flag over the houses that were in the process of being looted so that other looters would move on to another target. Stone raised the Turkish flag over the house containing Alethea and jogged to the corner where he could see the piazza in front of the Hagia Sophia. The Sultan's standard had replaced that of the Emperor and the doors of the basilica lay open. Those inside had been roughly shoved outside into the sunlight. Poor looking worshippers, the very old and very young, infants included, were killed outright, but the more prosperous looking were kept for ransom and other uses.

Alexandra Christopoulos, the mother of Alethea, saw the treatment meted out to ladies like herself. She heard the horrible cries of the nuns being dragged from the convents and raped in the streets. She broke from the crowd and flung herself down a nearby well, a plummet guaranteed to be fatal. A couple of other noble ladies followed her example before the Turks blocked off that escape. Stone witnessed this sad spectacle and returned to the house.

"We might save ourselves by letting them have her," one of the chubby younger Greek men said, the one who had tried to oppose Stone's entry into the house. "The patriarch Lot did it in the Bible."

Stone entered at that moment. "You are not Lot and I am not God; I am far less merciful than He. I will feed you to the Turks piece by bloody piece if you make a move towards her. She is under my protection and you are not," he warned with a glare.

Stone sat next to Alethea and whispered to her the news about her mother. She began to weep and laid her head on his chest. He held her and whispered encouragement to her for the next hour as the din outside began to abate.

By noon the Sultan had complete control of the city. The looting was curtailed and order was being restored. Mehmet toured the Hagia Sophia and summoned an imam to issue the Islamic testament of faith, 'There is no god but Allah and Muhammad is the Prophet of Allah.' The basilica was now a mosque. Leaving the new Grand Mosque he toured the ruins of the Great Palace, a mere stone's throw from where Alethea sat weeping. He marveled at the abandoned building's decrepit state when once it had been so magnificent. The more recent emperors had used the far more modest palace of Blachernae. "The spider spins its web in Khusrau's hall, the owl plays his music in the palace of Afrasiyab," he said, quoting a Persian poet. At twenty-one years old he had fulfilled the ancient dream of the Prophet Muhammad to capture Constantinople. He was now Mehmet the Conqueror.

Killings were soon replaced by captures as the excitement of the city's fall gradually ebbed. In the uniform of one of the dead Turks, Stone had little trouble escorting Alethea through the city since it appeared that she was his prisoner. They made their way by boat to the Genoan colony of Galata on the other side of the harbor. The next galley that sailed west had them on it. Eventually they found passage to Venice, already the home of many Byzantine expatriates. Alethea had a great uncle there and Stone managed to deliver her safely to his home. This was the occasion for another tearful goodbye for Alethea who thanked Stone and wept briefly on his shoulder. He caressed her cheek and bade her farewell. Neither thought they would see the other again, but the Fates had other plans.

28 July 1480, Otranto, Italy

Mehmet the Conqueror considered his work only half done with the conquest of Constantinople. Rome still beckoned and with its subjugation he would reunite the broken Roman Empire under Islamic rule and deal a deadly blow to Christianity. Faith in that rival religion would surely be shaken when St. Peter's Basilica was taken and used as a stable for Ottoman horses. His fleet set out for the conquest of Italy and appeared before the sleepy Adriatic coastal town of Otranto with ninety galleys, fifteen galleasses, forty-eight lighter vessels and eighteen thousand troops.

Otranto was situated on the heel of the Italian 'boot' and under the rule of the combined Kingdom of Naples and Aragon. From there a large land force might roll up the peninsula and capture Rome and more, especially if a toe-hold could be grabbed quickly. The Turks counted on terror leading to the quick surrender of blocking fortresses. Otranto would prove to be a poor choice. Despite having no cannons and few provisions for sustaining a long siege, despite having only four hundred men to oppose the approaching eighteen thousand, Count Francesco Largo was determined to hold. He sent messengers north to warn of the danger and prepared to resist to his uppermost.

The former Alethea Christopoulos lived in Otranto. She had married her husband, a fellow Greek named Nestor Michaelides, in Venice in 1460. They had two sons, Gregos, aged fifteen, and Alexander, age eleven. In 1473 the family relocated to Otranto where Nestor plied his trade as a shipbuilder, a skill he had honed for years in the famous Arsenal of Venice. Now the Turks were paying Alethea another visit.

The Ottoman commander, Gedik Ahmed Pasha, sent a messenger to the garrison with the generous offer to spare the lives of the inhabitants if the city surrendered. This offer was refused. A second messenger was chased away with arrows. Finally, Count Francesco Largo had the keys to the city cast into the sea from a tall tower in full view of the Turks. There would be no surrender; Largo knew he needed to buy time for the rest of Italy to mobilize its defenses.

Not all were so brave and bold, however. That night, all but fifty of the four hundred Neapolitan soldiers abandoned their posts and fled the city, leaving it to its fate. Townspeople, including the Michaelides, volunteered to defend the town. Nestor took a place on the walls while Alethea assumed the familiar role of supply courier. She would also aid in boiling oil and water to dump on the attackers' heads. The two boys would also assist as messengers and with bringing up supplies.

The siege began in earnest on the twenty-ninth of July. Cannonballs smacked the walls of the city, terrifying the inhabitants. Alethea, as a veteran of the siege of Constantinople twenty-seven years before, was a great steadying influence on her neighbors. Her encouragement and quiet courage in the maelstrom boosted the morale of all who worked near her. Numerous times she braved enemy fire to assist her husband in dumping the boiling oil on Turks assaulting the wall. She silently asked God to forgive her for the grim pleasure she took at the pain this inflicted on the attackers. Between assaults, her leadership was important in dividing the rations and in finding objects to hurl down at the Turkish assaulters.

The siege stretched on for days, buying the crucial time Italy needed to prepare. Finally on the morning of August twelfth, the Ottoman guns battered a breach in the wall and the Turkish troops stormed in, killing anyone in their path. Nestor was one of those who met them with sword in hand and was cut down. The Turks killed their way to the cathedral and burst inside. There they found the congregants praying with Archbishop Stefano Agricoli, Bishop Pendinelli, and Count Largo. The soldiers demanded that the Archbishop renounce his faith in Christ and embrace Islam. He refused and they beheaded him on the spot. They demanded the same of Bishop Pendinelli and Count Largo. These two also refused and, to the horror of those gathered, were slowly sawed in half.

Alethea had not been in the cathedral, remembering what had happened at the Hagia Sophia, but she was soon rounded up anyway, along with everyone else in the hapless town. All were made to watch as every Christian symbol was torn out of the cathedral and destroyed. The church building itself was promptly made into a stable for the Turks' horses, as was their custom. As at Constantinople, the Turks proceeded to massacre the very old and very young since these had little value in slave markets. Thousands were slain and thousands of others were destined for slavery.

Eight hundred of the men of military age were separated from the others. Both of Alethea's sons, including young Alexander who was big for his age, were in this group. They were positioned in the center of the piazza and made to sit while the women who were headed for the slave markets, including their own mother, were guarded at the edge of the same piazza where they witnessed what came next. Gedik Ahmed Pasha, the Ottoman commander, stepped forward and introduced an Italian gentleman who then addressed the assemblage. He was a former priest who had renounced his faith in Christ and embraced Islam. For this action he had received many honors and benefits from his Turkish overlords and he bid his listeners do the same.

One of the Otranto men, a tailor named Antonio Primaldi, stood up and made his own address:

"My brothers, until today we have fought in defense of our country, to save our lives, and for our lords; now it is time that we fight to save our souls for our Lord, so that having died on the cross for us, it is good that we should die for him, standing firm and constant in the faith, and with this earthly death we shall win eternal life and the glory of martyrs."

The men of Otranto roared in agreement with him and seemingly with one voice proclaimed their fidelity to Christ, come what may. Pasha had them beaten into silence and taken away to a holding yard. The women were kept under guard in the piazza, the only space large enough to hold them all. The next morning, the roughly eight hundred men reemerged, a line of bound and bedraggled souls being led out of town by their captors. They were marched by the women. If the Turks had hoped that the women would plead with them to renounce their faith and save their lives, they were disappointed. The women instead encouraged the men to hold firm. Alethea, who had scarcely any chance to mourn her husband, was no exception. She managed to catch the eyes of Gregos and Alexander shortly before they were led out of sight. She yelled to them that she loved them and that they must stand firm in the faith.

The eight hundred were marched up the nearby Hill of Minerva. One by one, the Turks beheaded each of them, casting the heads and headless bodies off the stony cliff. It was a lengthy ordeal that gave most of them plenty of time to reconsider after seeing the fate of their fellows, yet not one pleaded for mercy. Their bodies were buried in a mass grave and the Turks prepared to leave. Time had been lost in the siege of Otranto. It was hoped that word of the slaughter would serve to terrorize the Italian populace into compliance.

Three days later, Alethea and a dozen other women were loaded onto a cart for a drive down to the pier where a galley would take them to a slave market somewhere in the Ottoman Empire. Alethea suspected that she would soon face the same choice her mother faced in Constantinople. She had no doubt that she would also choose death over life in a harem. Fortunately, most of the women had not been violated yet, the Pasha feeling the need to press his troops forward lest he get bottled up in the Apulian Peninsula. Only a small garrison had been left in Otranto and they had been too busy, so far, to have their way with the women.

Bound and gagged, they endured the bumpy road as the wooden wheels seemed to hit every uneven cobblestone to jar the cart occupants. Two Turkish soldiers drove the cart and four horsemen rode at each corner as escorts. After a bend in the wooded road, out of sight of either the garrison or the pier, the ambush began.

First, one of the trailing riders found a crossbow bolt in his throat. He made an ugly rasping sound before tumbling lifeless from his saddle. The other trailing rider saw his companion's misfortune and sounded the alarm. Before he could withdraw his sword from his scabbard, another bolt struck him in the chest and he followed his companion in death. The man riding 'shotgun' on the cart wheeled around and pointed to the woods to the left of the road. He let a bolt fly from his crossbow in that direction, but he was shooting blind. The other two horsemen rode over there to find the sniper while the cart sped on.

Stone sprang from the tree line with a halberd and quickly used it to unhorse the first rider and then spun it around with the blade facing down to stab the sprawling man in the gut. He withdrew it and launched it javelin-like at the second rider. This hit home in the man's side and he fell dead from his horse. Stone picked up his crossbow, loaded another quarrel into it, and quickly mounted the nearest horse to pursue the cart. He soon caught up with it as the cart had made little progress.

Stone and the 'shotgun' riding Turk exchanged bolts with their crossbows. The Turk's sailed high but Stone's hit the Turk's arm, forcing him to drop the crossbow. Stone withdrew his sword and hacked the man down before he could reach his with his wounded arm. The driver was yelling for help but saw that he could not outrace Stone so he released the reins and let the cart slow as he drew his own sword. He slashed his scimitar at Stone who parried it and lunged back. The man dodged it and slashed at the face of Stone's horse, frightening it so that it bucked. Stone dismounted and the Turk picked up the reins again, but the cart still moved too slowly and Stone caught up with him on foot. The two renewed the sword fight, the Turk slashing in desperation, trying to use his height advantage by fighting from atop the cart. Stone parried these blows and awaited an opening. Soon enough it came and his riposte disarmed the man. A follow-up two handed blow removed his head.

Stone took the reins and drove the cart several miles into the Apulian wilderness, away from any road a Turkish patrol might use. Finally they escaped enemy-held territory and Stone released the women from their bonds. They continued riding until evening when they reached a town far from the Turkish occupation. Stopping at an inn for the night, Stone and Alethea got to speak together at last.

"I am sorry for your husband and your sons; I came as soon as I heard," Stone began.

"Thank you. They lived and died as fine Christian gentlemen. Now they are with God, just like my parents. And once again you have rescued me and I am forever grateful. How did you find me? Why have you not aged in all these years?" She now appeared to be the same age as he.

"I am not like you. I am on a different path. Its course is not as straight and its pace is not the same, but we will all end up in the same place, I believe," he answered, if such could be considered an answer.

"I do not understand. You look no different from the way I remember you in Constantinople."

"I promised your father I would look after you and that promise never expired. Again, I wish I could have done more."

"God's will," she said stoically, looking far away. It was the 'thousand yard stare' Stone had seen on the faces of so many survivors of trauma.

She turned back to him, "Will the Turks take Rome as they took Constantinople?"

"No, I think the sacrifice of Otranto has bought enough time to defend the Eternal City. The Turks have lost their advantage and will not be able to keep their toehold on Italy. I will see to that myself, if need be. I have heard just about enough from Mehmet the Conqueror. This time he will not get away with it," he took her shoulders and looked her in the eye. "I promise. And you know I keep my promises."

She nodded in agreement and her eyes grew misty with tears. They spontaneously embraced and their lips met in a long, passionate kiss. A kiss would be all there would be between them, and it was one of farewell. Alethea was a pious woman who honored her husband. She would honor him always and remain chaste for the rest of her days in a nunnery. But she felt compelled, in that brief moment, to give that one kiss to the first man she had ever loved.

Stone left her some money to travel and then set on his own journey. True to his word, he later infiltrated the military camp of Mehmet the Conqueror. He employed his ability to alter his form and disguised himself perfectly as Mehmet's private physician. No one ever discovered who it was that had poisoned the mighty conqueror, but he died suddenly at the age of forty-nine while plotting his next conquest.

Ahmed Pasha could not supply a large force in Italy indefinitely and withdrew all but the garrison at Otranto with the intention of renewing the campaign from there the following year. A combined Neapolitan and Hungarian force crushed that garrison and retook Otranto before he could return. Bayezid won the power struggle that ensued after Mehmet's death and Ahmed Pasha supported the winner. Another 'black op' by Stone planted evidence of treason on him, however, and Bayezid promptly had him executed. Within a little over a year since the massacre at Otranto, the Conqueror and the Pasha, who was his instrument, had both been dispatched to the next life for their final judgments. Alethea, for one, was able to rest more easily and devote the remainder of her life to prayer and good works, any thirst for vengeance having been quenched by her protector's intervention.

5 February 1900

Stone had omitted the gory details about the many deaths in the story. He did not mention the rape and pillage that took place. Nor did he mention his own involvement in the deaths of Mehmet and Ahmed. The tale was thus sanitized somewhat for the benefit of the young listeners. He did not tell them of the incredible kiss with Alethea, either. That transpired well before he had married their mother, but they would not understand. They sat spellbound through the telling of the edited story regardless.

"I hate the Turks! We should kill them!" Gideon announced.

"I like your spirit, but you have learned the wrong lesson," Stone told him. "The thing to learn from the martyrs of Otranto is that it is better to lose your head than your soul. I hope the two of you will grow to have the courage of your convictions and never compromise them. As for the Turks or anyone else, we don't hold all to account for the actions of a few. Ideas we may hate, but persons we only punish if they merit it for themselves.

At a place called Gallipoli, in a war yet to come from your standpoint, soldiers from far away Australia and New Zealand will invade Turkey and many will die there along with many Turks. The Turks win the battle, but the victorious Turkish commander will pay tribute to his fallen enemies when he says:

'Those heroes that shed their blood and lost their lives: – You are now living in the soil of a friendly country, – therefore rest in peace. There is no difference between the Johnnies and the Mehmets to us where they lie side by side here in this country of ours. You, the mothers, who sent their sons from faraway countries – wipe away your tears; your sons are now lying in our bosom, – and are in peace. After having lost their lives on this land they have become our sons as well.'"

"I suppose I don't hate all Turks," Gideon allowed.

"Good man. Now the two of you need to say your prayers and get some sleep."

As his children drifted off peacefully to enjoy the sleep of the just, Stone reflected on the strength of Alethea who watched first her parents, then her husband and children die. She bore it bravely and, while not without some bitterness, did not let hate control her life. In choosing to love Isis, Stone had left himself vulnerable to human emotion. Threats to her were disturbing to him, the thought of losing her seemingly unbearable. Their love had been fruitful and that emotional concern was magnified even more in regard to their children. The idea of harm coming to them was unthinkable, yet humans endured this ever-present fear all the time. He thought his species was the stronger, but now he had to reconsider his opinion. His kind was stronger in some ways, but certainly not in every way.

29 AUGUST 2005

Anonymous New Orleans memoir:

It seemed that the world was ending. Yes, I knew that the disaster was local. In the back of my mind I was aware that the rest of the world would carry on no matter what happened here. In fact I counted on that, having sent my wife and son to her parents' home in Tennessee. But here and now, with Hurricane Katrina landing a perfect uppercut on the chin of New Orleans and the surrounding area, the calamity seemed utter and complete. The levee had broken and the waters were rising. New Orleans lay famously below sea level. The failure of the levee was now making that bit of trivia a more salient feature of life here, to put it mildly. We had always dodged the bullet of the perfect storm, but with Katrina we took one right between the eyes.

The great city was fallen, a fall as great as any to a foreign invader. Indeed the criminal element within was taking advantage of the chaos and the looting spree was on. This irked me as I was law enforcement. I'd been with the NOPD for ten years. I was taking today off, though. No one was invading the sanctity of our home. I would save what I could from the rising flood waters and the rampaging hoodlums. The city was doomed; I was looking after my own. That much at least I could do. The city was beyond my ability to help. It was the god that failed. The levees should have held but didn't. The gods had made their judgment against us and our lives would never be the same. The disgusting floodwaters would ruin everything not burned or looted by the thugs running loose in the streets.

My conscience troubled me, though. What would Sergeant Stone say if he saw me? My FTO held me to high standards. No doubt he would be disappointed in me, but then he left the NOPD without hardly a word to anyone. He just up and vanished one day, never to return to work. Apparently something came up in his personal life so he had to split. Maybe he was dead. In any case, I struggled to put him out of my mind.

There was a knock at the door. I got my shotgun ready. It was an odd time for a polite knock at the door. With all the chaos outside, I doubted it was the neighbors wanting to borrow some sugar. Most likely it was a thief checking to make sure that no one was home.

I looked through the peep hole and saw the powder blue shirt of a fellow NOPD officer. His face was turned back to the street so I could not tell who it was. How the hell did he get here with all the flooding? With the phone lines down and cell service gone, was the department actually sending people out to check on the homes of its absent cops? You'd think they'd have other priorities. I considered not answering, but I wasn't hiding. I opened the door to confront my fellow officer.

To my utter astonishment, I opened the door and found myself face-to-face with Stone. My mouth fell open as if to speak, but I said nothing as his critical eye looked me up and down.

"You aren't in uniform," he observed testily.

"No. I'm not going in today," I said defensively, but my words had none of the conviction when spoken that they had in my head.

"That's funny because I've commuted an unimaginably long way so that I *could* be here to go to work today," he dripped with sarcasm.

"What the hell? You've been missing for like eight years or something and now you just show up out of nowhere as if you never left? As if it was just another work day!"

"No, I'm well aware that today is not like other days," he lectured me like a slow student. "That is why I have come so far to be here. The city needs me. It needs you, too, so get your damned uniform on double-quick!"

"Take a look around. There is no 'city' anymore. It's hopeless out there. What the hell can the two of us do?"

"If we save only one life we will have done a great thing." I had no retort to that so he let it sink in before going on.

"You don't put on that badge to write parking tickets and collect your paycheck. You are to protect and serve. You are the thin blue line of law and order that defends civilization against the very forces of chaos and evil. Right now those forces have the upper hand, but that is when you are needed most. This isn't the day you call in sick! Not all of our NOPD brethren are covering themselves with glory this day. Some, sad to say, are even on the side of chaos, but others are fighting the good fight and if we have a shred of honor left we must help them." He spoke with more passion than I recall him having before. Of course things had never been this dire.

He paused and went on, "There are old people trapped in their attics who won't last unless someone extracts them. There are patients languishing on the upper floors of hospitals that have no power. There is looting and thugs are taking potshots at police and rescue workers. People all over are stranded with little drinkable water. There is a ton to do. Now, I know where there is boat we can borrow. You get your uniform on and I'll brief you on some of the specifics I know…" he continued on as if not even considering that I might refuse.

I didn't. He continued to fill me in on the makeshift headquarters at Harrah's Casino and other operational details as I dressed. In a few minutes we were out of the door and on duty. I followed behind him and took his lead even though we were now the same rank and he wasn't technically even with the department anymore. No matter. We did a lot of good that day and for the rest of that week, rescuing lots of folks and stopping numerous crimes in progress while running on virtually no sleep and little food. It was the worst and best week of my life. When the worst was over and order was being restored, he said farewell and I didn't see him again; he did his disappearing act like some kind of ghost. I suppose it adds to his legend.

Later I realized that he did not return only to save storm victims trapped in attics, although that was, of course, very important. He also returned to save me, to inspire me to be the best version of myself. Thank God he was successful. I can continue to wear the badge with pride, my honor intact. That is a debt I can never repay.

THE FUNERAL OF
SERGEANT STONE

Lilith escaped destruction in the black hole, albeit by a narrower margin than had Stone whose own escape had been perilous enough. That had been her best ploy to destroy him, even if it would have meant destroying herself in the process. If Stone would not cooperate, if he would reject her, then destruction should be his fate and she cared not for her own survival if that is what it took. But she had played her best card and fallen short. Prior to that he had proved too much for her in single combat in spite of her rage-fueled attacks. She would need help for her next attempt on his life. Fortunately, willing partners abounded since Stone had made many enemies. He had destroyed an entire universe and isolated another in his detonation of the Cosmic Eraser. Survivors of those universes who had been traveling elsewhere when the Eraser hit were looking for revenge. That was why Stone laid low in New Orleans and its null region which made him impossible to detect from afar. But now his location was known and all she had to do was locate some of those enemies of his...

15 March 1908, New Orleans

"What is the importance of the Ides of March?" Isis asked Stone, linking arms with him after stepping off the St. Charles streetcar.

"The day they knocked off Big Julie, or Julius Caesar as he is more commonly known," Stone explained. "For once I had taken a day off for the festival of Jupiter. Bad things often seem to happen when I am off duty," he said, deliberately avoiding any reference to the assassination of New Orleans Police Chief David Hennessy, who was killed during their honeymoon. "Hopefully nothing bad will happen on this Ides of March while I am off duty."

So far it seemed to be going well. Stone had the day off and wore his finest suit while escorting his lovely wife Isis to a fine dinner and show. She was dressed to the nines in the latest fashion and looked terrific. The kids, Cassandra and Gideon, sixteen and fourteen respectively, were old enough to watch themselves and their grades in school so far were very good. Isis' long cherished desire to see the completion of the Chalmette Monument obelisk commemorating the Battle of New Orleans was finally coming to pass, so there was much to celebrate. Stone and Isis strolled contentedly down Canal Street towards Baronne, blending well enough into the crowd even though she was a princess from ancient Egypt and he an extra-dimensional alien. New Orleans was the type of city in which this odd couple did not appear odd at all since so many strange characters from so many places drifted through here.

They spotted their destination, the fourteen story Grunewald Hotel, and crossed Canal Street, dodging a couple of horseless Cadillac Runabout automobiles to do so. Most of the streets were paved now, a drastic improvement. The electric lights were improved, too, and had completely replaced gas lamps in the city. Isis had now lived in New Orleans for twenty years and she had seen remarkable changes in that time. It was all muddy streets, gas lights, and horse-drawn buggies when she had arrived. The horse-propelled vehicles were not so different from the chariots she knew in Egypt. These new engines, however, were a marvel she never would have imagined. Even these paled next to the new flying machines, or aeroplanes as they were called. Truly an age of wonders.

They reached the front of the hotel; the façade was not particularly impressive except for its height. The doorman opened the door for them to proceed inside, Stone acknowledging him with a nod. Isis caught her breath. The interior, in stark contrast to the ordinary concrete exterior, was magnificent. Marble floors and columns drew the eye up to the ornately carved wooden ceilings inlaid with gold leaf and illuminated by crystal chandeliers. It surpassed anything in the pharaoh palaces of her youth.

She glimpsed the main dining room, which was decorative enough, but Stone led her beyond it to a staircase that led downwards from the lobby to what was apparently the basement. Reaching the end of the stairs and turning the corner she spied the sign over the entrance to the next room. 'The Cave' it said, and the name was apt. Across the threshold the massive dining room turned into what appeared to be an underground cavern complete with stalactites reaching down from the ceiling and, amidst the tables and chairs, occasional stalagmites reaching upwards. In certain places, probably where they could be load bearing as well as decorative, these rocky protuberances met in the middle to form pillars. The lamps were low to preserve the cave effect and to set the mood. Somewhere there was the sound of water rushing. Isis' eyes searched out the sound and, surely enough, there was an indoor waterfall to further set the mood. There was a stage, too. It was occupied by a band doing their set up and part remained open for dancers.

"This is man-made?" she had to ask. The doubt in her voice indicated that she was not certain that the hotel did not just happen to be located over an actual cavern. The terrain of New Orleans made that unlikely.

"Remarkable, isn't it? They spared no expense to achieve the effect. Word has it that Louis Grunewald trucked in 700,000 pounds of plaster and cement to make this room look like the Mammoth Cave in Kentucky. I felt I owed it to him to come see it after so much effort. Do you like it?"

"It is fantastic," she smiled, squeezing his arm. Presently the host confirmed their reservations and showed them to their table.

Isis' delight was even greater when the band started playing jazz, a new musical form that was developing in New Orleans and beginning to spread around the country. It made Isis want to move her body more than any other music she had heard, but she controlled herself and listened from her seat. A line of chorus girls did a good bit of dancing on her behalf on the stage.

Between music sets and after the crawfish etouffee was finished, she leaned over to Stone and said, "Thank you for this. I needed a night out."

"Least I could do; you've given me seven happy years of marriage," he winked.

Isis did the quick math. "We've been married for over seventeen years!"

"Yes, total. So seven happy is not too bad," he chuckled. She feigned anger and then smiled.

"So, seventeen years and two children. It seems that our relationship is starting to get serious." She was learning to tease back.

"Here is to the next seventeen," he said, raising his wine glass.

She smiled broadly and joined him in the toast, "To the next seventeen years."

In a reality outside human-perceived space-time…

Lilith had little difficulty making contact with Commonwealth agents. Security was not as tight with the end of the war. She went straight to a dimension they dominated and soon found a planet that contained one of their overt headquarters. She explained to the personnel there that she had valuable intelligence of interest and they escorted her to an entirely different dimension for debrief. She soon found herself before Demetrius and Drusus, two uninteresting Commonwealth security bureaucrats.

"I have found something that you have lost," she replied confidently when Demetrius asked her to state her business.

"And what have we lost?" he asked.

"You remember the creature who ended the war for you, surely. Stone. I ran into him," she said almost nonchalantly.

"Ran into someone who resembled him, perhaps?" Demetrius offered.

"No, I know him. I am of his kind. There is no mistake."

"Stone was sealed inside a pocket universe forever. He could not have escaped. He will rot there until he eventually dies," Drusus explained.

"Well, if you are so certain I guess we have nothing to talk about." Before their eyes, Lilith transformed herself into an exact likeness of Demetrius, her flowing blonde locks melting away to be replaced by the buzz cut of the agent opposite her. When she spoke again, the voice was a match for his as well, only her clothing remained the same. "But I am telling you that I found him and whomever is locked in that pocket universe is not he. Let me guess, he went in with someone else into your limbo dimension, perhaps as part of a last request, and that someone else emerged later, right?" Demetrius shifted uncomfortably. "It is what I would have done."

"Melchior," Drusus murmured.

"Let me guess again," Lilith/Demetrius continued, "this Melchior later vanished." Drusus nodded in the affirmative. Actually several of Stone's adversaries met with accidents before 'Melchior' did his disappearing act. Drusus would have been in that number if Stone had known of his treachery. Drusus was still a mole who maintained contact with what remained of the Syndicate. That remnant would want revenge on Stone. Drusus, in the interest of self-preservation, would like to see them get it.

Lilith reverted to her true form and continued, "He broke your laws. He detonated a weapon you wanted for yourselves, wiping out an entire universe and sealing off all passage to and from another," Lilith reminded them.

"Yes, the strike that defeated the Syndicate and won the war for us," Demetrius observed.

"But you condemned him."

"There are those of us who believe that was an error," Demetrius stated flatly. Drusus looked sideways at Demetrius when he said this, but Demetrius went on, "We are not interested in pursuing him, even if he is out there, and the case is closed."

Lilith was boiling with rage on the inside but bit her tongue. She rose quickly to leave. "Sorry to have wasted your time," she said through gritted teeth, but she was not sorry. She was angry that she had wasted her own.

"Good day," Demetrius replied to her back as she departed the office.

Drusus rose as well. "Excuse me, sir. I must finish the report on the incident in Dimension 42T."

"Yes, thank you for assisting with that interview, short though it was," Demetrius said. He did not add that Drusus' help had been neither requested nor required.

After Drusus departed, Demetrius placed a call via his telepathic link headset to the non-corporeal agent, Aurora. As she had no solid form, she made an excellent spy.

"Aurora," he said through the mind link. Had she been nearby he might not have needed it, but the headset greatly extended his range to communicate with her.

"Yes?" she answered.

"I need you back at HQ right away. There is a woman who is just leaving," Aurora could see Demetrius' mental image of her. "I want you to follow her and report on her activities."

"On it," Aurora replied.

This Commonwealth planet was protected by jamming screens which prevented inter-dimensional transport of the type she preferred. She was compelled to buy a ticket on a transport spacecraft off-world so that she could get to where she wanted to go. She knew there were others interested in payback against Stone, but many were laying low themselves and it would take time to find them. Or perhaps not.

Drusus sat beside her in the waiting area. "I thought we might continue our discussion away from my superior's ears. You and I have a common interest which he does not share," he said with a grin. Lilith grinned back. Aurora observed all but was not observed herself.

30 June 1908, 1100 hours, New Orleans

Since 1897, prostitution had been legal in one 16 square block section of New Orleans known as Storyville. Named for the alderman who wrote the legislation that created it, Sidney Story, Storyville was commonly called 'The District' by most locals. The idea was that vice would be confined to one part of the city and well regulated to keep organized crime from dominating it and leading to violence. There were plenty of districts, but when one said simply, 'The District', Storyville was understood. Stretching from Iberville to St. Louis and from North Robertson to North Basin, it encompassed St. Louis Cemetery Number 1 and was adjacent to the French Quarter, forming its northern boundary just as the Mississippi River bounded it on the south.

'The District' housed the most ornately decorated pleasure palaces with the most expensive ladies of the night on the high end and lower class whore houses, known as 'cribs', on the other. A directory was published and available for purchase. This guide, called "The Blue Book," offered details on every prostitute that worked in The District to include her address, price, racial category (white, octoroon, quadroon, mulatto, black, etc.), any musical talents, and other pertinent qualities.

The nicer bordellos also offered fine musical entertainment. New forms of music were being brought into existence here. Talented, freestyling musicians were under no constraints in The District and their experiments with improvisation and syncopated rhythms soon yielded the musical form known as jazz. Many of the best early jazz musicians got their start right here in Storyville, playing piano, trumpet, clarinet, trombone, and so on. Jelly Roll Morton began his career in a Storyville brothel. When his grandmother found out, he was turned out of her house, leading him to begin his grand tour. Joe "King" Oliver was making the new sound at the Pete Lala "sporting house" and a young Louis Armstrong, who was delivering coal there, was listening. Soon enough, Oliver would mentor him in music and the rest is history.

Stone had all of this on his mind the night when summoned to The District by Detective Harriman. He rather enjoyed the music he could hear as he patrolled Storyville. But music was not the only thing on his mind. On this very day in faraway Siberia, he would come hurtling through the atmosphere ahead of the giant explosion known as the Tunguska Event. It had that name because it was unexplained by human science. Stone knew what it was since he had unleashed it. It was the last gasp of the Cosmic Eraser that he had detonated in a distant universe. Opening dimensional portals before himself in rapid succession to avoid the onrushing destructive energy, Stone thus directed its path to sever all connections between the Syndicate's home universe and every other. That done, he then let the destructive wave enter a universe that was home to a despicable race of predatory beings that existed only to feed on other sentient life forms, with humans being one of their favorite menu items. Here the Cosmic Eraser spent itself, erupting through Stone's last portal over 1908 Siberia with Stone himself barely escaping. That is, if crashing into the ground with meteoric velocity could be considered an escape. Stone winced at the memory. The long and short of it was that Stone was, if only briefly, now on Earth in two places at the same time. This was something that happened on occasion but which he consciously avoided because of the attention it drew. The Tunguska Event was already of interest to those inter-dimensional parties whose causes had suffered due to the Cosmic Eraser's detonation. In short, Stone's null zone hiding spot in New Orleans was now less secure than ever and at a time when he had more than ever to protect as a family man.

Miss Lulu White's Mahogany Hall was one of the higher class sporting houses in The District, if the word 'class' could be applied at all. The girls were considered to be of the highest quality, the music the most delightful, and the ornate interior the most elaborately decorated in all of Storyville. It was to this address, an impressive four story structure on Basin Street, that Detective Harriman had summoned him. Harriman was a long time veteran and a very competent detective, competent enough to know when he was in over his head. On the rare occasions when that occurred, he sent for Sergeant Stone, the lowly beat cop who artfully dodged promotion but who was informally the best homicide detective in the NOPD.

The police had the building cordoned off and one of the younger detectives, Fitzmorris, was questioning Miss Lulu White herself in the street outside. She was bedecked in fine jewels and an expensive dress, but what struck Stone was the look of abject horror on her face as she struggled to answer the detective's questions while stifling tears. She did not cry easily.

Stone was recognized and ushered in. Corporal Henderson led him up to the fourth floor ballroom, the most expensively decorated with marble floors and European furniture. Detective Harriman met him there and led him to the threshold of one of the bedrooms.

"I've preserved the crime scene as best I could. I wanted you to see this," he said.

"Thanks," Stone muttered.

"You won't thank me after you see it."

Stone stepped in and instantly understood the comment. The pool of blood covered the entire bedroom floor, making the marble slippery in the extreme. Blood splatters were on the floor and bed sheets and ceiling. On the floor were the two bodies, the prostitute and her john. Both of them had their heads and limbs severed and placed neatly around their trunks. This was the calling card of an old enemy, one Stone hoped had been permanently vanquished.

The last time he saw such a crime scene was in Boston in 1692. The entity in question fed not only on its victims but took delight in spreading chaos and fear. The one in Massachusetts was pleased to prey upon colonists so that they would blame the Indians and on the Indians so that they would blame the colonists, thus instigating retaliatory massacres by both sides. But that wasn't all; it was also pleased to spread fear of witches by its supernatural appearances in Salem, thus provoking the notorious trials. Stone chased that monster all the way to Jamaica where the energy unleashed by its violent demise caused the quake which devastated Port Royal.

The creature was one of a species that inhabited a dimension which paralleled that of Earth. They frequently crossed over to prey upon humans or abducted them to feed on them on their side. Isis was lured there but Stone crossed over to snatch her back, a very risky operation he barely survived. Their predations grew worse because they managed to influence twenty-third century Earth scientists to break down the barrier between the two dimensions. Stone averted that in the nick of time, but only at the cost of killing the scientists, a necessary solution which still troubled him. Billions would have been victimized by those monsters had he not acted promptly. When he detonated the Cosmic Eraser which sealed off the Syndicate from the rest of the multiverse, he made sure he directed its energy to also destroy the home universe of those disgusting slime beings. Unfortunately, at least one of them had been away from home when he did so. The handiwork of what could only be a surviving member of that wicked species lay before him on the floor of a New Orleans whore house. The odds of this calling card being here in his town on this day was either an astronomical coincidence or it was a message for him. Stone had not believed in coincidences in centuries.

"Witnesses?" Stone asked.

"No one was seen exiting the room. No one even heard any screams; they must have both been killed very quickly," Harriman sighed.

The prostitute had been a lovely and popular octoroon while the john was a prominent donor to Mayor Behrman's campaigns.

"What about the alley under the window? Any witnesses that way?"

"Not in the alley itself, but where it crosses the street, one kid saw a huge—"

"Black dog," Stone cut him off.

"Yes. How did you guess that?" Harriman was astonished.

"You were right to call me and it is not your fault that you struggled to find clues. I have seen the like of this crime before and only I can deal with it. You would be well advised to keep this one under wraps lest it spread panic, needless panic since I will make sure it doesn't happen again."

"Just what do you suggest?"

"Be creative. Jealous lover whacked them both. Leave out the gory details. Anything but the truth. I hate to say that, but it is essential. Now I must track this thing quickly," he rose to leave.

"The dog?" Harriman asked.

"I think you know it is no mere canine."

"What is it, then?" the detective asked with a shudder. He was not a coward, but this was beyond his experience.

"Something terrible that our penal system cannot handle. It will take too long to explain now," Stone went to the window and looked out. He turned back to the perplexed detective, "Sorry to leave you with cryptic nonsense, but I have to go. Hopefully I will see you again and explain more. Privately. Good luck," he said as he hopped out the fourth story window, landing on his feet with a thud before taking off at a trot.

Stone was on its trail. The creature left small traces of inter-dimensional energy behind like a trail of breadcrumbs, a trail only Stone could see. He trotted back to his motorcycle, a 1,000 cc two-cylinder 1908 Torpedo Tank road bike. Weighing only 120 pounds, it was a state of the art racer for its day and could reach a then-impressive 65 mph. Stone pushed it near to this speed now, zooming west down Basin Street. The trail was faint and growing fainter. If he did not hurry he might lose it. It turned sharply left on Canal Street and so did he, dodging in between two crossing streetcars as he did so. The trail slowly became easier to discern as he progressed to the creature's more recent steps. Unfortunately, the trail stopped cold at the riverfront. Stone knew the feeling of a bloodhound that has lost its scent; the energy band that only Stone could see was lost in the swirling water of the river.

Stone would have to do something he dreaded and travel to the West Bank. There he hoped to reacquire the trail, but time was of the essence. The Canal Street ferry was just pulling away. Damn! It was the last one of the night. Even if he could find some other transport and stumbled on the right spot once getting to the other bank, there was no guarantee that the trail would still be discernible. He found he could not teleport himself across in the right timeframe to pick up the trail, either. He was stuck with terrestrial means. Stone looked about, hoping for a solution to present itself.

One did, but it was not what he would have hoped. At the riverfront was a partially collapsed dock, the victim of an unscrupulous boat pilot some months back. The ferry would pass it in a few seconds. If Stone negotiated the obstacles just right and hit the upward pointing timbers with enough speed, the unintentional ramp might give him the distance to land on the ferry, just like in so many bad films that Hollywood would later make.

It was now or never. He gunned the engine and the bike surged forward. Confused onlookers murmured to themselves or pointed, but he paid them no heed, focusing on building just the right amount of momentum. If Evel Kneivel could do it…but then Evel didn't always make it. Jumping into the Mississippi while bound in manacles, Houdini had almost killed himself near here back in November, Stone recalled as the engine kicked into high gear with a loud whine.

He zipped past some unwary dockworkers and saw almost too late that the damaged section was cordoned off with a rope at waist height. With no way to jump, Stone laid the bike on its side and slid underneath the rope, righting himself after passing beneath it. He made it but now had to regain the speed he had lost. Gunning the engine again, he hit the broken, upward tilting timbers and hoped for the best. Within seconds he was airborne and destined to come down either with a crash on the ferry's deck or with a splash in the unforgiving waters of the Mississippi.

Stone sailed through the air for what seemed like a full minute, but it actually took no more than four seconds. He landed on the ferry deck with both wheels planting hard just inside the guardrails. Ferry passengers spilled in every direction to avoid the flying motorbike. Stone lost control on impact and he and the bike kept rolling forward in separate directions.

The opposite guardrail stopped the bike from riding into the river. Stone dusted himself off and switched off the engine. His luck was holding and the bike was still serviceable. Some of the passengers glared at him but none challenged him. He was in uniform and armed, after all.

One young man exclaimed, "That was the greatest thing I've ever seen!"

"It was the worst! I was trying to jump the whole river," he winked. Then he turned serious and warned, "Don't try it at home, kid. I'm a trained professional," he lied. He had never done anything so silly in all his countless years. But the situation had never justified it before.

The agonizingly slow ferry crossing gave him time to think. In spite of New Orleans' status as a null region where it was relatively safe for inter-dimensional fugitives to lay low, Stone had had very little trouble on that front. But then that was because most of them, even the malevolent ones, wanted to *lay low*. They did not commit such gruesome crimes for fear of drawing attention. A few years ago, Stone had a run-in with one troublemaker who used his telekinetic abilities to dazzle some followers and his telepathic powers to make a few into zombie slaves as he masqueraded as a Voodoo wizard. Who knew why? Perhaps he just enjoyed exerting power over weaker beings. That was something Stone detested. In any case, Stone convinced him after a short, sharp struggle to leave the planet for good and that was that. He had some initial trouble when the guy heaved heavy objects at him remotely with his telekinesis, but once Stone fought past that and belted him, he folded pretty quickly.

This confrontation would not be concluded so easily. These creatures were both wicked and powerful. It was not fleeing because it was afraid but because it was luring Stone into a trap. Doubtless it sought revenge for the destruction of its home universe. Stone was not sure if it chose the date of Tunguska for symbolism or because that event actually made the creature's travel here easier. He was sure that the grisly murder was but a ploy to lure Stone out for the chase, and Stone would chase this thing until it caught him. In ordinary police procedure he would call for backup with such an obvious trap, but none of his 1908 NOPD coworkers could be any help; they would only be victimized, too. Nor could he choose not to pursue this thing since it would keep killing until he did. He had little choice but to spring the trap on himself and deal with it the best he could.

Finally the ferry landed at Algiers on the Mississippi's west bank and disgorged its last passengers of the night. Stone sped off in search of the trail of 'bread crumbs' and found it with little difficulty. If there had been any doubt about whether this was a trap, it was gone now. There was no reason the creature had to climb back onto dry land so near the ferry landing unless it wanted to be followed. Stone sped the bike down Seguin Street which terminated at Verret. He followed the trail to the right for several blocks until it became Hancock. The trail continued on that street, leading into the small town of Gretna. With every mile, the trail became more discernible and easier to follow, allowing him to move faster.

The trail departed Hancock at a rail intersection and followed the tracks instead. Stone paralleled the train tracks as the trail headed west out of Gretna. With the town's lights behind him and the lights of New Orleans on the other side of the river, the night was dark indeed, but this only made the trail even easier to follow. Tracking this thing was not the hard part. Dealing with it when he caught it, on the other hand…

The tracks went over the Harvey Canal by way of a bridge. On the west side of the bridge, the trail departed the train tracks and turned south to parallel the canal instead. The night grew darker yet as the city lights receded. Now the tracking task became quite boring as the trail simply ran south alongside the canal for several miles. This area was sparsely populated and no gas stations were to be found. Was this thing headed for the Gulf of Mexico? He dreaded having to follow it by sea the way he had to follow its cousin in 1692.

Finally the trail veered west away from the canal along a lonely dirt road. He followed it and dreaded the long walk back to the city since the bike would not have the gas for the return trip. Should there be a return trip, he reminded himself. These creatures were so dangerous that his survival was far from certain. After a few more miles down the dark and desolate road, the trail, now fresher than ever, broke off into the woods. No, not woods. Swamp. There was some moonlight, but Stone's night vision was superb anyway. By it he could see where the creature had disturbed the pond scum as it passed through the bayou. Stone abandoned the bike and silently wished for better footwear. He started into the bog, careful to dodge the 'knees' of the cypress trees that jutted up through the water of the bayou. These ubiquitous knobby protuberances spread out around each tree and were yet another hazard to footing in the treacherous bog. His feet stuck in the marshy mud and his progress was slow. He was getting bogged down in the bog, he thought to himself amusedly. An alligator darted away off to his right. The mud made an unappealing 'schlup' sound every time he pulled his foot up for the next step. The swamp's stench of death intensified in his nostrils with every arduous step he took that disturbed the slimy mud. Isis would probably refuse to do his laundry this time as the mud was thick and smelly on his lower legs.

Gradually the ground firmed up as he came out of the bog to an island in the bayou. Here at least one could walk normally aside from the still numerous cypress 'knees' and palmettos almost everywhere. The trail was at its terminus at last. He could see the silhouette of the creature ahead in the darkness. All the way from Basin Street in The District this thing ran down here to a swamp in the middle of nowhere. Not a bad spot for an ambush, Stone thought. He felt the others approach before one of them spoke.

"Thank you for joining us on such short notice," one of the approaching figures said.

There were four in total now. Stone recognized the speaker as Severus, his opponent from the dogfight over 1920 Warsaw. With him was Drusus, the intelligence briefer who had sent him on that mission, a mission which had been blown. So Drusus was the mole. Also present was Grendel, the slime being that had tortured Stone after his capture. Unfortunately it had survived Stone's repulse. The fourth was, of course, the canine creature Stone had pursued and whom he called Anubis for its resemblance to the Egyptian jackal god. Not present was Severus' former partner in crime Nimrod, as he had been killed when pursuing Stone into the universe where Stone subsequently detonated the Cosmic Eraser. Four opponents and each of them was singly a match or nearly so for Stone. Make that five. A non-corporeal was there now to prevent Stone from jumping to another dimension and getting away. He recognized her: Jezebel. So she had survived the demise of the Syndicate as well. She would also have a personal ax to grind since her friend Morgana was killed by the same explosion that killed Nimrod. Stone had developed a counter-tactic since his run-in with Morgana wherein she secretly sapped his strength, so Jezebel would not be able to duplicate that feat. She would succeed in suppressing his travel, however, since he would not be able to overpower her while battling the four others. The ambush was well planned.

"You've assembled my fan club," Stone observed.

"We felt you deserved it," Severus replied.

"You didn't bring enough firepower," Stone warned through gritted teeth.

"Oh, I disagree. We have more than enough to see you to the next life."

"I have friends there. I'll introduce you to them..."

Isis woke with a start in the upstairs bedroom of the Stone family residence on St. Charles Avenue. She had been having a nightmare that her husband was in mortal danger, but that was not what woke her. No, she felt a malignant presence nearby. Fumbling for the electric lamp, she finally found it and switched it on. The dark room was suddenly bathed in light. Sure enough, a stranger sat in the chair in the far corner. Isis caught her breath but suppressed the urge to yell out.

"Greetings," the woman said. She had a flawless face framed by long, blonde hair. She would have been beautiful if not for the devilish smile she wore.

"Who are you and why are you in my home?" Isis demanded, springing out of bed and onto her feet.

"Fair questions. My name is Lilith and I am here for revenge. Did Stone never tell you about me, the other woman? I just wanted to meet you before your death. And his."

"He is not here; if you've come to kill him, you are too late."

"Oh, I know where he is. Do you? I came here to kill you," she stood from the chair, "and I will deal with him shortly."

Isis needed a weapon, but the handgun was in the end table on Stone's side of the bed and she likely would not reach it in time. Her husband always taught her to be cognizant of handy weapon alternatives. Sharp shears in the sewing table? Too far. Improvise, adapt, and overcome, Stone was always telling her. She reached down and grabbed the leg of the end table and snapped it off with a quick jerk. It broke unevenly and came off with a sharp point. She now had an improvised short spear with which to defend herself and her children who were also in the house.

Lilith laughed. "Oooh, a pointed stick. I think I'll make you swallow it before you die."

Cassandra and Gideon burst through the door having heard the crash of the table and the voices. It took them but a moment to size up the situation through their still clearing eyes.

"I didn't know we had a guest, Mother," Cassandra said drily. She had her father's wit.

"Offspring. You gave him half-breed abominations! Disgusting," Lilith spat.

"Our guest has poor manners, Mother. Shall I instruct her?" Gideon did not want to be outdone by his sister's sarcasm.

Lilith lunged forward, intent on killing them all. Before she moved a full step Gideon tackled her with such force that he crashed Lilith through the exterior wall of the house.

"Get Mom out," he called over his shoulder as he and Lilith fell into the backyard.

Cassandra did not argue. She did not have their father's strength as Gideon did, but she had something he did not. She placed a hand on her mother's shoulder and the two of them vanished in an instant. The girl had her father's ability to transit dimensional boundaries and move about in time and space.

Lilith wanted to end this quickly; she had much revenge to pursue this night. She seized Gideon in a firm grip as they wrestled on the ground and attempted to destroy him by means of transporting vital parts of his body to another dimension. The boy might not have the ability to transport himself, but he could summon the energy to deflect that kind of attack and Stone had shown him how. She would have to kill him the old fashioned way.

That would not prove too easy. When her attack failed, Gideon countered with a punch to Lilith's head that rocked her senseless for a second. The boy was strong, but not yet fully grown and she still had a modest strength advantage. They struggled to their feet and Gideon tried to press his attack. He was too eager and Lilith flipped him over her shoulder, crashing him into the wooden tool shed which burst to pieces with the impact.

He rose and continued the fight. His father had instructed him well, but he was still young and inexperienced. Lilith was ancient and had vast experience. He could not seem to land a blow, Lilith deftly deflecting them all. She countered with a side kick to his midsection that doubled him over and sent him crashing through the wooden fence into the alley behind the backyard. Gideon wondered how it was that she hit so much harder than his father until he reminded himself that his father was never trying to kill him.

Before he could rise again, Lilith was on him, beating him down. He tried to block the blows and did block some of them, but he could not maintain her pace. She was wearing him down and soon enough was astride him and choking him to death. His vision was closing in as he struggled vainly to free himself. Suddenly, Lilith stopped. She looked up as if distracted.

"Damn!" she blurted out. Things were not going as planned in the swamp. The kid could wait; she was needed elsewhere. She vanished, leaving Gideon to slowly recover from his beating and fear for the safety of his family. No way to assist them occurred to him besides prayer.

Back in the swamp raged a battle of the ages. Even Stone was convinced that his final hour had come and so he was determined to die well and, if possible, not alone. The odds were long against him as befits any good ambush. Each of his opponents would have been trouble enough one-on-one, but with four-on-one he had no chance to finish any of them off before one of their allies interfered. He made some deft moves, dodging attacks and misdirecting others in ways that obstructed a different foe. Grendel and Anubis lunged at him at once. He managed to deflect Grendel's tendril around Anubis so that both were knocked off balance and splashed headlong into the bayou. He followed up with a successful assault on Severus that smacked his skull into a cypress tree, snapping it in two. Before Stone could press his advantage, Drusus nailed him from behind and allowed Severus to recover and counter-attack with a savage uppercut.

Stone knew he had to eliminate one of them quickly to have a chance; the odds were overwhelming otherwise. He knew one move that could do the trick fast enough before the others could intervene. It was ruthless and deadly but would only work once since after that the others would be on their guard against it. Stone decided that it had the best chance to work on Drusus. Of all gathered here, he was the least battle-hardened, having sat behind a desk for a long time. He was also, quite literally, a back stabbing weasel who, unlike the others, never would have had the courage to face him alone.

Accordingly Stone turned all his attention on Drusus, forgetting for a moment that the others would shortly make him regret turning his back to them. He unleashed his full fury on Drusus who hesitated for a split second, unaccustomed as he was to such hyper-violence. It was all Stone needed. In an instant he had a hold of Drusus' neck and snapped it with a sickening crunch. Drusus twitched and then fell dead at his feet. One down, but Stone had no time to celebrate as Anubis plowed into him and nearly tore out his throat with his flashing fangs. Energized after felling one of his foes, Stone unloaded on Anubis with a flurry of blows, giving in to berserker rage as if he were still a Viking warrior. Stone knew deep down that the only key to success was to enjoy the battle. More than his adversaries he actually loved this, even if it ultimately killed him. At the moment, however, he felt invincible. Anubis crumpled under his fury, but Grendel ensnared him in his slimy tentacles, invading his mind with a psionic attack. This trick would not work a second time on Stone, however, who unleashed his berserker wrath mentally as well, easily repelling Grendel's tactile telepathic assault. It did slow him down enough for Severus to connect with a solid haymaker to the jaw that knocked him down, however.

Over on St. Charles Avenue, Lilith heard the death scream of Drusus through her telepathic link with Jezebel. She broke off her attack on Gideon and transported herself to the swamp. There she saw the unthinkable: Drusus dead, Grendel reassembling his dispersed gelatinous body, Anubis hurt and slow to rise, and Severus receiving a pummeling from an enraged Stone. How could things have possibly gone so wrong? She kicked Stone from behind, but he failed to notice. She placed a choke hold on him and he flung her over his head so that she crashed with her back onto a bed of cypress knees. She had given Severus a chance to recover, however, and now Anubis was back in the fight. Stone was wearing down from the effort. If they kept at it, they would still prevail, especially as it was again a four-on-one fight with Lilith's arrival.

Someone else had also arrived, however. Aurora was still tracking Lilith as she had all the way from Commonwealth territory. She nearly intervened to save Gideon when Lilith suddenly stopped herself and came here to the swamp. Aurora followed and detected Jezebel, a fellow non-corporeal and one of her opposite numbers from the defeated Syndicate. Jezebel had not detected her since her attention was focused on blocking Stone from transporting away. It would not be long before she did detect her, so Aurora decided that she had to act quickly. She blitzed Jezebel with all her energy and scored a quick knockout since her adversary's focus was not on defense.

This was fortunate for Stone who was clearly weakening now before the onslaught of so many powerful foes. Grendel had rejoined the fight and Lilith was relatively fresh to the battle, but Stone got no rest. As soon as he laid one enemy low, another was there. Their successful attacks hurt him and even their unsuccessful attacks drained his energy. With Jezebel suddenly out of the fight, however, Stone had the chance to change the game. He broke free of the grip Lilith and Severus held on him and established a telepathic contact with Aurora who offered to help. Stone thanked her but asked her only to look after his family. He gave her a mental image of who and where, but Aurora already knew this. She promised to protect them. With that promise gained, Stone stepped into the interphasing spheroids of space-time to change the arena. His foes were in hot pursuit since Aurora could not block them all and they would quickly land on him wherever or whenever he chose to exit. He recalled his earlier thought about how his NOPD colleagues could not help him…

2730 B.C., Memphis, Egypt

Cassandra was still relatively new to inter-dimensional travel. She had a few brief lessons with her father, unbeknownst to her mother, but these were short trips and never outside the New Orleans null region. The reason for that was so that the family would not be found by certain enemies. Stone had prepared Cassandra for the day they might be found, however, and instructed her to take Isis back to ancient Egypt and the court of her first son who was reigning as Pharaoh. He made her memorize the route.

Even though she was curious about her half-brother, she earnestly hoped she would never have to travel it. But alas, the terrible day had arrived.

Cassandra awkwardly had them materialize right in front of the royal court while it was in assembly. Oddly enough, the nightgowns they wore did not seem out of place and nearly matched the dress of those assembled. The fact that they appeared suddenly as a priestess was invoking the name of Isis in a blessing over the Pharaoh was nothing short of sensational. Dozens of courtiers were present and immediately bowed down before Isis and Cassandra to acclaim them as goddesses. This was embarrassing in the extreme to Isis, who was aware that a cult had formed around her. Now that cult had a boost that would be impossible to discourage. Isis commanded them to stop, but they did so only out of fear. She turned her attention to her son, Khasekhemwy, who sat on the throne with the combined crown of Upper and Lower Egypt atop his head, his mouth agape. Her first-born by her first husband Osiris was fully grown now and reigning as pharaoh, as rightfully he should. She ran up to him and he stood to receive her. They embraced joyfully, but then Isis asked if they could retreat to his private chambers to catch up. Once there and out of sight of the courtiers, minus a couple of royal attendants, Isis embraced her son again and introduced him to his half-sister. Cassandra had not learned ancient Egyptian while in New Orleans but found that she was picking it up rapidly, almost miraculously. She had always found languages to be very easy, another inheritance from her father.

Khasekhemwy had a surprise, also. He introduced his wife, Queen Nimaethap and their children, the boy Djoser and daughter Hetephernebti. Isis was a grandmother and Cassandra an aunt. Cassandra relished the chance to learn about her Egyptian heritage and enjoy family company, but somewhere across time and space her father and brother were in danger. She would go to them and help if she could. Mother could not help and it was her father's explicit instruction to bring her here. She had accomplished that, but Dad had never forbade her from coming back to help. She would do that also.

19 April 2068, New Orleans

Officer Paul Saladino was flying his patrol unit over the Central Business District when he spied what appeared to be a meteorite heading for the Superdome. The Dome had been heavily damaged in last year's battle to free the city and had not yet been repaired since other priorities delayed the work. Debris from the FiST gunship that crashed into the roof and collapsed it still littered the arena floor. As Saladino watched the meteorite he saw that it was in fact five separate objects streaking through the atmosphere at high speed. For a second he feared a renewed FiST attack. The ruptured one-world state was in abeyance for now but who could say with certainty that the remnant would not try again to assert its dominance?

The five streaks of light flew straight into the gaping hole in the Superdome's roof and away from Saladino's sight. He called in what he saw and banked his unit over to the Dome for a better look at the impact. Saladino hovered the unit over the hole in the roof and peered down inside but could see nothing. He did a vertical descent down into the Dome. The evening light streamed inside but all he could make out was pieces of wreckage from the crashed gunship and the roof itself. He finally set the unit down and dismounted for a better look.

Five figures stirred in the surreal landscape of the shattered arena. Three Saladino recognized immediately as human, but the fourth more resembled a werewolf. The fifth slithered in the shadows but when light finally hit it he was still at a loss. A dark gray blob of protoplasm that kept morphing its shape. It gave him a fright just to see it and he readied his plasma rifle. The NOPD rolled with heavy armament ever since the battle last year. Until now he thought that might have been an overreaction, but now he was glad. The other four figures were slowly gaining their feet. The blob had none to gain and was sliming its way across the concrete floor.

"You're going to want to call for backup, Paul. And don't let that thing near you," a familiar voice called. Stone had altered his appearance to match the one he had as an NOPD cop from the 2050s and 2060s, the one Saladino would recognize. His uniform was still of NOPD's 1908 vintage but it was almost completely ruined anyhow.

"Chief Stone? How the hell?" Saladino blinked at him.

"Flee human. This is not your affair," Severus warned, glaring only at Stone.

"Oh, let him stay and die," Lilith interjected. "As for you," she addressed Stone, "I wanted to show you your wife's severed head before your death, but I will settle for showing yours to her before I kill her."

"See, that is what I don't like about you; you're evil. It would never have worked between us," Stone deadpanned.

The three human-looking figures appeared to have just emerged from a war. On top of that, they had all just crashed into the Superdome floor at meteoric velocity and now were merely dusting themselves off. Saladino knew that there was something superhuman about Stone, but now it seemed that he had brought his friends. No, not friends, Saladino corrected himself.

With blinding speed, Severus lunged at Stone who caught him in a judo throw that sent him crashing into the concrete, splitting it. While Stone was thus engaged, Lilith hit from behind with a hard kick that sent him flying into an adjacent gunship bulkhead. Anubis pounced on the fallen Stone but was sent reeling back when Stone smacked him in the face with a chunk of heavy jagged metal from the wreckage. Stone regained his feet and sneered in defiance but he was clearly nearing exhaustion. His four adversaries circled him confidently like a pack of hyenas around an injured lion.

"Everybody freeze!" Saladino yelled in a convincing law enforcement tone which he reinforced by aiming his plasma rifle at Stone's attackers. "All units, Code Three inside the Superdome. Officer needs assistance!" he spoke into his comm link.

A voice from dispatch responded to Saladino, "926 we are sending units your way. What is the nature of the emergency?"

"Chief Stone is back and he needs help. Get here yesterday!"

A moment's pause. "10-4, all units converge on the Superdome," the comm link blared.

Anubis jumped first at Stone and Saladino hit him with the plasma rifle to little effect. The blue bolt crackled towards him and hit him square in the chest. He stumbled for a moment but then shook it off and pressed forward. Stone caught Anubis and threw him into Severus who was also springing forward. They crashed together into a heap of wreckage. Lilith thought she had another clear shot at Stone's back but he turned and faced her, catching her kick and dumping her head first into the ground. He delivered his own kick and sent her flying into Severus, knocking him down as he was trying to rise on an unsteady pile of rubble.

Stone had won another small victory, but it drained him. As he was trying to catch his breath, a tendril from Grendel had slithered unseen through the rubble he was standing on and ensnared his foot. It dragged him down and pinned him for a moment just as his other opponents were recovering. Saladino jumped on the rubble pile next to Stone and saw where the blob creature had caught his foot. He aimed his plasma rifle at the tentacle and fired at point blank range. He heard an unearthly screech in reaction to the shot and turned to see the main body of the thing with its gigantic mouth opened in a scream. So the plasma could hurt this one. Firing another shot at the main body of the blob, he hit it a glancing blow, and it quickly slithered away to hide in the wreckage.

Saladino helped Stone to his feet and then charged after the one monster he figured out he could actually hurt. But the thing moved fast for a blob and could morph its body shape to hide anywhere. Its dark gray body was hard to spot in the many shadows amidst the piles of debris. He heard Stone grunt under several blows as the fight was rejoined; it did not seem to be going well. Saladino thought he saw a piece of the monster and turned in that direction. Unfortunately Grendel had morphed into a pancake shape and slithered beneath several of the rubble piles surrounding the overmatched cop. Saladino saw the distraction Grendel wanted him to see while other tendrils seized him from behind and smashed his rifle.

"Stone! Help!" he managed to get out. Grendel dragged him closer to his wide open maw to devour him, but rather slowly to enjoy the primal fear in his victim.

Stone had a good grip on Severus and might have broken him the way he had broken Drusus. He was ignoring the teeth of Anubis sinking into his arm and the nasty blows from Lilith just to finish him off when he heard Saladino's call. Instead of killing Severus he tossed him into the open mouth of Grendel who immediately released Saladino in the ensuing chaos.

Stone had lasted so long in this uneven fight for one simple reason. For all of his existence he had eschewed the easy path. He sought out ennobling hardship and endured it again and again. He had faced fear and death as a mortal and undergone grueling torment and privation. One of his NOPD coworkers once commented that Stone, "smelled of hard times, bad places, blood and death." This had hardened him far beyond the mighty enemies he now faced. Still, while his courage and determination would not fail, his physical body ultimately would reach a rock hard limit. He neared that limit now and pushed bravely beyond realizing there was no turning back.

Then the cavalry arrived. An NOPD SWAT unit descended through the hole in the roof. More officers arrived on foot through the regular entrances.

Saladino aimed his flashlight at Grendel who was still spewing Severus out and trying to separate himself. He called into his comm link, "Plasma rifles on that one. Hit it!"

The half-dozen NOPD officers so armed unleashed a volley of blue plasma streams on Grendel from several directions. The dark gray blob sizzled and turned other colors under the intense heat. It screamed horribly for several seconds and then ceased as it lost all coherent shape, partially liquefied, and then finally sublimated away.

Saladino next directed fire on Anubis, "Restraining nets on that one!"

Other members of the force stepped forward and launched non-lethal netting from their compressed air guns. Four large nets entangled Anubis who struggled to break free. He was so strong that he was making progress, too.

"Hit him with the Fifty!" Saladino ordered.

The NOPD had seen the utility of the old Browning M-2 Heavy Machine Gun in the so-called Second Battle of New Orleans. Someone found drawings for the somewhat more modern, electrically driven GAU-19 three-barreled Gatling variety and produced a few with 3D printing. All the SWAT vehicles now had them mounted in turrets on top with the gunners operating them from inside. The GAU-19 roared fiercely at Anubis and pummeled him with the impact of the heavy rounds. They did not penetrate his hide but they beat him up like a pile driver and knocked him down.

As Stone wavered, Lilith left Severus to pound on him alone and leapt to deal with the new threat. She disregarded the plasma bolts that hit her and jumped atop the SWAT vehicle. Seizing the GAU-19 mount with her bare hands, she caused it to explode by means of an incomplete transport of it through a dimensional doorway. She then cast NOPD officers aside like ragdolls as she ran to Anubis. She freed him from the restraining nets and assisted him in rising to his feet. Meanwhile, Severus continued battering a rapidly weakening Stone. Lilith helped Anubis over to them so that they could all share in the kill.

Saladino was low on options. Stone's enemies, except for the one they had dealt with, were as impervious to plasma fire as he. Saladino thought back to the day of the great battle. Stone had proved susceptible to one thing only and the SWAT vehicle likely had it in stock. He ran inside to look, calling through his comm link for one of the localized EMP devices captured in the battle.

"Never mind why, just get it here!" he raged at the dispatcher.

Saladino found what he was looking for and ran back outside. Just when it seemed that Severus and Lilith were going to deliver the coup de gras to Stone, the slumped figure rallied with one more effort. He nailed Severus to the chin with an uppercut that dazed him and swept Lilith's legs, knocking her down. Anubis collapsed also, his strength gone. Stone grabbed both Severus and Lilith in a wrestler's hold to keep them pinned, but it was clear that he could not do so for long. Saladino came close and showed him the silver picobot globe.

"I thought you'd never ask. Yes, fall back and launch that on us right away."

"They don't discriminate; they'll attack you, too," Saladino explained.

"I can't hold them much longer and they will hunt down my family if you don't stop them. Use it, Paul. Now!" Stone urged him.

Saladino nodded. "Everyone to the unit. We're getting out of here!"

The NOPD officers fell back to the SWAT unit and piled inside. Its engines whined as it rose vertically to exit via the roof hole. Saladino looked down off the exit ramp and saw that Stone no longer held the brief advantage he had gained in the fight. Severus and Lilith were now wailing on him. Wait, it seemed they were trying to break free of him but he was grasping them close in a death grip they could not loosen. At least not yet. It was time to do what the former Chief instructed. Saladino pulled the pin on the grenade and dropped it on the combatants just before the SWAT unit flew them out of the Dome.

The silver orb dropped and hit the ground near the head of the unconscious Anubis when it exploded into trillions of tiny, unseen robots. The picobots were so small that they could infiltrate matter at the molecular level. Even the dense superhuman skin of Stone, Severus, Lilith, and Anubis could not keep out the invaders. The picobots then assailed every cell within their bodies with ruthless efficiency. Stone passed out, but Severus and Lilith shrieked in agony as their bodies were lit on fire on the inside, every cell in turn devoured by the fast moving picobots. Stone lost his grip on them and could no longer prevent their transport, but the damage was done and they could not escape now. Anubis awoke in agony as well and joined his voice to theirs, an unearthly screech that Saladino could hear far above the Dome.

The SWAT unit landed outside the Superdome on one of the concrete pedestrian ramps. There to meet them was the captured FiST tank with the directional EMP. Saladino commandeered it and drove it inside, crashing through barriers in his haste. A scan revealed that the picobots were no longer dispersing to seek out new targets; they would content themselves with what they had. It was safe to go back in.

All four combatants were down and Saladino dragged the apparently lifeless body of Stone away from the others. He directed EMP blasts at Stone once, twice, three times. Scans showed that he was thoroughly cleansed of the picobots but he did not revive. It was too late. Chief Stone was dead. So, too, were all his enemies, but that brought no comfort. The City had lost its sentinel.

It was then that Saladino did something rather odd. He arranged the body of Stone atop one of the piles of rubble neatly as would an undertaker for a wake. At Stone's feet he placed, after some dragging and with some help from fellow officers, the bodies of Severus, Lilith, and Anubis. These he set ablaze after some determined effort with a plasma rifle at highest setting and point blank range. Now that they were dead, the bodies were less indestructible and finally did catch fire after prolonged plasma torching. It took an entire rifle battery to do it, but finally Saladino had his raging fire that consumed the bodies of Stone's three foes. And Stone had the NOPD's impromptu version of a Viking funeral. His body was not burned, however. He was to be buried with full honors.

The formal funeral was held two days later with a Mass at St. Louis Cathedral said by the Archbishop himself. The Mayor was in attendance with most of her city council, as was the Chief of Police and all of the senior leadership of the NOPD and NOFD. The Archbishop recounted the highlights of what Stone had done to free the city from oppression and defend it against invasion. No family was present, so that place was taken by the officers who had served with him most closely, Saladino and Sanchez in particular. They would also be among the pall bearers.

At the conclusion of the Mass, the casket, which was draped with the new flag of the Constitutional Republic of America that New Orleans had lately joined, was led out of the cathedral under the sword arch of a police honor guard to the tune of "Amazing Grace" on the bagpipe. A thick crowd greeted the casket as it emerged into the sunlight of Jackson Square. It was probably the biggest crowd there since the visit of Pope John Paul II back in 1987, for which Stone had happened to work a security detail.

When the last note of "Amazing Grace" ended, a jazz brass band took over and led the procession down Chartres with a slow dirge rendition of "Nearer My God to Thee" as the pall bearers carried the casket by hand down the street. Mourners from the cathedral followed behind and after them came throngs of grateful citizens from all over the Quarter and in all manner of dress to form the 'second line'. The funeral procession turned down Dumaine Street and headed north, the song "Just a Closer Walk With Thee" replacing the earlier song on the slow march.

At Rampart Street the pall bearers unloaded their burden on a horse drawn hearse for the rest of the trip to St. Louis Cemetery Number One. New Orleans said goodbye in its own unique way and, in accord with tradition, the jazz band now played the joyous strains of "When the Saints Go Marching In". The second line dancers abandoned the slow, solemn march of the dirges and began dancing with abandon. Those who had handkerchiefs waved them and others produced parasols to dance with. Some of the revelers enjoyed intoxicating libations. This farewell was a celebration of life, and life was more worth celebrating in New Orleans thanks to the exertions of Chief Stone.

At the cemetery the formal ceremony was again solemn. Lines of police officers and firemen wearing black armbands saluted the casket as it passed. "Taps" was played on a lone bugle and a twenty-one gun salute was fired.

The Archbishop said more kind words before the casket was placed in the above-ground tomb. These were not easy to come by in St. Louis No. 1 in 2068, but a wealthy donor made it happen. The tomb was sealed and the ceremony concluded. Many stayed behind to pay their private respects, but finally these also left and the tomb stood quietly with others in the ancient cemetery. It had been a funeral of funerals for the city's benefactor, its sentinel, but life went on. It would do so because of him.

It took Aurora two more days to track down Stone's resting place. She found Cassandra and Gideon moping in their St. Charles home in 1908. They had conducted a search but had no idea how to track their father. They waited in the forlorn hope that he would return there. Instead they were met by Aurora who conveyed the bad news. The three of them then fetched Isis from ancient Egypt and, with Aurora leading the way, finally came to 2068 New Orleans and the grave site of one "Arthur M. Stone, Chief of Police and Savior of the City of New Orleans." Stone had used the name Arthur since he was, after all, the inspiration for the legends of King Arthur. Now there was another legend in his wake.

Isis placed her hand on the tomb and wept. The children embraced her and wept also. They regretted not having the chance to say goodbye. Aurora, too, said farewell in her own way but then she stopped herself. Something was amiss.

As the Stone family wept quietly beside the tomb, a thump could be heard within. They looked at each other, each seeking confirmation that the others heard it. Then there was another thump. And another, louder this time. Finally the side of the tomb exploded outward, sending white bricks and dust flying about. Isis and the children were stupefied. Out stepped Stone, dressed in the NOPD dress uniform his undertaker had placed him in and waving away at the dust cloud he had caused.

"How long was I out?" he asked.

Aurora answered, her voice emanating from above like that of an angel, "About four days."

"Not bad. If you had not happened along, it might have been far longer. Maybe never. I thank you," he nodded appreciatively to the unseen agent.

"My pleasure. I was delighted to discover upon closer inspection that you were only comatose and not quite dead," she replied. "Waking you was simple. For me, that is. They haven't the medical technology here."

"They have enough tech to almost seal my doom. It was a cloud of picobots that forced me to induce my own stasis; it was the only way to slow them down long enough. It still might not have been enough if one of my compatriots had not zapped them with an electromagnetic pulse a few minutes later. And without you reviving me, there is no telling when or if I would have awakened on my own," Stone explained.

Isis could stand it no more and ended this conversation. She threw herself around Stone and kissed him long and enthusiastically. Aurora bowed out and left the family in privacy for their reunion. It was time for her to report back to Demetrius. The last and deadliest of the remaining Syndicate cells had been dismantled, the mole had been discovered and eliminated, and Stone had been located but subsequently died. All in a day's work.

The Stone children and their mother continued shedding tears, only now they were for joy. Stone was not completely impervious to the emotion of the moment. He was reminded of so many soldiers' reunions with families he had witnessed after so many deployments. He had shared with those soldiers every bit of hardship they had endured, but the experience they had upon their returns to their loved ones was one that had always eluded him until now. He finally found an experience that he truly wished would never end as he stood there defying death in that cemetery and loving life while holding his wife and children.

They decided to stay there in New Orleans of 2068. It was an exciting time as the country was rediscovering its founding ethos and again asserting its liberty. Stone had reverted to the appearance he used in 1908 as Sergeant John Stone since he did not need to be recognized as the late Chief of Police Arthur Stone. Besides, Isis and the kids were more used to it.

Stone decided to live a quiet domestic life with the lovely Isis for as long as they had left. He would show Cassandra and Gideon some of the ropes and then leave the inter-dimensional and time traveling adventures to them. He had decided to retire from such a broad beat and focus on his adopted home town. "John Stone" rejoined the NOPD and was soon working again with Officers Saladino and Sanchez.

"You know we had a chief by the name of Stone," Saladino pointed out.

"You don't say?" Stone came back.

"Maybe someday, once you get some experience, you'll be a tenth of the man he was," Saladino teased.

"It is good to have a goal."

AFTERWORD

Alternative history is a fun genre, but this work is not part of it. The fun challenge of writing Sergeant Stone stories is to insert the character meaningfully into historical events without changing what *actually happened*. In other words, I tried to get it right concerning the historical events described herein. For Stone, time is not linear and history is fluid, but that is not true for me or for the reader. I do not deliberately do violence to actual history. Where certain details are unknown due to lack of historical knowledge, I will fill in my own, but not in a way that contradicts what we really know. In this afterword I will briefly separate fact from fiction in each of the stories in the book.

The story and the narrator in "Sergeant Stone and the Trial by Fire" are fanciful but the setting is real. Okmulkee (now Okmulgee) is a real town and the Creek Council House is a real landmark. The townspeople mentioned are fictional but Judge Isaac Parker and Deputy Marshal Bass Reeves were real people. Reeves is an almost legendary figure who might have inspired the creation of the Lone Ranger.

In "Sergeant Stone Visits St. Bernard" (the author's home parish), Captain Leathers was a real person and the steamship he commanded, the *Natchez VIII*, was also real. The descriptions of Governor Galvez's siege of Pensacola are taken from his own written narrative of the event, the *Diary of the Operations of the Expedition Against the Place of Pensacola, Concluded by the Arms of H. Catholic M., Under the Orders of the Field Marshall Don Bernardo de Galvez*. There was a lucky howitzer shot that exploded the powder magazine of the fort and I simply made the change that the hit was actually the result of our hero's skill once he lost patience with the siege.

"Sergeant Stone and the Second Battle of New Orleans" departs from the historical fiction genre and wades into the science fiction realm since it describes urban combat in 2067. The weaponry described is simply the author's own extrapolation from current developments in nanotechnology, high energy plasma, artificial intelligence, and the proliferation of drones to what may be around over fifty years from now. If any copies of this book are extant in the year 2067 and read by someone then, odds are that my predictions will be laughably wide of the mark. Just remember that the point of the book is fun.

"Sergeant Stone in the Company of Demons" is what I hope to be a faithful account of the Battle of Camerone. Stone participates but under the name of one of the actual Legionnaires who fought there. I drew from numerous internet resources to tell the story of the battle, but the Camerone chapter from Bryan Perret's *Last Stand! Famous Battles Against the Odds* was especially helpful.

In "Sergeant Stone Undone" we see Stone participate in the Battle of Warsaw from the Russo-Polish War of 1920, a real event that I tried to describe with accuracy. The Kosciuko Squadron and its exploits were real, as were the names of the members that I mention with the exception of Stone himself. Online excerpts from Janus Cisek's *Kosciuko, We Are Here: American Pilots of the Kosciuko Squadron in the Defense of Poland, 1919-1920*, were helpful.

"Sergeant Stone and the Vikings" drew inspiration from Icelandic sagas but meshed historic events into the narrative described in the *Saga of Harald Hardrada*, particularly details of his career and that of Earl Hakon. The description of the Battle of Stamford Bridge relied on both that source and the *Anglo-Saxon Chronicle*. The sources agree that a single Viking held off the entire Anglo-Saxon army at the bridge, killing forty of them with his battle-axe before being cut down himself. The warrior's name was not known, but now it can be revealed that it was none other than our own Sergeant Stone while under amnesia. This story also dovetails with that of another of my

Uncle James S. Prine's indelible characters, Bjorn of "Bjorn's Adventure in the Unknown Lande" from his short story collection, *Tales From the Id*, the same fantastic book that introduced Sergeant Stone to the world.

"The Wedding of Sergeant Stone" depicts a pre-Vatican II Catholic wedding. The officiating priest, Father Gambera, was an actual priest of the diocese and partner to St. Frances Cabrini for her New Orleans operations. Father Manoritta was the actual pastor of St. Anthony of Padua Church in New Orleans at the time. The assassination of Chief David Hennessy happened just that way by all accounts.

"The Honeymoon of Sergeant Stone" is a thoroughly concocted story that weaves in real persons and places. Giuseppe Esposito was a real Mafioso whom Hennessy had put behind bars, but I invented his tie to the murder as well as his jailhouse stand-in and henchmen. The Matrangas and Provenzanos were real enough, the Esplanade shooting really happened, Ucciardone Prison and St. Dominic Church in Palermo are real places.

"The Temptation of Sergeant Stone" is a fanciful story but with the factual backdrop of the Hennessy murder trial and the lynchings of the acquitted by a New Orleans mob. I used several sources but I owe much to the book, *The Crescent City Lynchings: The Murder of Chief Hennessy, the New Orleans "Mafia" Trials, and the Parish Prison Mob*, by Tom Smith for the historical details in this story and for the two previous stories. He in turn relied heavily on contemporary newspaper accounts. The Olde Absinthe House was and is real.

Sources are scanty for "Sergeant Stone Versus the Beloved of the Gods" since it is set in ancient India. The weapons depicted were likely in use then with the possible exceptions of the urumi sword and Stone's katars. The urumi cannot be dated with certainty back that far and the katars almost certainly developed later, so I took some liberty here. The broad outline of the Kalinga War is true as far as we know and Ashoka's famous change of heart appears to have been genuine. He never waged another aggressive war and devoted his efforts to spreading Buddhism and improving living conditions for his subjects.

"Sergeant Stone, Warrior Monk" describes the story of Tianyuan who, according to contemporary accounts, did singlehandedly defeat eight challengers for the right to leadership of the monastic forces. Not much else is known about him, but now it is revealed that he was none other than

Stone, our wandering hero. For details on the Shaolin of this period and their war with the pirates I drew from Meir Shahar's essay, "Ming-Period Evidence of Shaolin Martial Practice" from the *Harvard Journal of Asiatic Studies*, Vol. 61, No. 2. (Dec., 2001), pp. 359-413.

"Crescent City Sentinel" was a completely made up event. The narrator, his team, and the U-885 submarine were also fictitious. Lieutenant Walter Kappe and Operation Pastorius were quite real, however. He did indeed arrange for teams of German saboteurs to be delivered to American beaches by way of U-Boats. The Japanese mini-sub did exist, as did the Higgins Boat Factory. I did try to get the other places and street names correct as well.

Details of the siege of Constantinople for "Sergeant Stone at the Fall of the Empire" are drawn from the eyewitness account of one of the defenders, Niccolo Barbaro. *A Short History of Byzantium* by John Julius Norwich was also helpful. Alethea and her family are made up, naturally, but the events of the siege itself and the fate of Constantine XI and other inhabitants are factual. Internet sources were used for the Otranto siege and the Catholic Church, which carefully vets such stories, has canonized the martyrs of that town. Mehmet II did die under mysterious circumstances.

"29 August 2005" is more of a mood piece than a work of historical fiction. Katrina is not some far off historical event for me to research. It deeply affected almost everyone I know and care about. Sergeant Stone would have been with his favorite city in one of its darkest hours.

"The Funeral of Sergeant Stone" features a nightclub called 'The Cave'. It existed up until 1930 inside the Grunewald Hotel, later renamed the Roosevelt, then the Fairmont, and now the Roosevelt again. Storyville was real as was the Mahogany House, but both are long gone now and housing projects stand on the former location of The District. Several famous Jazz musicians did get their starts there. Lulu White was the actual proprietor and operator of the Mahogany House but the grisly double murder featured in the story is fabricated.

Thank you for coming along on this adventure. I hope you enjoyed reading it as much as I enjoyed writing it. God bless you and yours!

Sincerely,
Daniel Barker

Printed in the United States
By Bookmasters